Jelera

☑ **W9-BMG-233**

Feb/20/00

LUKE, I THOUGHT, SURROUNDED NOW BY pretty coeds, healthy, happy girls . . . girls who can walk and laugh and do fun things with him. Maybe he had delayed coming to visit me because he couldn't stand to see me the way I was. I would surprise him; I would look stronger, better, and I would be better . . .

As I thought of him, I embraced myself, imagining him beside me, his fingers twirling my hair, his eyes so close to mine as we gazed longingly at each other, tormented by our desire and our forbidden love at the same time.

Thinking about him this way warmed my body and made it feel alive again. Surely if visions of Luke loving me had such a wonderful effect, it couldn't be all bad, I reasoned. With Luke at my side, I would overcome this tragedy . . .

I looked up at my empty room. I could hear people talking and moving about downstairs. A door was closed. A gust of wind whistled through some shutters. And then, it was quiet again.

Oh, Luke, I thought, what could possibly be your reason for not moving heaven and earth to see me? . . .

V.C. Andrews® Books

Published by POCKET BOOKS

For orders other than by individual consumers, Pocket Books grants a discount on the purchase of **10 or more** copies of single titles for special markets or premium use. For further details, please write to the Vice-President of Special Markets, Pocket Books, 1633 Broadway, New York, NY 10019-6785, 8th Floor.

For information on how individual consumers can place orders, please write to Mail Order Department, Simon & Schuster Inc., 200 Old Tappan Road, Old Tappan, NJ 07675.

Gates of Paradise

V.C. ANDREWS ®

POCKET BOOKS

New York London Toronto Sydney Tokyo Singapore

The sale of this book without a cover is unauthorized. If you purchased this book without a cover, you should be aware that it was reported to the publisher as "unsold and destroyed." Neither the author nor the publisher has received payment for the sale of this "stripped book."

Following the death of Virginia Andrews, the Andrews family worked with a carefully selected writer to organize and complete Virginia Andrews' stories and to create additional novels, of which this is one, inspired by her storytelling genius.

This book is a work of fiction. Names, characters, places and incidents are products of the author's imagination or are used fictitiously. Any resemblance to actual events or locales or persons living or dead is entirely coincidental.

An *Original* Publication of POCKET BOOKS

POCKET BOOKS, a division of Simon & Schuster Inc.
1230 Avenue of the Americas, New York, NY 10020

Copyright © 1989 by the Vanda General Partnership
Cover art copyright © 1989 Richard Newton

All rights reserved, including the right to reproduce this book or portions thereof in any form whatsoever. For information address Pocket Books, 1230 Avenue of the Americas, New York, NY 10020

ISBN: 0-671-72943-8

First Pocket Books printing June 1989

23 22 21 20 19 18 17 16 15 14

POCKET and colophon are registered trademarks of Simon & Schuster Inc.

V.C. Andrews is a registered trademark of the Vanda General Partnership.

Printed in the U.S.A.

Prologue

For as long as I could remember, the only person I could share my deepest secrets with was Luke Casteel, Jr. It was as if I were truly alive only when he was with me, and in my secret putaway heart, I knew he felt the same way, even though he had never dared say anything about it. I wanted to look at him, look into his soft dark sapphire eyes forever and ever and tell him what I really felt, but the words were forbidden. He was my half brother.

But there was one way I could look continually at him and he at me without either of us being self-conscious about it or feeling someone would discover our secret, and that was whenever I painted him. He was always a willing subject. With the easel between us and my world of art serving as a window, I could stare closely at his perfectly shaped, high-cheeked, bronze face and I could capture the way those unruly, jet-black strands of hair always fell over his forehead.

Luke had my aunt Fanny's hair, but my father's deep blue eyes and perfect nose. There was strength in the lines of his mouth and in his sharp, smooth jawline. I couldn't help seeing the clear resemblances to my father, and even to myself. He had the same tall, lean build Daddy had and kept his shoulders back the same way. The resemblances always saddened me because they reminded me that Luke wasn't simply my half brother; he was my illegitimate half brother, born out of a passionate indiscretion between Daddy and my aunt Fanny, my mother's sister, something we all understood was best kept unmentioned.

We tried to leave it behind us, stuffed away in the shadows, even though we both knew people whispered and gossiped about us in Winnerrow. Although my family was the most prominent in Winnerrow, we were a very odd family indeed. Luke, Jr. lived with his mother, who had been married twice: once to a man much older who had died, and once to a man much younger, who had divorced her.

Everyone in Winnerrow remembered the court hearing over who would win custody of Mommy's and Aunt Fanny's half brother Drake, after their father Luke and his new wife Stacie were killed in a car accident. Drake was only about five at the time. The argument was settled out of court, with Mommy getting custody and Aunt Fanny getting a lot of money. Drake hated to hear about it, and more than once got into a fight at school when some boy teased him about "being bought and paid for." Mother said Drake had her father's temper anyway. He was handsome, muscular, and very athletic, as well as very bright and determined. Now he was a student getting his M.B.A. at Harvard Business College. Even though he was really my uncle, I always thought of him as a big brother. Mommy and Daddy raised him as they would raise a son.

Most everyone in Winnerrow knew about Mommy, how she was born and raised in the Willies, how her

2

mother had died giving birth to her, how she had lived in a shack most of her young life, and then gone off to live with her mother's rich family, the Tattertons.

She lived at Farthinggale Manor, or "Farthy," as she often called it whenever I could get her to talk about it, which wasn't very often.

But Luke and I talked about it.

Farthinggale Manor ... it loomed high in our imaginations ... this magical, yet sinister place, a castle filled with a thousand secrets, some of which we just knew had to do with us. It was still the home of the mysterious Tony Tatterton, the man who had married my great-grandmother and who still ran the great Tatterton Toy empire, now only loosely associated with our Willies Toy factory. For reasons Mother would not discuss, she refused to have anything to do with him, even though he never failed to send us all birthday and Christmas cards. He had sent me dolls from everywhere in the world every birthday for as long as I could remember. At least she let me keep them ... precious little Chinese dolls that had long, straight black hair, and dolls from Holland and Norway and Ireland with colorful costumes and beautiful, sparkling faces.

Luke and I wanted to know more about Tony Tatterton and Farthy. Even Drake was very curious, although he didn't talk about it half as much as Luke and I did. If only our home, Hasbrouck House, was as open and revealing about the family's past as it was on holidays when Mommy and Daddy's friends and their families wandered freely through it. There were so many lingering questions. What finally had brought my parents back here from the rich, lavish world of Farthinggale Manor? Why did my mother want so much to return to Winnerrow where she had been considered lower than everyone because she was a Casteel from the Willies? Even when she had been a teacher here, she hadn't been fully accepted by the rich, snobby townspeople.

So many secrets haunted the shadows around us, hanging in the corners of our minds like old cobwebs. For as long as I could remember, I felt something was supposed to be told to me about myself, but no one had told it: not my mother, not my father, and not my uncle Drake. I sensed it in the silences that sometimes fell between my parents and between them and me, especially between my mother and me.

I wished I could come to a clear, clean canvas and lift my paintbrush and pull the truth out of the blank white sheet before me. Maybe that was why I had always been obsessed with my painting. Hardly a day passed when I didn't paint something. It was as much a part of me as . . . as breathing.

Part

1

Part

I

Family Secrets

Oh no!" Drake exclaimed, coming up behind me without my realizing it because I was so involved in my painting. "Not another picture of Farthinggale Manor with Luke, Jr. gaping out a window at the rolling clouds." Drake rolled his eyes and pretended to go into a faint.

Luke sat up quickly and brushed the strands of hair off his forehead. Whenever anything embarrassed or unnerved him, he always went to his hair. I turned slowly, intending to scowl at Drake the way Miss Marbleton, Luke's and my English teacher, would every time anyone misbehaved or spoke out of turn; but Drake wore his impish smile, and his coal-black eyes glimmered like two dew-covered stones. I couldn't make myself angry at a face like that. He was so handsome, but no matter how often he shaved, he had a dark cloud in his complexion. My mother was always running her hand over his cheeks affectionately and telling him to shave away the porcupine quills.

"Drake," I said softly, practically pleading with

him not to say anything more that might embarrass Luke and me.

"Well, it's true, Annie, isn't it?" Drake persisted. "You must have done a half dozen pictures like this with Luke inside of Farthy or walking about the grounds. And Luke wasn't ever there!" He raised his voice to clearly remind us that he had been. I tilted my head to the side the way my mother did when something suddenly occurred to her. Was Drake jealous of my using Luke as an artistic subject? It never occurred to me to ask him to pose because he rarely sat still long enough for me to paint his likeness.

"My pictures of Farthy are never the same," I cried defensively. "How can they be? I'm working only from my own imagination and the little tidbits I've been able to pick up here and there from Daddy and Mommy."

"You would think anyone would realize that," Luke remarked, his eyes remaining fixed on his English literature textbook. Drake widened his smile.

"What, has the great Buddha spoken?" Drake's eyes danced with glee. Whenever he could get Luke to rise to one of his taunts, he was happy.

"Drake, please. I'm losing my mood," I pleaded, "and an artist has to seize the moment and hold it the way you would hold a baby bird . . . softly, but firmly." I didn't mean to sound so pretentious, but there was nothing I hated more than Luke and Drake getting into an argument.

My beseeching eyes and pleas worked. Drake's face softened. He turned back to me, his posture relaxed. Mother always said Drake strode through Winnerrow with a Casteel's pride. Because he was six feet two with broad shoulders, a narrow waist, and muscular arms, that wasn't hard to imagine.

"I'm sorry. I just thought I could wrench Plato

here away for a while. We need a ninth man for softball over at the school," he added.

Luke looked up from his textbook, genuinely surprised at the invitation, his eyes small and inquiring. Was Drake sincere? Since he had come home for his spring break, he had spent almost all his time with his older friends.

"Well, I . . ." Luke looked to me. "I had to study for this unit test," Luke explained quickly, "and I thought while Annie was painting me . . ."

"Sure, sure, I understand, Einstein. Einstein," Drake repeated, gesturing toward Luke, his voice dripping with sarcasm. "It's not all books, you know," he said, spinning to face him again. This time his face was serious. "A lot of it has to do with getting to know people, getting them to like you, respect you. That's the secret of success. More executives are coming off the playing fields than out of the classrooms," he lectured, waving his long, right forefinger. Luke said nothing in response. He ran his fingers through his hair and fixed that stoical, yet piercing, analytical gaze on Drake, something Drake couldn't stand. "Ah . . . why I am wasting my breath?"

Drake turned to my painting again.

"I told you that Farthy was gray, not blue," he corrected softly.

"You were only five at the time you were there and you said yourself, you were hardly there. Maybe you forgot," Luke said, quickly coming to my defense.

"You don't forget the color of a building as big as that!" Drake exclaimed, pulling in the corners of his mouth. "No matter how young you are at the time or how short you stay."

"Well, you once told us there were two outside pools and then Logan finally corrected that, telling us there was only one outside, but one indoors," Luke continued.

9

When it came to Farthy, both he and I were as exacting as we could be, cherishing whatever small details and truths we knew. So little had been given to us about it.

"Is that so, Sherlock Holmes?" Drake replied, his eyes growing smaller, colder. He didn't like being corrected, especially by Luke. "Well, I never said there were two outside pools; I just said there were two pools. You just don't listen when I tell you something. It amazes me you're doing so well in school. What'dya do, cheat?"

"Drake, please!" I exclaimed, grasping his wrist and squeezing softly.

"Well, he doesn't listen. Unless it's you who does the talking," he added, smiling, content because he had struck a sensitive spot. Luke blushed, his blue eyes swinging my way briefly before he turned away, his face turning sad.

I looked beyond him, just over the first rise in the Willies at a wisp of a cloud that the wind had molded into the shape of a tear. Suddenly I felt like crying myself and it wasn't only because of the conflict between Drake and Luke. It wasn't the first time this melancholy mood had come over me like a dark cloud passing over the sun. What I did realize was that the sad feelings often stimulated my desire to paint. Painting brought me relief, a sense of balance and peace. I was creating the world I wanted, the world I saw with inner eyes. I could make it forever spring or make winter dazzling and beautiful. I felt like a magician, conjuring something special in my mind and then bringing it to life on the empty canvas. While I was sketching in my latest image of Farthy, I felt my heart grow lighter and the world around me grow warmer and warmer, as if I were lifting a shadow off myself. Now because Drake had really interrupted the mood, my sadness returned.

I realized Drake and Luke were both staring at me, their faces troubled by my gray expression. I fought back the urge to cry, and smiled through the shadow over my face.

"Maybe each of my paintings of Farthinggale Manor are different because it changes," I finally said in a voice barely above a whisper. Luke's eyes widened and a smile rippled across his soft lips. He knew what that tone in my voice meant. We were about to play the fantasy game, to let our imaginations wander recklessly about and be unafraid to say what other seventeen- and eighteen-year-old teenagers would find silly.

But the game was more than that. When we played it, we could say things to each other that we were afraid to say otherwise. I could be his princess and he my prince. We could tell each other what we felt in our hearts, pretending it wasn't us but imaginary people who were speaking. Neither of us blushed or looked away.

Drake shook his head. He, too, knew what was coming. "Oh no," he said, "you two don't still do this." He covered his face in mock embarrassment.

I ignored him, stepped away and continued.

"Maybe Farthy is like the seasons—gray and dismal in the winter and bright blue and warm in the summer." I was looking up as if everything I thought was suggested to me by the patch of blue sky. Then I shifted my eyes toward Luke.

"Or maybe it becomes whatever you want it to become," Luke said picking up the thread. "If I want it to be made of sugar and maple, it will be."

"Sugar and maple?" Drake smirked.

"And if I want it to be a magnificent castle with lords and ladies-in-waiting and a sad prince moping about, longing for his princess to return, it will be," I responded, lifting my voice above his.

"May I be the prince?" Luke asked quickly and stood up. "Waiting for you to come?" Our eyes seemed to touch and my heart began to pound as he stepped closer.

He took my hand, his fingers soft and warm, and stood up, his face only inches from me.

"My Princess Annie," he whispered. His hands were on my shoulders. My heart pounded. He was going to kiss me.

"Not so fast, Twinkle Toes," Drake suddenly said, leaning over and pulling up his shoulders to make himself look like a hunchback. He folded his fingers into claws and came toward me. "I'm Tony Tatterton," he whispered in a low, sinister tone, "and I've come to steal the princess from you, Sir Luke. I live in the darkest, deepest bowels of the castle Farthy and she will come with me and be forever shut up in my world to become the princess of the darkness." He pealed off an evil-sounding laugh.

Both Luke and I stared at him. The look of surprise on both our faces made Drake self-conscious. He straightened up quickly.

"What drivel," Drake said. "You've even got me doing it." He laughed.

"It's not drivel. Our fantasies and our dreams are what make us creative. That's what Miss Marbleton told us in class recently. Didn't she, Luke?" Luke only nodded. He looked upset, deeply wounded, his eyes down, his shoulders turned in the way Daddy's would be when something disturbed him. Luke had so many of Daddy's gestures.

"I'm sure she didn't mean making up stories about Farthy," Drake responded and smirked.

"But don't you always wonder what Farthy is really like, Drake?" I asked.

He shrugged.

"One of these days, I'll take off some time from college and just go there. It's not far from Boston," he added nonchalantly.

"Will you really?" The idea filled me with envy.

"Sure, why not?"

"But Mommy and Daddy hate to talk about it," I reminded him. "They would be furious if you went there."

"So . . . I won't tell them," Drake said. "I'll only tell you. It'll be our secret, Annie," he added, looking pointedly at Luke.

Luke and I looked at each other. Drake didn't have our intensity when it came to talking about the past and Farthy.

Occasionally I would sneak a look at the wonderful pictures of Mommy and Daddy's fabulous wedding reception held at Farthinggale: pictures of so many elegant people, men in tuxedoes and women in stylish gowns, tables and tables of food and servants rushing about everywhere, carrying trays of champagne goblets.

And there was a picture of Mommy and Tony Tatterton dancing. He looked so debonair, like a movie star; and Mommy looked so vibrant and fresh, her cornflower-blue eyes, the eyes I inherited, dazzling. When I looked at that picture, it was hard to believe that he could do anything so terrible to turn her against him. How sad and mysterious it all was. It was what often drew me back to the pictures, as if studying them would reveal the dark secret.

"I wonder if I will ever see how elegant and fabulous it really is," I said, half as a question and half as a wish. "I'm even jealous that you were there at the age of five, Drake. At least you have that memory, as distant as it is."

"Sixteen years," Luke said skeptically.

"Still, he can close his eyes and remember something, see something," I insisted. "What I see of Farthy is only what I create out of my imagination. How close have I come? If only my mother would be willing to talk about it. If only we could visit. We could ignore Tony Tatterton; we wouldn't even look at the man. I wouldn't say a word to him, if she forbade it, but at least we could wander about and . . ."

"Annie!"

Luke jumped to his feet as my mother stepped around the corner of the house where she had obviously been listening to our conversation. Drake nodded as though he had expected her to make such an abrupt appearance.

"Yes, Mommy?" I retreated behind my easel. She looked at Luke, who quickly shifted his eyes away, and then she approached me, avoiding any look at my canvas.

"Annie," she said softly, her eyes filled with a deep, inner sorrow, "haven't I asked you not to torment yourself and me by talking about Farthinggale?"

"I warned them," Drake said.

"Why don't you listen to your uncle, honey. He's old enough to understand."

"Yes, Mother." Even as sad as she looked, she was beautiful, her complexion rosy, her figure as firm and as youthful as it was the day she and my father were married. Everyone who saw us together had the same reaction, especially men. "You two look more like sisters than mother and daughter."

"I've told you how unpleasant it is for me to remember my days there. Believe me, it is no fairy-tale castle. There are no handsome young princes waiting to swoon at your feet. You and Luke shouldn't . . . pretend such things."

14

"I tried to stop them," Drake said. "They play this silly fantasy game."

"It's not so silly," I protested. "Everyone fantasizes."

"They act like grade-school children sometimes," Drake insisted. "Luke encourages her."

"What?" Luke looked at my mother, his eyes lighting with fear. I knew how important it was to him that she like him. "No he doesn't," I cried. "It's just as much my fault."

"Oh, please, let's not dwell on it," Mother pleaded. "If you must pretend, there are so many wonderful subjects, places, things to think about," she added, changing her tone of voice to a lighter, happier one. She smiled at Drake. "You look so collegiate in your Harvard sweater, Drake. I bet you're anxious to get back," she said, and then turned to Luke. "I hope you'll be as excited about college as Drake is, Luke."

"I will. I'm looking forward to going." Luke glanced at my mother and then quickly turned back to me. For as long as I could remember, there was that shyness in Luke whenever he was in my mother's company. He was normally shy anyway, but he was afraid to have her catch him staring at her, and I couldn't remember him having long conversations with her, or with Daddy for that matter, even though I knew how much he admired them.

"Well, it's wonderful how well you have done in school, Luke," she told him, hoisting her shoulders back and raising her head with what some in town called "her defiant Casteel pride." I knew most of the women in Winnerrow were jealous of her. Besides being beautiful, she was a successful businesswoman. There wasn't a man who didn't adore her and respect her for being as efficient as she was sweet. "We are all proud of you."

"Thank you, Heaven," he replied, brushing his hair back and pretending interest in his textbook while his heart was bursting with happiness.

Suddenly he looked at his watch.

"Didn't realize the time," he said. "I'd better be heading home."

"I thought you were going to eat with us tonight," I protested before he could step away.

"Of course you should eat with us tonight, Luke." My mother looked with adoration at Drake. "It's Drake's last night home before his return to college," she said. "Would Fanny mind?"

"No." A subtle, sarcastic smile appeared at the corners of Luke's mouth. "She won't be home to-night."

"Okay then," my mother said quickly. She didn't want to hear the details. All of us knew about Fanny's escapades with younger men, and I knew how much it embarrassed and bothered Luke. "It's settled. I'll have another place set."

She turned, her eyes resting for a long moment on my canvas. I looked at it and then quickly turned to her to see if there was any sign of recognition in her face. She tilted her head slightly, her eyes suddenly far off as if she had been serenaded by a distant song.

"It's not finished yet," I said quickly, afraid she might say something critical. Even though both she and Daddy had been very supportive of my painting ever since I had begun, paying for all the lessons, providing me with the best brushes and paints, I couldn't help but feel insecure. Daddy had such wonderful artisans in his factory, some of the most talented people in the country. He knew what real art was.

"Why don't you paint a picture of the Willies, Annie?" She turned and pointed toward the mountains. "I'd love to hang something like that in the dining room. The Willies in spring with its blossoming forests full of birds; or even in fall with the rainbow colors of the leaves. You do so well when you paint a scene in nature."

"Oh Mommy, my work isn't good enough to be displayed. Not yet anyway," I said, shaking my head.

"But you have it in you, Annie." Her blue eyes softened with love and reassurance. "It's in your blood," she whispered, as though she were saying something blasphemous.

"I know. Great-grandpa whittled wonderful rabbits and forest creatures."

"Yes." My mother sighed, the memories bringing a soft smile to her face. "I can still see him, sitting on the porch of the shack, whittling away for hours and hours, taking a shapeless piece of wood and turning it into a lifelike little forest creature. How wonderful it is to be artistic, Annie, to come to a blank canvas and create something beautiful on it."

"Oh, Mommy, I'm really not that good yet. Maybe I'll never be," I cautioned, "but I can't stop wanting to be."

"Of course you will be good, and you can't stop wanting to do it because . . . because of your artistic heritage." She paused as if she had just told me some great secret. Then she smiled and kissed me on the cheek.

"Walk in with me, Drake," she said. "I have some things I'd like to discuss before I forget and you're off to college."

Drake stepped over first and gazed at my painting.

"I was just kidding you before, Annie. It's good," he said, practically under his breath so my mother wouldn't hear. "I know how you feel, wanting to see bigger and better things than Winnerrow. Once you leave this one-horse town," he added, turning a little toward Luke, "you won't have to spend your time pretending you're somewhere else."

With that he joined my mother. She threaded her arm through his and they started toward the front of Hasbrouck House. Something Drake said made her laugh. I knew Drake occupied a special place in her heart because he reminded her so much of her father. She loved walking through Winnerrow with him, arm in arm.

Sometimes I would catch Luke staring at them together, a look of longing in his face, and I understood how much he wanted to have a real and complete family. It was part of the reason he loved coming over to Hasbrouck House, even if he only sat quietly and watched us. Here there was a father, the father he never had, but should have had, and here there was a mother he would have rather had.

I felt Luke's eyes on me and I turned around. He was staring at me, a troubled, sad look on his face, as if he could read my thoughts and knew how sad I felt for all of us sometimes, despite our wealth and position in Winnerrow. Sometimes, I found myself envying much poorer families because their lives seemed so much simpler than ours . . . no secret pasts, no relatives to be ashamed of, no half brothers and half uncles, not that I would trade away anyone in my family. I loved them all. I even loved Aunt Fanny. It was as if we were all victims of the same curse.

"Do you want to continue with your painting, Annie?" Luke asked, his blue eyes bright, hopeful.

"You're not tired?"

"No. Are you?" he asked.

"I never get tired of painting and I never get tired of painting you," I added.

TWO

Birthday Gifts

Luke's and my eighteenth birthday was a very special day for us both. My parents came into my room that morning to wake me. Daddy had bought me a gold locket with his and Mommy's pictures in it. It was on a twenty-four-carat gold chain and glittered brighter than any charm. He put it on me and kissed me and hugged me so hard, my heart fluttered. He saw the look of surprise on my face.

"I can't help it," he whispered. "You're a young lady now and I'm afraid I'm losing my little girl."

"Oh Daddy. I'll never stop being your little girl," I cried.

He kissed me again and held me to him snugly until Mommy cleared her throat.

"I have something I would like Annie to have now," she announced. I couldn't believe what she had in her hand: something I knew was more important to her than the most expensive jewels she had. In fact, I couldn't think of any possession that was more precious to her, and now she was going to give it to me!

19

I thought about the days when I was a little girl before I was old enough to begin school. I remembered my mother spending what seemed to me to be hours and hours brushing my hair in her room by her vanity table while we listened to the music of Chopin. She would take on this dreamy look, a small smile playing on her beautifully shaped lips.

Near us on another, but much smaller table, was what I used to call her dollhouse, even though it wasn't really a dollhouse; it was one of the few examples of a Tatterton toy we had in our home. It was a replica of a toy cottage with a maze of hedges near it. I wasn't permitted to touch it, but sometimes, she would take the roof off and let me look at the inside. There were two people in there, a man and a young girl. The man was sprawled on the floor, his hands behind his head, looking up at the young girl, who seemed to be listening intently to something he was saying.

"What is he saying to her, Mommy?" I asked.

"He's telling her a story."

"What kind of a story, Mommy?"

"Oh, a story about a magical world where people are always snug and warm, where there is only beauty and kindness."

"Where is this world, Mommy?"

"For a while it was in the cottage."

"Can I go to that world, too, Mommy?"

"Oh, my darling, sweet Annie. I hope so."

"Were you there, Mommy?"

I could still see her face just before she answered me. Her eyes brightened bluer than the sky ever was, and the smile on her lips widened and deepened until her whole face grew softer and more beautiful. She looked like a little girl herself.

"Oh yes, Annie, I was. Once."

"Why did you leave, Mommy?"

"Why?" She looked around as if the answer were written down on a piece of paper she had left somewhere. Then she swung her eyes back to me, the tears glistening over them, and she embraced me. "Because, Annie . . . because it was too wonderful to bear."

Of course, I never understood and still couldn't. How can something be too wonderful to bear?

But I didn't think more about it. I wanted to look in at the tiny furniture and dishes. They were so perfect, I wanted to touch them. But I was forbidden to do that because everything was too fragile.

And now she was giving it to me. I looked at Daddy. His eyes were small as he stared intensely at the cottage. I never knew what it meant to him.

"Mommy, no. It means so much to you," I protested.

"And so do you mean so much to me, honey," Mommy said, handing me the cottage. I took it into my hands carefully, lovingly, and quickly put it safely down on my dresser.

"Oh thank you. I'll cherish it always," I said, knowing I would not only because it had been so special to her, but because whenever I was permitted to look in at the man and the woman, I thought about Luke and myself running off and living happily ever after in such a cottage.

"You're welcome, honey."

My parents stood there smiling at me, both looking so young and happy. What a wonderful morning to awaken, I thought. I wished my eighteenth birthday would go on and on forever, that my whole life was just one long, happy day when everyone was in a pleasant and glorious mood and all of us were kind to one another.

After they left, I took a shower and dressed and stood before my closet, spending time considering what I would wear on such a special morning. I decided to wear the pink angora sweater and white silk skirt, an outfit similar to the one the young girl in the toy cottage wore.

I brushed my hair down and pinned it back at the sides and put on very light pink lipstick. Happy with myself, I rushed out of my room and bounced down the soft, blue carpet stairs. As if all the world were celebrating my birthday, the sun was shining with a rich golden splendor. Even the leaves and long, spidery thin branches on the weeping willow trees just outside the front windows looked translucent. Everything green was greener. Every flower that had blossomed was brighter. The world was full of color and warmth.

I stopped at the foot of the stairs because there wasn't a sound in the house . . . no one talking, no servants moving about.

"Hello? Where is everybody?"

I went into the dining room. The table was set for breakfast, but there was no one there. I looked in the living room and sitting room and den, but there was no one in any of those rooms. Drake, who had come home from college the night before, just for my birthday, wasn't even up and about.

"Mother? Daddy? Drake?"

I even went into the kitchen. The coffeepot was perking, eggs were scrambled and readied for the skillet, slices of bread were in the toasters ready to be pushed down to be toasted, the juice was poured into glasses and placed on the silver trays, but there was no one in the kitchen. Where was Roland Star, our cook, or Mrs. Avery, our maid? And I hadn't seen Gerald Wilson, our butler, in the hallways or standing quietly in a corner.

"What is going on here?" I smiled with confusion

and excitement. Finally, I went to the front door and opened it to look out.

There they were: my mother, my father, Drake, the servants, and standing off to the side, Luke, all of them with this Cheshire cat smile on their faces.

"What's going on here?" I asked, and started out. "Why are you . . ."

And there it was. Somehow, the night before, my father had snuck a brand-new Mercedes convertible onto the driveway. It was light blue with sparkling aluminum wheels. They had it wrapped in two large pink ribbons. Before I could say anything, they all broke out into a rendition of "Happy Birthday." A lump came to choke my throat as I walked around and around the car and saw the license plate with my name.

"Happy birthday, Annie honey," my mother said. "May you have many, many more as happy as this one."

"I don't think that's possible," I cried. "How could I ever be happier than this? Thank you, everyone."

I kissed Daddy and hugged Drake.

"I don't know about anyone else," my father announced, "but I'm starving."

Everyone laughed and the servants filed past, kissing me and wishing me a happy birthday as they all went back to their duties. Only Luke lingered behind. I knew no matter how he was treated, he always felt like an outsider.

"Come along, Luke," my mother called, seeing how he remained just where he had been standing. "Logan and I have something special for you, too."

"Thank you, Heaven."

My mother looked at Luke and then at me and then joined the others. Luke didn't move.

"Come on, silly," I said. "It's our special day."

He nodded.

"What a beautiful car."

"We'll take a ride in it right after breakfast, okay?"

"Sure," he said, but he looked confused. "Heaven invited my mother, but she has a hangover. I don't know if she's going to make it," he explained.

"Oh Luke, I'm sorry." I took his hand. "Let's not let anything make us sad today, and if anything does, we'll go right to the gazebo and travel away from it." That made him smile. When we were very little, we would spend a lot of time there. It became a special place for us, a center for our fantasies. Without ever coming out and saying so, we understood that whenever we wanted to do or say something special, we would go to the gazebo.

Stepping up the three steps was like rising up out of the real world. It was a large gazebo, with a circular bench attached to the railings. My parents had had it repainted a bright white and green. There were small lanterns spaced along the ceiling beams so at night it could be lit up, something Luke and I thought made it even more magical.

We were practically the only ones to ever use it. It was more like a decorative piece. I couldn't remember a time my father had ever been in it. Drake never cared for sitting in it. He would much rather sit in the study, even on sunny warm days. Unless, of course, I wanted to go out there and he had nothing else to do. Then he would go along, but complain endlessly about the bugs or the hard wooden benches.

"We've got to go there anyway," Luke said. "I've got something for you," he added.

"And I've got something for you. See? This will be a wonderful day. Happy birthday."

"Happy birthday, Annie."

"Good. Now let's eat. I'm starving. All this excitement made me hungry."

He laughed and we rushed into Hasbrouck House.

Luke was wrong about his mother. Aunt Fanny made one of her usual dramatic entrances. We had all just sat down to have breakfast when she came bursting through the front door.

"Jist like ya all not ta wait for me," she declared, her hands on her hips. She was wearing a wide-brim black satin hat with a bright green ribbon and had her hair pinned up. Luke must have been right about her hangover because she wore her sunglasses in the house. Aunt Fanny often wore something outlandish, especially whenever she visited us. I thought she was just trying to annoy Mommy, but my mother never seemed to pay much attention to Fanny's clothing. Today she wore a dark green, short leather skirt and leather vest over a frilly pink blouse. All her colors made her look like a Christmas tree.

"We are sitting down nearly a half hour late as it is, Fanny," Mommy said.

"Oh, are ya?" She swept her hat from her head in one motion and sighed. Then she stepped forward and pulled out the gift-wrapped box that was snugly under her right arm. "Happy birthday, Annie darlin'."

"Thank you, Aunt Fanny." I took it gracefully and turned to the side so I could unwrap it without disturbing the table. Daddy sat stone faced, his hands folded, his chin against them. Luke looked down at the table and shook his head. Drake wore a wide smile. Of all of us, Drake enjoyed Aunt Fanny the most. I think she knew that because she always looked his way and winked as if there was something special between them.

Her gift was rather unique and quite unexpected—a hand-carved, ivory jewelry box that played "Memories" from the musical *Cats* when it was opened. Mommy's eyes widened. She was impressed.

"That's beautiful, Fanny. Where did you get it?"

"Got somethin' you couldn't git in Winnerrow, Heavenly. Sent a . . . gentleman friend of mine ta New York City, specially fer ya, Annie."

"Oh thank you, Aunt Fanny."

I kissed her and she beamed.

"Luke's gift is home. Too big ta carry around. Got him his own color TV."

"Oh. That's very nice, Luke," Mommy said, but Luke only shook his head slightly. He didn't watch much television. He was a reader.

"Wish ya two had been born a few months apart," Aunt Fanny said, taking her seat at the table. "Woulda made it easier come ya birthdays." She followed that with a peal of laughter. "Well what ya all gaping at? If this is breakfast, let's eat. I ain't et since . . . early yesterday," she added, and laughed again.

Despite Aunt Fanny's wild antics at the table and loud comments now and then, we all had a wonderful time. This birthday was the most magnificent and wonderful birthday of my life. It was truly a unique day, a day filled with music and laughter and sunlight, a day that would take up pages and pages in my diary. And I couldn't wait to have Luke pose for what I would call his "Eighteenth Birthday Portrait."

Everyone made me feel like a princess. Even the servants had bought me presents. Then, another special thing happened.

Before I could take Luke for a ride in my new car and then sneak away to the gazebo, my mother called me aside and asked me to go upstairs with her. We went to her and my father's bedroom. It was an enormous room with a great king-size bed that had a hand-carved hickory-wood headboard and large hickory-wood pillars. It looked like it would take a dozen men to lift it.

Over the bed was one of the few things I knew my mother had taken from Farthinggale Manor, and because I knew it came from Farthinggale Manor, it was always something extraordinary, even magical to me. Of course, as an artist, I appreciated it as well. It was a painting of the old cabin in the Willies with two old people seated in rockers on the porch.

My mother had redecorated and redesigned the room a few times since coming to Hasbrouck House. Now she had elegant, blue satin drapes lined with gold over the windows. The wall covering was a light blue velvet cloth and the matching light blue carpet was so thick and soft, I loved walking barefoot over it.

Two of the newer and younger craftsmen at the factory had been employed to build customized dressers and closets out of the same rich hickory wood as the bed. My mother's vanity table had been extended nearly the entire length of the right wall, which was now covered by a wall-length mirror. She took me directly to the vanity table and opened a middle drawer.

"There is something I want you to have," she declared, "now that you have turned eighteen. Of course, you will wear it only on special occasions, I'm sure, but nevertheless, I wanted to give it to you today."

She reached in and took out the long, coal-black jewelry case that I knew contained her most precious diamond necklace and matching earrings.

"Oh, Mother!" My lips gaped open at the realization of what she was about to do.

She opened the case and held it toward me. We both stared down at the sparkling diamonds. I could see that when my mother looked at them, she remembered special moments. How I wished that simply by wearing them, they would give me all the secrets of our past, plant my mother's precious memories into my mind as well, and teach me what wisdom and knowledge she had gained from her painful as well as her wonderful experiences.

"This belonged to my grandmother Jillian, who lived like a queen."

"And who wouldn't let you call her Grandmother," I whispered, remembering one of the few things she had told me about her life at Farthinggale Manor.

"No." She smiled. "She was very, very vain and wanted to hold onto her youth and beauty forever, clinging to every fabrication, to every illusion with the tenacity of a drowning woman clinging to a slab of driftwood. Beautiful jewelry and beautiful clothing were some of the things she clutched. Of course," she continued, that gentle smile still on her lips, "she had the face-lifts and the spa treatments and bought all the miracle ointments. She wore hats with wide brims whenever she was in the sun because she was afraid the sunlight would bring on wrinkles.

"Her skin did stay smooth and her complexion rich," she continued. I held my breath, for this was one of the longest descriptions of her grandmother she had related to me and I didn't want it to end. "And although she was twenty years older than Tony, those who didn't know, couldn't tell. She would spend hours and hours at her vanity table." My mother's smile widened.

She paused, lost in a memory for a moment.

"Anyway," she said, regaining her awareness, "this is something I inherited and it's something I want you to have now."

"They're so beautiful, I'd be afraid to wear them."

"You shouldn't be afraid of wearing and owning beautiful things, Annie. There was a time when I was.

I used to feel guilty having so much and remembering how poorly I and my family had lived in the Willies." Her blue eyes suddenly took on a determined look. "But I soon discovered that the rich are no worthier than the poor to inherit and enjoy the richest and most wonderful things this life has to offer.

"Never think you're better than anyone because you've grown up privileged," she continued with a vehemence that told me her words were offspring of much pain and suffering. "The rich are often driven by the same base motives as are the very dirty and very poor. Maybe even more than the poor," she added, "because they have more idle time to drift into their private madness."

"You learned these things at Farthinggale?" I asked softly, hoping she had chosen my eighteenth birthday as the occasion to tell me all her darkest secrets.

"Yes," she murmured. I waited breathlessly for her to say more, but then something snapped and she pulled herself up and out of that stream of memories instantly. Her eyes widened and brightened as if she had just come out of a hypnotic state. "But let's not talk about anything unpleasant. Not today of all days, honey." She leaned over and kissed me on the cheek and then placed the diamond necklace and earrings into my hands. "It's time to pass them on to you. Of course, I might come to you once in a while and ask to borrow them."

We both laughed as she hugged me.

"I'll just put them safely away and then go down," I told her as I rose from her embrace. I want to take Luke for a ride in my new car."

"And don't forget Drake. He's looking forward to it, too, Annie." Mother was always insisting on my being close to Drake.

"But there are only two seats!" I cried out in

29

dismay. I would have to chose between them and risk hurting the feelings of one or the other.

"Drake came all the way from college for your birthday, Annie. He made such a special effort. Luke is always here, and anyway, you spend far too much time with him. I've noticed you haven't had a date for months now. Other boys in town are probably becoming discouraged."

"The boys in my class are silly and immature. All they care about is going somewhere and drinking themselves into a stupor to prove their manhood. At least I can have an intelligent conversation with Luke," I pleaded, aware that I was close to whining.

"Still, Annie," she said, lowering her eyes, "it's not healthy." Her words fell like heavy drops of rain because I knew what she was saying was right. I nodded and tried to find a voice that didn't quiver.

"I feel sorry for him."

"I know, but soon he'll be going off to college to start his own life and you'll be traveling through Europe and meeting different people. Besides, his mother has money for him and he is very intelligent, your class valedictorian. There's no reason to pity Luke now. Why," my mother said smiling, "I bet he would resent it if he knew."

"Oh please, never tell him I said that!"

"I would never do such a thing, Annie. Don't you think I care for Luke and realize what he has had to go through and live with all these years? It's why I admire him for what he has become," she concluded, stroking my hair. "Now, go on, put your diamonds away and take Drake for a ride and then take Luke. There will be no tears or sad words today. I absolutely forbid it. I might even have the mayor of Winnerrow pass an instant ordinance against it," she said, laughing. I smiled away my worries.

"Thank you for being so wonderful to me," I told her.

"I could be no other way, honey. I love you too much."

She kissed me again and then I hurried off to put the diamonds safely in my jewelry drawer. When I went downstairs, I found Drake, Luke and my father in a serious discussion about the economy. They were arguing about the trade deficit and the need for protective legislation. I listened for a moment, admiring the way Luke held his own against the two of them. Then I burst into the study to announce rides in my Mercedes would begin.

"We'll do it by age," I said diplomatically. "First Daddy, then Drake, and then Luke. Three times down Main Street and back."

Daddy laughed.

"Can you imagine what the residents are going to be saying?" he asked. "They'll think we're just parading our wealth."

"If you've got it, flaunt it," Drake boasted. "I don't see the point in being ashamed of wealth. It's a phony, liberal attitude."

"I'm just talking about a ride," I protested. They all turned to me and then suddenly, the three of them broke out into laughter because of the expression on my face and the way I was holding my hands on my hips. "Men," I said, and started to turn away.

"Oh Annie," Daddy quickly said, and rushed to put his arms around me. "It's just that you're so cute when you're angry. Come on, let's see if that car is worth all the hullabaloo."

I took them each for a ride. Drake insisted I stop at the luncheonette so he could visit with some old friends for a few minutes, but what he really wanted to do was show off the car. Luke was reading a magazine on the gazebo when Drake and I returned. Drake decided to complete one of his college assignments so he could have the rest of the day off and go out to dinner with all of us later.

"I'll be right there," I called to Luke and ran into the house and up the stairs to my room to get his gift. Mommy and Daddy looked up surprised as I rushed by the sitting room.

"Slow down!" my father called. "Or you'll be eighty before you're fifty." I heard him laughing at his own joke as I closed the front door behind me and flew around to the gazebo, my heart pounding. Flushed with excitement, I bounced up the steps and plopped down beside Luke.

"Happy birthday," I said, and thrust out my hand. He studied the small package a moment and then plucked it out of my palm.

"Might be keys to another Mercedes," he jested. He opened the package and then lifted the cover of the small box to display the black onyx, solid gold pinky ring. "Wow!"

"Look inside the band."

He turned it to read the tiny inscription that said, "Love, your sister Annie."

It was the first time either of us had written anything that acknowledged our true relationship. Luke's eyes moistened with feeling, but he kept the tears imprisoned within their lids, not wanting to seem unmanly by shedding them, even out of happiness. I saw him try hard to close off his emotions and clamp down hard on them.

"Put it on," I said quickly. He slipped it over his finger and held it up in the sunlight. How the stone sparkled.

"It is so beautiful. How did you know I liked this jewel?"

"I remember you said so once when we were looking at a magazine."

"You're amazing." He stared down at the ring and ran the tip of his right forefinger over it and over it. Then he looked up quickly, his eyes bright with mischief. He reached behind himself and brought forward a flat, thin box in pink gift wrap. First, I opened the card.

Amazingly, as if we had both agreed that our eighteenth birthday should end all pretense, his card was "To a Sister on the Occasion of her Eighteenth Birthday." Whenever he gave me a card, he often wrote his own, more personal lines next to the printed ones.

The years may come and go, and time, like the magical maze we've dreamt about, might separate us. But never fear my ability to solve the puzzle and find you wherever you might be.

Happy Birthday,
Luke

"Oh Luke. These words are gift enough. More precious to me than even my new car."

His smile was small and tight.

"Open the gift."

My fingers trembled as I tried to tear away the paper neatly. I wanted to save it, save the ribbon, save every moment and everything associated with this wonderful day. Under the paper was a cream-colored box. I lifted the cover and saw tissue paper. Peeling it back, I gazed down at a bronze picture of a large house, beneath which was inscribed, "Farthinggale Manor, Our Magic Castle, Love, Luke."

I looked up with some confusion and he leaned forward, taking my hands into his as he explained.

"One day I was looking through an old trunk of my mother's in the attic and I came upon this newspaper clipping she had saved. It was from the social pages and it had a write-up of your parents' wedding reception. In the background of this picture of the guests and the party, was a clear view of Farthinggale Manor. I took it to a photographer who isolated the building in the photograph and then had the bronze replica made. That's actually it."

"Oh Luke." I ran my fingers over the embossed metal.

"Just so wherever you are and whatever you do, you'll never forget our fantasy game," he said softly.

"And I never will."

"Of course," he said sitting back quickly, aware of how closely our faces were to one another's, "that's the way it was years and years ago. Who knows what it looks like now."

"It's a wonderful gift," I cried, "because it has special meaning for us. Only you would think of something like this. I'll have to keep it hidden from my mother. You know how she gets when we make any references to Farthy."

"Oh, I know. I was going to suggest that myself. I don't have to have any other reasons for her not to like me."

"Oh she likes you, Luke. You should hear how she talks about you. She is very proud of you, really!" I exclaimed.

"Really?"

I saw how important that was to him.

"Yes, really. She never stops talking about your being our class valedictorian. She thinks it's just wonderful how you've overcome obstacles to reach great heights."

He nodded with understanding.

"Tall mountains may be harder to climb, Annie,"

34

he said, "but the view from the top is always worth it. Go for the tall ones. That's been my motto." He stared at me so hard. The mountain between us was just too tall.

"Come on now," I said, gathering the card and wrapping paper with the gift. "It's time for your ride in my new car."

I took his hand and hurried across the lawn to the car. Afterward, I snuck my gift up to my room and put it with my most private and personal things. Drake came to me that night before we went to dinner to ask what Luke had given me. He knew about the way we had exchanged birthday presents since we were twelve. I showed the plaque to him only after he promised not to tell my mother. I didn't show him Luke's card.

"That doesn't look like it," he said when I uncovered the box. "Not the way I remember it."

"But it must be, Drake. He found a picture and took it to the photographer."

"I don't know." He shook his head. "Magic castle. You're still really intrigued with that place, aren't you?"

"Yes, Drake. I can't help but be."

He nodded, his eyes small and thoughtful. I put the gift away and we joined my parents for my birthday dinner. But that night, before I went to sleep, I took it out again and looked at it and wondered if Drake was right to continue to make fun of our fantasy game. Would I ever really find such a magical and wonderful place? I wondered.

One day a few weeks later, I received a letter from Drake. He often wrote to me to describe his college life or give me advice. Even though he could be a tyrant at times and at times cruel to Luke, I missed his wit and humor and big brother–like antics. I looked forward to receiving mail from him and having him call me from time to time. His letters were usually filled with anecdotes about college girls or fraternities and events at Harvard. He told me about the picture of the championship rowing team in which my uncle Keith, Drake's stepbrother, a man neither of us saw much or heard from, appeared. So I wasn't surprised to receive this letter from him. What surprised me was the thickness of it. The envelope was so stuffed, I thought he had put something else in it beside a sheet of his personalized stationery.

I sprawled out on my lace quilt and opened Drake's letter.

Dear Annie,

I have news that I know will excite you. It has been very exciting for me, but you do your best to keep this from Heaven.

After your wonderful birthday, all the way back to college I thought about your fascination with Farthinggale Manor, and since your childhood days how you and Luke have built it into something fantastical. I decided the only reason you two act so silly about it is because you, as well as I, don't really know much about it or about the mysterious Tony Tatterton, my step-great-uncle and your step-great-grandfather. So I did something I know would upset Heaven, but I did it mostly for you.

Annie, I wrote a letter to Tony Tatterton, introducing myself and asking him if I could come visit. What must have been moments after he received it, I received a phone call from a man with a very distinguished-sounding voice, who invited me to Farthinggale Manor. That man was Tony Tatterton and I accepted his invitation.

Yes, Annie, I have just returned from your

magical kingdom and I have some rather sad, tragic, and yet fascinating news to tell you.

First, let me say it is a truly enormous place. And that wrought-iron gate is there. Oh, not quite as big as you and Luke always pretend it to be, but a rather big gate with large letters.

But, that's where the fantasies begin and end. The house is dark and dilapidated. Believe me, I am not saying this because I have often ridiculed you and Luke whenever you pretended Farthinggale was your magic castle. There is nothing magic about it now; only something tragic.

The big doors actually squeaked when they were opened. A butler who looked as old as Methuselah greeted me and I entered the enormous building. The entryway seemed as big as the gymnasium in the Winnerrow High School, but it was dimly lit and the curtains were drawn everywhere so that I felt chilled.

I saw the long stairway and some of my childhood memories flashed across my mind. The butler showed me to an office off right, and there I met our Tony Tatterton. He sat behind a large, dark mahogany desk with only a single small lamp casting any illumination in the room. In the shadows he appeared gaunt, but when I was announced, he stood up quickly and had the butler open the curtains.

Although he didn't fit my image of what a multimillionaire would look like, I found him warm, intelligent and very friendly. He was very interested in my career and as soon as he heard I was studying a business curriculum, he offered me an opportunity to work in his enterprises. Can you imagine?

Of course, our conversation dealt mainly with

your mother and with you. He was very interested in learning about you. At the end I felt somewhat sad, for he looked so lost and lonely in that huge house, hungry for anything I would tell him about the family.

Of course, we never got to talk about the reasons why Heaven and he no longer communicate, but I will tell you this. After spending time at Farthinggale with Tony Tatterton, I wished the breach between them could somehow be mended.

When I see you again, I will go into greater detail. At last you won't have to depend upon your and Luke's imagination to discover what Farthinggale Manor is all about. You have a witness who will tell you the truth. You might not want to paint any more pictures of it, but maybe that will be good because you can go on to happier and brighter subjects.

Can't wait to see you again.

Love,
Drake

I put the letter down. For some reason it had brought me to tears, tears I hadn't realized were streaming down my face the entire time I had been reading Drake's description of Farthy and Tony Tatterton. It was like I had been reading the obituary of a dear friend.

Drake meant no harm, I'm sure. He did only what he thought I would have wanted him to do, but in doing it, he had brought the curtain down on fantasy and illusion and on childhood dreams, and left me feeling empty and sad.

More than ever now, I wanted to know what it was that had driven my mother away from Farthinggale and left that distinguished elderly man alone in those enormous rooms and deep shadows.

I couldn't help myself. My soft weeping grew more and more intense until I was sobbing ˙like a baby. When I exhausted myself with it, I fell asleep with Drake's letter clutched in my hands and woke with the ringing of my phone. I was so happy to hear Luke's voice.

"What is it?" he asked immediately. There really was something special about us being born on the same day. We always seemed to know instantly when the other was upset.

"Drake has written me a letter. He went to Farthinggale and he saw Tony Tatterton." For a moment he didn't respond.

"Really?"

"You'll have to come over so I can read it to you," I told him. "Oh Luke, it's not what we dreamt it was."

"I don't care what Drake's written or what it really is," Luke said defiantly. "Our dreams are important to us because they fill our lives with hope and light."

"Oh Luke," I said smiling at his determination to hold on to our precious, secret fantasies, "I hope you will always be nearby when I need someone to cheer me up."

"Of course I will," he promised.

But I couldn't help wondering if that too was just another one of our childhood fantasies.

THREE

Scary Crossroads

Drake couldn't return from college until after the end of June because he had finals to take, but he phoned me a few days after he had mailed his letter to be sure I had received it and to tell me more about Farthy.

"Tony Tatterton showed me what was once Heaven's room when she first came to Farthy to live," Drake said in a voice lowered in confidence.

"He did!" My heart beat faster, louder, at just the thought of his being there, being where so many secret things involving our family had taken place. Of all of us, Drake had been closest to the answers to the questions that haunted. Were there any clues he might have missed that I would have seen?

"Or what was also your grandmother Leigh's room. I got a little confused about that because one moment he was telling me about Heaven and the next he was talking about Leigh."

"Maybe he's the confused one; maybe he's senile," I suggested.

"I don't think so. He still handles some of the business affairs for the Tatterton Toy Company, and when we began to talk about my career and the economy, he seemed very sharp and up on everything."

"How does he look? Like he did in the pictures?"

"Not anymore. He's completely gray, and when I saw him, he obviously hadn't shaved for a few days. He was wearing what looked to be expensive clothing, but his jacket needed pressing, as did his pants, and his tie was stained. I don't think the butler, a man called Curtis, is much good any longer. His eyesight is apparently poor and it takes him ages to move from one room to another."

"Weren't there any maids?" I asked, a little astounded. I would have thought a man as rich as Tony Tatterton was surrounded by a staff of servants.

"I didn't see any, but I'm sure there must be at least one to clean up the areas he lives in. I met the cook because he helped serve the meal. His name is . . . get this . . . Rye Whiskey."

"Oh, I remember hearing Mommy mention that name," I squealed with excitement. Just hearing the name made the few stories from the forbidden past come alive for me. "He must be very old, too."

"Probably, but he doesn't show his age as much as the butler does. He was so grateful for another mouth to feed, he piled enough food for three on my plate. I liked him. He has a great sense of humor, and I could see he cares a great deal about Tony."

"How I wish I had been there too," I cried. Every moment would reveal a discovery and a new and better understanding of my family's past, I thought. To walk up those stairs and step into what had been my grandmother's and my mother's room! Perhaps I would have seen something that would immediately solve the mystery of why my mother disliked Tony Tatterton so much and refused to go back, even for a visit.

Most of all I would be in Luke's and my dream world. Would it prove to be anything like we imagined? Would it be the place where we could be free and true, where we would be isolated and protected from all the harsh, nasty, ugly, and distorted things that make life a burden sometimes?

To paint it as it really was! How exciting that would be. I could see myself set up on the big front lawn, the enormous building spread before me.

"You wouldn't want to be there," Drake said in a tone of discouragement. "Believe me. It was too sad. I promised I would keep in touch with him, so I think I'll phone him in a few days. I rather like the possibility of working in his company, as an executive, of course. But don't tell Heaven I said that."

"Of course not." Once again I was surprised at Drake's willingness not only to keep all this from my mother but to pursue a relationship with Tony Tatterton, something which she would despise intensely. What sort of a man could Tony Tatterton be, I wondered, that he could have such a dramatic effect on Drake and be such a strong influence, even now?

"Well, anyway, I'll see you in a few weeks. I'm afraid I will have to miss Fanny's big birthday party, which is something I regret. She wrote to tell me she's going to have a band, and that she's having it catered. She's invited loads of people, many of your parent's friends, too. She even hired people to decorate her house and grounds. Can you imagine throwing yourself such a big celebration! I just know she's setting up her own audience for one of her outlandish shows. Take notes so you can tell me all the ridiculous and embarrassing things she does. I imagine she will invite all her young boyfriends, who will gather around her like suitors at the feet of a queen. I laugh just thinking about it."

"It's not funny for Luke," I said, sorry to see that even Drake had to make fun of Fanny. "He doesn't even want to go! He dreads it!" I exclaimed.

"So?" Drake said with surprising indifference and insensitivity. "Tell him to hide in his room. I'll call you again after I speak with Tony again, and let you know anything else of interest."

I couldn't stop thinking about what he had seen and what he had done.

"Oh, Drake, you were the only one of us who was ever there and now you've been back and will go again," I whined like a jealous little girl. I couldn't help it.

"You'll be there, too, through me," Drake promised, his voice softer, kinder, "and it won't be any fantasy game. Talk to you soon. Bye."

I couldn't wait for our lunch break the following day at school, so I could tell Luke all about Drake's phone call. I never expected him to be as excited as I was, because he didn't have family roots at Farthy and wasn't as concerned about the ancestors and the mysteries surrounding my mother's past, but he usually got involved because of our fantasies. He sat munching on his sandwich listlessly and listened, but I could see he was terribly distracted and troubled. Unlike his usual self, he refused to talk when I questioned him. I thought about him all the rest of the school day, and after it ended, asked him to walk me home, just so I could question him some more.

It was one of those late spring days that was more like the peak of summer, with puffy, fat white clouds sliding lazily across the turquoise sky. As Luke and I walked along, we heard the clink and clank of ice in pitchers of lemonade. Elderly people sat out on their porches and stared out curiously. Once in a while we could hear someone say something like, "That's the Stonewall girl," or "Ain't that a Casteel?"

I hated the way they pronounced "Casteel," making it sound like a curse word, like a family less than human. I knew much of why people saw the Casteels the way they did was because of my aunt Fanny's behavior over the years, and the fact that the Casteels were people from the Willies, mountain people who were not as educated and had a fraction of the wealth town people had. Town people were disdainful of the way Willies people dressed and lived, and a lot of that was understandable, but why couldn't they see how wonderful Luke was and how much he had overcome? He was right. "Go for the tall ones!"

I especially loved this walk home from school in spring because the streets were lined with flowering trees and shrubs, lawns were fresh and kelly green, tulips, irises and azaleas were blossoming, walkways and patios were scrubbed clean. Starlings sat like sentinels on telephone lines, watching the traffic of cars and people below. Robins, perched on branches, peaked out with curious eyes between cool, rich green leaves. Only an occasional hummingbird flew nearby. They seemed to have endless energy no matter how hot it was. The world looked fresh and alive.

For most of the walk home, Luke was closed-lipped and walked with his head down. When I stopped at the entrance to the walk of Hasbrouck House, I could see he was unaware we had arrived.

"Do you want to sit in the gazebo for a while?" I asked hopefully, for I wanted to keep him with me until he told me exactly what was bothering him.

"No, I'd better get home," he said, his voice filled with melancholy.

"Luke Toby Casteel!" I finally exclaimed, my hands on my hips. "You and I are not in the habit of keeping secrets from one another, even if they are painful ones."

He stared at me a moment, looking as if he had suddenly woken up and realized I was there. Then he shifted his eyes away.

"I was accepted to Harvard yesterday on a fully paid, tuition scholarship," he said with a surprising absence of feeling and excitement.

"Oh, Luke, how wonderful!"

He put his hand up to indicate that wasn't all he was going to say about it, and then looked down again and gathered his strength to continue as I waited with a lump in my throat.

"I never even told my mother I had applied to Harvard. Every time I used to mention it, she would go into one of her tirades about the blue bloods and this ungrateful family that thinks it's so much better than her. She would rant and rave about Uncle Keith and Aunt Jane and how they won't ever call her or write her or acknowledge her existence. It bothers her that she was never invited to Farthinggale, not even to your parents' wedding reception. In her mind she links it all together: Harvard, the Tattertons, wealth, and those she calls "Bean Town Snobs."

"But Luke, that's so unfair to you," I consoled him. He nodded.

"Anyway," he continued, "I didn't tell her about my application. Yesterday the acceptance announcing the scholarship came in the mail and she opened it. Then she got drunk and ripped it up. I found the pieces on the floor in my room."

"Oh, Luke, I'm sorry." I cringed just thinking what it must have been like for him to walk into his room and discover such an important piece of mail scattered all over the floor.

"That's all right. Her ripping it up won't stop me

from going. It was the ugly things she said while she was in one of her drunken states."

Without his having to tell me, I knew what direction her ugly words had taken.

"About my father?" He nodded. I took a deep breath to prepare myself. "You might as well tell me." I closed my eyes and winced at the anticipated ugliness.

"I won't tell you all of it because some of it was so vicious and hateful, I don't want to remember it myself, much less repeat it to you. The worst part was when she accused me of being more like Logan than her, being more loyal to his goody-two-shoes side of the family than to her, but really, Annie, your parents treat me better than she does. She's hardly ever home to make dinner, but she hates me for spending so much time at your house!"

"Oh, she doesn't hate you, Luke."

"She hates half of me, the Stonewall half, so she gets drunk and runs off with one of her young boyfriends and then chastises me because I don't like her when she's drunk and with them!"

"I'm sorry, Luke, but soon you'll be going off to college and you'll be away from all this," I promised, even though I hated the thought that he and I would be separated.

"The thing is, I don't hate her, Annie. I hate what she does to herself sometimes, and I feel sorry for her and the life she's had. So I worked hard and did well and made it possible for her to be proud and walk with her head high, not that she wouldn't anyway," he added. I smiled. Aunt Fanny wouldn't hesitate to flaunt any of her success to anyone in Winnerrow. "But instead of being happy I was accepted to Harvard on a full scholarship, she accuses me of deserting her."

"She will change her mind," I assured him. Poor

Luke, I thought. He had worked so hard to make us all proud of him and his mother had torn that pride into pieces and left it lying like garbage on the floor. How his heart must have broken. I wanted to comfort him, to soothe his mental anguish, to hold him in my arms and help him to feel content and happy once again. I could do it, if only . . . if only there wasn't so much preventing me.

"I don't know. Anyway, I'm not looking forward to her birthday party. She has invited every man who's taken her out and some of her low-class friends, just so she could rub it into the family." He shook his head. "It's not going to be nice or any fun for us."

"My mother will handle it; she always does," I said as my admiration for my mother brightened my spirits. "She can be a lady no matter what. I hope I'll have half her strength when I'm her age."

Luke nodded knowingly, that deep analytical look in his eyes as he came to his conclusion.

"You will. You're just like her."

"Thank you. There is no one I would rather be like. And don't worry about the party. I'll be there with you to help if Aunt Fanny gets out of hand," I assured him, my eyes as intense and my face as determined as Mommy's could be when she was decided about something.

"You haven't seen her really out of hand, Annie," Luke warned. Then he shook his head and smiled, his face brightening. "Anyway, thanks for listening. You've always been there when I've needed you and it's always made a difference. You don't realize how much of a difference, Annie. Just knowing you were there for me helped me to go on, to climb those taller mountains, to want to see that view. When I was accepted to Harvard, I thought to myself, Annie will be proud and it's because of Annie that I want this so much, want to make so much of my self. Sometimes, I feel you're the only real family I have. Thank you, Annie."

"You don't have to thank me for that, Luke Toby, Jr." I didn't like the way it sounded, like I was just a good friend. I was more; I had to be more. I wanted to be more. "You have often listened to my troubles, too."

He smiled at my reminder, his blue eyes turning as soft and warm as the sky above us.

"I'll miss you when you go off to Europe to study art. I know how important it is to you, though," he added softly. "And I know it's going to help you become the wonderful artist you are meant to become."

"I'll write to you all the time, but I'm sure after the first week, you'll have yourself a "bean town" girlfriend." How I wanted to tell him that I would always be his girlfriend, but how could I? We were brother and sister and it seemed as if the whole world stood between us and what we really wanted, for I knew in my heart that he felt some of what I felt and there was a part of both of us that cried and mourned and wished we could stay together forever and ever.

So we had to pretend, to talk about each other finding someone else, even though in our hearts, we hoped and prayed it would never happen.

His smile disappeared and he turned as serious as a deacon on Sunday.

"I don't know. After having you for a friend all my life, she's going to have to be pretty perfect whoever she is." His shiny blue eyes swung my way again, filled with warmth and affection, but it was more than just a brotherly affection. He looked at me with such longing I felt a flush move up my neck and settle into my cheeks. He was looking at me and I was looking at him the way two young lovers would.

There was no denying it. Every part of me cried out to embrace him; I could almost feel his lips against mine. He waited, looking for some encouragement. I had to stop it before it went too far.

"I'll call you later," I whispered in a breathy voice, and ran down the walkway to the front entrance of Hasbrouck House. When I looked back, he was still standing there. He waved and I waved back. I slipped into the house and rushed up to my room quickly, my heart thumping harder than ever. Why did Luke have to be my half brother, closer to me than anyone my age could be? We shared so much, our happiness and our sadness.

How I wished that he was a stranger going to Harvard, and I was visiting Tony Tatterton at Farthinggale, and Luke and I had just met in Boston. Perhaps we would meet in a department store. He would come up beside me and say something like, "Oh that's not your color. Here." He would reach for the aqua shawl. "You want to bring out the blue in your eyes."

I would turn and look into the most handsome face I had ever seen and instantly fall in love.

"Forgive me for being so forward, but I couldn't stand by and watch you make a mistake." He would speak with his familiar self-confidence and sweep me off my feet. I always felt more secure when I was with Luke.

"Then I'll have to thank you," I would say, batting my eyelashes coquettishly. "But first I have to know your name."

"Luke. And your name is Annie. I already took the trouble to find out."

"Really?" I would be flattered, impressed. Afterward we would go for coffee and talk and talk. We would go to movies and dinner every time I came to

Boston. Then, he would come to see me at the estate and we would get to know one another in that palatial setting, only it wouldn't be the way Drake had described it; it would be the way Luke and I had fantasized: a castle filled with rainbow rooms of dreams. If only I could go to sleep and when I woke up, the fantasy be a reality.

But that couldn't be. Time was like a roller coaster and we were approaching the peak of the steepest hill. We were both about to graduate high school and then we would go rushing downward into our futures that might easily take us into far different directions. We couldn't even turn around to look back.

After I stood by my bedroom window and watched him walk off, I lay there on my bed, staring out the window through the pink and white curtains, hearing the birds serenade each other and listening to the thumping of my own heart. It made me so sad that I cried for what seemed like hours. Mother's soft, concerned voice rescued me from my own tears.

"Annie, what's wrong?" She came in quickly and sat beside me on the bed. "Honey?" I felt the comfort of her hand on my hair, stroking the long, dark brown strands with concern. I turned my tear-filled my eyes toward her.

"Oh Mother, I don't know," I moaned. "Sometimes, I just can't help crying and feeling just terrible. I know I should be happy. Soon I'll be graduating and going off for an extended visit to Europe, seeing all those wonderful places most people only read about or see pictures of, and I have so many things other girls my age don't have, but . . ."

"But what, Annie?"

"But suddenly everything seems to be happening too fast. Luke is getting ready to go off to college and become someone else. We'll probably hardly ever see each other again," I cried.

"But this is what it means to grow up, honey." She smiled and kissed my cheek.

"And all the things that used to look so big and important to me look small and . . . and simple. The gazebo . . ."

"What about the gazebo, Annie?" She waited with her smile frozen on her lips as I tried to find words that made any sense to me as well as to her.

"It's just a . . . gazebo now," I protested.

"Well, that's all it ever was, Annie."

"No, it was more," I insisted. So much more, I thought. It was our dream place and dreams were falling away too quickly.

She shook her head.

"You're just going through something everyone your age goes through, Annie. Life can be scary when it comes to these crossroads. All this time you've been a little girl, protected and loved, and now you're being asked to be grown up and responsible."

"Did this happen to you, too?" I asked.

"A lot earlier, I'm afraid."

"Because your father sold you and your brothers and sisters?"

"Even before that, Annie. I didn't have much of an opportunity to be a little girl. Before I knew what was happening, I had to be a mother to Keith and Jane."

"I know. And Fanny was no help," I repeated. I had heard this before and was afraid it was all I would hear now.

"No." She laughed. "Hardly. Fanny has always been able to discard her frustrations like a garment easy to rip off. But your uncle Tom was a great help. Tom was wonderful and strong and very mature for his age. How I wish you could have known him," she added wistfully, her eyes, so much like my own, taking on a faraway look.

"But your life got so much better after you went to

live at Farthy, didn't it?" I prompted, hoping she might tell me more. She appeared startled, as if she really had been in some other world.

"Not right away. Don't forget I was a girl from the Willies suddenly going to live in a fancy, sophisticated, luxurious world, sent to a posh school attended only by rich, snobby girls who made me feel unwanted." Her face hardened as she remembered. "Rich girls can be very cruel because their money and wealth protects them like a cocoon. Don't ever be inconsiderate and unsympathetic to those who have less than you do, Annie."

"Oh I won't," I insisted. Surely Mother had instilled that in me from the time I was old enough to talk.

"No, I don't think you will." She smiled softly. "Try as he might, your daddy hasn't succeeded in spoiling you," she said, her eyes twinkling with love.

"Mother, will you ever tell me why you hate Tony Tatterton so much?" I swallowed and bit down hard on my tongue to prevent myself from telling her about Drake's letter and visit to Farthy.

"I don't hate him as much as I pity him, Annie," she said, her voice firm. "He may be one of the richest men on the East Coast, but he's a pathetic creature as far as I'm concerned."

"But why?"

She stared at me. Could she look at me and see the things I already knew, the things Drake had written about and told me about on the phone? I had to shift my eyes away from hers, but the truth was, she wasn't looking at me; she was looking through me, looking at her own memories. I saw the way they turned and twisted her lips, narrowed her eyes, brought a smile and then a scowl to her face.

"Mother?"

"Annie," she replied, "a long time ago, someone

52

once told me you trap yourself sometimes, by thinking desire and need is love. He was right. Love is something far more precious, but something far more fragile. As fragile as . . . as one of our tiniest, most intricate, most delicately crafted toys. Hold on to it too tightly, and it will crumble in your fingers, but hold on to it too loosely, and the wind might blow it away and shatter it on the cold ground. Listen to the voice in your heart, Annie, but be absolutely sure the voice comes from your heart. Will you remember that, Annie?"

"Yes. But why are you telling me this? Does it have something to do with your life at Farthy?" I held my breath.

"Someday I'll tell you everything, Annie. I promise. It just isn't the time yet. Trust me, please."

"I trust you, Mother. More than anyone in the world." I couldn't help being disappointed. For so many years I had heard this promise. When would be the time? I was already eighteen years old, a fully grown woman. She had given me her most valuable diamonds, her most precious replica cottage. When would she give me the real story of her life?

"My Annie, my precious, precious, Annie." She hugged me to her and pressed her cheek against mine. Then she sighed and stood up. "Well, I haven't bought your aunt Fanny a birthday gift yet. Want to help me pick something out?"

"Yes. Luke's so upset about her party though."

"I know. Why we cater to her is a mystery to me. But don't underestimate your aunt Fanny. She talks like a hillbilly, but she's far from dumb. She makes us feel guilty before we have a chance to say no. There's no one else like her," she added shaking her head and smiling with amusement.

"Talk to her about Luke, Mother. Make her stop making him feel bad about going to Harvard."

"He was accepted?" Delight lifted her voice.

"Yes. And with a full scholarship!"

"How wonderful!" She straightened into a flag of pride. "Another descendent of Grandpa Toby Casteel goes to Harvard," she announced as if to the whole town. Then her eyes softened. "Don't worry about Fanny. She will say and do something dramatic, but in her heart, she's proud of Luke, and I'm sure she will find some reason to pay him a visit and stroll over that campus like a queen."

She folded her arms under her breasts like Aunt Fanny often did, and threw her head back.

"Well, ma son goes here, so ah think I kin stroll over this grass if I've a mind ta."

We both laughed and then she hugged me again.

"That's better. Now you're the Annie you're supposed to be, happy, delicate, alive. You're everything I could have wished for myself, honey," she said softly. My tears were tears of happiness now.

My mother, how quickly she could drive away my dark clouds. Suddenly my world was full of bright, golden sunshine again, and the songs of the birds were no longer sad songs. I hugged and kissed her and went into the bathroom to wash my tear-streaked cheeks so I could go shopping with her for a birthday gift for Aunt Fanny.

FOUR

Aunt Fanny's Birthday Party

It was a wonderful night for a party. The sky was a backdrop of rich black velvet with tiny diamonds cast randomly over it. The air was fragrant and still. My parents and I were dressed and ready. Roland Star greeted us outside on the porch as we left the house. "This is the calm before a mighty storm," he drawled.

"But there's not a cloud in the sky!" I remarked. When it came to predicting weather, Roland was rarely wrong.

"They're hoverin' about up there, just over the horizon, Annie. They's the kind that sneak up on ya. Be a while yit, but watch fer the first streaks of lightnin'. Then head for the indoors."

"Do you think it will rain?" I asked my mother. A spring thunderstorm could bring torrents and flood everything, turning any party into a disaster.

"Don't worry. We won't be at the party that long." She looked to my father for confirmation, but he just shrugged. Then we got into our Rolls-Royce and started for Fanny and Luke's house.

They had a nice home, modest in comparison with Hasbrouck House, but most every home in Winnerrow was. After Aunt Fanny "mysteriously" inherited a great deal of money—an inheritance Drake, Luke, and I came to realize had something to do with Drake's custody hearing—she had her home redesigned and expanded. She had bought the original home with money she had gotten from her first marriage, to someone named Mallory. I never knew his first name because she referred to him only as "Ole Mallory." Her second marriage, to Randall Wilcox, was short-lived. He had long since moved away. Then Aunt Fanny legally returned her name to Casteel, partly to rub it into the faces of the townspeople, I always thought.

Aunt Fanny was always threatening she would have a third marriage. It seemed like an empty threat because for as long as I could remember, she hadn't ever gone out with anyone near her own age. All her boyfriends were in their twenties. One of her more recent ones, Brent Morris, was just four years older than Luke.

Her house was on a hill overlooking Winnerrow, and the rock band had set up speakers so huge that the music rolled right down to Main Street. We could hear the music blaring as we drove up the mountain. Mother thought that was outrageous, but Daddy only laughed.

By the time we arrived, the party was in full swing. The rock band had set themselves up in Fanny's garage and the expanded and widened driveway served as a dance floor. Over the garage door a banner spelled HAPPY BIRTHDAY FANNY! in fluorescent red paint. Paper lanterns hung from tree limbs, and streamers were draped everywhere on her property.

Mommy asked Daddy to park our car where it

couldn't be blocked in by anyone, so we could make a quick getaway when she determined we had had enough, but Daddy didn't seem as eager to secure an escape route. He seemed in an unusually jolly mood. I suspected he had had a few drinks at home to fortify himself for the occasion. No matter how many years had gone by and how wonderful Mommy was about it, Daddy was always agitated in Aunt Fanny's presence. Her conversations were usually stocked with innuendos that made almost everyone uncomfortable. I had to admire Mommy for the ladylike way she always handled Fanny's carrying-on. I only hoped Luke was right—that I would be as strong and steady as she was when I was on my own.

Aunt Fanny came running over to us as soon as we stepped out of the car. She had her hair crimped and blown out and wore the tightest black leather dress imaginable. It looked like a second layer of skin. The dress had a very low neckline, the base of the V dipping well below her cleavage. She wore no jewelry, almost as if she didn't want anything competing with her rich cream complexion and rose-tinted bosom. Mother didn't look surprised, but Daddy's eyes widened with masculine appreciation. I looked around for Luke, realizing how embarrassed he must already be.

Fanny scooped one of her arms under Mother's right arm and the other under Daddy's left so she could escort them into the party, announcing their arrival as she did so. I followed closely behind.

A long bar with two bartenders had been set up in front of the house, and the bartenders were pouring drinks very generously, not even measuring how much alcohol they were putting in the glasses. Adjacent to the makeshift bar was a full keg of beer submerged in a vat of ice. A steady stream of men, many of whom lived in the Willies, stood in line to fill their quart-size mugs.

Fanny had had strings of multicolored lights strung across the lawn from the house to adjacent trees. She had hired a half-dozen women to prepare and serve the food. All wore button-down white cotton dresses and dished out the food from behind long tables covered with buckets of fried chickens, platters of fish, bowls filled with a variety of salads, mashed potatoes, and steaming vegetables.

"Ma rich sista and brotha-in-law, the king and queen of Winnerrow, the Stonewalls!" Fanny bellowed.

"Oh, Fanny, please. Behave yourself," Mother chastised.

"Oh, let her enjoy herself," Daddy said. I think he liked being called the king of Winnerrow. "It's her night. Happy birthday, Fanny," he said.

"Why thank ya, Logan, dear, but don't I get at least one birthday kiss? That'd be all right with ya, won't it, Heavenly?"

"That's entirely up to Logan, Fanny. I don't tell him who he can kiss and who he can't."

Mother's reply struck Fanny funny. She laughed and laughed and then suddenly stopped and rubbed up to my father so seductively, it interrupted conversations all around us. Everyone stopped and stared. Mother turned away, but I couldn't take my eyes off the two of them. Daddy smiled nervously and then he leaned forward to give Fanny her birthday kiss.

When his lips met hers, Fanny seized his shoulders and pulled him closer. I saw her work her tongue in between his lips and then press her breast against his arm. Some of the men from the Willies cheered and whooped lasciviously. When their lips finally parted, Fanny pulled Daddy onto the dance floor as he looked back helplessly at Mother and me. Fanny started to gyrate before him, egging him on to join her in what she called "these modern dances."

She made him loosen his tie.

"Ya didn't have ta get all fancied up for lil' ole Fanny," she announced. She directed everything she said to the audience of young men that hovered around her. They laughed and smiled and nudged one another. The band played even louder.

I looked again for Luke, but didn't see him anywhere outside.

"I'm going to get something to eat, Annie," Mother said tightly, "and put Fanny's present on the pile over there. Do you want something to eat?"

I looked at her face and wondered how she felt about Daddy and Aunt Fanny being the center of attention, especially with all the gossip about their affair years ago. But even in these circumstances, Mommy had a wonderful way of holding in her true feelings. Only someone like me, someone who had known her so long and was as close to her as I was, could see the cold, hard look in her blue eyes and know that not only wasn't she happy, she was in a rage.

How could she be so controlled? I wondered. What if something similar to this happened to me and my husband? Could I carry on as she was or would I just explode? If it were Luke and he were kissing another woman . . .

Daddy was trying to swing his hips in time to Fanny's as she reached out and rested her palms on his shoulders. I thought she looked ridiculous, dancing like a lewd teenager. He looked baffled. How unfair Daddy and Aunt Fanny were being to Mommy, considering what she had to go through while they performed for this raucous crowd. I wanted to shout out to Daddy to stop, and I wanted to bawl out Aunt Fanny for not considering Mother's feelings, too.

There was a limit to selfishness and how much should be excused in the name of a good time, I concluded. I needed to talk to Luke.

"First I'll find Luke, and then we'll join you."

"All right, honey," she said, and glanced back once at Daddy and Aunt Fanny. Fanny had her arms around his waist now and she was swinging her hips wildly from side to side. For a moment I wondered if I shouldn't cut in and take Daddy from Fanny, but then I thought she might make a bigger scene and embarrass us even more. I went searching for Luke and finally found him in the house, sitting alone on the couch in the living room.

"Luke, why are you sitting by yourself in here?"

He looked up. When he saw me, his smile broke through the icy layer of rage that covered his face.

"I just couldn't stand it anymore out there, Annie. I decided the best thing to do was come in here and wait for it all to end. She's throwing herself on all of them, and the way they kiss her and the way she kisses them back . . ." He shook his head. "What is she trying to prove?"

"That she can be young and beautiful forever, maybe; that forever and ever young men will desire her."

"Why doesn't she just act her age? Why can't she have class, like Heaven?"

"She's making a scene with Daddy now, and Mother's getting angry," I said, not masking my anger.

He looked up quickly. "Is she? I had a nightmare about that. What is your father doing?"

"I think he's just trying to be polite and not have her escalate into any more embarrassing scenes, but I don't know how long Mother will put up with it. I feel so sorry for her, Luke."

"I guess I had better get back out there. Maybe I can do something. I'm sorry," he said.

"You can't spend your life apologizing for your mother, Luke."

"Seems that's all I've been doing since I can remember." He straightened up. He looked very handsome, dressed in a light blue sports jacket and tie. His rich black hair was soft and wavy. He looked like a man, I thought, not a boy anymore, a man who could handle a situation like this. I followed him out.

The band had changed the music. Suddenly they were playing a Willies hoedown, and the men from the shacks had formed a circle around Aunt Fanny and Daddy, who looked like he was holding on for dear life now as she swung him around, his once neatly brushed hair now flying about wildly.

I spotted Mother off to the side, standing under a pine tree. She had a plate of food in her hands, but she wasn't eating any of it.

"Your father's making a fool of himself," she muttered when Luke and I stepped up beside her. "I'm just waiting for him to come to his senses, but by my count he's had four drinks already."

"I'll cut in on them," Luke volunteered. He lunged forward before my mother could respond. He pulled two men apart and entered the circle, seizing Aunt Fanny's loose right hand and pulling her toward him and away from Daddy, who spun around in confusion for a moment. He got his footing, saw Fanny was dancing with Luke, and backed out of the center of the circle. Mother stepped forward.

"You'd better put something in your stomach, Logan, and soak up some of that alcohol," she said, her voice as hard as nails.

"Huh?"

He looked at me and then at the circle of men and women clapping and now joining Luke and Fanny in their dance. Then he wiped his face with his handkerchief and nodded.

"Your sister's crazy," he said. Mother just glared at him. "I am starved," he added quickly, and headed for the tables of food. I watched him stumble along, and when I lifted my eyes toward the sky, I saw Roland Star's sneaky clouds begin to crawl over the dark purple mountains, heading directly for Winnerrow.

Daddy filled a plate with food and flopped into a seat by one of the tables Fanny had set up on the lawn. Mother and I joined him, and we ate as we watched the crowd of revelers working themselves into a wilder and wilder frenzy. I recognized many people from town. Fanny had obviously invited everyone she came across, I thought, determined to make her party a memorable occasion for Winnerrow.

Most of the people were laborers and service folk. None of my parents' high-class friends had attended, not even out of respect for them; but I knew that was something Mother would forgive them for. I couldn't remember ever seeing my Mother look as uncomfortable as she did now.

Suddenly Aunt Fanny stopped the dance and went to the leader of the band. He nodded, and the band played a short introduction followed by a drum roll. Aunt Fanny turned over a small garbage can and had two of her young male admirers help her up onto it.

"I got a few words ta say," she began.

"Only a few?" someone shouted, and there was a hubbub of laughter.

"Well, maybe a dozen or so more," Aunt Fanny countered, and there was more laughter. "I'd like ta thank ya all fer comin' ta my fortieth birthday party. That's right, I said forty, an' I'm darn proud of it, proud ta be forty but look like twenty." She spun around on the turned-over garbage can to show off her figure, thrusting her breasts out. The men around her whistled and stomped their feet.

I looked at Luke. He had retreated to the sidelines and lowered his head. I felt terrible for him and wished I could take his hand and lead him away, far away.

"Other women, especially the high and mighty ones in Winnerrow who couldn't bring themselves ta come ta ma party, lie about their age. They gotta. When they were twenty, they looked forty."

There was more laughter. Then one of her young men shouted, "I'm twenty, Fanny. How many times does twenty go into forty?"

The laughter grew louder. Fanny beamed, put her hands on her hips and turned to him.

"Not once," she exclaimed, and her audience howled. "Anyway, you dummies, I gotta lot ta be happy about tonight. Ya see my son Luke standin' over there, lookin' as though he would like to crawl under a rock. Well, he's done me proud. He's been accepted ta Harvard, and they want 'im so bad they goin' ta pay the whole darn bill. How's that fer a Casteel, eh?"

Luke looked up, his face so red I thought he would just burst into flame. Everyone had turned to stare at him.

"Well, ya want ta make a speech about it, Luke honey, or don'cha think these hillbillies could understand ya?"

Luke didn't respond.

"That don't matter none, honey. I kin speak enough fer the two of us, and when I git to Harvard, I'll show those professirs a thin' or two."

"You sure will, Fanny," someone shouted.

Then the band struck up "Happy Birthday" and the audience started to sing. Fanny, posed on the turned-over can, smiled widely at Mother and me. When the song ended everyone applauded while a half-dozen young men rushed forward to help Fanny down.

Moments later our attention was drawn to two men who began pushing each other. One accused the other of cutting into the beer line ahead of him. Their friends, instead of separating them, egged them on until one swung at the other. People rushed to break them up. The whole thing struck Daddy as funny.

"I'm ready to leave, Logan," Mother announced firmly. "This party is only going to get worse and worse."

"In a minute," Daddy said, and rose to get closer to the fight. The two men were hurling curses at one another. I could hear Aunt Fanny's laughter over the din. The wind had intensified and the bulbs strung over the lawn began swinging back and forth. Aunt Fanny's banner snapped as it was driven up and back, so that it now waved loosely in the night like a flag of war.

Aunt Fanny came charging forward to the scene of the brawl.

"What's this 'bout fightin' on ma birthday?" she demanded, her hands on her hips. Three of her young boyfriends gathered around her and began describing the fracas. She was wobbling on her feet as she listened. Luke came up behind her, looked my way and shook his head. Mother suddenly surged forward and seized Daddy's arm.

"Logan, I want to go home. Now!" she insisted. He stared at her a moment and then nodded. She led him over to where I stood.

"Let's go, Annie." The rage in her face looked like it was about to explode.

I got up and followed her, my father trailing behind, but before we made it to our car, Fanny spotted us and screamed.

"Where ya goin', Heavenly? Ma party's jist gettin' started!"

I looked back, but Mother told me just to keep

walking to the car. Fanny's laughter followed us like a tail on a kite. Daddy stumbled behind us and caught up after I got into the back seat.

"Can you drive?" Mother asked him.

"Of course I can drive. I don't see what you're getting so excited about. Two guys had a little disagreement. Nothing to it. They're best of friends again already."

He got in and fumbled through his pockets for his keys.

"You drank too much, Logan. I know you had something before we left for the party, too."

"Well? That's what a party's for, isn't it?" he said with surprising curtness.

"No," she said forcefully.

He found his key and concentrated on getting it into the ignition. I couldn't remember ever seeing him so confused. Suddenly a drop of rain struck the windshield with a splat. It was followed by another and then another.

"It looks like it's going to rain on the party, anyway," he said sullenly. "Roland was right."

"That's the best thing that could happen," my mother said. "It will cool everyone down, and everyone," she added, looking at him pointedly, "could use a little cooling down."

Daddy started the car and we lunged forward.

"What's that supposed to mean?" He turned to Mommy and looked at her belligerently.

"You shouldn't have let her kiss and maul you like that, Logan. Everyone saw it."

"Well, what was I supposed to do—beat her off?"

"No, but you don't have to be so cooperative."

"Cooperative? Oh, come on, Heaven. That's not fair. I was stuck, I—"

"Slow down, the rain is getting harder, and you know how these roads can get," Mommy admonished.

"I didn't want to dance like that with her, but I figured if I pulled away, who knows what she might say. She's as drunk as a Saturday-night Indian and—"

"Slow down!" she yelled, more vehemently this time.

Sheets of water were pouring over the windshield now, and the wipers were unable to clear it away.

I hated to see them like this. I realized that the only time they had these fights was when Aunt Fanny was involved. Somehow, she always managed to cause trouble between them, scratching at old wounds or pouring salt over new ones. Too bad she didn't run off with one of her young men and leave Luke to live with us, I thought. Then we could truly be a happy family and never have to worry about angry situations like this one.

"I can't see anything!" Mommy exclaimed, but Daddy wasn't listening.

"Can you imagine what's going on back there?" he said, and laughed. He looked at Mommy. "I'm sorry if I caused you any pain, Heaven. Honest, I was just trying to—"

"Logan, keep your eyes on the road. These turns . . ."

The road down to Winnerrow was steep and sharply curved. The rain, coming in from the east, was pounding the mountainside now. Daddy's erratic driving had me swinging from side to side in the rear. I reached up and took hold of the handle above the window.

"You know I didn't mean to do anything—" he began again, but Mommy cut him off.

"All right, Logan," she stated emphatically. "We'll talk about it when we get home." Suddenly, as we approached a sharp turn, a vehicle coming up the hill was too far on our side.

I heard Mother scream and felt the car swerve to the right. Then I felt the brakes lock.

The last thing I remember was Mommy's shrill scream and my daddy's now instantly sobered voice call out my name.

"Annie . . . Annie . . . Annie . . ."

I heard Mother scream and felt the car swerve to the right. Then I felt the brakes lock.

The last thing I remember was Momma's shrill scream and my daddy's now-infantile voiced voice call out my name . . .

"Anne . . . Annie . . . Annie . . ."

FIVE

The Greatest Loss

I opened my eyes, but it seemed to take an enormous effort, my lids felt as if they had been sewn shut. I blinked and blinked, each time my eyelids opening and closing with less effort.

Where was I? The room was so white. An ugly, plastic light fixture was at the center of the ceiling. And this bedding . . . it smelled starchy and felt so rough. And there was a tiny ringing in my ears.

"Annie! Nurse, she's opening her eyes. Nurse . . . nurse!"

I turned slowly, my head feeling as if it had been turned to stone, like the bust of Jefferson Davis in the front yard of the Winnerrow School. A woman in white—a nurse—took my right wrist into her fingers to check my pulse, and I saw the I.V. tube attached to my arm.

I looked to my left. There sat a gray-haired elderly gentleman with the brightest light blue eyes I had ever seen. I turned back to the nurse. She was busying herself writing on a chart and only glanced quickly at the man, who took my left hand into his hands and leaned closer to me, close enough for me to get a whiff of his sweet after-shave.

"Who are you?" I asked. "What am I doing here?"

"Annie, I'm afraid that it has fallen to me to deliver the most terrible news you will ever hear. I hope you won't hate me for being the bearer of this great sorrow." He closed his eyes and took a deep breath as if it had taken the air out of him to say just those few words.

"What sorrow?" I tried to raise myself up, but below my waist my body felt numb. I was able only to lift my shoulders a few inches from the mattress.

"You were in a terrible car accident, and in a coma."

"Accident?" I blinked. Then it all came rushing back to me: the rain, my mother's scream, my father calling "Annie!" The walls of my heart quivered. "Oh, my God! Where are my parents? Where is my mother? *Mommy!*" I screamed, suddenly feeling frantic. I looked at the nurse. "Where's Daddy?" A cold, wet panic claimed me.

The strange man closed his eyes and then opened them slowly, tightening his grip on my hand.

"Annie, I'm very sorry."

I felt as if I were living in a slow-motion nightmare. I looked at the man and saw the pain in his eyes melt into tears. He lowered his head and then raised it to look at me. "I'm so sorry, Annie."

"No!" I wanted to deny his words before he spoke them.

"They were both killed," he said, tears streaming down his cheeks. "You have been in a coma for two days."

"No!" I pulled my hand from his strong fingers and turned my face into the pillow. *"No, I don't believe you."* I felt numb all over now, frozen, dead myself. I

didn't want to be here, and I wanted this man to go away. All I wanted was to be home again, to be with my parents. Oh God, I prayed, please make this happen and please make this terrible nightmare disappear. Please, please . . .

"Annie, poor Annie." I felt him stroking my hair the way my mother often had. "I came as soon as they called me, and I've been at your bedside ever since."

I turned around slowly and peered over my fingers. The man's face was full of sympathy and sorrow. He was mourning and hurting sincerely.

Suddenly it dawned on me who he was. This was the mysterious Tony Tatterton, the prince of Farthinggale Manor, and he was here at my bedside.

"I hired round-the-clock nurses and flew in my own physicians for you, but the facilities here are far from adequate. I must get you to Boston and then to Farthinggale," he continued. Everything he said rushed by me like words mumbled in a dream. I shook my head.

"Mommy. I want to see her. Daddy . . ."

"They are dead and await burial back at Farthinggale Manor. I'm sure it's what your father would have wanted," he said softly.

"Farthinggale Manor?"

"The Stonewalls, your paternal grandparents, are both dead, or I would consult with them, but I'm sure they would want the same things—a proper interment for your parents and my using every available dollar toward getting you healthy and well again."

I stared at him a moment, and then the tears that had pressed themselves up against the floodgates behind my eyes broke free and I sobbed and sobbed, my entire upper body shaking. Tony Tatterton leaned forward to embrace me and hold me as best he could.

"I'm so sorry, my poor, poor Annie. Heaven's

70

beautiful daughter, Leigh's granddaughter," he muttered as he kissed my forehead and gently pushed back strands of my hair. "But you won't be alone; you'll never be alone. I'm here now, and I'll always be here for you as long as I live."

"What's wrong with me?" I asked through my tears. "I can't seem to move my legs. I don't even feel them!"

"You received a bad blow to your spine and your head. The doctors believes the trauma about your spine has affected your motor coordination, but you don't worry about what's happened to you, Annie. As I said, I'll make you well again." He kissed my tear-soaked cheek and smiled, his blue eyes soothing.

"Drake," I said. "Where's Drake? And Luke Junior. Where's Luke? Aunt Fanny," I muttered. I needed my family around me now, not this stranger. Oh God, what was going to happen to me? I felt lost, bereft, empty, floating off like some kite in the wind whose string had torn. What would I do now?

"Drake's in the lobby, waiting. Luke and Fanny have been by a few times, and I'll let them know you've come out of the coma," Tony said. "But first I'll send my physicians in here."

"No. I want to see Drake first, and please call Luke and Fanny and tell them to come right away."

"All right, I will. Whatever you want." He kissed my cheek again and stood up. He smiled down at me in a warm but strange way and then left. Moments later Drake entered the room, his face glum, his eyes bloodshot. Without speaking, he embraced me and held me so tightly to his chest, my tears burst out again. My sobbing brought pain into my back and heart. He kissed me and held me and rocked me like a baby, pressing his face to mine, his own tears mixing with mine.

71

"You know they were more like my parents," he said. "My real mother couldn't have loved me any more than Heaven did, and Logan always treated me the same as he would have treated his own son. Once, when I went for a ride alone with him, I remember him telling me that he always thought of me as his son. 'What's mine is yours,' he said 'and always will be.'"

"Oh, Drake, can it really be true? Are they truly dead and gone?"

"Yes, and it's a miracle you're alive. I saw the car. It's a total wreck."

"I can't move my legs. They don't even feel like they're there."

"I know. Tony told me what the doctors think. He's going to do everything for you, Heaven. He's an amazing and wonderful man. As soon as he heard the news, he turned the full power and wealth of his Tatterton empire to work. Doctors have been flown in and will be at your side continually. He's moved in one of his managers so that Logan's factory in Winnerrow can continue, because, as he says, it was so important to Logan and Heaven that the people here have something significant. He swears it will never go out of business and will even expand. He's already asked me if I would consider running it someday, after I graduate from college.

"And then he told me he plans to fix up Farthinggale again, just so you can recuperate in a wonderful setting. We're lucky to have him, Annie, at a time of such great need."

"But I don't want to go to Farthinggale! I want to go home, Drake! Farthinggale wasn't supposed to be a hospital; it was supposed to be . . . a special place, a paradise. Please, Drake."

"Annie, it's hard for you to think clearly now. You've got to leave that to other, older and wiser people who are not as close to the tragedy as you are. We've got to do what's best for you. You want that, don't you? You want to walk again, to go on with your life."

"My life? Without Mommy, without Daddy? Away from everyone? Luke? You? All the people I love? How can I go on with my life?"

"You must, Annie. It's what Heaven would want, what Logan would want, and if I didn't tell you to do so, I would be at fault. Your parents weren't the kind of people who gave up on anything, Annie. You've got to be the same way. No matter what the obstacles, go forward and overcome them."

No matter what the obstacles, I thought. Go for the tall ones, I thought. Luke's advice, too.

"I won't be far away from you, Annie. I'll be nearby. I'll be going back to Boston today, and I'll come visit you at the hospital there. I know it's impossible for you to think of all this now because it's all happening so fast, but trust in those who love you. Please," he pleaded.

I took a deep breath and lowered my head to the pillow. The weight of the world seemed to press on me. My lids were heavy again and I felt very dizzy and tired. Maybe if I fell asleep and woke up, this would all be one terrible nightmare, I thought, and I would awaken in my own room at Hasbrouck House.

It would be morning and Mommy would come in full of her usual energy, talking about the things we were going to do this morning. Downstairs, Daddy would be having his coffee and reading his *Wall Street Journal*. I would shower and dress and bounce down the stairs to greet a new and bright day, and he would kiss me good-bye before he went off to the factory, just as he did every morning. I settled into my misty dream.

73

"Roland has my breakfast ready," I muttered.

"Huh?" Drake said.

"I've got to eat and get started. Mother and I are going shopping today. I need a new dress for Maggie Templeton's birthday party, and we want to get something special as a present. Don't make fun of us, Drake. I see you smiling."

"Annie . . ." His hands cupped my head, but I couldn't keep my eyes open, so he let my head settle back on the pillow.

"The toy cottage . . . it's so beautiful . . . so beautiful . . . thank you, Mommy. I'll cherish it forever and forever and forever. . . . "

"Annie . . ."

Was that Daddy's voice still calling? Daddy, don't stop calling me, please. Daddy . . .

Into the warm and comforting arms of sleep, I turned and lowered myself slowly, shutting away the ugly and horrible light that wanted to come bursting into my fantasy world and burn it away.

"Let's not let it do that, Luke. Let's not. I know . . . Go for the tallest mountains . . . the view, the view . . ."

"Oh, Annie, you must get well again," Drake whispered, and took my hand into his. But in my dream I took Luke's hand and we rushed across the lawn toward our make-believe paradise where I felt safe and secure again. And I could sleep.

When I awoke, Tony's doctors and private nurse were looking down at me. A tall, dark man with a thin reddish-brown mustache and soft hazel eyes held my hand and smiled down at me.

"Hello there," he said. "I'm Dr. Malisoff and I'll be taking care of you until you're well again."

I looked up at him, his face slowly coming into sharper and sharper focus until I could even make out the small, thin wrinkles that crossed his forehead as if someone had drawn lines there with a pencil.

"What's wrong with me?" I asked. My lips were so dry, I had to keep running my tongue over them. Instead of answering me, he turned to the younger doctor at his side. He had blond hair and light skin and there were patches of tiny freckles under his eyes.

"This is my assistant, Dr. Carson. We'll both be attending you."

"Hi," the younger doctor said. He was studying a chart the nurse beside him held.

"And this is Mrs. Broadfield, your private nurse. She will be with you from now until the day you are healthy and well enough to be on your own again."

"Hello, Annie," she said, and blinked a smile that flashed as quickly as a camera light. She had hair as black as Aunt Fanny's, but cut very short, and she was round-faced and chunky, with broad shoulders like a man's. She wore no makeup and her lips were a pale burgundy.

"Where's Drake?" I asked, and then vaguely recalled his telling me he had to return to Boston.

"Drake?" Dr. Malisoff said. "There are two people waiting in the lobby to see you. One is your aunt Fanny and the other, I think, is her son?" He looked to Mrs. Broadfield, who nodded quickly. "I'll have them come in in a moment. First, let me tell you what we're planning to do with you, Annie.

"Apparently, when your father's car turned over, you hit something rather hard, and the blow to your spine just at the back of your head created what we call a trauma which is interfering with your motor control and causing paralysis of your lower body. We don't know exactly where the damage is or how much yet, because this hospital doesn't have what we need to make a precise diagnosis, so we are preparing to fly you to Boston, where you will be examined by a

75

neurologist who is an associate of mine. There they
have sophisticated instruments such as a CAT scan to
pinpoint your problems and help us arrive at a proper
diagnosis, therapy, and prognosis."

"I don't feel any pain in my legs right now," I said.
He smiled at that.

"No, you wouldn't if they were paralyzed. If you do
feel pain, that will be the sign that your nerves and
muscles are returning to functioning order. I know it
sounds funny to hope for pain, but in a real way, that's
what we've got to do. My guess is that once we treat
the trauma, you will regain the use of your legs.
However, it may take some time, and during that
time, you'll need more than just tender loving care.
You'll need professional therapy."

I was impressed and encouraged by his confident
tone, but I wanted Daddy to be beside me holding my
hand; I needed Mommy to tell me I would be all right
again, and not just doctors and nurses. I'd never felt so
alone, so deserted and bereft in the strange, cold
world.

"So," the doctor continued, releasing my hand and
standing straight again, "just relax until all the prepa-
rations are completed. You'll go by ambulance to the
airport and be flown by air ambulance to Boston." He
smiled again and patted my hand. "In the meantime,
Mrs. Broadfield will give you something liquid to eat,
okay?"

"I'm not hungry." Who could think of food at a
time like this? I didn't care if I ever ate again.

"I know, but I'd like you to have something liquid,
some nourishment besides what you're getting
through the I.V. All right?" He paused and gave me
another smile meant to reassure me, where never
again could anything do that. "I'll have your family
come in to see you now."

He turned, and he and the younger doctor left. Mrs.

Broadfield prepared a small carton of cranberry juice for me by opening it and inserting a straw.

"Just suck gently," she advised, adjusting my bed so I was in a sitting position. Her short, stubby fingers and large palms reeked of rubbing alcohol. This close to me, I could see the tiny black hairs peeking out the bottom of her round chin. I wanted my mother, my beautiful, loving, sweet-smelling mother to be the one taking care of me, not this ugly stranger.

She placed the juice in my free hand and rolled the table over the bed. The change in my posture made me dizzy again and I had to close my eyes.

"I'm getting nauseous," I cried.

"Just try a little," she insisted. I took in some juice quickly and swallowed. My throat ached and I moaned.

"Please, roll me down again," I pleaded.

"You're going to have to try, Annie, just a little every day. Doctors can't do it all," she said, a note of disapproval, even impatience, in her voice.

"I'm not ready," I insisted. She shook her head and pulled the table away. I took one more suck on the straw and then handed her the juice. She pressed her lips together, her rubbery face filled with annoyance. When I looked more closely at her, I saw how pocked her skin was and wondered why a nurse would have such a poor complexion.

Just as she lowered me into a fully reclining position again, Aunt Fanny burst into the room with Luke right behind her. I was never so glad to see them. Aunt Fanny wrung her hands before me.

"Oh Gawd . . . Oh Gawd!" she screamed. Mrs. Broadfield nearly dropped her tray.

"Oh, Annie, darlin', poor chile. My poor niece." Tears were streaming down her face and she was dabbing her cheeks with her silk handkerchief. "Oh Gawd, Gawd . . . look at her in that bed. Sweet child," she wailed, and leaned against Luke. Her shoulders shook. Then she took a deep breath and came to my side and kissed me on the forehead. I welcomed the scent of roses, her personal perfume she had sent in from New York once a month.

She held me and sobbed, her body shaking mine. I looked to Luke, who seemed embarrassed by his mother's outward display of sorrow. I reached forward to indicate he should come closer. Aunt Fanny was holding me as if for dear life. Her sobbing got louder.

"Ma," Luke said. "You're making things worse. Please."

Aunt Fanny snapped back.

"What?" She dabbed her eyes again. "Oh . . . Oh Gawd, Gawd."

"Ma, please. Think of what Annie's been through," Luke pleaded, lowering his voice for emphasis. Mother used to say that when it came right down to it, no one could handle Fanny as well as Luke could.

"Oh dear, dear Annie," she said and kissed me on the cheek, her tears dripping onto my face. She wiped them away and stood up.

"Poor Luke and me been sittin' out there fer hours waitin' for the doctors and the nurses ta let us in," she added, flashing a chastising look at Mrs. Broadfield. Suddenly her great sorrow turned into great anger.

"Try not to excite her," Mrs. Broadfield commanded, and left the room.

"Don't ya jist hate doctors and nurses. They all have these faces that looked pinched. Remind me of muskrats. And I hate hospital smells. Why don't they spray some deodorants in the halls and bring in flowers? If I ever get sick, Luke, so I don't know what I'm doin', hire a private nurse like Annie has and keep me in ma house, y'hear?" Aunt Fanny declared. It was as if her grief had been merely a cape she could pull off when she had a mind to.

Luke stepped up to my bed. He looked so handsome, so young, his eyes two pools of fear and pain.

"Hi, Annie."

"Luke, oh Luke."

He took my hand softly into his own. The tears glistening in his eyes filled my heart with even more sorrow. He was as deeply in mourning as I was, for despite the way we all had ignored who and what he really was all these years, the truth was he had lost his father, too. And my mother was often more kind and loving to him than his own.

"Now there's no sense in us all jist standin' around an' cryin' our hearts ta pieces," Aunt Fanny suddenly said. "We can't bring 'em back, though I'd give all I have ta do it. I loved Heaven more'n I ever told her. I'm sorry I was so mean ta her all these years, but I jist couldn't help my jealous self. She understood that and forgave me time after time, which was more'n I done fer her." She touched her eyes gently with her lace handkerchief and then took a deep breath and pulled her shoulders back.

"But," she announced, "I jist know she'da wanted me ta take control'a things now. I jist know it." Aunt Fanny nodded in agreement with herself as her pride marched out in full dress parade. "I'm jist as capable as . . . as that dirty, old rich man who calls himself yer great-grandpa." She shook her head and ran her palms over the sides of her hair as if she had walked into a cobweb.

"Ma." Luke touched her left hand and nodded toward me. "This isn't the time—"

"Nonsense. We gotta do what we gotta do. Now he says yer parents' wills put him in control, but I say—"

Luke glared daggers at Fanny.

"Ma, Annie is in no condition to discuss all this right now. She has other things on her mind at this moment."

"Well, I think that's good, him gettin' ya the best medical treatment," Aunt Fanny went on, undeterred by Luke's admonishments and pleadings, "but as far as Hasbrouck House and—"

"Ma, please."

Frustration pulled her lips back, her pearly white teeth contrasting sharply with her dark Indian complexion.

"All right, then, I'll wait until yer feelin' better, Annie. Jist don't ya worry yerself none about what that old beantown millionaire's goin' ta do with yer fortune."

"He's been very nice so far, Aunt Fanny," I said, unable to make my voice much more than a loud whisper.

"Yeah, well, he's got reasons."

"Reasons?"

"Ma, please." Luke turned on her, his eyes fiery. "I said this isn't the time."

"Okay, okay."

Mrs. Broadfield returned to my room and came up behind them, moving so quietly in her soft white nurse's shoes, none of us heard her enter. She was suddenly just there, like a milk-white ghost.

"I'm afraid you'll have to leave now. We are preparing Annie for her trip."

"Leave? We jist walked in. This is ma niece, ya know."

"I'm sorry. We have a schedule to follow," the nurse insisted authoritatively.

"Well, where ya takin' her?" Fanny demanded.

"A Boston hospital. You can get all the specific information at the nurse's desk on this floor," Mrs.

Broadfield said. Aunt Fanny shook her head in anger, but Mrs. Broadfield simply went around my bed to adjust the I.V.

"Now Annie, honey, ya don't worry 'bout nothin' but gettin' yerself up and around again, hear?" She kissed me on the cheek and squeezed my hand. "I'll be comin' out to that fancy Boston hospital in a day or so ta be sure they're doin' the right things fer ya," she added, and glared at Mrs. Broadfield, who continued to work as if Fanny were no longer there.

"I'll come with her, Annie," Luke said. He took my hand back into his.

"Oh, Luke, I'm going to miss graduation and your speech now," I cried.

"No you won't," Luke said with his characteristic reassurance. "I'll read the whole speech over the phone to you, and before I go to school that day, I'll go to the gazebo and sit there just as if you were there, too, and pretend that none of this happened."

"What kinda talk is that?" Aunt Fanny asked, a half-curious and half-appreciative smile on her face.

"Our kind of talk," Luke said. Truth was in his eyes. Love for me was there as well. He leaned over and kissed my cheek just as Tony Tatterton reentered the room.

"Well, how are we doing?" he asked. He glanced at Luke, who snapped back and looked at him suspiciously. "I'm Tony Tatterton," Tony said quickly. He extended his hand. "And you must be . . . ."

"Ma son Luke Junior," Aunt Fanny announced. "You know who I am, I assume. I'm Heaven's sister." She pronounced her words as sharply and as hatefully as I had ever heard her. I looked to Tony to see his reaction, but all he did was nod.

"Of course. Well, we've got to turn our attention to Annie now and get her started. I'll be down at the ambulance," he added, and shot a glance at Luke again. Luke's eyes were working overtime, analyzing and studying Tony critically.

"We'll be with you in Boston, too," he repeated, and then he and Aunt Fanny left. Before I had a chance to burst into tears, the hospital orderlies arrived with the stretcher and began loading me onto it as Mrs. Broadfield directed. In moments I was being wheeled out of the room and down the corridor.

And there was no one at my side holding my hand, no one I loved who loved me. All the faces around me were strange and empty, the faces of people who saw me as just a part of their job. Mrs. Broadfield tucked the blanket around my shoulders efficiently when we arrived at the doorway to the parking lot where the ambulance awaited.

Even though the sky was overcast and gray, I closed my eyes the moment the outside light struck my face. It was only seconds, though, because I was quickly lifted from the hospital stretcher to the ambulance stretcher. I opened my eyes again as the doors were closed and Mrs. Broadfield took her seat beside me. She adjusted the I.V. and sat back. I felt the ambulance jerk forward and start down the hospital driveway on its journey to the airport and the plane that would jet me away to a big-city hospital.

I couldn't help but wonder if I would ever see Winnerrow again. Suddenly all the things I used to take for granted seemed so very precious and dear, especially this little town that Drake called "one-horse."

I wished I could sit up and look out the window as we rushed away. I wanted one last look at the village proper to take with me, and a last farewell to the broad green fields and the neat little farms with their summer crops planted. And especially I wanted one last vista of the mountains with their coal-miner shacks and moonshiner cabins dotting the hills. I wanted to say good-bye to the Willies.

I was being ripped out of my world, torn from the people and places I loved and cherished and identified with. There would be no magnolia trees, no sweet scents of fresh flowers blossoming on the street as I walked to school. There would be no magic gazebo, no tiny cottage music box playing Chopin. I closed my eyes and imagined Hasbrouck House at this moment. All our servants surely sat around dumbstruck, not yet able to fully mourn my parents' deaths.

My head began to thump. Tears flowed freely from my eyes. I shook with sobs.

Never to see them again? Never to hear my father calling when he arrived home: "Where's my girl? Where's my Annie girl?" When I was little, I would hide behind the high-back blue chintz chair in the living room and press my tiny fist against my lips to suppress a giggle as he pretended to look everywhere for me. Then he would take on a worried expression and my heart would burst at the thought I could bring him any sadness.

"Here I am, Daddy," I would sing out, and he would scoop me up and cover my face with kisses. Then he would take me into the den where Mommy was sitting with Drake, listening to his school stories. We'd plop down on the leather couch with me in my daddy's lap and listen, too, until my mother said it was time we all got cleaned and dressed for dinner.

Those days seemed always full of sunshine and laughter. But now the clouds had come over us and dropped shadows like sheets of cold rain, like funeral shrouds. My mother and father were dead, my happy sunshine days colored black.

"Try to sleep, Annie," Mrs. Broadfield said, jerking

me out of my reverie. "Lying there and crying will only make you weaker and weaker, and you have many big battles ahead to fight, believe me."

"Have you had a patient like me to care for before?" I asked, realizing that I needed to make friends with this woman. Oh, how I needed friends, someone to talk to, someone older, wiser, someone who could help me know what to do, who to be now. I needed someone with wisdom, but someone with warmth and loving feeling, too.

"I have had a number of accident victims, yes," she said, her voice full of arrogance.

"Did they all recuperate?" I asked hopefully.

"Of course not," she said flatly.

"Will I?"

"Your doctors are hopeful."

"But what do you think?" I wondered why someone who was supposedly dedicated to helping others, especially others in such great need, would be so cold and impersonal. Didn't she know how important warmth and tender care were? Why was she so stand-offish?

Surely Tony must have known something about this woman before hiring her. My recovery was so important to him, he would certainly have gone looking for the very best, and yet I wished he had found someone who could be more warm and confiding, perhaps someone younger. Then I remembered what Drake had said, how I should put myself into the hands of older, wiser people who were able to think more clearly than I could now.

"I think you should try to rest and not worry about it now. There's nothing we can do right now, anyway," Mrs. Broadfield said, her voice still cold, factual. "Your great-grandfather is getting you the best possible treatment money can buy. You're lucky to have him. Believe me, I've been with many a patient who had far less than you have."

Yes, I thought. How quickly he had come to my aid, and how fully committed to helping me get well again he seemed. It made me wonder even more what it could have been that had driven my mother, who was capable of such great love, away from a man who apparently had such a generous heart.

Would I ever find out, or had the answers died on that Willies mountain slope with my mother and father?

I was tired. Mrs. Broadfield was right: there was nothing to do but rest and hope.

I heard the ambulance siren blare away and vaguely realized that it was for me.

SIX

Tony Tatterton

I slept through the rest of the journey to the airport, but I awoke as they were transferring me to the air ambulance, and the realization of what was happening struck me like a hard, cold slap to the face. None of this was a dream; it was all true, all really happening. Mommy and Daddy were really dead, gone forever. I was seriously injured, paralyzed, all my dreams and plans, all the wonderful things Mommy and Daddy had hoped for me, obliterated in one fateful, horrible moment on a mountain road.

Everytime I awoke I relived the terrible memory, saw the rain blinding the car windshield, heard Mommy and Daddy arguing about Daddy's behavior at the party, and saw that car coming at us. The visions made me scream inside, and ache so much that I was grateful when I started growing groggy again. Each time sleep came, it brought relief. Only each time I awoke, I had to face the reality and relive the horror once again.

Mercifully, I fell asleep again until we arrived at

the Boston airport for transfer to the Boston hospital ambulance. Whenever I was awake I was impressed with Mrs. Broadfield's tone of authority and the way orderlies and attendants snapped to action when she issued a command. Once I heard her say, "Easy, she's not a sack of potatoes, you know." And I thought, yes, Drake was right. I'm in good hands, professional hands.

I drifted in and out of a deep sleep and awoke when we arrived at the hospital and I felt someone holding my hand.

I opened my eyes and looked up at Tony Tatterton. At first he didn't realize I had awakened, and I thought he had such a dreamy, far-off expression on his face, it was as though looking down at me had taken him away somewhere and left him there. When he finally noticed I was staring up at him, his face brightened with a smile.

"Welcome to Boston. I told you I would be right here when you arrived so I could greet you and be sure you had whatever you needed. Was your trip all right?" he asked with great concern.

I nodded. Yesterday when I had seen him at my bedside, everything was so unreal that my memory of him was vague. Now I had a chance to really see in the flesh the man I had imagined so many times. His eyebrows were perfectly trimmed and he was closely shaven. His hair was trimmed neatly, too, and the gray looked silky and rich, as it would after being washed and treated by a professional stylist. He was wearing an expensive gray and white pinstriped silk suit with a dark gray tie. All of his clothing looked brand new. When I looked at my hand in his, I saw his long, patrician fingers were well-manicured. The nails shone. Yes, he was far different from the Tony Tatterton described by Drake. His letter and phone call now seemed part of the imaginary world I had sometimes entered and abruptly left for this cold, cruel, real existence.

Tony let me scrutinize him and rested gentle, affectionate eyes on me as I did so.

"I slept through most of the journey," I said, my voice barely more than a whisper.

"Yes, Mrs. Broadfield told me. I'm so glad you're here, Annie. Soon you'll be going through the battery of tests the doctors have planned and we'll get right to the bottom of your problems so we can fix them." He patted my hand and nodded with the confidence and assurance of a man who was used to having things his way.

"My parents," I said.

"Yes?"

"Their funeral . . ."

"Now Annie, you must not think of that. I told you back in Winnerrow. I'm taking care of everything. You turn your strength and concentration toward getting yourself well," he advised.

"But I should be there."

"Well, you can't be there right now, Annie," he said gently. "But as soon as you are able to, I will have another service held at their grave sites and you and I will be there together. I promise. But for now, you're off to the best medical treatment money can buy." Then he turned thoughtful.

"But don't let my concern for the here and now and your immediate needs make you think I didn't love your mother very much. I was very, very fond of your father, too. As soon as I met him, I knew he was executive material, and I was so happy when he agreed to become part of my business. When your mother and your father lived at Farthy and we all worked together, I had some of the happiest years of my life.

"The years afterward, when they were gone, were the saddest and hardest years of my life. Whatever I had done to cause a rift between us, I want to undo by helping you, Annie. Please let me do all I can so that I can make it up to them. It's the best thing I can do to honor their memory." His eyes filled with pleading and sorrow.

"I don't want to stop you, Tony, but there are so many questions I need to have answered. For a long time I tried to get Mommy to talk about her days at Farthy and why she finally left, but she held it back, always promising to tell me everything someday soon. Just recently, right after my eighteenth birthday, she made that promise again. And now . . ." I swallowed hard. "Now she won't be able to."

"But I will, Annie," he said quickly. "I'll tell you everything you need and want to know. Please trust and believe me." He smiled and sat back. "In fact, it will be something of a relief to me to have you listen and judge."

I studied his face. Was he sincere? Would he do what he promised or was he just saying these things to get me to like him and trust him?

"I tried to make amends every way I knew how," he continued. "You received my presents, I hope, and I hope your mother let you keep them."

"Oh yes, I have them all . . . all the beautiful and wonderful dolls."

"That's good." His eyes brightened; he looked younger. There was something in his face that reminded me of Mommy's . . . the way he could telegraph his thoughts and moods with a twinkle in his eyes. "Whenever I traveled, I made sure to find a special gift for you. I wanted you to have authentic artifacts, and those dolls were just the thing. I've lost track of how many I sent, but I bet it's quite a collection by now, isn't it?"

"Yes. They take up an entire wall in my room. Daddy always says I'm going to have to open a store. Everytime he comes in, he . . ." I paused, realizing Daddy would never come in and never say those things again.

"Poor Annie," Tony consoled. "You've suffered a great, great loss. I'll never be able to do enough to ease your pain completely, but believe me, Annie, I'll do whatever is humanly possible. It's my mission in life now," he added with the same look of determination I had seen so often in Mommy's eyes.

I couldn't harden myself against him as Mommy had. Perhaps it was all part of some horrible misunderstanding. Perhaps Fate had decided I would end it.

"I know you can't help but be suspicious of me, Annie, but believe me. I am a man with a large fortune who has nothing and will be grateful only for the opportunity to do something noble and worthwhile in the autumn of his life. Surely, you won't deny me that chance," he said softly.

"As long as you promise to tell me it all as soon as you can," I said.

"You have the solemn word of a Tatterton who comes from a long line of distinguished gentleman on whose words many, many people had relied," he promised, his face solid, serious. Then he turned to the orderlies who stood waiting nearby. "She's ready. Good luck, my dear." He patted my hand as they took hold of my stretcher.

They began to wheel me down the corridor. I lifted my head as high as I could to see Tony, who remained behind. I saw the look of love and concern in his face. What a wonderful soft-spoken man he was, and yet he was also a man who had obviously had a stream of power and confidence running beneath his every word. I couldn't wait to learn more about him. My parents had rationed each tidbit as if the small amount of knowledge I was to have of the man had to last me a lifetime.

Of course, I knew he had built up a unique toy business. "An empire," my father always called it, worth millions of dollars with foreign as well as local markets. "The Tattertons are kings of the toy makers," he told me during one of those rare times when he would talk about it. "Just like our toys, they are toys meant for collectors."

"Tony's toys are toys only for the rich," my mother countered. I knew she was proud that the toys we made in Winnerrow were bought by all sorts of people, not only the very wealthy. "Tatterton Toys are for wealthy people who don't need to grow up and forget their childhood, when they had nothing to find under their Christmas trees and never enjoyed a birthday party. Tony's kind of people," she added, anger bolting through her eyes like lightning.

Now, I wondered how he could be so much different from the kind of people my mother, my father, and I were. Although I sensed his power and authority, I sensed his softness and his vulnerability, too. He cried real tears for my parents and me.

For the rest of the day I set my mind on cooperating with my doctors, who appeared to run me through every test known to medical science. I was probed and prodded. They turned every kind of light on me, X-rayed me every which way, conferred and consulted.

As Dr. Malisoff had predicted, I didn't feel any pain in my legs during the tests. I was able to move my upper body, but my legs were like rag-doll legs, dangling freely when I was lifted to examination tables and placed carefully on beds. At times I felt as if I had stepped into icy water waist deep and it had numbed me from my feet to my hips. My reflexes didn't respond, and I looked down in awe as Dr.

Malisoff's assistant and a Dr. Friedman, the neurologist, actually poked me with a pin. I didn't feel it, but seeing it go into my skin made me squirm.

"Annie," Dr. Malisoff told me at one point, "it's almost as if we have given you what is known as a spinal anesthesia to mask pain during an operation. We believe the inflammation caused by the trauma around your spine is responsible for your paralysis right now. There are a few more tests we would like to do to confirm our suspicions."

I tried to be a cooperative patient. My condition made me so dependent upon everyone. I had to be lifted from one place to another, strapped in and rolled about on movable stretchers. It was very hard for me to sit up. Every attempt to do so exhausted me. The doctors kept reassuring me that in time I would be able to do it, but I felt as though half my body had been killed in the accident along with my parents.

Being so helpless was not only frustrating but irritating. We all take so much for granted—walking, sitting, being able to get up and go wherever we like when we like. My injuries seemed like salt upon wounds, for beside the devastating loss of my parents, I now had this physical disability to contend with. How much can one person bear? I screamed to myself. Why was I being put through such a horrible torture? All the things that mattered to me had been snatched away.

Despite the way I felt, I couldn't help being awed by my surroundings and the staff who worked on me. It was an impressive hospital, with corridors twice as wide as the hospital corridors in Winnerrow. There were people rushing about everywhere, everyone looking important and busy. I saw rows of stretchers filled with patients being wheeled up and down corridors and in and out of elevators. Every minute there seemed to be an announcement for or the paging of some doctor. I learned that there were over twenty floors to the building and what seemed to me to be an army of nurses and technicians working there. I thought Aunt Fanny and Luke would get lost trying to find me.

And yet, even in this setting with all these people working on so many different patients, I felt important; I sensed Tony Tatterton's presence and money at work. From the moment I was rolled away from him, I was surrounded by a team of doctors and technicians who remained with me until they finally wheeled me into what would be my private hospital room. Mrs. Broadfield was waiting for me there.

In order to get me into bed, she had to roll the stretcher up beside it and pull me gently, setting my dead legs over the bed first and then moving the rest of me. She said nothing much while she worked; she didn't even grunt.

After she got me comfortably into the bed, she fed me some juice. Then she closed the curtain around the bed so I could sleep, telling me she would be sitting right by the door in case I had need of anything. Exhausted from my examinations, I fell asleep again, and woke when I heard voices around me. I looked up at Dr. Malisoff, who was at my bedside. Tony Tatterton was standing beside him.

"Hello again. How are you doing?" the doctor asked.

"I feel tired."

"Sure. You've got a right to be. Well, we've come to a final decision about you, young lady. My initial theory was correct. The blow to your spine just at the back of your head has inflamed the area, and that's what is causing your paralysis. There has already been a discernable, small amount of improvement, so we are not going to have to operate to release any pressure. Instead, we're putting you on a medicine therapy, and after a while, on physical therapy.

"But you won't have to remain in the hospital all that time," he added, smiling at my look of concern. "Fortunately, Mrs. Broadfield is a nurse with training in physical therapy, and she can manage your recuperation program at Farthinggale Manor. Are there any questions I can answer for you?"

"I will walk again?" I asked hopefully.

"I see no reason why not. It won't happen overnight, but it will happen in due time. And I will be coming out to see you periodically."

"When will I stop feeling dizzy?"

"That comes from the concussion. It will take a little time, too, but you will improve steadily each day."

"Is that all that happened to me?" I asked suspiciously.

"All?" The doctor laughed and Tony stepped closer, smiling warmly. "Sometimes I forget how wonderful it is to be young," the doctor said to him. Tony nodded.

"It is wonderful, and if you can't be young, it's wonderful to have someone as young and beautiful as Annie near you." His smile was small and tight, amused.

"But I'm going to be such a burden," I protested. It was one thing to be a burden to people you loved and people who loved you, but to go off with a stranger and be in this condition made me feel very awkward. How I needed the comfort and affection of Mommy and Daddy now, but Fate had decided that I would never again have it.

"Not to me. Never to me. Besides, I have servants who are bored because they have so little to do now, and you have Mrs. Broadfield."

"I'll see you outside," Dr. Malisoff said to him in a voice just above a whisper, a doctor's conference voice, and left my room. Tony remained staring down at me.

"I'll come twice a day," he promised. "And each time I'll bring you something." He put a light, happy tone into his voice, as if I were still a child who could be cheered up by toys and dolls. "Is there anything special you want?"

I couldn't think of anything; my mind was still too clouded with the tragic events and the impact of all that was to happen next.

"It doesn't matter. Let me surprise you each time." He stepped closer so he could lean over to kiss my forehead, and for a moment his hand lingered on my shoulder. "Thank God you're going to be all right, Annie. Thank God you're going to be with me and that I can do something to help you." He kept his face so close to mine, I felt his cheek graze my own. Then he kissed me again and left the room.

Mrs. Broadfield took my blood pressure and washed me down with a sponge and warm water. Afterward I lay there in a kind of daze with my eyes open, fighting back any tears. Finally I closed my eyes and dozed off.

Drake came to visit me the next day. I was so happy to see him. I was in a strange place, far from home, but I had family nearby, and family was one thing I always cherished.

He came to my bed and kissed me, hugging me gently, as if I were made of eggshells and he thought I might crack.

"You have some color in your cheeks today, Annie. How do you feel?"

"Very tired. I keep drifting in and out of sleep, in and out of dreams, and whenever I wake up, I have to tell myself where I am and what has happened. My mind won't hold onto the truth. It keeps throwing it out like last week's meat loaf."

He smiled and nodded and stroked my hair.

"Where have you been? What have you been doing?" I asked quickly, anxious to see how he had been handling the tragedy and his own sorrow.

"I decided to stay at school and finish the semester."

"Oh?" Somehow, I thought the whole world had stopped working for a while. Even the sun had refused to appear. Night had a tight grip on the earth. How could anyone work or live or be happy ever again?

"My teachers wanted to excuse me, but I thought if I didn't keep my mind on something, I would go mad with grief," he told me after he had pulled a chair up to the side of the bed. "I hope you don't think me too hard or indifferent for doing that, but I couldn't just sit around. It was too painful."

"You did the right thing, Drake. I'm sure it's what Mommy and Daddy would have wanted you to do."

He smiled, grateful for my understanding, but I believed what I was saying was true. No one handled hardship as well as Mommy could. Daddy always said she had a spine of steel. "CA-steel," he joked. What I wouldn't give to hear one of his jokes now. "How wonderful that it's all behind you, Drake. No more studying for a while."

"But I'm not returning to Winnerrow. It will be too painful for me to return to that big empty house right now, and anyway, Tony Tatterton has made me a wonderful offer for the summer months."

"What sort of offer?" I asked, curious at how quickly Tony Tatterton had taken up the management of our lives.

"He's going to let me work as a junior executive at his offices, can you imagine? I'm not even out of college yet, but he's going to let me have some responsibility. He's even set me up with an apartment here in Boston. Doesn't that sound exciting and wonderful?"

"Yes, it does, Drake. I'm happy for you." I looked away. I knew it wasn't fair to Drake, but happiness seemed out of place at this moment. The whole world should be in mourning for me and my parents, I thought. The dark veil that had fallen over everything still clung to me. No matter how blue the sky really was, it would be gray to me.

"You don't sound too happy. Is it because of the medicine you're taking?"

"No." We stared at one another for a moment and I saw the sadness creeping back into his face, bringing shadows over his eyes and making his lips quiver. "No," I continued. "I've just been thinking a lot about Tony. I can't help wondering why he has come rushing into our lives and why he's being so wonderful to us. For the longest time, our family treated him as if he didn't exist. You'd think he'd hate us. Don't you wonder, too?"

"What's there to wonder about? A terrible, terrible tragedy has occurred and he . . . he's part of the family in a real way. I mean, he was married to your great-grandmother and my step-sister's grandmother, and he has no one. His younger brother committed suicide, you know," Drake added in a deep whisper. Mrs. Broadfield was walking in and out of the room.

"Younger brother? I don't remember any mention of him."

"Well, Logan once told me something about him. Seems he had always been a very introverted man who kept to himself and lived in a cottage on the other side of the maze instead of in that big, wonderful house."

"Cottage? Did you say a cottage?"

"Yes."

"Like the one my mother had in her room, the toy-model music box she gave me for my birthday?"

"Well, I never thought about that, but . . . yes, I suppose so. Why do you ask?"

"I keep dreaming about it, remembering it and the music and the times she let me look at it when I was a little girl. Sometimes, when I awaken from one of my short naps, I think I'm back home and I look around for my things, listen for Mommy's or Daddy's voices, think about calling for Mrs. Avery, and then . . . it comes back to me, rushes over me like a cold, dark wave, almost drowning me in the horrible, ugly truth. Am I going crazy, Drake? Is that part of what's happening to me, but no one wants to tell me? Please, you tell me! I've got to know!"

"Your mind's confused by all that's happened, that's all," he said reassuringly. "Memories are jumbled. It's understandable, considering what you've been through. You should have heard the gibberish you were saying when I visited you in Winnerrow." He smiled and shook his head.

"What gibberish?" I was frightened for a moment. Had Drake eavesdropped on my most secret thoughts? Thoughts about Luke?

"All sorts of silly stuff. Don't worry about it," he said, waving the topic away. "And don't worry about how you're going to be treated or about being alone. I'll be nearby all summer, and I can come visit you at Farthinggale Manor on weekends. You're my big responsibility now, Annie, and I mean to take good care of you. But I've got to develop my career objectives and be on my own, too. Independence is in my blood. I'm not looking for any handouts from Tony Tatterton. I'll earn what I get and work my way up," he said proudly.

He went on and on about working for Tony and

what it could mean for him. His words ran together and I lost track of what he was saying. After a while he saw I wasn't listening. My eyes kept closing.

"Here I am, putting you to sleep, and I just keep on and on," he said and laughed. "Maybe they ought to hire me to help with the insomniacs."

"Oh, I'm sorry, Drake. I didn't mean not to listen. I heard most of what you said and—"

"It's all right. I've probably stayed too long anyway." He stood up.

"Oh no, Drake! I'm so glad you're here!" I cried.

"You need your rest if we expect you to recuperate. I'll come see you again soon. That's a promise. Bye, Annie," he whispered as he leaned over to kiss my cheek. "Don't worry. You'll always have me nearby."

"Thank you, Drake." It was reassuring to know that he would be close, but I couldn't help wishing that Luke would be nearby, too, that somehow he could stay with me at Farthy and help me to recuperate. Maybe then my life wouldn't be as different from what it was back at Winnerrow. I was already dreaming about Luke and I sitting in the bigger gazebo at Farthy, about Luke pushing me about in a wheelchair or sitting at my bedside reading to me as I rested.

The moment Drake left, Mrs. Broadfield approached the bed and pressed the button to raise me into a sitting position.

"It's time for some nourishment," she announced.

I closed my eyes to keep the room from spinning, but I didn't complain this time. More than anything, now, I wanted to get well as fast as I could and get out of this hospital where I was dependent on someone for my food, for my bodily necessities, for my every personal need. And I wanted, more than anything else, to get myself well enough to be taken out to the site of my parents' graves.

I had yet to say good-bye.

SEVEN

Season of Darkness

Tony was true to his promise: everytime he visited me, he brought a different surprise. He came twice a day, once in the late morning and once in the early evening. At first he brought boxes of candy and armfuls of flowers; then he simply had vases of fresh roses delivered every day. The fourth time he visited he brought me a bottle of jasmine perfume.

"I hope you like it," he said. "It was your great-grandmother's favorite."

"I remember my mother wore this scent sometimes Yes, I love it. Thank you, Tony."

I sprayed some on immediately, and when he inhaled the scent, his eyes turned glazed and distant for a few moments. I saw him drift in and out of a recollection. What a complex man he was, and how much like my mother! How soft and caring and very like a little boy, and yet how strong and authoritative he could be! Like a child on a swing, he went back and forth from one personality to the next. A word, a scent, a color would drop him into the past, sink him into a pool of memories. And then, moment, he emerged bright, keen, alert, charge.

Maybe we weren't so unalike. How often mother or father come upon me to find m in a melancholy mood. The simplest things sometimes made me sad: a lone bird on a willow-tree branch, the sound of a car horn in the distance, even the laughter of little children. Suddenly I would find myself lost in my own heavy thoughts, and then, just as suddenly, I would step out of the shadows and return to the sunlight, unable to explain why I had been sad. Once, my mother found me with tears streaming down my cheeks. I was sitting in the living room, staring out at the trees and blue sky.

"Why are you crying, Annie?" she asked, and I looked at her with confusion at first. Then I touched my cheeks and felt the warm drops.

I couldn't explain why the tears had burst forth. It just happened.

The next time Tony arrived at the hospital, his chauffeur, a man called Miles, accompanied him to carry several boxes. Tony directed him to place them on the table beside the bed. He opened box after box containing different silk nightgowns. The last box held a crimson silk robe.

"It was a color that looked wonderful on your mother." His eyes were bright with his recollection. "I still remember a wonderful crimson dress and jacket I bought her when she attended the Winterhaven School for Girls."

"Mother wasn't happy there," I said, interrupting his pleasant memory. "She said the other girls treated her mercilessly, and even though they were rich girls, they were not as compassionate and kind as poor people in the Willies could be."

"Yes, yes, but it built her character to contend with

them. What strong character she had! Winterhaven was and still is a highly academic school. They make their students work, and they supply them with intelligent teachers. I remember telling your mother that if she reached the top of their academic lists, she would be taken to teas and meet the people who really counted in Boston society. But you're right; she didn't like the people she met there. Oh well," he added, moving off the topic quickly, "at least you'll be the best-dressed patient in the hospital."

I wanted him to talk more about the years my mother lived at Farthinggale Manor, but I thought it best to leave that until I was actually there myself.

When one of the Pink Ladies—sweet, elderly women in pink aprons who volunteered to do charity work at the hospital—came by with the mail the next day, she had a small stack of get-well cards for me from some of my friends back in Winnerow, from my teachers, from Mrs. Avery and Roland Star, as well as cards from Drake and Luke. I asked Mrs. Broadfield to tape them all on my wall. I saw she wasn't happy about it, but she did it anyway.

The day after his card arrived, Luke and my aunt Fanny came to visit. Because I had a private room, they could come any time. My door was open, so I could hear Aunt Fanny coming down the hospital corridor. I probably would have been able to hear her even if the door had been closed. She and Luke stopped first at the nurse's station.

"We're here to see ma niece," she bellowed. "Annie Stonewall."

I couldn't even hear the nurse's response, she spoke so low, but Aunt Fanny didn't take a hint.

"Well, why are ya private rooms so far away from the elevata? If ya payin' more, ya should get the convenience. This way, Luke."

"My aunt's coming," I warned Mrs. Broadfield,

102

who sat like a statue of stone by the door and read the latest issue of *People* magazine. Tony had sent up dozens of the latest magazines that morning, and Mrs. Broadfield had organized them by the windowsill. My room looked like a library. Some of the regular nurses came by and asked if they could borrow this or that during their breaks. Mrs. Broadfield permitted them to, but she wrote down each and every one of the names next to the name of the magazine on a little pad.

"Just remember where you got them," she warned.

She shifted in her seat when Aunt Fanny's footsteps grew louder. I could tell from the clickity-clack that she was wearing high heels and was all dolled-up for this visit. She stepped into my doorway wearing a wide-brim panama hat with a black velvet sash, a short-sleeved black denim jacket and tan demin skirt over a small striped tank shirt. Naturally, the skirt hugged her hips.

Despite the way she lived and the things she said and did, I had to confess my aunt Fanny was a very attractive woman, especially when she dressed fashionably. It was no wonder young men buzzed around her like bees around a hive.

Luke came in right behind her. He wore a simple blue cotton short-sleeve shirt and jeans, but I could see he had taken extra care with his hair. He was so proud of his rich, dark hair. Other boys, envious boys, teased him because he gave it so much attention, never allowing a strand out of place.

Mrs. Broadfield stood up as soon as Aunt Fanny entered the room. She backed away as if she didn't want to chance rubbing elbows, and slapped her magazine on the sill.

"Annie, dear!" Aunt Fanny rushed over to my bed and threw her arms around me.

Mrs. Broadfield headed for the doorway.

"Don't hurry, honey," Aunt Fanny responded. I nearly laughed aloud when Fanny turned back to me, her eyes wide, her lips curled as if she had just swallowed sour milk.

Luke came up on the other side of my bed, looking timid and out of place.

"How are you, Annie?"

"A little better, Luke. I can sit up without getting dizzy, and I've begun to eat solid foods."

"That's wonderful, honey. I jist knew once they gotcha inta a fancy place like this, they'd have ya up an' about in no time." Fanny peered down at me. "That glum-faced nurse treatin' ya okay?"

"Oh yes, Aunt Fanny. She's very efficient," I reassured her.

"Looks it. I guess ya gotta have someone like that ta count out the drops'a medicine properly, only she'd be enough to keep someone in a coma."

"Everyone at school sends regards to you, Annie, and sends their condolences," Luke interjected, trying to steer the conversation away from Fanny's insults.

"Thank them for me, Luke. And thank them for the cards. I just loved your get-well card." I nodded toward the wall.

"Thought you would." He beamed.

"Where's the card I sent ya?" Aunt Fanny demanded after she perused the cards on the wall.

"You sent a card, Aunt Fanny? When?"

"Days ago. I spent a lotta time pickin' out the best one, too. And I know I put a stamp on it, Luke, so don't accuse me'a forgittin'," she added quickly, anticipating Luke's theories.

"Maybe it will be here tomorrow, Aunt Fanny."

"And maybe that dreadful nurse threw it out before ya got it," she said, sneering.

"Oh, Aunt Fanny, why would she do that?"

"Who knows. She didn't like me the moment she

set her eyes on me, and I didn't like her much neither. I don't trust her as far as I could kick her."

"Aunt Fanny!"

"Ma," Luke warned.

"All right," she mumbled.

"All set for graduation, Luke?" I asked, trying to sound cheerful. I would miss my own graduation.

"Three days to go." He ran his forefinger over his throat to suggest it would be a disaster. "This is the first time I'll be doing something really important without you at my side encouraging and supporting me, Annie."

It was wonderful to hear him tell me I was as important to him as I hoped I would always be, but I knew he would do well even though I wasn't beside him. There were few young men his age as capable as he was when it came to a challenge or a responsibility. Our teachers loved it when he volunteered to do something, because they knew they didn't have to be on his back the way they had to with most teenage boys.

"You're going to do fine, Luke. I just know you will. I wish I could be there to hear it," I said, my eyes telling him just how much I wished it.

"He keeps makin' the speech ta the trees in the back of the house, but I ain't heard no applause yit," Fanny interjected. Luke scowled. He was growing impatient with her and so was I. "Well, I'll tell ya this, Annie. If those snobs in Winnerrow don't give Luke a standin' ovation—"

"Ma, I asked you—"

"He's only worried I won't behave and give them snooty people somethin' more ta talk about," she explained. Then she paced around, her voice growing louder as she worked herself up. "Luke, git me that chair over there, the one Annie's nurse was layin' eggs on."

105

I looked to the door quickly to see if Mrs. Broadfield had returned and overheard any of this. She had apparently decided to stay away until my aunt left.

Luke brought the chair over for her and she sat down, taking her hat off carefully and placing it at the foot of my bed. She had her hair pinned back neatly. I did think there was something different about her, a new, more serious look in her blue eyes. She fixed her gaze on me intently for a moment, pressing her lips together, and then took my hand.

"Annie, honey, I've been doin' a lot of thinkin' lately, nothin' but thinkin'. Right, Luke?"

"That's all she's been doing," Luke said sarcastically. Aunt Fanny saw the way we were looking at one another.

"I'm serious here."

"Okay, Aunt Fanny. I'm listening. Go on." I folded my hands under my breasts and sat back against the pillows. My legs were still like two dead appendages. I had to shift them from side to side with my hands, and twice a day Mrs. Broadfield had to massage them and work them up and down.

"I decided that I would move into Hasbrouck House while yer recuperatin', jist ta be sure it's kept up properly and those servants do what they're paid ta do. I'll take one of the guest rooms. There's enough of 'em, and whenever Luke comes back from college ta visit, he can take one of the others."

"I'm starting college this summer," he explained. "Harvard has a summer program that I can enter, and my full-tuition scholarship applies to that as well."

"That's wonderful, Luke. But Aunt Fanny, have you told Drake your plans?"

"I don't see as I hafta get Drake's permission fer anythin' I do. I got certain rights and obligations. Ma own lawya's been goin' over the wills. Yer motha was

106

kind to me, Annie, and I feel I have an obligation here. Nobody's goin' ta tell me different, not Drake, and certainly not Tony Tatterton."

"I don't see why Tony would object anyway, Aunt Fanny."

"Well, Drake's still finishin' college, and since no one's sayin' I'm not the oldest livin' relative here, I'm goin' to do what has ta be done fer ma family. Drake will be away; yer goin' ta be away; someone's gotta take charge. Heaven would want me to do it, I'm sure."

"I don't mind you and Luke moving into Hasbrouck House, Aunt Fanny. I appreciate what you want to do."

"Well thank ya, Annie, honey. That's sweet of ya ta say. Ain't that sweet of her, Luke?"

"Yes," Luke said, staring at me the way he did that day after he had told me what Aunt Fanny did to his acceptance letter from Harvard. I felt myself blush, and swung my eyes back to Aunt Fanny quickly.

"I only wish ya was comin' back ta yer own home ta recuperate, Annie, instead a goin' off ta that big stone house ta live amongst strangers. I could take jist as good care'a ya as that leather-faced nurse Tony Tatterton hired. Bet she's expensive, too. Anyway, yer motha was never happier than when she was livin' in Winnerrow. When she was older and rich, I mean. 'Least, that's what I think."

"Why, Aunt Fanny?" I wondered how much of the secret past she knew.

"She didn't like all them beantown phonies," she said quickly. "And she had some bad times with that loony granny'a hers. Tony, too. Everybody always mixin' everyone else up till a person didn't know who him or her was. She killed herself, ya know," she stated flatly and cast a fish-eye on me.

"I thought that was an accident, Aunt Fanny."

"Accident, ma . . . no accident. One night she jist got sick'a bein' locked up like a loony, I suppose, and took too many sleepin' pills. Can't tell me that was an accident."

"But if she didn't know what she was doing or who she was . . ."

"Annie's right, Ma. It could have been an accident."

"Maybe, but it still didn't do yer ma no good ta hafta live in that big house with all that craziness goin' on. And I don't think she woulda wanted ta be buried in that ritzy cemetery. She probably woulda preferred the Willies, out there in the woods, right next ta her real ma."

Luke and I shot quick glances at one another. He knew that I had often gone up to that simple grave in the Willies alone to stare at the tombstone that simply read, "Angel, Beloved Wife of Thomas Luke Casteel."

"'Course, yer daddy probably woulda wanted the huge monument and all."

"You saw it?" I looked back at Luke quickly. He nodded and bit down on his lower lip.

"Yeah, Luke and I went ta the Tatterton family cemetery on our way here and stopped by ta pay our respects."

"You were at Farthy, Luke?"

"Well, it was on the grounds, but we didn't go to the house. The cemetery had its own entry road and was some distance away."

"No one invited us, anyway, Annie. And from where we was standin', that mansion looked cold and deserted," she said, and embraced herself as if just the memory gave her a chill.

"We couldn't see much, Ma," Luke said, looking at her with chastisement.

"It looked like one'a them old castles in Europe," she insisted. "That's why I'd rather ya was where I could look in on ya, than stuffed away in that ole mansion. It's probably haunted. Maybe that's why yer great-grandma went loony."

"Oh, Ma," Luke moaned.

"Well, Logan once told me how Jillian—that was her name, Jillian—claimed to see the dearly departed," she whispered.

Luke looked away. Any reference to my father and his mother always embarrassed him. I squeezed out a silly little laugh to change the mood.

"You don't have to worry about that, Aunt Fanny. Tony's going to fix Farthy up to make it very comfortable for me," I said. "He's got all kinds of plans . . ."

"Sure." She shifted her gaze from me as if she didn't want me to read her thoughts in her eyes.

"Aunt Fanny, do you know why my mother didn't want to have anything to do with him?"

Still looking at the floor, she shook her head.

"That was between yer daddy, yer motha, and him. It all happened jist before Drake's custody hearin', and me and yer ma wasn't very sisterly then, so she didn't tell me everythin' and I didn't ask. After we mended fences, she wanted ta keep her unpleasant memories buried, and I didn't push none ta know. But I'm sure she had good reason, so maybe ya oughta reconsider what yer doin'," she added, her eyes small now and her lips pursed.

"But Aunt Fanny, Drake thinks Tony's wonderful, and he's done so much for me. He's promised Drake a job for the summer, an important job, too."

"Yeah, well, jist ya keep yer wits about ya when yer in that castle, Annie, and if anythin' upsets ya, that nurse or anythin' at all, ya jist give yer aunt Fanny a call and I'll be there in a jiffy ta bring ya back where ya belong, hear?"

Aunt Fanny sounded funny and her ideas were often weird, but I couldn't help wondering if she wasn't right about Tony Tatterton. Were there any other reasons for his doing all that he was doing? Was Aunt Fanny right about the stream of madness that ran through the family? For now I decided I would wait and see. At least I felt secure because Drake and Luke would be close by in Boston. In fact, I'd be closer to Luke if I stayed at Farthy. His going to Harvard, which I had thought would separate us forever, would now mean we would be near each other again.

"Thank you, Aunt Fanny, but I think I'll be fine, and there is all this special medical attention I need now."

"She's right, Ma."

"I know she needs special care. I jist thought . . . anyway, I'll be where ya kin find me. Now." She straightened up again, trying to look like my mother did when she conducted business. "Seems yer parents neva changed that part of their wills that left management of their finances up ta Tony Tatterton. So I suppose he's got control'a what happens with the factory and such."

"And Drake will have a lot to do with it. Someday he'll probably run it himself."

"Wouldn't my pa be proud'a that," she said, beaming. She shook her head and reached into her handbag for a lace handkerchief with which to dab her eyes. "You and Luke's the only family I really got, Annie, and I mean ta do well by ya both. I'm gonna really try to behave and be a decent motha and aunt. I swear it." I could see she was convincing herself as well as me.

"Thank you, Aunt Fanny," I said, grateful for her intentions, intentions I suspected she would have trouble sustaining.

We kissed each other's cheek. Her eyes glistened with tears. It saddened me to see it, but I fought back crying, too. She straightened up again and stuffed her handkerchief back into her bag.

"I'm jist goin' ta go down ta that fancy cafeteria fer

a cup a coffee. Promised Luke I'd let ya two have some time alone, though why there's gotta be secrets kept from me, Ah don't know." She cast a suspicious eye on Luke.

Luke blushed.

"It's not secrets, Ma. I told you."

"All right, all right. I'll be back in ten minutes."

She got up, squeezed my hand, and left. As soon as she went out the door, Luke moved closer to my bed. I reached up and took his hand into mine.

"How have you really been, Annie?"

"It's been hard, Luke; especially when I'm awake and I can think and remember. All I do is cry," I whimpered, and I began to cry again, to really sob as Luke sat on the side of the bed and comforted me with his strong arms. We remained like that for a long time, until my heart got stronger and my tears receded.

"I wish there was something more I could do for you." He looked down and then looked up quickly. "I dreamt I had gone to college and become a doctor and I was able to treat you and make you well again very quickly."

"You would be a wonderful doctor, Luke," I said as my sobs subsided.

"I wish I was one now." He fixed his eyes on me.

"Everyone's been wonderful," I insisted. "Drake comes every day, and Tony is really doing a lot for us." He nodded. "Anyway, I'm finally going to Farthy. I just wish it were for different reasons."

"I'll come see you, Annie. If they'll let me."

"Of course they'll let you," I assured him.

"As soon as I get my first opportunity. And if you're still in a wheelchair, I'll wheel you all about and we'll see all those places we dreamt about. We'll even go to the maze and—"

"Perhaps you'll take me to their grave site, Luke. If I don't get there before you come," I said solemnly.

111

"Oh, I'd like that, Annie. I mean—"

"Maybe I'll soon be able to wheel myself, so we can separate and try to find each other like we dreamt we would," I said quickly. It seemed to wrong to turn Farthy into a sad place, especially after we had built it up to be so fantastic in our minds.

"Yes, and we'll go down to the big pool and the tennis courts—"

"And you'll still be my prince?" I teased.

"Oh, more than ever now." He stood up and took a princely pose. "My lady," he said with a wide sweep of his arms. "Might I wheel you through all the gardens this morning? We'll go to the gazebo, where we'll sit until the sun goes down, talking softly and drinking mint juleps."

"Afterward, do you promise to sit with me in the concert hall so we can listen to music by the grand piano, Prince Luke?"

"Your wish is my command, my lady," he said, kneeling beside the bed and taking my hand to his lips. He kissed my fingers and stood up. His eyes dazzled as another fantasy returned.

"Or we can be Southern aristocracy again," he offered.

"And get all dressed up for elegant dinner parties?" I asked smiling.

"Of course. I'll wear a tuxedo and you'll come floating down the long stairway, looking like Scarlett O'Hara in *Gone With the Wind* with your dress trailing behind you. And you'll say—"

"I'll say, 'Why, Luke Casteel, it's so nice to see you.'"

"Annie, you're looking more beautiful than ever," he recited, imitating Clark Gable in the movie. "But I must keep my wits about me. I know the way you manipulate men with your dazzling beauty."

"Oh, not you, Luke. I would never manipulate you."

"Oh, but Annie, there is no one I would rather have manipulating me," he said with such sincerity in his eyes, I was speechless for a moment.

"It's not good if you let me know you know I'm doing it, Luke Casteel," I finally responded, my voice breathy.

We laughed. And then I looked up.

"Luke, there's something else I want to see; something I want to see very, very much now."

"What?" he asked, his sapphire eyes sparkling.

"A cottage that is on the other side of the maze. It's something I feel I've got to see. It's something I feel I've got to do."

"So we'll do it. Together," he added confidently.

"I hope so, Luke." I squeezed his hand for emphasis. "Promise me, really promise."

"Every promise I make to you, Annie, is a real one," he said hoarsely, looking more mature and more determined than I could ever remember. For a moment our eyes remained glued together and I saw his love for me like a warm cleansing lake, big enough to swim in. Then Mrs. Broadfield returned, bursting in on us like a cold wind.

"Time to change your head bandage," she announced.

"Just wait outside a moment, Luke."

"I'll go check on my mother. She might be turning this place upside down by now."

Fanny and Luke returned for a while after lunch, and before they left, Luke and I agreed on a time when he would call me the next day to read me the final version of his speech.

"I've added something to it," he said. "Something I want you to be the first to hear."

Later than afternoon Tony and Drake arrived.

"I heard your aunt was here visiting," Tony said as he came through the door.

"Yes." I turned right to Drake. He was dressed so

handsomely in a silk black-and-white pinstriped suit just like the ones Tony wore. I thought he looked years older already and very mature and successful. "Drake, Aunt Fanny wants to move into Hasbrouck House to watch over things. I said it was all right for her to do so."

"What? Now wait a minute, Annie."

"Now, now," Tony interjected. "That's a big house, from what I hear." I saw the look he gave Drake, the look that said, "Don't do anything to disturb Annie." The fire in Drake's eyes extinguished quickly. He shrugged.

"That's true. I suppose it's all right. For a while, anyway. I'm going to be too busy, and you'll be at Farthinggale, so she can't bother either of us."

"She's trying to do something decent, Drake." I tried to defend Fanny, wanting so much to believe the best of her. "She wants family again. I believe her, and I just didn't have the heart to turn her away. Not now."

He nodded.

"That was very kind of you, Annie," Tony said. "To be thinking of other people's needs while you have so many yourself. It's going to be refreshing to have a person such as you at Farthinggale. You'll warm the place as it hasn't been since . . . since your mother lived there.

"And now," he added quickly, "I have a surprise. Dr. Malisoff tells me that you can be released by the end of the week to continue your recuperation and begin your therapy at Farthinggale. Isn't that wonderful?"

"Oh yes. I can't wait to get out of here!" I exclaimed.

Both Tony and Drake laughed, Drake shifting his eyes to Tony a split second beforehand to see if he would laugh first. I was amazed at how quickly Tony had made a disciple of Drake. How different Drake was with Tony! I had never seen him so deferential to anyone!

Tony took my hand. "I hear what a wonderfully cooperative patient you've been. Why, Mrs. Broadfield just raves about you," he added, looking toward her. Instead of flashing one of her imitation smiles, she looked at me and nodded, her eyes full of real appreciation and warmth.

"Thank you," I said, smiling at my nurse.

"However, Annie, there is something very important that you have been hiding from me," Tony said.

"Hiding?"

"Drake tells me you're quite an artist."

"Oh, Drake. Did you exaggerate my abilities?"

"I just told the truth, Annie. You are good," he declared, confident of his opinion.

"I'm just learning," I told Tony. I didn't want him to be too disappointed when he saw my work.

"Well, I'm going to find one of the best art instructors in town and have him come out to Farthinggale to give you lessons. I won't let you be bored; I promise you that. We need a new portrait of the Manor, and I can't think of anyone better to do it than you, Annie."

"But Tony, you haven't even seen what I can do."

"I think I know what you can do," he said, his sharp, penetrating gaze resting on me with deep consideration. Thoughtfully, with narrowed eyes, he waited as I stared at him and wondered what he thought he knew. What did he see in me that I couldn't see in myself?

"One more surprise." Tony reached into his pocket and produced a small jewelry box. I took it from his palm and opened it slowly to gaze down at a magnificent pearl ring in a gold setting. "I searched and searched through your grandmother's things until I found what I thought would look best on your hand." He plucked the ring out of the box and took my left hand into his to slowly put the ring over my finger. He didn't seem surprised that it was a perfect fit.

"Oh, Tony, it's beautiful," I marveled. And it was! The pearl was large and set in rose gold.

I held my hand up and turned it about so Drake could see. He nodded in appreciation.

"Beautiful," he agreed.

"In time everything I have and everything that was your grandmother's will be yours, Annie."

"Thank you, Tony, but you've given me so much and done so much, I don't know how to thank you."

"Just come to Farthinggale and get well there. That will be more thanks than I had ever hoped to receive."

It was on my lips to ask why, but once again I told myself that all the questions, and hopefully all the answers, would be uttered at Farthinggale Manor, and suddenly it seemed so right that the mysteries of my mother's past would be solved for me where they had been born for her.

The next day, at the time we had arranged, Luke called to read me the new part of his speech.

"Everyone in Winnerrow knows about our family tragedy, Annie. When they look up at me after the principal introduces me as the valedictorian, it's going to be in their eyes. So I thought and thought about Heaven and how she would want me to react and what she would want me to say.

"Annie, you know your mother was an inspiration to me, maybe the biggest inspiration in my life, because she was born to a hard, poor life and struggled up and out of it more or less on her own, battling so many hardships and emerging with dignity and beauty. I mean, she never let me feel out of place in your

116

home, and I know it had to be painful for her to see me there."

"Oh, Luke, she never—"

"No, Annie, it would only be natural for her to feel that way. I understood and . . ." His voice nearly cracked. "And I loved her for it. I really did. God forgive me, more than I love my own mother."

"I think she knew that, Luke."

"I know she did. Anyway," he said, pulling his voice up, "I decided to add this paragraph. Ready?"

"My ear's glued to the phone, Luke."

I envisioned him on the other end, his posture straight, seriousness tightening his face as he held out his script and read.

"The Bible tells us there is a season for everything. A time to be born and a time to die; a season of light and a season of darkness. This is a happy day, a wonderful day, a day during the season of light; but for my family it is still the season of darkness. However, I feel certain that my aunt and my . . . my father would want me to remain in the season of light, to brighten the darkness and think only of what this day means for my family. It means hope and opportunity. It means another descendant of Toby Casteel and his loving wife Annie has emerged from the poverty of the Willies to become all he is capable of becoming. So I dedicate this day to the memory of Logan and Heaven Stonewall. Thank you."

My tears gushed. I couldn't hold the phone against my ear. I dropped the receiver into my lap and cried and cried. Luke called my name: "Annie? Annie? Oh, Annie, I didn't mean for you to cry so hard. Annie?"

Mrs. Broadfield, who was just outside the door talking to a floor nurse, came charging in.

"What is it?" she demanded.

I took deep breaths until I could plug up the sadness

117

and agony enough to speak. Then I picked up the receiver.

"Luke, I'm sorry. It's beautiful. They'd be so proud of you, but do you think," I gasped, "do you think you should say . . ."

"My father? Yes, Annie. On this day especially, I want to put away any deception and stand proud for who I am. Do you think he would mind?"

"Oh no. I was just thinking about you and afterward."

"Afterward doesn't matter. I'm going off to college, and frankly, this is one time I agree with my mother—I don't care what the hypocrites of Winnerrow think."

"I only wish I could be there beside you, Luke."

"You'll be beside me, Annie. I'll know it."

I started to bawl again. I hid my face in my palms. Mrs. Broadfield, her face screwed in anger, rushed forward.

"Now you have to stop this!" she exclaimed. "Hang that phone up. The call is too disturbing."

She took the phone before I had a chance to pick it up again.

"This is Mrs. Broadfield," she said. "I'm afraid you'll have to end this conversation. Annie is too weak for this kind of emotional strain."

"Please, give me the phone, Mrs. Broadfield," I demanded.

"Well, bring this to an end," she said. "You'll make yourself sick."

"I'll be calm. I promise."

Reluctantly, she returned the phone.

"I'm sorry," Luke said immediately. "I didn't—'

"It's all right, Luke. I'm all right. I'll be strong. I'm crying because I'm happy, too, happy for you."

"Be happy for the both of us, Annie."

"I'll try."

"I'll call you right after graduation and let you know how it goes."

"Don't forget."

"I'd as soon forget to breathe," he said.

"Good luck, Luke," I cried, and surrendered the phone to Mrs. Broadfield, who quickly cradled the receiver.

I fell back against the pillows.

"You don't understand your condition, Annie," she began. "You've not only been damaged physically, but emotionally as well. This kind of thing can set you back for months."

The tears and the agony made my heart feel like a brick in my chest. Suddenly I was struggling to breathe. I gasped and reached up. I felt the blood draining from my face, my cheeks turning cold. The room began to spin. The last thing I heard was Mrs. Broadfield yell, *"Stat!"*

Then the season of darkness claimed me again.

119

EIGHT
Doctor's Orders

I felt as if I were falling down a long, dark tunnel, but as I fell I began to see a light at the end. I was drawing closer and closer to it, and soon I began to hear voices. First it sounded like many people whispering; then their whispering grew louder, until it sounded more like hundreds of flies buzzing around a screen window on a hot, sticky, late summer day. Then the buzzing turned into words and I fell through the bottom of the tunnel into the bright light.

I blinked and blinked.

There really was a very bright light pointed at my face.

"She's coming to," someone said, and a head moved away from the light and pushed it away so the brightness was directed to the side. I looked into Dr. Malisoff's concerned hazel eyes.

"Hey there, how are you doing, Annie?"

My lips felt so dry I thought I would scratch the tip of my tongue over them. I swallowed.

"What happened?"

I blinked again and turned to see Mrs. Broadfield over by the sink talking with Dr. Malisoff's assistant, Dr. Carson. She was shaking her head, too, and gesturing excitedly with her hands as she spoke, apparently describing what had happened to me. I'd never seen her so animated.

"Well, Annie, part of this is my fault. I should have explained to you how emotionally weak you are. We seem to be concentrating only on your physical problems, when indeed there are emotional and mental ones, too. Your injuries go a great deal deeper than might first appear."

He took the cold cloth from my forehead and handed it to Mrs. Broadfield. Dr. Malisoff didn't move from my bedside. He sat down and took my left hand into his hands.

"Remember when you asked if that was all that was wrong with you and I laughed?" I nodded. "Well, I shouldn't have laughed. I should have told you there were emotional and psychological injuries as well. Maybe then more would have been done to prevent something like this from happening."

"But what happened? All I remember was feeling this weight on my chest and . . ."

"You passed out. Emotional strain. The thing is, Annie, you didn't realize how weak you were because we have you relatively comfortable and well taken care of here. But the truth is you've been crippled in a number of different ways, one of which is emotionally. Just as the skin on your body has been torn and bruised, so has the skin over your feelings and thoughts. I'm sure you've heard it said, 'He's thick-skinned.' Right?" I nodded. "Well, that's not as silly as it sounds. We protect our emotions, protect our minds in many ways, and your protecton has been badly damaged. So, you're easily upset, vulnerable, exposed. Understand?"

"I think so."

"Good."

"Now our major concern here is that your physical recuperation will be hampered, maybe even totally prevented, if you continue to suffer emotionally. One part of you is tied to the other part. A person can't be physically healthy if he or she is psychologically and emotionally sick. That's where I was a little careless. I should have kept you more protected, at least until you are stronger, until that emotional skin gets thick again. That's what we have to do now."

"What does that mean?" I couldn't help being afraid. I had thought that I was doing well emotionally. Who could have stood up under such tragedy? Who could have gone on not only losing both her parents, but finding herself paralyzed, her life turned upside down and inside out? I felt like spending my entire day crying and mourning, but I kept my tears locked in my heart so others wouldn't be continually uncomfortable in my presence. And yet here was the doctor telling me I was an emotional mess. It was as if I had only to look into a mirror to see a crushed and broken me. I shivered at the thought.

"Well, Mrs. Broadfield has told me about your visitors and your phone calls." He squinted so that wrinkles and folds broke out over the bridge of his nose. Then he shook his head. "We've got to slow that sort of stuff down for a while so we can protect you. I know you won't be happy about that in the beginning, but for a while, at least, will you trust us and let us do what is best for you so you can make a full recuperation and return to a normal life that much faster?"

"I didn't have that many visitors . . . just Tony and Drake and my aunt and Luke. He's the only one who's called me," I protested.

122

He turned to Mrs. Broadfield, who shook her head as if I were babbling like a madwoman.

"Well, it's not how many people come to see you or call you; it's what those visits and calls can do to you," Dr. Malisoff explained with painstaking concern. "You're very lucky, though. You've got a place to go for your recuperation that will be as good as any therapeutic hospital. You'll be in a beautiful, quiet setting, insulated and protected. Your body and your mind will have a chance to mend much faster than they would if you were exposed to everyone else's problems and feelings."

He patted my hand and stood up.

"Do I have your trust and cooperation, Annie?"

"Yes," I said, in a voice so small it reminded me of a little girl's voice. Maybe he was right; maybe I had become a little girl again. I had returned to a time when the smallest things could make me cry and fill my heart with sorrow, only I didn't have my mother or my father to turn to for sympathy and solace.

"Good."

"Does this mean I have to stay in the hospital longer now?"

"We'll see."

"How is she?" I heard Tony demand. He was suddenly in my doorway. I lifted my head to see him. His face was flushed, his silky gray hair mussed, and his double-breasted dark blue suit creased and out of shape. He looked like he had run all the way.

"She's fine now," Dr. Malisoff reassured him. "There was no need for you to come rushing over, Mr. Tatterton." He shifted his eyes quickly to Mrs. Broadfield, who busied herself with washcloths and towels.

"Thank God," Tony said, rushing to my bedside and looking down at me. "I thought . . . well, what happened?"

"Oh, a case of emotional exhaustion. Annie and I have just had a good discussion about it, and she understands now what has to be done, right, Annie?" I nodded. He patted me on the hand again and started out of the room.

"Just a minute," Tony called after him. He and the doctor walked out together. I could just hear them mumbling in the hallway. Mrs. Broadfield came to my bed and straightened my blanket and fluffed my pillow. She looked stern, cold, her eyes fixed and beady.

"No one's going to blame you, are they?" I asked her, thinking she was worried about that.

"Me? Why should anyone blame me? I couldn't red tag your visiting hours or cut off your phone calls."

"I just thought—"

"Oh no, Annie. I think now, if anything, everyone agrees with me," she said. A wide, sharp smile of self-satisfaction crawled over her face, making her look more like an arrogant cat settling on a fine sofa for a nap.

A few moments later Tony reentered my room and came to the side of my bed.

"Are you really feeling better now?"

"Oh yes, Tony."

He looked so worried, his blue eyes cloudy, the wrinkles in his forehead deepening.

"I was careless, too. I should have realized . . ."

"Now everyone can't go around blaming everyone else and themselves. It's over," I said. "Please, let's forget it."

"Oh, we're not going to forget it. The doctor told me everything he told you. I've already agreed with him. New orders are being given."

"New orders?"

He nodded at Mrs. Broadfield and she went right to my telephone and disconnected it from the wall.

"My phone!" I protested

"No calls for a while, Annie. Doctor's orders."

"But Luke is supposed to call me right after graduation to tell me how his speech went," I cried in dismay.

"I'm going downstairs to the telephone operator right after I leave this room, Annie, and have them redirect all your calls to my office, where either I or Drake can take them for you. I'll bring all the news and information to you immediately. I promise, and you know I keep my promises, right?"

I looked away. Luke would feel so terrible; he would blame himself, and it was so important for him to talk to me after the speech. I felt the tears trying to work themselves up again, and my pitter-patter heart quickly became a heavy thumping drum in my chest. But I remembered Dr. Malisoff's lecture. I had to develop the thick skin or I would slow down my recuperation. For a while, just for a while, some sacrifices had to be made.

"We're all trying to do what is best for you, Annie, as directed by the best physicians and nurses money can buy. Believe me. Please."

"I believe you, Tony. I just feel sorry for Luke."

Tony looked at me with great fondness and sympathy. "I'll tell you what. I'm going to send him a telegram from you right now wishing him good luck. Won't that buoy his spirits?"

"Oh yes, Tony. What a great idea," I said excitedly.

"And . . . and I'll call him personally and tell him you're all right, but the doctor has made new orders and for a while you have to remain quiet and undisturbed," he instructed.

"Please, tell him not to blame himself for calling me."

"Oh, of course I will. And if I think he doesn't

believe me, I'll have the doctor call him, too," he offered with a gentle smile.

"You would?"

"Annie," he said, his face turning serious, "I will do anything in my power to get you back on your feet and return you to happiness. I know that's going to be hard to do because you lost the people you most cherished in your life, but all I ask is an opportunity to replace them in a small way. Will you let me try?"

"Yes," I said softly, impressed with the intensity of his eyes and the determination in his voice. Was this the same voice my mother heard pleading for forgiveness? How could she turn him away?

"Thank you. Well now, I'll let you rest, but I'll be back this evening," he promised.

He leaned over and kissed me on the forehead.

"Drake's waiting to hear about you, too."

"Give him my love."

"I will. He's doing exceptionally well. He'll make a very good executive because he has self-assurance and ambition. In some ways he reminds me a little of myself at his age," he added, a note of pride in his voice. Mrs. Broadfield accompanied Tony out of the room, closing my door softly behind her.

No more phone calls; no visitors. Oh well, it would be just for a little while, I thought, and soon I'd be at Farthy. Perhaps the magic Luke and I believed resided there would work its way into me and speed up my recovery.

Mrs. Broadfield, because of what I assumed were the doctor's orders, turned herself into a fortress. Even the Pink Ladies had to go through her to get to me. Most of the time, now, my door was kept closed. I hated all this protection. Whenever I was left alone, I cried for my parents. When Mrs. Broadfield found me drenched with tears, she chided me and warned me about bringing on another emotional collapse. But I couldn't help it. All I could see was my mother's beautiful smile, a smile I would never see again; all I could hear was my father's wonderful warm laughter, laughter I would never hear.

True to his promise, the next day Tony came to the hospital immediately after he had spoken with Luke. I listened as he related Luke's description of our graduation.

"The weather was perfect, not a cloud in the sky. He said the audience fell into a hush after he was introduced and took his position at the podium. He wanted me to be sure to tell you that when he was finished, he received a standing ovation." Tony smiled. "He said his mother was the first to jump up, but everyone followed right along. And everyone asked about you."

"Oh, Tony, I feel so bad about his not being able to call me," I said, and moaned.

"No, no. He understands completely. He's a fine lad, concerned only about your welfare. He told me repeatedly to let you know you shouldn't worry about him. Just recuperate as quickly as you can." Then his face lit up like a beacon and he gathered himself up into an announcer's posture. "And now, the words you've been waiting for: Dr. Malisoff has signed your release. I'm taking you to Farthy tomorrow morning."

"Really?" The news both excited me and made me anxious and sad. I was finally going to see Farthinggale Manor, the place I had dreamt of going to all my life, my fairy-tale castle. But now I was going under a cloak of mourning. My mother and father weren't taking me there, and I wasn't going to walk up those tall and wide steps and through that arching front door. I'd be carried up and enter Farthinggale a crippled orphan.

"Why so sad a face?" His smile weakened.

"I was just thinking about my parents and how wonderful it would have been if all of us would have gone to Farthinggale together."

"Yes." His eyes took on that glazed, far-off look again. "That would have been wonderful. Anyway," he said, snapping back quickly, "I've gotten you the msot comfortable wheelchair made. It will arrive this afternoon and Mrs. Broadfield will help you get used to it."

"Thank you, Tony. Thank you for everything you've done and are doing."

"I told you how to thank me—get better quickly."

"I'll try."

"Tomorrow, then, you will begin your journey back to happiness and health."

He leaned over and kissed my cheek, but paused and closed his eyes before his lips touched my skin. He inhaled deeply.

"Wearing the jasmine, I see. Well, we've got gallons of it at Farthy." He kissed me, his lips lingering longer than I expected. He stood up straight and gazed down at me with the most intense look I had yet seen. "There is much that awaits you at Farthy, much that is yours to inherit and enjoy."

"I can't wait to see it."

About an hour after he left, the wheelchair was delivered. Tony had had them wrap it in a large pink ribbon. Mrs. Broadfield took it off quickly and folded it out. It had shiny chrome arms and legs, a brown, soft-leather seat and back, and suede armrests. Even the footrests were padded.

"Mr. Tatterton must have had this custom built,"

Mrs. Broadfield commented. "I've never seen one like it."

She wheeled the chair alongside the bed, and I got my first taste of what it was going to be like to be lifted out of bed in the morning and into my chair.

First she brought the head of the bed up as far as it would go so I was in a sitting position. Then she came around and peeled the blankets off my body. She lifted my legs and turned me so my legs dangled over the side of the bed. They felt loose, barely attached, although there was no pain in them, no feeling whatsoever.

After she had turned me, Mrs. Broadfield came around, put her arms under my armpits, and lifted me so that I could slide off the side of the bed and into the chair, the right arm of which was folded down for my entry. It embarrassed me. I felt like an infant. I hated the dependency, but there was nothing I could about it.

Once I was in the chair, she snapped the right arm back into place and adjusted the footpads so my feet were safely placed on them.

"This little lever will lock the chair so it won't roll. You don't have to push hard to get it moving. Just make gentle, easy strokes and let the momentum carry you forward. Take hold of this metal rim when you want to make a turn to the right, or that metal rim when you want to make a turn to the left. Go on, practice now," she commanded, and I wheeled myself about the room.

How I wished Drake or Luke were here, too, I thought. I longed for their support. Drake would say I looked like a little girl in a toy wagon or on my first tricycle. Luke would look for something humorous to say, too, only his eyes would reveal his deep sadness. Mrs. Broadfield watched me, gave me more advice, and then decided I had had enough. She wheeled me back to the bed and reversed the order of movements to return me to it. Then she pushed the chair away and went out to see about my dinner.

I lay there staring at the chair, realizing that it and I would have to become good friends. Although Tony had gone to great effort to make it look like an ordinary chair, a comfortable chair, he couldn't hide its true purpose. I was an invalid, a cripple sentenced to dependence on other people and mechanical aids. All the money and all the expensive help in the world couldn't change that. Only I could change that; and I was determined to do so.

There was so much excitement around me the next day that Mrs. Broadfield almost shut my door to isolate me until it was time to go. Regular hospital nurses who had often stopped by to chat or borrow a magazine came to say good-bye and to wish me good luck. Some of the nurse's aides and orderlies came by, too. And my Pink Lady made a point to get to me as early as possible.

The night before, Tony had brought me a box containing a mauve dress. Although it looked brand new, I realized it was a style worn twenty-five or thirty years ago.

"It was your mother's," he explained. "I bought it for her when she went to the Winterhaven School. You're about the size she was at the time. Do you like it?"

"It's a beautiful dress, Tony. It's not the kind of thing girls wear today, but since it was my mother's . . ."

"She looked beautiful in it, and anyway, Annie, you don't want to be a slave to fads. Something that is beautiful is timeless. Most young girls today don't realize that; they're victimized by fashion, by advertising, by passing trends. I'm sure you've inherited your mother's good sense and you'll appreciate style that is enduring."

I didn't know what to say. My mother wanted me to look nice, but she always allowed me to pick out my own clothes. She never tried to impose her tastes on me, and my father enjoyed seeing me in oversize sweatshirts and jeans. Sometimes he called me "Miss Be-Bop."

Although, I suppose Tony was right, I did enjoy dressing up more than most girls my age. That was something I had inherited from my mother.

"I brought it for you to wear tomorrow, a special day, the day you leave the hospital and return to Farthy."

"Return?"

"I mean, return with me to Farthy," he corrected quickly. "Besides, wearing something of your mother's will bring you good luck."

I didn't need convincing. The next morning Mrs. Broadfield helped me put on the dress and wheeled me to the mirror over the sink in my hospital room. I couldn't see below my waist, but what I saw was enough to convince me that I did resemble my mother in the dress. Mrs. Broadfield was kind enough to help me with my hair so that I was able to brush it down the way I had seen my mother wear it in some early pictures. Although hers was a shade darker than mine, we had the same fine texture, and when we wore our hair in a similar style, we almost appeared like twins.

When Tony came, his face lit up at the sight of me in the dress. I could feel his eyes almost drinking me in. He stared so long without saying a word that I began to feel uncomfortable. "I'm ready, Tony," I said to break whatever spell had come over him.

His eyes suddenly snapped to attention. "Yes, yes,

Annie, let's go." He beamed as I had never seen him beam. He looked years younger, perhaps because he was wearing a summer-weight light blue suit that brought out the blue in his eyes. Gone was the paleness I had seen from time to time around his eyes. His cheeks looked rosy, his hair thicker and shinier than ever. With Tony at my side, Mrs. Broadfield began to wheel me out of the hospital room, down the corridor to the elevator. Once again the nurses on the floor wished me good luck and waved as I wheeled past.

My heart was pounding in my ears. The echo of that terrible accident on the Winnerrow road had died a little, but the sound of my father's voice when he called my name still lingered.

I looked back at the hospital floor as the elevator doors closed. The nurses and doctors had returned to their duties. I was just another name to be taken off the charts, a file to be stored now. Just before the doors closed, I remembered something.

"My cards! We left them on the wall!"

"Cards? Oh, your get-well cards. Don't worry. I'll have them brought out to Farthy," Tony promised, but it made me even sadder to think I had left them behind. Luke's funny card, Drake's beautiful card ... I suddenly realized I wasn't bringing along anything from Winnerrow, anything from Luke. I wasn't even wearing the charm bracelet.

The elevator doors opened again and I was wheeled out to the limousine.

"Annie, this is my chauffeur, Miles. He knew your mother very well," Tony said, eyeing Miles.

"Please to meet you, Miss Annie, and glad you've been released from the hospital," Miles said and tipped his cap to me. I saw the smile in his eyes and on his lips, a smile of appreciation and happiness. I was sure I reminded him of my mother.

"Thank you, Miles."

He opened the rear door. Mrs. Broadfield then directed my shifting from the chair into the car. Tony insisted on helping. He went into the car first and took me from Mrs. Broadfield, holding me tightly against his chest as he pulled me gently onto the seat. His lips grazed my cheek and he held me snugly against him. I was surprised at how tightly he held me, and thought he wasn't going to let go. But he did, and then he directed Miles to fold the chair and put it into the trunk. Mrs. Broadfield joined us in the rear and Miles started the car and began my journey to Farthinggale Manor, a journey I was sure I would never forget.

Part

2

Part

2

NINE

Over the Threshold

Mrs. Broadfield and Tony sat me on the rich suede rear seat so I could look out the window at the scenery. The day looked disappointingly overcast, but suddenly a brilliant sun peeked through the dreary clouds and I saw a wide patch of soft, aqua blue that reminded me of lazy summer days back at Winnerrow. Perhaps God was going to shine his light on me after all.

When I gazed back, I saw just how enormous Boston Memorial was, especially compared to our Winnerrow Community General Hospital. We passed through the gates and through some of downtown Boston before getting on the major thoroughfare that would take us to Farthinggale Manor. The rows of houses came to an end and woods and long green lawns appeared with houses spotted here and there along the way.

"Comfortable?" Tony asked. He adjusted the pillow that Mrs. Broadfield had inserted behind my lower back and the rear of the seat.

"Yes."

I was content just staring out the window now, watching the scenery fly by as we continued down the highway that would take us to Farthinggale Manor.

"I remember the day Jillian and I first picked your mother up at the airport to bring her to Farthy. Just like you, she looked so innocent and young, so wide-eyed and eager. I knew she was nervous. Jillian, your great-grandmother, didn't realize Heaven was coming to stay with us forever. She thought it was just going to be a short visit."

He laughed. "Jillian was very concerned about looking young and being thought of as young, so she asked—no, she demanded—your mother to refer to her as Jillian, and never as Grandmother."

"My mother was upset about that."

"She didn't let on that she was. She was a very wise and beautiful young woman, even at that early age." Tony stared silently out the window, lost in thought. Then he sighed, and snapped out of his reverie. "We'll be there soon. Turn your head to the right and look for a break in the treeline. The first glimpse of Farthinggale Manor is a sight to remember."

"How old is Farthy?" I asked.

"It was built by my great-great-great-grandfather in 1850, but don't let its age fool you. It's a grand place, as luxurious as any modern-day mansion. Many a movie star and entrepreneur have sent me offers."

"Would you sell it?"

"Not at any price. It's as much a part of me as . . . as my own name. When I was a boy, there wasn't a house anywhere in the world as fine as the one where I lived. When I was seven, I was sent to Eton because my father thought the English knew more about discipline than our private schools do. I was terribly homesick from the day I arrived to the day I left. Sometimes I'd close my eyes and pretend I could smell the balsam, fir, and pine trees, and the briny scent of the sea." He closed his eyes, as if inhaling the perfumed air of Farthinggale right here in the limo, which smelled only of fine leather.

I felt the limo slow down and then turn onto a private road, and then there it was, looming above us: the fabled high wrought-iron gates with ornate embellishments that spelled out FARTHINGGALE MANOR. Imps and fairies and gnomes peeked between the iron leaves.

"It's almost as big as Luke and I dreamed." I sighed.

"Pardon?"

"Luke and I used to play a game, a fantasy game, imagining what Farthinggale looked like."

"You're about to find out, firsthand."

The driveway seemed to go on forever and ever, and then a huge house made of gray stone suddenly appeared. It did resemble a castle. The red roof soared above the trees, and there were the turrets and small red bridges . . . just as they were in the plaque Luke had given me.

But there was much that was different from the Farthy of our dreams and fantasies, I thought, as I scanned the grounds. Drake's description, unfortunately, was the more accurate one.

The grounds were overgrown and unkempt, bushes untrimmed and flower beds overrun with weeds.

The house was as breathtaking in size as Luke and I had dreamt it would be, but it looked like it hadn't been lived in for years and years. Wherever there was wood siding or trim, it was peeling and cracked. The house looked gray and cold, the windows dark, the curtains closed like the eyelids of a dying old woman.

When the sun slipped behind the heavy clouds, the front of the great house took on a gloomy look.

Suddenly I felt chilled, apprehensive, and ever so lonely. I embraced myself. Here I would need all the warmth I could find.

Tony, on the other hand, smiled widely, his face full of excitement. He gave not the slightest indication that the degeneration of the grounds and the dilapidated look of the great building embarrassed him. It was as if he didn't see it. I looked at Mrs. Broadfield to see if she was as surprised as I was, but she sat stone-faced.

"Farthy goes on for acres and acres," he explained proudly. "It is some of the richest land in the area, and we have our own private beach. When you're ready and able, I'll wheel you about and show you our stables, the pool and cabana, the tennis courts, the gazebo . . . all of it," he promised. "And you must think of it all as yours. Don't ever think of yourself as a guest here; you're more than a guest, far more," he pronounced as Miles brought the car to a stop.

Mrs. Broadfield got out quickly and came around to wait for Miles to get the wheelchair out of the trunk. I looked up the stairway at the great arching door. Even it had lost its grandeur. The wood had chipped off on the right side, as if some giant animal had clawed at it, trying to gain entrance into the house. How could Tony enter and exit from it every day and fail to have it repaired?

"You're here!" Tony exclaimed. "You're actually here! Well, what do you think?"

"I . . ." I fumbled, not knowing what to say. I was disappointed, so very disappointed to see my dream mansion crumbling in disrepair.

"Oh, I know the place needs a little work," Tony interjected, "and I'm going to get right to it now, now that I have a reason to do so." His eyes fixed solemnly on me. My heart fluttered beneath my breast. Something in me, some part of me I couldn't name, rang out an alarm.

"It's a magnificent place, and once you get it shipshape, I bet it will look like it did when you were a little boy," I said, not wanting him to notice my trepidation.

"Exactly. That's exactly how I want it to look. Oh, I knew you would understand, Annie. I'm so happy you're here."

Mrs. Broadfield opened my door. Miles and she had the chair unfolded and ready. She reached in to help guide me out.

"Oh, let me help," Tony insisted, and came around quickly. Mrs. Broadfield stepped back. Tony reached in and embraced me around the waist with his left arm and scooped his right under my thighs. Then, taking great care, he inched back, lifting me up and out of the car as if I were . . . I was about to think: infant, but there was something in the way he held me and smiled at me that made me think of a new bride instead, a new bride about to be carried over the threshold of her new home.

"Mr. Tatterton?" Miles asked, wondering, as I was, when Tony was going to lower me to the chair.

"What? Oh yes, let's do that."

He placed me into the chair gently and then he and Miles lifted me, chair and all, up the stairs to the front entrance. A tall, lean, gray-haired man with dark gray eyes and pale gray skin, creased and wrinkled into small folds over his forehead and neck, stood like a mannequin in the doorway.

"This is Curtis, my faithful butler," Tony announced.

"Welcome," Curtis greeted, bowing slightly and stepping aside so I could be wheeled into the great house.

They brought me into the foyer, carpeted with a Chinese rug that had seen its best days years ago. There were spots that were actually worn through to the hardwood floors. A single chandelier cast pale illumination over the stone walls. It needed a half-dozen bulbs but had only one. Ancestral portraits lined the walls, yellowish faces of stern New England men and women, the women's faces pinched, as if the smiles were ironed out of them; the men making great efforts to appear serious, important, as solid as the rock upon which they had built their magnificent home.

"In time I'll show you all of it," Tony promised, "but for now we'll get you comfortably ensconced in your quarters. I'm sure, after all that you've been through, even a short journey, such as the one we have just made, tires you out."

"I'm too excited to be tired, Tony. Don't worry about me."

"Oh, but that's exactly what I intend to do from now on, Annie: worry about you. You're my new number-one priority."

He continued pushing me farther into the house.

"My office is right here; I'll give you just a short look at it because it's not fit for feminine eyes. Needs a good cleaning," he confessed, kneeling down so his lips actually touched my earlobe.

Even though we didn't enter the room, I saw he was not exaggerating. The single lamp in the corner threw long fingers of anemic white light over the large mahogany desk and the black leather chairs. The books in the dark pine bookcases looked dusty. Rays of sunlight filtered through the curtains over the windows at the rear, capturing the dust particles as a spotlight would. They danced about freely, arrogantly. When had someone last taken a dust mop or vacuum cleaner to this room? I wondered. Tony's desk was piled high with paperwork. How could he find anything?

"Now that you're here, of course, I'll have to get all this into order. Right now I wouldn't think of wheeling you into that unkempt sanctuary, for all the fugitive dirt and grime this house could have. Men," he added, kneeling down again, "when they live alone, tend to ignore the finer things. But that's coming to an end . . . thank God, it's coming to an end," he muttered, and turned me away.

At least there was nothing disappointing about the stairway. It was just as we had dreamt—long, elegant marble steps with a shiny mahogany balustrade. Just gazing at it was enough incentive to make me want to get well again so I could glide down those steps like a princess, just as Luke and I had envisioned I would—wearing a long flowing gown, my wrists and neck bedecked with jewels, jeweled combs in my hair. Oh, how I wished Luke could be here with me now to see it.

"Yes, unfortunately that staircase is an obstacle for you right now, but hopefully not so for long."

We started toward it, but when I looked to my right again, I saw the large living room and the grand piano, and there were pictures painted on the walls and ceiling!

"Oh wait. What a magnificent living room! What are those pictures?"

He laughed and wheeled me to the doorway. It was a very large room, with dowdy satin curtains that were once white but were now gray with dirt and age. Some of the furniture—the velvet couch and love seat and the deep cushioned chair—were covered with plastic that showed the dust, too. The marble tables, the grand piano, the vases . . . everything looked rich and elegant, but decayed and in desperate need of cleaning and polishing.

The faded murals on the walls and ceiling were exquisite, depicting scenes from fairy tales— shadowed woods with sunlight drizzling through, winding paths leading into misty mountain ranges topped with castles and a sky painted overhead with birds flying and a man riding a magic carpet. There was another mystical, airy castle half hidden by clouds. But all the light was gone from the fairy-tale scene, grayed and darkened by years of neglect, so the scene had the dismal, mournful feel of dreams long dead. I shivered.

"Your great-grandmother did all that, Annie. Now you know from where you have inherited your talent for art. She used to be a famous illustrator for children's books."

"Really?"

"Yes," he said, his eyes taking on a faraway look, "in fact, that's how I met her. One day when I was twenty I came home from playing tennis and I looked in and saw up on this ladder the shapeliest legs I had ever seen. When this gorgeous creature came down and I saw her face, she seemed unreal. She had come with a decorator and suggested the murals. 'Storybook settings for the king of the toy makers,' was the way she put it, and I fell for the idea hook, line, and sinker." He winked. "It also gave me a reason for having her come back."

"What a wonderful, romantic story," I cried. Then I fixed my eyes on the grand piano.

"Who plays?" I asked, intrigued.

"Pardon?"

"Do you play the piano, Tony?"

"Me? No. A long time ago my brother used to play," he said. I looked back because his voice had become so thin. "His name was Troy," he said, "and because of our age difference, and because both our parents had passed away by the time he was barely two, I was more like a father than a brother to him. He loved to play, especially Chopin. He died a long time ago."

"My mother loved listening to Chopin."

"Oh?"

"And the small Tatterton Toy cottage that she has. She had," I corrected, "plays a little of a Chopin nocturne when you lift the roof."

"Really? Toy cottage, you say?"

"Yes, with the maze."

I turned to him because he didn't respond. He had stepped to the side of the chair so he could look at the living room with me. Suddenly his faraway eyes focused on me and his face changed. His eyes narrowed and there was a tiny trembling in his lips.

"Tony?"

"Oh, I'm sorry. Daydreaming a bit. Remembering my brother," he added and smiled again.

"You must tell me about him. Will you?"

"Of course."

"I'm depending on you to tell me everything, Tony," I said, feeling it was finally the time to do so. "I want to know all about my family—my great-grandmother, my grandmother, and what you remember of my mother when she lived here."

"If I do all that, you'll get tired of me."

"No. I want to know it all. And Tony," I added, my eyes as determined as they could be, "I want finally to know what it was that caused you and my mother to stop seeing and talking to one another. Promise to tell me all that, no matter how painful it might seem?"

"I promise, and you know by now I keep my promises. But please, for a while, let's avoid anything unpleasant so that you can get well on the way toward a full recovery."

"I'll wait, as long as you've promised."

"Good. Now," he said cheerfully, "onward and upward."

Mrs. Broadfield had gone upstairs ahead of us to prepare my room. Miles was waiting patiently behind us. Tony signaled to him and he came to lift me in the chair. Then, with careful steps, making me feel like some dowager queen returning to her palace quarters, they carried me up the magnificent marble stairway.

"I'm such a trouble," I said, seeing the strain in both their faces as we started the final third of the stairway.

"Nonsense. Miles and I need the exercise, eh, Miles?"

"No trouble, Miss Annie. Glad to do it anytime."

They set me on the floor and I looked down the long corridors that seemed to extend for miles in either direction. Tony turned me to the left.

"I have a wonderful surprise for you. The room you will be in," he said as he continued wheeling me down the corridor, "was your grandmother's room and then your mother's. And now," he said, turning me into a double doorway, "it is yours!"

He put his hand over mine. "As I always knew in my heart it would be someday."

I turned quickly to look at him. His eyes held my own and seemed to send silent messages. He looked so determined, so self-satisfied, that for a moment I felt afraid. Sometimes I got the feeling that Tony had long ago planned out my whole life for me.

My heart fluttered like the wings of a confused canary unsure whether it should enter the golden cage. Truly it would be taken care of, pampered, fed, loved; but it knew also that once it entered the cage, the tiny door would be closed and it would look at the world forever through those golden bars.

What should it do; what should I have done?

As if he sensed my fears, Tony hurriedly wheeled me forward.

She turned and gave me a warm smile. She was a note-faced woman with dull brown eyes, a rather round chin and puffy cheeks. I imagined that perhaps she was aided with a simple body; a small bosom, and hips so wide they made her look like a church bell. She was doomed to be a domestic servant, always cleaning and polishing in someone else's house.

"I'm pleased to meet you, miss." She made a small curtsy. I saw that Tony was disgusted at it, the way he grimaced and turned to release the door stopper.

"Very good. Thank you, Millie. Let's see to your bedroom." Tony said, pushing me on through the sitting room. We stopped just inside the doorway and

TEN

My Mother's Room

T ony wheeled me through two wide, double doors into the first room of the two-room suite. The sunlight through the pale ivory sheers was misted and frail and gave the sitting room an unused, unreal quality. Just like the living room below, this room seemed more like a museum than a room to live in. The walls were covered in a delicate ivory silk fabric, subtly woven through with faint Oriental designs of green, violet, and blue.

A maid in a mint-green uniform with a lace-edged white apron was removing plastic covers from the two small sofas, both upholstered in the same fabric as the fabric that covered the walls. She fluffed the soft blue accent pillows which matched the Chinese rug. After having had Mrs. Avery as our maid for so many years, I thought of maids as elderly women, and so I was surprised to see so young a woman working at Farthy. She looked no more than thirty. Tony introduced her.

"This is Millie Thomas, your personal maid."

She turned and gave me a warm smile. She was a plain-faced woman with dull brown eyes, a rather round chin, and puffy cheeks. I imagined that because she was cursed with a dumpy body, a small bosom, and hips so wide they made her look like a church bell, she was doomed to be a domestic servant, always cleaning and polishing in someone else's house.

"Please to meet you, miss." She made a small curtsy and turned to Tony. "I've finished up in the bedroom and just had these covers to remove and store."

"Very good. Thank you, Millie. Let's go see your bedroom," Tony said, pushing me on through the sitting room. We stopped just inside the doorway so I could take it all in. I could hear Mrs. Broadfield in the bathroom washing out basins and preparing things.

As I slowly scanned the room, I kept trying to imagine the first time my mother had seen it. She had been living with Cal and Kitty Dennison, the couple who had paid five hundred dollars to her father for her.

Now I thought, she had lived in a shack in the Willies, poorer than a church mouse, and then lived with this strange couple, the Dennisons, and then suddenly arrived here in this mansion where she was presented with a magnificent suite of rooms. She must have paused in this doorway, just as I was now pausing, and looked with charmed, astonished eyes at what was before her: a pretty four-poster bed with an arching canopy of blue silk and ivory lace, a blue satin chaise, crystal chandeliers, a long dressing table with a wall of mirrors, and three chairs that matched the sofa and love seat in the sitting room.

The room looked as though it had been left as it was the day my mother departed. Silver-framed photographs sat on the long dressing table, some standing, some facedown. A hairbrush lay on its side. A pair of wine-red velvet slippers were tucked under the chair by the table, slippers that matched the robe Tony had brought me at the hospital. Was it a new robe, as I had thought, or had he taken it from these very closets?

I detected a vague, musty odor, as if the doors and windows had been kept closed for years. Fresh flowers had been placed everywhere to freshen the staleness.

The closets were full of garments, some in plastic bags, some looking as if they had just been hung. I saw the dozens and dozens of pairs of shoes, too. Tony realized I was staring at the clothing.

"Some of those belonged to your mother and some to your grandmother. They were remarkably close in size. Just your size. You won't need to send for a thing. You have an enormous wardrobe right here, waiting for you."

"But Tony, some of these things have to be out of style."

"You'd be surprised. I noticed that many of the old styles have returned. Why should we let all that go to waste, anyway?"

Mrs. Broadfield came out of the bathroom and turned down the blanket on the bed.

"I was going to have a regular hospital bed brought in," Tony explained, "but I thought this would be more comfortable and pleasant. We have extra pillows, a hospital table, and a pillow with cushioned arms for when you want to sit up and read."

"I don't want to go right into bed!" I insisted. "Wheel me to the windows so I can see the view, please, Tony."

"She should get some rest," Mrs. Broadfield advised. "She doesn't realize how tiring it is to leave a hospital and make such a trip."

"A few more moments, please," I begged.

"Just let me show her the view."

Mrs. Broadfield folded her arms under her heavy bosom and stood back, waiting. Tony wheeled me to the windows and opened the curtains wide so I could look out over the grounds. From this perspective, looking to my left, I could see at least half of the maze. Even in the late-morning sunlight the paths and channels looked dark, mysterious, dangerous. When I looked out to my right, I saw beyond the driveway and the entrance to Farthinggale. In the distance I recognized what had to be the family cemetery and I saw what I was sure was my parents' monument.

For a long moment I could not speak. Pain and mourning claimed me and I felt lost, helpless, paralyzed with grief. Then, shoving the memories away and taking a deep breath, I leaned forward to get an even clearer view. Tony saw what had caught my attention.

"In a day or so, I'll take you out there," he whispered.

"I should have gone right to it."

"We've got to worry about your emotional strength. Doctor's orders," he reminded me. "But I promise to bring you out there very soon." He patted my hand reassuringly and stood up straight again.

"I guess I am tired," I confessed, and sat back against the chair, closing my eyes and taking a deep breath. Two tears slipped between my lids and fell like drops of warm rain onto my cheeks, zigzagging to the corners of my mouth. Tony took out his folded handkerchief and gently wiped them away. I mouthed a thank-you and he turned my wheelchair and brought me to the bed. He helped Mrs. Broadfield lift me onto it.

"I'll get her into her nightgown now, Mr. Tatterton."

"Fine. I'll be back in a few hours to check on things. Have a good nap, Annie." He kissed me on the cheek and left, closing the bedroom doors softly behind him.

Just before the doors closed, I caught a glimpse of his face. He looked ecstatically happy, his eyes blazing and bright like the blue tips of gas-fed flames. Did doing things for me fulfill his life so? How ironic it was that one person's misery provided an opportunity for another person to regain his happiness.

But I could not hate him for it. It wasn't his design that brought me here, and what would I fault him for anyway—providing the best medical treatment money could buy? Turning his home and his servants over to me for my recuperation? Doing everything he could to ease my pain and my agony?

Perhaps it is I who should pity him, I thought. Here he was, a lonely, broken man living alone in a mansion echoing with memories, and all that could bring him back to life was my own misery and misfortune. If our family tragedy hadn't occurred, I wouldn't be here and he couldn't do what he was doing. Surely one day he would realize this and it would make him unhappy again.

Mrs. Broadfield began to undress me.

"I can do this myself," I protested.

"Very well. Do what you can yourself and I'll help you with the rest." She stepped away and took out one of my nightgowns.

"I want the blue one," I said, deliberately rejecting whatever she had chosen. Without comment she put the green one back and took out the blue one. I knew

I was being petulant, but I couldn't help it. I was angry about my condition.

I unfastened my dress and tried to lift it over my head, but when I had been placed on the bed, I had sat on the back of the skirt. I had to lie on my side and work the garment up awkwardly, grunting and struggling in a way that I was sure made me appear pathetic. Mrs. Broadfield just stood aside and watched me, waiting for me to call for help. But I was stubborn and determined and I turned and twisted my upper body until I worked the garment over my waist and then tugged it up over my bosom. For a few moments I felt stupid because I wasn't able to get it over my face. And I had exhausted myself with the effort. I had to catch my breath, and I couldn't believe how my arms ached. I was far weaker than I had realized.

Finally I felt Mrs. Broadfield take hold of the dress and complete the job. I said nothing. She placed the nightgown over my head and brought it down after I put my arms through the sleeve holes.

"Do you have any bathroom business?" she asked.

I shook my head. Then she guided my head to the pillow and brought the blanket up and over my body, tucking it snugly around the bed.

"After your nap, I'll bring you some lunch."

"Where do you sleep, Mrs. Broadfield?"

"Mr. Tatterton has set up a room for me across the hall, but I will spend most of my time in your sitting room and leave your bedroom doors open."

"This must be a very boring job," I said, hoping to encourage her to reveal something about herself, her feelings. I had been with her practically every waking moment for over two weeks, but I didn't know the first detail about her life.

"It's my life's work." She didn't smile after she said

that, as most people might. She said it as if it were something that should be immediately obvious to me.

"I understand, but still . . ."

"It's not every day that I get to look after a patient in such rich surroundings," she added. "This looks like a very interesting house with very interesting grounds. I'm sure I won't be bored. Don't you worry about that. Worry about doing all you have to do to get yourself well again."

"You've never been here before?" I inquired.

"No. I had no reason to be here. Mr. Tatterton hired me through an agency."

"But the grounds . . . the building . . ."

"What about it?"

"Don't you think it's all quite run-down?"

"That's none of my concern," she said sharply.

"You're not surprised?" I really wanted to say "disappointed," but I was afraid she would think me a very spoiled and ungrateful person.

"I imagine it must be an enormous expense to keep such a place up, Annie. Besides, as I told you, that's not my concern. Your health and recuperation are my only concerns. You should put most of your concentration on that, too, and not worry about how the grounds are being maintained. Are you going to try to get some rest now?"

"Yes," I said weakly. She was a good and efficient nurse, perhaps even an expert nurse when it came to someone in my condition, but I missed having someone warm and friendly to be with. I missed my mother, being able to run to her with every trouble, even if it was just a bad feeling. I missed bathing in the warmth of her eyes and the softness of her voice; I missed having someone who loved me as much if not more than she loved her own life. Mostly, I missed her wisdom, a wisdom I knew came from years of hardship and difficult experiences.

"Hard times ages ya like bad weather ages the bark on a tree," her Willies granny used to say, the very granny I'd been named for. "If yer smart, that's the tree ya'll lean on."

It hurt me to think I had no one to lean on anymore. Drake was already quite involved in his new and exciting business world. Luke was off to college and certainly occupied by all his new interests and responsibilities. I wasn't sure about Tony yet. He was so kind to me, and yet, yet, shadows hung over my thoughts. Why had Mommy been so set against him?

"I'll return in a few hours," Mrs. Broadfield said. "If you get thirsty, there's a fresh glass of water right here on the night table. Can you reach it?"

"Yes."

"Fine. See you soon."

She turned off the lights, closed the curtains tightly, and left the room.

Now that I was alone, I sat up in the bed to really study the room. What could it have been like for my mother the first night she was here? She had come to live with people she had never seen before, strangers to her, even though they were relatives. In a real way we had both come here as orphans: she made an orphan by her father, who sold away her family; and I, made an orphan by Death, jealous Death, who came and stole away my parents.

And she knew almost as little about her family background as I did. She must have gone through Farthy like an explorer, out to discover who she really was. Only, she wasn't at the mercy of nurses and servants and confined to beds and wheelchairs. She could at least explore.

Oh, I couldn't wait to get well again, to be on my

feet and be whole. I couldn't wait for Luke to come and explore our childhood dreams with me.

Luke. How I missed him, needed his comfort. I hadn't heard from him for days now, because of what had happened in the hospital. But surely I would hear from him soon. I turned to look at that night table.

No phone!

There's no phone. How could he call? A flush of heat and panic swept up through my chest.

"Mrs. Broadfield!" I called. "Mrs. Broadfield!" Had she gone away, thinking I would fall asleep? *"Mrs. Broadfield!"*

I heard the scurrying footsteps, and a moment later she appeared.

"What's wrong?" She flicked on the lights.

"Mrs. Broadfield, there is no telephone in this room."

"My God, was that why you screamed like that?" She put her palm against her chest.

"Please, have Tony come up here."

"Now, Annie, I told you to take a nap, and you said—"

"I won't take a nap until I see Tony," I insisted, and folded my arms under my bosom the way Aunt Fanny often did when she insisted on having things her own way. I could be just as stubborn and determined to have my own way.

"If you insist on acting like this, you'll prolong your recuperation for months. Maybe you'll never recuperate."

"I don't care. I want Tony."

"Very well." She spun on her heels and left the room. Very shortly afterward I heard Tony coming, so I worked myself up into a sitting position.

"What's wrong, Annie?" he asked, his eyes full of alarm.

"Tony, there is no telephone in this room. I can't

155

call anyone and no one can call me. It was all well and good at the hospital. I understood because I had had a bad time, but I'm going to be here for a while; I must have my own phone."

Tony's face and shoulders relaxed. He glanced quickly at Mrs. Broadfield, who stood beside him in a stiff posture of annoyance.

"Oh, of course you will. In time. I spoke to the doctor about that just before we brought you out here. He requested that we keep you quiet for a while longer and then ease you back into things. In fact, he'll be here himself day after tomorrow to give us an evaluation of your recuperation and let us know just how to proceed."

"But surely talking to someone like Luke or Drake or some of my old friends—"

"Drake will visit you today, and if Luke wants to come later on, he may. I'm following the doctor's orders, Annie. If I didn't and something else happened to you, I would feel entirely to blame."

I stared at him. He had his hands out, almost as though he were pleading for me to do what was good for myself. I felt ashamed and shifted my eyes toward the windows.

"I'm sorry. I just . . . I'm in a strange place and—"

"Oh please, don't think of this as a strange place. This is your ancestral home, too."

"My ancestral home?"

"Your great-grandmother lived here, your grandmother lived here, and your mother lived here. Very soon you'll feel right at home. I promise."

"I'm sorry," I said again, and dropped my head back to the pillow. "I'll take my nap now. You can turn out the lights."

He came to the side of my bed and fixed the blanket. "Sleep well."

After he left I looked toward the doorway and saw Mrs. Broadfield silhouetted in the light from the hallway. She looked like a sentinel standing guard. I imagined she was waiting to be sure I was going to do what I had been told.

I was tired and defeated and lost, so I closed my eyes and thought about my mother and the first time she had closed her eyes and put her head down on her pillow on this bed. Did she wonder about her own mother in this room and her life at Farthy? Were there just as many mysteries about her mother's past as I felt there were about mine? It was as if I had inherited my grandmother's and Mommy's fears.

Surely, my grandmother Leigh must have felt strange and alone when she had first been brought to Farthy by her mother, my great-grandmother Jillian. Everything might have been newer and fresher in Farthy, the colors brighter, the rugs and curtains clean and new, the halls shiny and the windows clear. There were many servants about, gardeners, housekeepers, but still, from what I understood, Leigh had been uprooted, taken from her father to live a new life here at Farthinggale with a step-father, Tony Tatterton. She had gone to sleep listening to the same sea breeze push at the windows and thread through the shutters.

And then years and years later, her daughter, my mother, found herself here, going to sleep to the same sounds, perhaps feeling just as alone. In time the great house became home to both of them, as it might now to me. In a real sense Tony was right. I shouldn't feel like a stranger in Farthy. Too much of my past lived here. But all the unanswered questions, the lingering mysteries, the dark shadows that surrounded me and my presence here, made it so confusing.

Perhaps with every passing day another shadow and another mystery would disappear, until Farthy was brilliant with light again the way it might have once been for my grandmother Leigh and for Mommy.

Funny, I thought, but it's as if I'm in the middle of the maze outside, trying to find my way back.

But back to where?

Back to what?

I fell asleep counting questions instead of sheep.

CHAPTER OF PARADISE

ones. Now mature he looked. How grown-up, as if I had been gone for five years and seen, as a little girl, the Kip Van Winkle, and awakened to find my friends had passed me in the night. Would I also look as grown-up and beyond my time?

Drake wore a tuxedo-breasted, satin blue silk suit, a suit shirt under to the satin bows vest. His hair was cut shorter and brushed back, and down on the top like shorter. If I had come upon him on a city street, I might not might not have recognized him.

"Why, Drake, you look like a — a banker," I chuckled.

"But a businessman," he . . . . to look the part Annie. People expect that. It's something I've quickly learned. So let me all about your arrival here, as you — Come in." He turned the knob over the door and closed auto adits, allowing so I could . . . to an . . .

ELEVEN

Drake

I awoke to the sound of laughter in the hallway and recognized Drake's voice. He would never know how much I welcomed that sound, something familiar, something from home. The laughter stopped and then I heard footsteps. A moment later he appeared carrying my lunch on a solid silver tray. He snapped on the lights and came into the room.

"Oh, Drake!"

"Annie, I've come all the way from Boston to serve you your lunch."

He laughed and brought the tray to the bed table. Then he kissed me and held me firmly for a few seconds. A film of tears formed over my eyes, but they were tears of happiness, and tears of happiness did not burn; they simply clouded my vision and made me sniffle.

"Oh, Drake, I'm so happy to see you."

"You're okay, aren't you?" he asked, backing away and looking at me with concern. Handsome, tall, dark Drake, I thought, with his bronze skin and ebony

159

eyes. How mature he looked, how grown-up, as if I had been asleep for years and years as a little girl, like Rip Van Winkle, and awakened to find everyone had passed me in the night. Would Luke look as grown-up and beyond me, too?

Drake wore a double-breasted, light blue silk suit, a suit identical to the suits Tony wore. His hair was cut shorter and brushed back and down on the top like Tony's hair. If I had come upon him on a city street, I thought, I might not have recognized him.

"I'm okay. Drake, you look like a . . . a banker."

He laughed.

"Just a businessman. You've got to look the part, Annie. People respect that. It's something I've quickly learned. So, tell me all about your arrival here, as you eat, of course." He pushed the table over the bed and helped adjust my pillows so I could sit up.

I glanced at the doorway and he caught my look.

"Oh, I gave your nurse time off, told her I would give you lunch."

"Where's Tony?"

"He's in his office, trying to straighten out the mountains of papers strewn about. Says he's got to get it looking decent enough for you to visit someday, so you can watch him work. He says that was something your grandmother used to do."

"Drake," I whispered, pausing between spoonfuls of hot soup, "it's exactly as you described in your letter and phone call . . . all of it looks like it hasn't been touched for years and years."

"It hasn't been."

"But Drake, Tony doesn't seem to see it that way. Haven't you noticed?"

He swung his eyes away and thought for a moment.

"He can't get himself to see it as it really is right now. I suppose it's too painful for him. He remembers it the way it was . . . a magnificent estate."

160

"But—"

"Give him time, Annie. He's like a man who has been in a coma for years and is just coming out of it."

"He's nice, very considerate and all . . . but sometimes he scares me." There, I'd said it out loud.

"Oh, why, Annie? He's a harmless, elderly man who lost everything that had any real meaning in his life: family. If anything, you should pity him."

"I do. It's just . . ."

"What? You'll get whatever you want. The doctors will be coming to you, instead of you going to them. Tony's asked the doctors to order any machine, any therapeutic device, that would speed up your recuperation, no matter what the cost. You'll be attended by a professional nurse and waited on hand and foot by an army of servants. Tony has already hired an additional maid and two more groundskeepers. He's doing so much for you."

"I know." I gazed at the photographs in the silver frames. "I guess it's just that I miss Mommy and Daddy so much."

"Oh, of course." He sat down beside me and took my hand into his. "Poor Annie. I miss them, too. Sometimes, when I get a break for an hour or so, I think maybe I should call Heaven, and then I remember all that's happened."

"I keep hoping this is all just a dream, Drake; and I'll wake up and you'll be coming home from college to see me."

He nodded. Then he leaned over and kissed me warmly on the cheek, but so close to my lips that the corners of our mouths touched. He seemed embarrassed. I noticed that he was wearing a different cologne, a scent I had recognized as Tony's cologne.

"Hey," he said quickly, "if you don't eat, they'll blame me and never let me bring you a meal again."

I spooned some more soup and took a bite of the sandwich.

"Have you seen or spoken to Luke? You heard about his wonderful graduation speech, didn't you?"

"Yes. Mark Downing told me. He was in Boston and came by to see me. He said everyone was shocked when Luke referred to Logan as his father, even though they all knew it to be true."

"I'm so proud of him. Aren't you?" He nodded. "But Drake, haven't you spoken with him since? You called him to congratulate him, didn't you?"

"Frankly, Annie, I wasn't in the mood to congratulate anyone for anything. I've been keeping myself as busy as I can just so I don't think about things."

I nodded softly, understanding what he meant.

"So you haven't spoken to him at all?"

"I spoke with him briefly yesterday, after he arrived at Harvard."

"He arrived at Harvard! Oh, then he's nearby and he'll come to visit or he'll call Tony. Maybe he's called already."

Drake's eyes darkened and the lines in his mouth tightened.

"You have to give him time to get settled in. It's quite a thing to arrive at college. There's mountains of things to do, forms to fill out, arrangements to make. He was so excited about it all, and he's making so many new friends at his dorm. Dorms are coed now, you know. Some of his new friends will be girls. You should expect that he will find a real girlfriend someday."

My heart sank. A real girlfriend? Someone who would replace me as the person to whom he trusted his most intimate and secret thoughts, someone with whom he would share dreams—and that someone wouldn't be me. In my secret heart I knew this would happen someday, but I wouldn't listen to the voices whispering the warnings, and now Drake was telling me in his usual nonchalant manner that Luke would fall in love with someone else and go on to live happily ever after somewhere else. What's more, perhaps my condition would speed it all since I wouldn't be there for him. I'd be stuck here, crippled and alone.

I shifted my eyes quickly so Drake couldn't read my thoughts.

"Oh, of course, but I'm sure as soon as he gets free . . ."

"You know," Drake said. He was so eager to change the subject, it made me nervous. "Now that you're not going to be able to travel through Europe, you should think about your education, too. I think we should arrange for you to have a tutor so that you could pick up a college credit or two while you're recuperating. As long as the doctors approve, of course." He looked about the room. "You might just be terribly bored otherwise."

"That's a good idea."

"I'll speak to Tony about it."

"Why don't you just take care of it for me, Drake. Talk to people at Harvard. Have me tutored in one of the courses Luke's going to take. That way, when he comes by, we can go over the work together." It would make it less boring for Luke to come here, too, I thought.

"I'll see what I can do. You must not underestimate the power and influence of a man like Tony. True, he's kept himself out of things for quite a while, permitting managers to run his toy empire, but everywhere I go in Boston," he added, smiling and straightening his back and shoulders with pride, "they have heard of the Tattertons. Just the mention of the name opens doors and sets people scurrying about, treating me as if I were a millionaire myself.

"And there is so much a man like Tony can teach me," he continued, going on like a runaway car downhill. "His wisdom comes from experience and not just books. He knows whom to see, how to handle people, what to say, especially when it comes to negotiations." He laughed. "I bet he's a great poker player."

"That's wonderful, Drake. I'm glad you're happy with him. Tell me, though," I said, putting the remainder of my sandwich aside, "does he ever talk about my mother and about the things that happened between them?"

"Oh no. And I don't ask. If Heaven's name comes up, his face brightens and he mentions only happy, wonderful things. Maybe it's best we just let sleeping dogs lie. Why bring about any more unpleasantness? Think of it this way, Annie," he added quickly, "what good will it do anyone now?"

"I'm not insisting on anything like that right now, Drake; but I can't stay here without knowing these things. Sometimes," I said, shifting my eyes to the bed, "I feel as if I've betrayed Mommy by letting Tony do all that he has done for me."

"Oh, Annie, that's nonsense. If anything, Heaven would have wanted you to have the best possible recovery. She would never resent anything that was good for you. She loved you too much."

"I hope you're right, Drake."

"I know I'm right. Do you think if it had been the other way around, if Tony would have needed Heaven's help, that she would have turned him out?"

"I don't know. She turned him out of her heart for so long. I've got to know why. Don't you see, Mommy—"

"Well now," Tony's voice boomed, "how's the patient doing?"

He came in so quickly, I wondered if he hadn't been standing just outside the room listening to our conversation. Drake didn't seem to be concerned. He stood up immediately and beamed. It was clear how much he truly respected and admired Tony.

"She's doing fine, Tony," he replied quickly. "There couldn't be a better place for her to recuperate."

"That's wonderful. Did you have a good nap, Annie?"

"Yes. Thank you, Tony."

"Please, don't thank me. It is I who should be thanking you. You don't know what your presence at Farthy, even for only a short time, has already done. There's a new brightness about the place. Everything feels fresh and exciting again. Even my old servants—Curtis, the butler; Ryse Williams, the cook—are moving around as if they were years and years younger, just because they know you're here."

"I'd like to meet Rye Whiskey." I remembered he was one of the few people at Farthy Mommy liked to talk about.

"I'll send him up as soon as I can."

"And I'd like to explore the house. Maybe Drake will wheel me about."

"Oh, I'd like to, Annie, but I have to get back to Boston before the stock market closes today."

"Today's a little soon for explorations anyway," Tony said. "Give yourself a day or two to get strong and then I'll take you around myself and tell you all the history and romance associated with each and every nook and cranny."

"But I'm tired of just sitting in bed," I moaned.

"Mrs. Broadfield has things planned out for you,

Annie. You have physical therapy to do and a hot bath and—"

I pouted.

"If Tony promised he'll take you around, he'll take you," Drake muttered. I kept my head lowered but raised my eyes at him. I saw the smile ripple through his lips just the way it used to when I caught him watching me across a room back in Winnerow. That familiar look warmed my heart.

"I'm behaving badly, I know. Everyone's trying to help me and I'm just being a brat."

"But a beautiful brat," Tony said. "So you're forgiven."

"See what a charming man he is," Drake said.

"I see. Oh, Tony, did Luke call yet? Drake tells me he's been at Harvard since yesterday."

"Not yet. The moment he does, I'll have the message delivered to you."

"Just tell him to come whenever he can."

"Fine." Tony clapped his hands to end that topic of conversation. "Well, we'd better let Mrs. Broadfield get started. Don't want to stand in the way of your progress."

"Excuse me, sir," Millie Thomas said. She stood timidly in the doorway. "But I came to see if Miss Annie was finished with her tray."

"I'm finished." She came in quickly to take it. "Thank you, Millie." She smiled. "Whenever you're free, come up to see me."

"Oh." Her frown came fast but slight, as if such an easygoing and friendly mistress unsettled her, but our servants at Hasbrouck House were always treated like part of the family. Millie looked up at Tony quickly. "Yes, Miss Annie."

"And please, Millie, just call me Annie."

She scurried out of the room with mousy steps.

"I hope she will work out," Tony muttered after her. "Got her on rather quick notice from a new agency."

"She seems very nice, Tony."

"We'll see."

"I'd better be going," Drake said. "I'll come by again in a day or so, Annie. Is there anything I can bring you?"

"There are things back at Winnerow that I want, Drake. When are you going to make a trip there?"

"Not for a while, Annie, but I suppose we could send for them." He looked to Tony for confirmation.

"Of course."

"I can just call Aunt Fanny, too. I'm sure she's going to want to come out to see me."

"I'm sure Drake can get away for a day," Tony decided. "It's important enough."

"Make a list, Annie, and I'll pick it up when I return."

"Thank you, Drake."

"See you soon." He gave me a quick peck on the cheek and hurried out of the room.

Tony stood there gazing down at me. Suddenly the expression on his face changed. His blue eyes brightened and his face lifted as though he had just come upon something he thought he had lost. There was a strange look in his eyes as he turned toward the windows.

"Well now, we can open these curtains. The sky has cleared and it's a magnificent day." He pulled open the curtains and looked down. "Flowers are in bloom everywhere. I'm going to have that pool filled tomorrow. I know how you like to swim."

"Swim?" Who told him I liked to swim, I wondered, and how could he fill that pool tomorrow? It looked like it needed a lot of repair work.

167

"I'll have to see about Scuttles, too. I know as the days get warmer you're going to want to ride that pony."

"Scuttles? What a funny name for a horse. You really think the doctors will let me get on a horse, Tony?" He didn't reply. He continued to stare down. "Tony?"

He turned around as if he had just realized I was there.

"Oh. Lost myself in a daydream. So, I'll tell Mrs. Broadfield to get started," he said. He slapped his hands together and then started out of the room.

Shortly after, Mrs. Broadfield came in and took me through some therapeutic exercises and gave me a leg massage. Even though my legs were lifted and turned this way and that, I felt nothing, no pain, no aches, just as Dr. Malisoff had predicted. There was only a slight sensation over my toes, but perhaps even that was in my imagination.

"I see your fingers there, but I don't feel them, Mrs. Broadfield." She nodded and worked on as though I were a piece of clay she was molding.

After that she helped me into the wheelchair so I could sit up and wheel about while she prepared a hot bath. When she went into the bathroom, I wheeled myself to the window and looked down as Tony had.

Flowers in bloom? The flower beds were so overrun with weeds and grass, nothing dainty could compete. Maybe he meant he would do something about them now so there would be flowers in bloom. Just as he said, he must have been daydreaming, I thought. Scuttles . . . horseback riding. I shook my head. It was strange, almost as if Tony were living in another time and thought me to be someone else.

"Let me prepare you for your bath now, Annie," Mrs. Broadfield said, coming up behind me. I was in such deep thought, her voice made me jump. She put her hand so softly on my shoulder, I quickly relaxed. She could be gentle when she wanted to be. "Are you all right?"

"Yes, yes, I was just thinking. Mrs. Broadfield, do you think I could go horseback riding in the near future?"

"Horseback riding." She laughed. I think it was the first time I had heard her do so. "I'm just hoping you'll be able to get yourself in and out of this chair in the near future. Whoever put such a thought in your head?"

I stared up at her.

"No one," I said.

"Well, I'm glad you're thinking positively. It helps." She wheeled me into the bathroom and helped me strip off my nightgown. Then she guided me into the hot tub. At the hospital, doctors, nurses and Mrs. Broadfield poked and explored my body and I had no self-consciousness about it. Modesty seemed ridiculous and out of place. Who cared who saw me naked? I was more like a dead person.

But now, stronger, more aware of myself, I did blush. Not since I was a very little girl had anyone helped me bathe. Mrs. Broadfield held me under my arms as I lowered myself into the hot water.

"It's so hot."

"It has to be that way, Annie."

When I was settled securely, she released her grip but kept her hands on my shoulders. Under the hot, bubbling water, my legs looked leaden. I still couldn't feel them at all. Her strong fingers, made muscular by hours and hours of massaging and lifting patients, kneaded my small shoulders and the back of my neck.

"Just relax," she said. "Close your eyes and relax."

I did what she said and leaned back. Steamy vapor filled my lungs, misted the air so Mrs. Broadfield and I seemed miles and miles away. I drifted into a dreamy land where soft music played. I felt drunk from lack of energy. I heard her dip a washcloth into the bubbling water and then felt her bring it to my arms.

"I can do that."

"Just relax. It's what Mr. Tatterton has hired me to do."

It was difficult for me to relax while someone else scrubbed my body. She moved the soft cloth slowly over and under my arms. She washed my neck and shoulders and had me lean forward so she could wash most of my back.

"Doesn't this feel good, Annie?"

I simply nodded, keeping my eyes closed. It was easier for me that way. Whenever I opened them, I saw Mrs. Broadfield bent over the hot tub, her face tight and intense, like a skilled technician worried about detail.

"You have a nice, firm young body, Annie. Strong. You're going to recuperate, if you cooperate and follow the therapy."

The hot steam drew beads of water in lines across her forehead and over her puffy cheeks. They looked like tiny pearls. Her face was very flushed, almost as red as someone who had fallen asleep in the hot sunlight.

She dipped her arms as deeply into the water as she could to reach my legs and thighs, washing and massaging. Finally she sat back, looking short of breath. She saw how I gazed quizzically at her and she quickly rose to her feet to wipe her forearms.

"Just sit there and soak for a while longer," she said, and went into the bedroom.

I did all that I could to help assist her in lifting me out of the tub. I wiped down my upper body while she wiped my feet and legs. Then she helped me into a new nightgown and brought me back to the bed. I wanted to remain in the wheelchair, even though the hot bath had tired me out.

"Just for a short while," she said. "I'll be back and help you into bed so you can take a brief nap before dinner."

I waited until she left the room and then I wheeled myself to the window. The afternoon sun had fallen far enough below the great house so that the building now cast a long, dark shadow over the grounds and the maze. Still, it looked warm outside.

I had come to the window because I wanted to look again at the Tatterton family cemetery. I hadn't been there yet, but just seeing my parents' monument would make me feel closer to them, I thought.

Suddenly I saw a man appear as if out of the air. He must have been standing off in a shadow. I leaned as close to the window as I could and gazed at the figure made small by the distance. At first I thought it might be Luke, but as my eyes focused in more accurately, I realized he was a taller, thinner man.

He stepped up to the monument and stared at it for the longest time. Then he dropped to his knees. I could see him lower his head, and although I was much too far away to be sure, I even thought I could see his body shudder with sobs.

Who was he? It wasn't Tony, although there was something about the frame of his body that reminded me of Tony.

Was it one of the help who remembered my mother well?

I blinked because my eyes grew tired and began to tear from staring so intently, and then I leaned back and wiped them with the back of my hand.

When I leaned forward again to look out at the cemetery and the monument, the man was gone. It was as if he popped into thin air, disappearing like a bubble.

I sat back because something that occurred to me filled me with a shudder and a chill.

Had I imagined him?

Frustrated and exhausted, I backed away from the window.

TWELVE

Ghosts in the House

T ony found me asleep in my wheelchair by the window. I woke when I felt him wheeling me back to the bed.

"Oh, I didn't mean to wake you. You looked so beautiful, like a sleeping princess. I was just about to be the prince and kiss you to wake you," he said warmly, his eyes bright.

"I can't believe I fell asleep so quickly. What time is it?"

Dark, brooding clouds had slid across the sky, blocking the sun and making it hard to tell what time of day it was.

"Don't be concerned. I'm sure your fatigue is a result of the therapy and the hot bath Mrs. Broadfield gave you," he explained with a father's comforting tone. "They'll wear you out in the beginning. You must remember that you still don't have much strength. That's why the doctors are so concerned that you have a peaceful, restful time while trying to recuperate. At least at the very beginning."

I saw by the way he pressed down on his lips that this was meant as a reminder and as mild chastisement for the tantrum I threw when I discovered I had no phone.

"I know. I just get so impatient, so frustrated," I offered as an excuse. His face lightened instantly.

"Of course you feel that way. Why shouldn't you? Everyone understands. You have to come back slowly, in small increments, doing a little more each day. Mrs. Broadfield says that when patients try to rush things along, they retard their recuperation."

"The strange thing is, I don't feel that weak," I cried. "It's almost as if I could walk again immediately if I were forced to do it. At least, that's the feeling I get every once in a while."

He nodded with understanding. "Your feelings deceive you. Dr. Malisoff told me that might happen. It's expected. The mind doesn't want to face up to the limits of the body."

I wanted to show him that he and Mrs. Broadfield and the doctors were wrong, so I didn't ask him to help me up and out of the chair and into the bed. My hands wobbled on the arms of the chair as I tried to raise myself. But even putting all my weight on only my upper body, my lower body now just a ball and chain, I was unable to lift myself very high and fell back into the chair, my heart pounding from the effort. I felt a sharp pain across the middle of my brow and moaned.

"As I said. It seems like you can do everything you used to do for yourself, but you can't. It's the mind's way of trying to deny what happened." He looked away for a moment. "And sometimes, sometimes even the best minds, the strongest minds, refuse to believe what their bodies . . . what reality tells them is true. They invent, pretend, fantasize, do anything to avoid hearing the words they dread," he explained, his voice dropping to a whisper.

I stared up at him. He had spoken so passionately, so vehemently, that I felt overwhelmed. All I could do was nod. Then he turned back to me, his face changed again, a look of loving compassion in his eyes. He leaned down over me, his face so close to mine, our lips nearly touched, and he hooked his hands under my arms to lift my body out of the chair and onto the bed. For a long moment he held me, embracing me, his cheek pressed against mine. I thought he whispered Mommy's name, but then he swung me gently to the bed and I fell back against the pillow.

"I'm not too rough, I hope," he said, still leaning over me, his face still very close to mine.

"No, Tony." I knew it was unfair and even silly to think it, but I hated my body for betraying me and leaving me dependent upon the mercy and kindness of other people.

"Perhaps you should take a nap before dinner," he said. I didn't need the suggestion. My eyelids felt so heavy it was hard to keep them open. Everytime I did look up, it seemed as if Tony were leaning closer and closer over me. I know I wasn't supposed to be able to feel anyone touch me from the waist down, but I thought his hands were over my legs, caressing them. I fought to keep myself awake in order to confirm or deny what I was seeing, but I dropped off quickly, like one under sedation, my last thought being Tony's lips were moving down my cheek toward my lips.

I next awoke to the sound of Millie Thomas setting my supper tray on the bed table beside me. Apparently I had slept through a summer thunderstorm, for I could smell the fresh, wet scent of rain, even though the sky was now only partly cloudy.

When I recalled Tony helping me to bed and thought about the image of his hands on my legs and his lips close to mine, I considered it some kind of dream. It seemed too ethereal, too misty a memory, anyway.

"Didn't mean to wake you, Miss Annie," she said timidly.

I blinked and blinked and focused in on her. With her arms pressed tightly against her body and her hands overlapping at her waist, she looked penitent, like one of the people from the Willies who had just been lectured by old Reverend Wise. He was always harder on them than he was on the people from Winnerrow proper.

"That's all right, Millie. I should be awake. It rained, didn't it?"

"Oh, like the dickens, Miss Annie!"

"Please, don't call me Miss Annie. Just call me Annie." She nodded slightly. "Where are you from, Millie?"

"Oh, from Boston."

"Do you know where Harvard is?"

"Of course, Miss . . . of course, Annie."

"My uncle Drake goes there, and I have a . . . a cousin going there now, too. His name is Luke."

She smiled more warmly and fixed my sitting pillow behind me. I pulled myself up into position to eat and she wheeled the table to the bed.

"I don't know anyone who went to Harvard."

"How long have you been working as a maid, Millie?"

"Five years. Before that I worked as a stock girl at Filene's, but I didn't like the work as much as I like working as a maid."

"Why do you like working as a maid?"

"You get to work in such nice houses. All not as big

176

as this one, of course; but nice ones. And you meet people of better breeding. That's the way my mother put it. She was a maid, too, for years and years. Now she's in a rest home."

"Oh, I'm sorry."

"That's okay. She's happy. I'm sorry for you, Annie. I know your tragedy. All the servants were talking about your mother this morning, the ones who remembered her, that is."

"You mean like Rye Whiskey?"

She laughed.

"When the groundskeeper called him that, I thought he was ordering a drink."

"My mother used to call him that, too. But that reminds me. When you go back down to the kitchen, you tell Rye Whiskey that I want him to come up to see me. Right away. Tony was supposed to send him up, but he must have forgotten. Will you do that, please?"

"Oh, of course, I will. I'll go right down now. Would there be anything else you might want with your supper?"

"No, this all looks fine."

"Then you'd better eat it before it all gets cold," Mrs. Broadfield snapped as she came into the bedroom and crossed to the bathroom, carrying an armful of fresh, white towels. "Didn't I ask you to bring up these towels?" she said, turning at the bathroom door. Millie blushed.

"I was going to do just that, ma'am, as soon as I served Annie her supper."

Mrs. Broadfield grunted and continued on into the bathroom. Millie started away quickly.

"Don't forget Rye Whiskey," I called to her in a loud whisper.

"I won't."

Mrs. Broadfield came out and stopped at my bed to look over my meal. She frowned at the small piece of chocolate cake.

"I distinctly told that cook not to put rich desserts on your tray. Just Jell-O for now."

"That's all right. I won't eat the cake."

"No, you won't," she said, and reached over to take it off the tray. "I'll see that you get the Jell-O."

"It's not important."

"Following my orders is important," she muttered, and then she pulled her shoulders back like a general and marched out of the room. Poor Rye Whiskey, I thought. I hadn't even met him yet, and now, because of me, he had gotten into trouble. I finished my meal, eating more out of necessity than out of pleasure, chewing and swallowing mindlessly. Each piece of broiled chicken tasted as if it were made of stone. It wasn't the fault of the carefully prepared food. I was just too tired and too depressed to care.

Just as I finished, I heard a knock on my outside door. I looked out and saw the elderly black man I knew had to be Rye Whiskey. He still wore his kitchen apron and carried a small dish of Jell-O.

"Come in," I called, and he came forward slowly. As he drew closer I saw that his eyes were wide, the whites around his black pupils so bright, it was as if a candle burned behind them like the candles in pumpkins on Halloween. What he saw in me obviously took his breath away.

"You must be Rye Whiskey."

"And you surely is Annie, Heaven's daughter. When I first set eyes on you from the doorway there, I thought I was lookin' at a ghost. Weren't the first time I thought I saw somethin' like that in this house, neither."

He tipped his head to whisper some prayerful words and then looked up, his face a portrait of

178

sadness and worry. I knew he had been here through all of it: my grandmother's flight from home, my great-grandmother Jillian's madness and subsequent death, my mother's arrival and eventual unhappy parting with Tony Tatterton, and now my tragic arrival.

His thin hair was as white as snow, but he had a remarkably smooth, wrinkle-free face and looked very spry for a man I estimated to be close to if not over eighty.

"My mother often spoke fondly about you, Rye."

"I'm glad ta hear dat, Miss Annie, for I was sho' fond o' yer mama." His smile widened and he nodded, his head bobbing as if his neck were a spring. He glanced at my supper tray. "Food all right?"

"Oh, very tasty, Rye. I'm just not that excited about eating right now."

"Well, ole Rye Whiskey's goin' ta change that." His eyes crinkled in a smile and he nodded his head again. "So, how you gettin' along, Miss Annie?"

"It's hard, Rye." Funny, I thought, but I felt comfortable being honest with him right from the start. Maybe it was because of the way Mother had spoken about him.

"Oh, I expect it would be." He leaned back on his heels. "I can remember the first time yer mama came ta the kitchen ta see me. Remember it just like it was yesterday. Just like you, she was so much like her own mama. She would come in an' watch me cookin' for hours, sittin' there on a stool, restin' her head on her hand and pepperin' me with all sorts of questions 'bout the Tattertons. She was 'bout as curious as a kitten who got inta a linen basket."

"What did she want to know?"

"Oh, jes' 'bout eveythin' I could remember 'bout this family—uncles, aunts, Mr. Tatterton's pappy and grandpappy. Whose picture was that on the wall, whose was this? 'Course, like in any family, there was things decent folk don't gossip 'bout."

What things, I longed to ask him, but I held my tongue, biding my time. Rye slapped his hands to his thighs and sighed.

"So, is there anythin' special I can make you?" he asked to quickly change the subject.

"I like fried chicken. My cook in Winnerrow makes a batter—"

"Oh, he does . . . well, you ain't tasted mine yet, chile. I'll make you that this week. Unless your nurse says otherwise." He looked back to be sure Mrs. Broadfield wasn't there. "She come inta the kitchen with a list of do's and don'ts. Made my assistant, Roger, as nervous as the Devil on Sunday."

"I don't see how Southern fried chicken could hurt, Rye," I said, swinging my eyes toward the window, "Farthy was a much prettier place when my mother lived here, wasn't it?"

"Oh, and how! Why, when the flowers would bloom, it looked like Heaven's Gate."

"Why did Mr. Tatterton let it fall apart?"

He shifted his eyes away quickly. I saw that my question made him nervous, but that only made me more curious about his answer.

"Mr. Tatterton's had a hard time, Miss Annie, but he sho' has changed a whole lot since yourself arrived. Almost back to the way he was—talking 'bout fixin' this and buildin' that. Things are comin' back to life 'round here, which is good for us and bad for the ghosts," he whispered.

"Ghosts?"

"Well, like any big house that had so many people movin' through it, spirits linger, Miss Annie." He nodded for emphasis. "But I ain't one to challenge that, and neither is Mr. Tatterton. We live side by side with 'em and they don' bother us none and we don' bother them."

I saw he was serious.

"Are there many servants here now who were here when my mother lived here, Rye?"

"Oh no, Miss Annie. There's jes' myself, Curtis, and Miles. All the maids and grounds helpers are gone, mostly dead and gone."

"Is there a tall, thin man working here, too, a man much younger than Curtis?"

He thought a moment and shook his head.

"There's groundsmen, but they're all short and stocky."

Who was that man at my parents' tomb? I wondered. Rye continued to gaze at me, a fond smile on his face.

"Has it been hard for you these past years, Rye, because of the way Mr. Tatterton was?"

"No, ma'am, not hard. Sad, but not hard. 'Course, I stayed in ma room after supper and left the house to the spirits. Now," he smiled, "they gonna retreat and hover 'bout their graves mostly, 'cause we got light and life again. Spirits hate young people roamin' 'bout. Makes 'em jittery 'cause the young folks got so much energy and brightness 'bout 'em."

"You really heard these spirits in the house, Rye?" I tipped my head and smiled, but he didn't smile back.

"Oh yes, ma'am. Many a night. There's one spirit, very unhappy one, who roams the halls, goes from room to room, searchin'."

"For what?"

"Don' know, Miss Annie. Don' talk to 'im and he don' talk ta me. But I've heard him walkin' 'bout and I've heard the music."

"Music?"

"Piana music. Sweet music."

"Did you ever ask Mr. Tatterton about it?"

"No, Miss Annie. Didn't have to. Saw it in his eyes."

"Saw what?"

"That he heard and saw the same things I did. But you forgets all about that, Miss Annie. You get strong and better fast. Ole Rye will cook up a storm now that there's someone to cook for."

I thought a moment.

"Rye, is there a horse here called Scuttles?"

"Scuttles, Miss Annie? There ain't no horses now. H'ain't been any for some time. Scuttles?" His eyes went from side to side as he thought, scanning his memory. I saw him stop thinking, a realization coming to him.

"Scuttles, why that was the name Miss Jillian gave to her ridin' pony. She lived on a horse ranch when she was a young girl. I remembers her talkin' 'bout that pony all the time. But we never had one here named Scuttles. Her horse was called Abdulla Bar. A devilish animal," he added, his eyes brightening with fear.

"Why do you say that, Rye?"

"He let no one but Miss Jillian ride 'im, so Mr. Tatterton kept everyone else off, 'cept that one terrible time. But it wasn't his fault," he added quickly.

"What terrible time, Rye?"

"Oh, this ain't the time to talk 'bout sad things, Miss Annie. You got your own hardship ta bear."

"Please, Rye, I don't want to ask Mr. Tatterton, but I want to know."

He looked back and stepped closer to the bed. He shook his head and lowered his eyes.

"It was his brother, Mr. Troy, Miss Annie. One day he jes' hopped on that stallion and rode him into the sea. Only a Devil horse woulda done it. Any other horse woulda refused to go in."

"So that's what Drake meant when he said Troy

committed suicide. He rode my great-grandmother's horse into the ocean and—"

"And he drowned, Miss Annie. Seems this house has had more'n its share of hardships ta bear, hasn't it, Miss Annie?" He shook his head. "Sometimes it's harder ta live ta a ripe ole age. Yer haunted by the many bad memories and ya hear the many lonely spirits."

"But why did he do such a thing, Rye?"

"Oh, I wouldn't know," he said quickly; too quickly, I thought. "Troy was as handsome a young man as ya'll ever see, and talented, too. He made many of the toys, ya know. Only, I never called 'em toys. They was more like art." He shook his head and smiled, recalling. "Lil' houses and lil' people, some made inta music boxes."

"Music boxes?"

"Beautiful melodies . . . like soft piana music."

"Chopin," I muttered. The memory of my mother's musical cottage sent my heart pitter-pattering, overwhelming me with a flush of sadness.

"What's that, Miss Annie?"

I shifted my eyes away quickly, not wanting him to see my tears.

"I was just thinking of a composer."

"Oh. Well, I best get my ole self back down ta the kitchen and see what Roger's up to. He's my—what do you call 'im—apprentice. Ole Rye can't expects he'll be workin' in that kitchen forever, and Mr. Tatterton needs a good cook when I gets the call to join my maker. 'Course, rights now, I play deaf to that, Miss Annie," he said, smiling widely. We laughed.

"Oh, I almost forgot yer Jell-O." He put the dish on my tray.

"Sorry I can't have your chocolate cake, Rye. It looked delicious."

"Oh yes, she brought that right down again." He

looked back and then leaned toward me. " 'Course, I'll find away to sneak a piece back up. Jest ya wait."

"Thank you, Rye. And come back to see me, please."

"Sho' will."

"Well, what's this?" Tony said, suddenly appearing in my doorway. "The chef checking up to see how well his food's gone over?"

"Someone had ta bring up some Jell-O, and I thought it was as good a time as any to pay my respects, Mr. Tatterton." He turned back to me and winked. "Gots ta be gettin' back ta my kitchen now."

"Thank you, Rye," I called as he hurried out. Tony watched him leave and then turned to me.

"Why didn't Millie bring up the Jell-O?" he wondered aloud.

"I asked Millie to send him up."

"Oh?" His blue eyes narrowed.

"I hope that was all right," I said quickly. He looked upset.

"I was going to tell him to come see you after dinner. It's all right," he added, his eyes softening. "He's still one of the best chefs on the East Coast. I'd wager his Yorkshire pudding against any."

"He's everything my mother said he was. He must be over eighty, right?"

"Who knows? He can't really remember his birthday, or he lies about his age. So, how are you doing? Feeling a bit stronger?"

"Tired from the therapy, and frustrated. I want to get out and about the mansion and the estate."

"Well, maybe Mrs. Broadfield will approve a short trip down this corridor late tomorrow morning. The doctor will be here the day after."

"Has Luke called?" I asked hopefully.

"Not yet."

184

"I don't understand why not." My heart plunged. Had Drake's predictions already come true?

"Just giving you a chance to get settled in, I'm sure."

He brought a chair up beside the bed. When he sat down, he crossed his legs and meticulously ran his fingers down the sharp crease of his gray trouser leg.

"It's not like him. We're very close," I explained. "Did you know we were born on the very same day?"

"Really? How extraordinary!"

Luke's and my birthday was such a major touchstone in my life that it seemed incredible Tony would know nothing about the coincidence. How completely my father and mother had shut him out of their lives, I thought. I wondered if he knew that Luke and I were really half brother and half sister.

"Yes. And since then our relationship has been sort of what my mother's was like with her brother Tom, the one who died tragically in that circus accident."

"Oh yes." He gazed at me with the same intensity again, staring so hard I could almost feel his eyes drilling into my soul. "Your mother had a very hard time of it, but she was a very strong woman, as I am sure you will be. 'What doesn't destroy me, makes me stronger,' as my father used to tell me. He'd borrowed the expression from some German philosopher, I can't remember which one.

"Anthony, he'd say," Tony recalled, pulling himself up stiffly into what he must have remembered as his father's posture, "you've got to learn something from every defeat in life or life will defeat you." He relaxed and smiled. "Of course, I was barely five or six when he was giving me all this advice, but oddly enough, it stuck with me."

"The Tattertons are a fascinating family, Tony."

"Oh, I'm sure some of my relatives are quite

boring. I've never spoken to half my cousins. Dreary people. And Jillian's side of the family wasn't much better. Both of her sisters and her brother passed away some time ago. Actually, I only found out by reading the obituaries. Once Jillian died . . ." His eyes became somewhat glassy as he got lost in a memory.

"Tell me about your brother, Tony. Please," I added quickly, seeing his face begin to harden and his eyes say no.

"I should really let you rest."

"Just a little. Tell me just a little." Perhaps because he was no longer here, or perhaps because I had learned only a tidbit here and a tidbit there, Troy lingered in my mind as someone mysterious. "Please."

His eyes warmed and his smile trembled through his lips. Then he leaned over and surprised me by stroking my hair just the way Mommy often had.

"When you plead like that, you remind me so much of Leigh as a young girl, pleading with me to take her here or there, to show her this or that. She would burst into my office, interrupting anything I was doing, no matter how important, and ask me to take her on the sailboat or horseback riding. And no matter how busy I was, just like now, I would relent. Tatterton men spoil their women, but," he added, his eyes twinkling, "they enjoy doing it."

"About Troy?" Did he purposely drift off so much or was it something he couldn't help?

"Troy. Well, as I told you, he was much younger than I. When he was a little boy, he was sick so much of the time, I'm afraid I considered him a millstone around my neck. You see, our mother died when he was very small, and soon after that our father. Troy grew up thinking of me as his father and not just his older brother.

"He was a very bright young man, however, and graduated from college when he was only eighteen."

"Only eighteen!" I exclaimed in astonishment. "And then what did he do?"

"He worked in the business. He was a talented artisan and designed many of our most famous toys. So, there you are," he said, intending to end his tale of Troy.

"But why did he commit suicide, Tony?"

His soft blue eyes hardened as if they had instantly turned to ice.

"He didn't commit suicide; it was an accident, a tragic accident. Who said it was suicide? Did your mother tell you that?"

"No. She never mentioned him," I replied, swallowing hard. He looked so angry. His lips grew so tight and thin that a white line developed around them. This change in his face frightened me, and I think he saw that because he quickly softened his look. In fact, he looked very sad, very distraught.

"Troy was a melancholy man, very sensitive, deep, convinced that he wasn't going to live long. He was very fatalistic about life. No matter what I did, I couldn't change him. I don't like talking about him because . . . because I feel somewhat responsible, you see. I couldn't help him, no matter what I did."

"I'm sorry, Tony. I didn't mean to make you feel bad." I saw that he couldn't face up to the idea that his brother killed himself. It was cruel of me to try to make him do so.

"I know you wouldn't do anything to hurt me; you're too sweet, too pure." He broke out into a wide, warmer smile. "Let's not talk about sad things. Please. For a while, anyway, let's just concentrate on the beautiful, the pleasant, the hopeful, and the miraculous. Okay?"

"Okay," I said.

"Now, if you feel up to it, I've made a list of books you should read, and I'll have them brought up to your room. Also, I'm having a television set brought in here tomorrow. I'll go through the television guide and underline some of the better programs for you," he added.

How odd, I thought. How did he think I was brought up? I knew what books to read and what programs to watch. My mother often praised my taste in literature. Tony acted as if he thought I was some hillbilly who needed direction and instruction. But I didn't want to complain and hurt his feelings. He looked so happy to be doing all this.

"And I've got to make that list of things for Drake to bring from Winnerrow," I reminded him.

"Right. He'll be here in the afternoon. Let's see, is there anything else?"

I shook my head.

"All right, then. I have to do some work. I'll see you in the morning. Have a good night's rest, Heaven."

"Heaven?"

"Oh, I'm sorry. It's just you had me thinking about your mother then and I—"

"That's all right, Tony. I don't mind if once in a while you make a mistake and call me Heaven. I loved my mother very much." My tears came so fast, it was as though they had been just waiting for an opportunity to show themselves.

"There, now I've gone and made you sad again."

"No, it's not your fault."

"Poor Annie." He leaned over and kissed me softly on the cheek, his lips lingering. He inhaled deeply, as if he wanted to drink in the scent of my hair. Then he pulled himself back abruptly, realizing how long he was taking to kiss me good night. "Good night," he said, and left the room.

I rested my head on the pillow and thought about

some of the things I had learned. How right Rye was. This house had had more than its share of tragedy. Was this the way it was with all great families; rich, powerful families who had so much and yet suffered so much?

Was there a curse on the Tattertons and all who came into close contact with them? Perhaps Rye Whiskey wasn't so wrong about spirits wandering about. Perhaps that man I had seen in the distance visiting my parents' tomb was one of them.

Maybe Drake was right; maybe I should leave the sad things alone. I knew that I couldn't, though. There were things I just had to know. They itched, and just like a persistent itch, they had to be scratched.

At the moment one of the things that bothered me was Luke's silence. It just wasn't like him to keep away this long. It was so frustrating not being able to call him, not even to know which dorm he was in.

Millie came in to get my supper tray, and I thought of something.

"Millie, would you look in the desk drawer there to see if there is a pen, a sheet of stationery, and an envelope, please."

"Yes, Annie." She did so and found the stationery and a pen. "It's perfumed stationery," she said, bringing the sheet to her nose and inhaling. "Still smells very nice."

"I don't care. I just want to write a quick letter. Please come back in fifteen minutes to get it and have it mailed out for me."

"I will."

She left with the tray, and I used the bed table to write my letter to Luke.

Dear Luke,
    I know you have spoken to Tony since gradua-

189

tion, and I was happy to hear about the reception you received for your speech. You deserved it. I wish only that I could have been there, that my mother and our father could have been there.

Drake has visited me at Farthy and told me of your arrival at Harvard. The doctors want me to continue my quiet rest and recuperation, so I have no phone yet, otherwise I would try to call you rather than send this letter. I'll ask that it be sent special delivery, so you should get it quickly.

I can't wait to hear from you and to see you. I'm already planning just how to go about our explorations of Farthy.

Please call or come as soon as you can.

Love,
Annie

I addressed the letter to Luke Toby Casteel, Dormitories, Harvard College, and wrote "Special Delivery" on the bottom of the envelope. When Millie returned, I called her to the side of my bed to give her special instructions.

"Take this to Mr. Tatterton, please, and ask him if he would put the rest of the Harvard address on here for me and send this right out in the morning."

"Right away, Annie," she said.

I watched her go, and thought Luke would surely respond immediately when he received that. Confident that he would be with me in a day or so, I lowered my head to the pillow and closed my eyes. I opened them slightly when I heard Mrs. Broadfield come in. She took my blood pressure and checked my pulse, fixed my blanket and then put out the light.

With the sun down and the sky overcast again, darkness fell around me like a heavy curtain. It was my second night at Farthy, but unlike the first, I had something to listen for: Rye Whiskey's spirits. Maybe

I dreamt it because he had been so dramatic when he spoke, but sometime during the middle of the night, I thought I heard the soft tinkle of a piano playing a Chopin waltz.

Was it only my desperate need to remember, to envision my mother's soft smile as she gazed at me while she brushed my hair? Or was Rye Whiskey right? Was there a spirit that wandered through the house searching and searching?

Maybe he was searching for me. Maybe I had always been expected.

THIRTEEN

Mystery Man

Mrs. Broadfield yanked open the curtains so abruptly the morning light burst upon me like a bomb blast. She looked as though she had been up for hours, but I thought she always looked that way.

"You should want to get up early, Annie," she said without really looking at me. She talked as she moved about the room setting things up—unfolding my wheelchair, getting a robe from the closet, finding my slippers. "It takes you longer to do everything now, and you will need the extra time.

"After a while you will be able to get yourself up and out of that bed and into the wheelchair to do your bathroom business and have your breakfast, but you're going to have to build up to it, just like an athlete builds up to a task. Understand?" she asked, finally pausing to look at me.

I pulled myself up and sat back against my pillow and nodded.

"All right, then, let's get you out of bed, washed, and into a clean nightgown."

Still groggy from what had turned out to be a very deep night's sleep, I simply nodded. Quietly, almost as if the two of us were performing a mime show, she assisted me out of the bed and into the chair. She wheeled me into the bathroom and took off my nightgown. I washed my own face and she brought in the new nightgown. Then she brought me back into the room and left me by the window.

"I'll get your breakfast now," she said, starting out.

"Why isn't Millie bringing it up?" I was anxious to find out if she had given my letter to Tony to mail. Mrs. Broadfield paused at the doorway and turned back.

"Millie was discharged last night," she said, and left before I could respond.

Discharged? But why? I had liked her and even thought she would be good company. She was so pleasant and kind. What could she have done to get herself fired so soon? The moment Tony looked in on me, I demanded to know.

"Tony, Mrs. Broadfield just told me you fired Millie. Why?"

He shook his head and pressed his lower lip up and under his upper.

"Incompetent. Made a mess of things from the day she arrived. I was hoping she would improve, but she just seemed to get worse and worse. Jillian wouldn't have countenanced her more than a day. You should have seen the fine help we used to have here, their professionalism, their—"

"But Tony, she was so nice," I said.

"Oh, she was nice enough, but nice isn't enough. I found out that her references weren't accurate, anyway. She couldn't get a position for some time and worked as a waitress, not as a maid. But don't fret, one of my people is already looking for someone new."

Mrs. Broadfield arrived with my tray and set it down.

"Well, I'm off," Tony said. "I'll let you have breakfast."

"Tony, wait! I gave her a letter to give to you last night to mail to Luke."

He smiled quizzically.

"Letter? She gave me no letter."

"But Tony—"

"I called her in around seven-thirty and gave her two weeks' severance pay, but she mentioned no letter."

"I don't understand."

"Why not? It's just as I said: she was incompetent. She probably had it in her apron and forgot it. Honestly, I don't know what it is with young people today; they seem so distracted all the time. No wonder it's so hard to get decent help."

"It was a letter to Luke!" I cried.

"Your eggs are getting cold," Mrs. Broadfield pointed out.

"I'm sorry," Tony replied. "Write another letter today, and I'll see to it myself this time, okay? I'll return this afternoon to take you on a short tour of this floor. That is, if Mrs. Broadfield approves," he added, looking her way. She didn't reply.

He left before I could say another word on the subject of my letter, and when I looked at Mrs. Broadfield, she wore her mask of annoyance.

"We have to get to your morning therapy, Annie, and then you have to rest or I can't see you taking any tour. Now, please eat your breakfast."

"I'm not hungry."

"You've got to eat to gain strength. Your therapy is just like a workout would be for an athlete, and just as he or she wouldn't be able to do well without food energy, neither will you. Only," she said, raising her shoulders and straightening her posture to emphasize her point, "instead of simply losing a tennis match or a football game, you will remain an invalid."

I lifted my fork and began to eat. Thank God for Rye Whiskey, I thought as I chewed and swallowed. He had a way of making the simplest foods extra tasty.

My morning therapy session began just like the one I had the day before, but there was something different this time. I was positive I felt Mrs. Broadfield's fingers on my thighs. There was a stinging sensation, like pins being poked through my skin, and I screamed.

"What?" she demanded, looking up impatiently.

"I felt something . . . it stung."

"That's just your imagination," she said, and started again. Again I felt the sting.

"I do feel something . . . I do!" I protested. She paused and stood up.

"It's what we call hysterical pain. You're in a worse mental state than I thought. Even this is happening to you now."

"But the doctor said—"

"I know what the doctor said. Don't you think I've worked with more than one or two doctors in my time?"

"Yes, but—"

"Just try to relax as I work your legs, and when you think you've felt something, control yourself."

"But—"

She started again. The pain was there, but I simply grimaced and stifled my groans. The effort exhausted me, so I had to nap before lunch. Mrs. Broadfield brought me my lunch and told me Tony had phoned and would be back shortly to take me through a short tour of the floor. Funny, I thought, how something so simple had become something to look forward to, the way I would have looked forward to a special date or a party or dance. Right now, being wheeled out of this room was as exciting as a trip across the country. How my life had changed! How much I had taken for granted!

One of the grounds people arrived and set up a television set for me. It came with a remote control so I could work it from bed. He was a stocky man with a face that looked like old, dry leather. Hours and hours of working in the sun had cracked his skin and crisscrossed his forehead and even his chin with deep lines. He said his name was Parson.

"Have you been working here a long time, Parson?"

"Oh no, just a little more than a week."

"How do you like it?" At first I thought he didn't hear my question; then I realized he was thinking of how he would answer. "I suppose there's a lot for you to do," I added to encourage him to respond. He paused in his work to attach wires to the television set and looked at me.

"Yeah, there's a lot of work, but every time I start on something, Mr. Tatterton changes his mind and starts me on something else."

"Changes his mind?"

Parson shook his head. "I don't know. I was hired to repair the pool, so I started mixing the cement, but I only just got started when Mr. Tatterton come out and asked me what I was doin'. I told him and he looked at the pool and then at me as if I was crazy. Then he says his father told him never to fix somethin' 'less it was broke. 'Huh?' I says. 'The hedges have to be trimmed all along the pathways in the maze,' he tells me, and sets me off to do that. Meanwhile, all the cement I mixed gets hard and is wasted.

"But he pays good." Parson shrugged and went back to the television set.

"But what about the pool?"

"I ain't askin'. I do what I'm told. There, now this should work just fine." He turned on the set and fiddled with the channels and controls. "Want this on?"

"Not right now, thank you, Parson."

"No problem."

"Parson, what is it like in the maze?"

"Like?" He shrugged. "I don't know. Peaceful, I guess. When you get deep in it, that is. You can't hear much on either side, and then . . . I guess because it's so quiet, you imagine you hear things." He laughed to himself.

"What do you mean?"

"Couple a times I thought I heard someone walking about in one of the corridors nearby, so I shouted, but there was no one. Late yesterday, I was sure I heard footsteps, so I got up and found my way over a path and then another and another, and what do you think happened, ma'am?"

"What?"

"I got lost, that's what." He laughed hard. "Took me nearly a half an hour to get back to where I was working."

"What about the footsteps?"

"Never heard 'em after that. Well, I gotta get goin'."

"Thank you," I called.

After he left I stared out the window. The sky was as blue as Mommy's eyes when she was radiant and happy. My eyes must be gray now, I thought, as dull as a faded, old blue blouse. But the world outside sparkled with life and light; the grass was deep green and looked cool and fresh, the trees were in full bloom, and the small, puffy clouds looked clean and soft like freshly plumped pillows.

Robins and sparrows flitted from branch to branch, excited by the prospect of a warm, wonderful afternoon. I would gladly change places with one of them, I thought, and become a mere bird, but at least a creature who could move about at its own will and enjoy what life it had.

Mommy and Daddy were gone, Luke was seemingly beyond reach, and I was shut up in this old house with only therapy and hot baths and medicine and doctors to look forward to. And for how long, I did not know, nor would anyone be able to say.

I snapped out of my self-pity when I saw Tony's Rolls-Royce approaching. When the car came to a stop near the cemetery, I wheeled myself as close to the window as I could get. I saw him get out and go to my parents' monument. He knelt before it and lowered his head. He remained that way for a long time, and then, suddenly, the mysterious man appeared again, approaching from the wooded area. Tony didn't seem to hear or see him approaching.

The figure stood beside him and then placed his hand on Tony's shoulder. I watched and waited, my heart suddenly thumping, but Tony didn't look up. After a few more moments the man left him and went back to the darkness of the woods. Then Tony got up and went back to his car.

It was as if only I knew the man had been beside him. I couldn't wait for Tony's arrival. I wheeled myself to the front of my bedroom and faced the door.

It was nearly two hours before Tony came to my room. I was dying to ask him about the man at the cemetery. I wanted to call for him, but I thought my curiosity was too trivial to justify making him come right up. He'll be here any moment, I kept telling myself, only the clock ticked and ticked and he didn't come. What was it Roland used to tell me whenever I was impatient—"A watched pot never boils"?

I tried to fix my mind on other things and looked over the books Tony had had sent up to my room. They were all novels by authors I had never heard of. Nineteenth-century writers like William Dean Howells. Some were described as "period pieces." Others were "novels of manners." It was as if Tony wanted me to live in a bygone age.

At last he appeared. Immediately, almost frantic with curiosity by this time, I asked him about the man in the cemetery.

"What man?" Tony's smile remained frozen on his face, but the warmth that had been under it momentarily slipped away.

"I saw him step up beside you when you were at my parents' monument."

He stood there in my doorway blinking as though he had to refocus on the real world. Then he released a deep breath and came forward, his smile warming again.

"Oh, I keep forgetting you can see the family cemetery from your window." He shrugged. "He was only one of the grounds people. To tell you the truth, I was so involved with my sorrow at that moment, I can't remember which one he was or what he wanted."

"Grounds people? But Rye Whiskey said—"

"Anyway," Tony chirped, slapping his hands together, "it's time for your first tour of Farthy. Mrs. Broadfield says you have earned it. Are you ready?"

I gazed out the window again, looking in the direction of the cemetery and the woods. Clouds, as long and thin as witches' fingers, blocked the sun, laying shadows over my parents' monument.

"I should go to the cemetery, Tony."

"As soon as the doctor okays it. Hopefully tomorrow. In the meantime I'll show you something special, something nearby."

He came around my chair and grasped the handles. Why wasn't he telling me the truth about the man? Was he afraid it would disturb me? How could I get him to tell me the truth? Maybe Rye would know. I'd have to arrange it so Tony wouldn't know I had asked.

I felt his warm breath on my forehead, and he planted a soft kiss on my hair. The gentleness of that caress took me a bit by surprise. He must have seen it in my eyes.

"It's so good, so wonderful to have you here, and to be able to take you back through time with me."

"But I'm an invalid, Tony, a sick, crippled person." I don't think he heard me.

"To regain the beautiful memories, to seize happiness once again. Few men get such an opportunity once they have lost it."

He began pushing me out of the room.

"Where are we going?"

"The first thing I want you to see is the suite of rooms I had prepared for your parents when they came to Farthy for their wedding reception. They were so lovey-dovey, just as newlyweds should be."

I had often tried to imagine Daddy and Mommy as young people, newly discovering one another. I knew they had first met when Daddy moved to Winnerrow. Mommy told me they fell in love the moment their eyes met.

But she had never described her good memories at Farthy. I was sure there had to be some. So I listened keenly as Tony rattled on, describing how they laughed and clung to one another, how excited my father was to see Farthinggale, and how much Tony had enjoyed showing him around.

"When I first set eyes on your mother, I couldn't get over how much she resembled her own mother," he added as we turned out of the suite and headed down the long corridor. "Just as you do, my dear. Sometimes, when I close my eyes and hear you speak, I think I'm back in time and listening to Heaven, and when I open my eyes, there is a moment when I'm not sure. Have all the years since she left me been simply a nightmare? Can I return to the happier times? If you want something enough, pray for it enough, can't it happen?

"All of you run together in my mind sometimes . . . as if you are not three, but one woman, Leigh, Heaven, and now you, so similar in voice, in demeanor, in looks. You're like sisters, triplets, instead of mothers and daughters," he said softly, hopefully.

I didn't like the way he clumped us together. It was as if I weren't an individual, my own person with my own thoughts and feelings. Of course I wanted to be like Mommy, even look like her, but I wanted to be myself, to be Annie, not Leigh; Annie, Heaven's daughter, not a clone. Why was Tony so intent on ignoring that? Didn't he know how important it was for everyone to feel like her own person? How would he like it if people called him "just another Tatterton, like all the rest"? I made up my mind that later on I would bring up the topic. I wasn't the only one who could be taught new things.

I turned my attention back to the tour of the house. I hadn't noticed much about the upstairs portion of the house when they first brought me in and up to my room, but now I saw how heavily worn and frayed the hallway rug was. Many of the chandeliers that hung from the ceiling had blown bulbs, and there were cobwebs clinging to the fixtures. The drapes over the few windows were closed, so that the corridor was dark, especially the section into which Tony was wheeling me.

"This entire section of the house had been left untouched for years. The rooms were originally my great-grandparents', but in honor of your parents, I had them redecorated and refurbished. I knew what pleased your mother and had it all ready when she arrived. You should have seen the surprise on her face when I opened those double doors."

He laughed, but it was a strange, thin laugh, the laugh of someone who was laughing at things no one else could share, the laugh of someone locked in his own, very private world. When I leaned back and turned my head to look up at him, I saw that he was looking far off into his own memories.

Couldn't he see how worn and frayed the corridor was? Didn't he smell the musty odor?

"No one travels these hallways anymore. I don't permit anyone to go into these rooms," he added, as if he had read my mind and knew I wondered why he hadn't sent the maids in to clean and dust and polish.

When we crossed into the area he said had been reserved, we seemed to move into even darker quarters. Large cobwebs caked with dust draped between the corridor's ceiling and walls. I wondered if even he, himself, had been back. He stopped before two great double doors made of pickled hickory wood. Each had long, thin waterstains down its front. Some of the stains looked fresh.

Tony dug a ring of keys out of his jacket pocket. When he unlocked the doors and turned to me, his face took on a strange brightness, his eyes awash with excitement. He must have looked like this the day he surprised my parents with the suite, I thought. Were his recollections so vivid that he could cast himself back through time and behave as though it were all happening for the first time today?

"The suite of Mr. and Mrs. Logan Stonewall," he announced, as if they were alive and standing beside me.

He threw open the doors, which groaned on their hinges, moaning warnings. Unable to wait for him to come back around to push me, I took hold of the wheels myself and moved the chair forward, and to my utter astonishment, my complete surprise, before me was an impeccably maintained suite of rooms: clean and polished and dusted, sparkling behind these deceiving old doors in this apparently deserted section of the great house. It was as if we really had stepped over some invisible border of time and reentered the past.

Tony laughed again, this time at the expression on my face.

"Beautiful, isn't it?"

Everywhere I saw my mother's favorite color: wine red. The French Provencial furniture was upholstered in that color fabric, picking up the colors in the large Persian rug. The walls were done in a floral-patterned cloth paper, which picked up on the reds and whites in the upholstery and rug. Over the two large windows hung antique silk drapes, behind which were sheer curtains. But everything looked brand new!

Tony confirmed my thoughts.

"Everything has been replaced and restored to what it was. This is the way the sitting room looked the day your mother and father stepped into it for the first time."

"Brand new?" I asked, puzzled. He nodded. "But . . . why?"

"Why? Why . . ." He looked around as though the answer were obvious. "Why, maybe someday you and your husband will come to live here. Anyway," he said quickly, "it makes me feel better to bring things back to the way they were when we were all happier. And I can afford to do it, so why not? I told you I was going to bring Farthinggale Manor back to the way it was in its most glorious days."

I shook my head. Someone might say this was the way a very wealthy, elderly man indulged himself. But why bring back a painful memory? Mommy refused to have anything to do with him all these years, and all these years he held on to his memories of her and Daddy, refusing to permit time to erase them. Why?

"I'm afraid I still don't understand, Tony. Why was it so important to keep it . . . as it was?" I pursued. His face hardened.

"I told you. I have the means to do it."

"But you have the means to do many things, new things. Why dwell on the past?"

"The past is more important to me than the future," he replied, almost snapping at me. "When you're my age, you'll realize how precious good memories are."

"But with the rift between Mommy and you, I would have thought this painful for you. She was gone from your life; she was—"

"No!" He looked furious. "No," he repeated, more calmly. Then he smiled. "Don't you see, by doing all this"—he extended his arms—"I've kept Heaven as she was to me . . . always. I've cheated Fate." He laughed, a thin, hollow laugh. "That, my dear, is the true power of great wealth."

I simply stared up at him. He looked at me and shook the wild look from his face.

"But now come look at the bedroom. See what I have done here." Tony moved ahead and opened the bedroom doors. More tentative, a little reluctantly, I wheeled myself up to the entrance and gazed within.

Even the huge king-size bed looked lost in this enormous room, the floors of which were covered with a beige carpet so soft and thick, I had trouble wheeling over it. It was like wheeling through marshmallow. It was obvious that this, too, was a brand-new carpet.

All the linen was new. The bedspread matched the apricot canopy, and there were rust-colored throw pillows as well. I turned to the right and looked at the white marble vanity table, resting at the middle of a marble counter that ran nearly the length of the room. Under the counter were drawers framed in wood the shade of the marble counter. Above it was a wall of mirror, the edges of which were trimmed in gold.

Something on the vanity table caught my eye, so I wheeled myself closer. There was a hairbrush there with strands of hair still caught in it, silvery-blond strands. I took the brush into my hand and studied it.

"That was Heaven's," Tony whispered beside me. "When she had hair like Leigh's. She had done it herself, as if Leigh had come back through her, don't you see?" he asked, his eyes wide, wild and bright. My heart began to pound. "The hair is . . . it is Leigh's hair. It wasn't just Heaven's hair dyed . . . Leigh was coming back. I . . ."

He saw the look of amazement on my face and shrugged, taking the brush from my hands and gently running the tip of his finger over the strands of hair.

"She looked so beautiful with that hair; that color was so right for her."

"I liked her better with dark hair," I said, but he didn't seem to hear me. He stared at the brush a while longer and then put it back on the table as though it were part of some valuable museum collection. As I looked over the counter and dressing table, I spotted other personal artifacts—hairpins, bobby pins, combs, even crumpled tissues, tinted yellow by time. Some of the things I saw were very personal things.

"Why would my mother leave these things here?" I turned when he didn't answer immediately and saw he was staring down at me, his mouth curved into a half smile. "Tony?" He continued to stare. "Tony, what's wrong?" I turned my chair about so that I faced him completely. It snapped him out of his daze.

"Oh, I'm sorry. Seeing you seated there in your chair . . . I saw Heaven seated at her vanity table, dressed in her nightgown, brushing her hair just before she would go to sleep."

How odd, I thought. Why would he be in Mommy's room watching her prepare for bed? That was more like something a husband would do with a wife, not a step-grandfather with a step-granddaughter. He was talking about Mommy as if she were Jillian, the wife he had lost. It was spooky. Maybe he was losing his mind and I had the misfortune of being here just as all that was beginning.

"You watched her preparing for sleep?" I couldn't help but ask.

"Oh no, I would just come by and knock, and while I was standing in the doorway, she would answer my questions or converse while she continued to brush her hair," he said quickly; too quickly, I thought. He had the tone of a man guilty of something.

"Oh. But Tony, why did my mother leave so much after she left Farthy?" The counter was still covered with her powders, her bottles of perfume and cologne, cans of hair spray.

"She had doubles of everything so she didn't have to pack that much whenever she went to Winnerrow," he replied, also with that quickness that made me wonder if he were telling the truth.

"It looks more like she fled from here, Tony," I replied, so he would know I had not accepted his explanation. I wheeled closer to him. "Why did she leave so suddenly, Tony? Can't you tell me now?"

"But Annie, please—"

"No, Tony, I must tell you that I appreciate all you have done for me and for Drake, but I worry, knowing how things were between you and my mother. Sometimes I feel there are things you are hiding from me, bad things, things that would frighten me away."

"But you must not think—"

"I don't know how much longer I can remain here without knowing the truth, no matter how ugly or painful that truth might be," I insisted.

His sharp, penetrating gaze rested on me with deep consideration. His eyes blinked when he made his quick decision, and then he nodded.

"All right. Maybe you're right; maybe it is time. You seem a lot stronger today, and I do feel badly about the hard feelings between your mother and me. Also, I don't want there to be a wall of secrets between you and me, Annie. I'll do anything to prevent that."

"Then tell me all of it."

"I will." He pulled a vanity chair from the table and sat down in front of me. For what seemed to be an eternity, he sat with his elegant, well-manicured hands templed under his chin, saying nothing, and then he lowered his hands and looked around the room. "This is the right place to confess . . . in her rooms." He looked down and then up at me, his eyes as sad as a motherless puppy's, a puppy longing to be cuddled and loved. I took a deep breath and waited for him to begin.

CRIES OF HEAVEN

FOURTEEN

Tony's Confession

A nnie," he began, his eyes two marbles of blue ice, "I don't ask you to condone or to forgive me for what I did. All I ask is you try to understand why I did it and how badly I felt about what I had done afterward, especially after Heaven found out and hated me for it."

He paused, waiting for me to reply, but I said nothing. Perhaps he hoped for some encouragement before he started, but all I could think was I was about to hear something so terrible, I would immediately ask—no, demand—to be taken from Farthinggale Manor.

I realized Tony was right about one thing—this was a perfect place for me to be to hear the story. Some of my mother's clothing still hung in the closets, and from the way the garments looked, I didn't doubt Tony had had them cleaned and pressed—all part of his obsession to keep the past alive, to keep his memories happy memories. I was positive I smelled the familiar scent of jasmine, and, although I knew I had to be imagining it, I thought I even heard the tinkle of a Chopin melody being played on a music box.

"Annie, you can't imagine what it was like for me after my brother passed away. I had always hoped he would overcome his fatalism and depression and find someone to love. He would marry and have children. Little Tattertons would once again be laughing and running through these great halls. There would be heirs and the family line would continue on and on."

"Why didn't you and Jillian have children of your own, Tony?" The question seemed natural and obvious to ask, but I could see from the reaction in his eyes and the way his lips tightened that it brought him great mental anguish. He shook his head slowly.

"Jillian wasn't a young woman when I married her, and she was a very vain woman who believed that after she had Leigh, she had lost some of her beauty. She claimed she had to battle to win back her figure.

"In short, Jillian did not want to have another child. Of course, I pleaded. I begged her to consider the Tatterton heritage and my desire for an heir."

"What was her response?"

"Jillian was like a child, Annie. She couldn't conceive of her own death; she couldn't even face getting old. That problem just didn't exist for her.

"During the earlier times, she would drive me away by saying Troy should be the one to have heirs. After he died . . . well, it was too late for Jillian by then."

"But what does this have to do with why my mother refused to have anything more to do with you?"

"This is all by way of preface, Annie, so that you will understand my motives for what I did. By that time Troy was gone; Jillian was . . . well, Jillian was so lost in herself, she was well on her way to the world of insanity she was to inhabit until the day she died.

"When Heaven first came along, you can't imagine how my heart cheered when I set eyes on her, Jillian's granddaughter. Troy was already in deep depression by then, living alone, convinced he was to die soon. Jillian was wrapped up in herself, in her beauty regimen.

"Heaven was bright and alive and eager to learn and to become someone. As you know, I enrolled her in an expensive private school, lavished her with expensive clothing, made sure she had everything she could ever want. When she wanted to go back to Winnerrow and try to bring her Casteel family back together again, I financed her." He leaned toward me and lowered his voice as if he didn't want any of his ancestors to hear. "I would even have permitted her to bring the whole clan back here, as long as she would remain and become my heir.

"You can't imagine how it broke my heart when she decided to go back to Winnerrow to become a schoolteacher. I couldn't believe she had given all this up for a teaching position in a small town, where the people didn't even appreciate her, where they still looked down on her and called her a 'scumbag Casteel.' "

"It was her lifelong dream to be there for the children just the way her teacher had been there for her," I said. "I remember how proud she was of what she had been able to do as a teacher."

"Yes, yes, I know. And I was wrong to belittle that. I realized it too late.

"Anyway, after I learned she was going to marry your father, I panicked. This would surely keep her away from Farthinggale forever, I thought. She would marry and set up a modest little home in Winnerrow, and . . ." He swallowed. "And she would make up with her father Luke Casteel and be rooted solidly in that world again.

"Can you understand how I felt?" he pleaded. "It was all going to end with me . . . Tatterton Toys, Farthy, all of it. What had it been for? Nights I would walk through these dark halls feeling the angry eyes of my ancestors on me looking down from the portraits. I began to despise the echo of my own footsteps, to hate the face that gazed back at me from the mirrors, to wish I had never been born a Tatterton.

"And then, one day, I thought, why can't there be a way to bring Heaven and her world to Farthy?

"When I learned of Heaven's engagement to Logan, I contacted him and we discussed his future. I saw that he was a bright and perceptive man, ambitious and eager. I offered him an important position with my company and I requested that he and Heaven permit me to make them a wedding reception here."

"I know. I've seen the pictures. It must have been wonderful."

"There hasn't been a party like it since. It was that day, just before that party, that I presented Logan and Heaven with the idea of joining my company and building the factory in Winnerrow. Your mother consented, and then I showed them this suite." He stopped and stared at the memory of victory. "And she was overwhelmed. I had won her back. I had used all my resources, used all I was, and all I had, to do so."

"But Tony, why did she hate you?"

He looked down and turned his hands about in his lap as though inspecting them for scars.

"She hated me for the one additional thing I had done to secure my plan." He looked up.

"What was it, Tony?" My voice was soft and breathless.

"I was afraid of the relationship she would develop with Luke Casteel. I knew how much she loved him

211

and wanted him to love her. After all their years apart, she was going to forgive him for selling her and her brothers and sisters; she was inviting him and his new wife Stacie to her wedding in Winnerrow. And I knew that Luke would go. I was positive that once she had made up with him, she would have no need of me—not my money, not the factory, nothing would make any difference. I felt I had to stop it."

"What did you do?" I asked, with anticipation.

"I knew from my discussions with Heaven that Luke had always dreamt of owning his own circus. At the time he worked for a man named Windenbarron. I bought the circus from Windenbarron and offered it to Luke for one dollar."

"One dollar!"

"One dollar and one stipulation . . . he was not to go to the wedding and he was not to have any contact with Heaven. If he did, he would lose the circus."

I stared at him; even though I was unable to speak, I couldn't help the flood of thoughts that rushed through my mind. One dollar! Tony had been like the Devil buying a man's soul, tempting him with all that he wanted and dreamt of having, but making him surrender the things that should have been most precious to him. I felt sick, disgusted, as weak as I would had I just learned my own father traded me for a circus, and only for a dollar!

The silence between us seemed eternal. How I wished I could get up and run from that room, run from these terrible revelations. What kind of a man was Luke Casteel? Luke Jr. surely hadn't inherited these traits, I prayed. Not the Luke Jr. I knew and loved.

"Luke agreed?" I finally asked, knowing the answer full well.

"Yes, and lived up to his agreement until the day he

and his wife were killed. It was only then . . . Heaven found out what I had done. I tried to explain it to her, just as I am explaining it to you. I begged her to forgive me, but she was so enraged she left Farthinggale immediately and never returned."

He lowered his head.

"She left me a broken, guilt-ridden man, wandering alone in this enormous house to ponder my selfish acts. After what I thought was a sufficient time for the wounds to heal, I tried to get Heaven to talk to me, to answer my calls and letters, but she would have nothing more to do with me, and nothing I could do would make a difference.

"I retreated to the shadows, and I have been there ever since." He looked down and then he looked up quickly. "But what kept me alive was learning about you and about Heaven and Logan's life in Winnerrow. I had my people bring me reports about your progress, your growth into the beautiful young lady you've become, as well as reports about the success of the Willies Toy Factory and Heaven and Logan's wonderful life in Winnerrow, where they came to be respected and envied. I . . . I couldn't help wanting to see you, to learn about you.

"Many times I toyed with the idea of simply appearing there, risking being thrown out of the house. I even planned to go to Winnerrow in a disguise and watch you from a short distance," he said, but in such a way that I wondered if he had indeed not done such a thing.

"You can't imagine how much it has meant to me during all these dry and lonely years to live with you and Heaven even vicariously, through stories," he said, and I saw the tears in his eyes and realized how deeply sincere he was. He had been waiting all these years for either Mommy's or my appearance at

Farthinggale. How he had longed for it. I couldn't help but pity him for his desperate longing.

"Oh, Annie, don't think for one moment I wouldn't give all that I have to go back in time and change what I had done, but I couldn't. Please . . . please don't hate me for it. Give me the chance to correct my wrong by helping you, by making you whole and well and happy again."

He took my hands into his, his eyes pleading, begging, beseeching me to accept him. I looked away and took a deep breath. My heart was pounding. I thought I might swoon again if I didn't get back into bed.

"I want to go back to my room, Tony. I need to rest and to think."

He nodded sadly, resignedly.

"I don't blame you for hating me, too."

"I don't hate you, Tony. I believe you are sorry for what you did, but I also understand now why my mother was so sad when it came to talking about her father and why she was so upset whenever we talked about Farthinggale and mentioned you. He died before they had a chance to reconcile with each other after so many years of estrangement. Unlike you, Tony, my grandfather never had a chance to ask for forgiveness."

"I know, and that knowledge will accompany me into hell." He wiped a tear from his cheek.

Forgive me, Mommy, I thought, but at this moment I couldn't help but feel sorry for him, too.

"Let me get some rest, Tony. Drake's coming this afternoon to get the list of things I want from Winnerrow, isn't he?"

"Yes."

He got up and came around my chair. I heard him take a deep breath and sigh. Then he began wheeling me out of the suite, out of the past and back into the present.

Tony sent Mrs. Broadfield up immediately after he brought me back to my room, and she helped me get back into my bed.

"I'll be right back," she said after I was settled in, "and we'll begin your therapy."

"I don't want to do therapy today," I replied.

"Of course you do. You can't skip a day. We have to develop a rhythm that your body will learn and depend upon," she lectured. "Now rest a few moments and I'll return for our exercises. Your legs must be massaged, the blood made to circulate through your muscles. You don't want your legs to rot and fall off, do you?" she asked, smiling again, this time like some wicked witch. She pivoted about and walked out before I could respond, but that grotesque image remained with me.

I was like putty in her hands when she returned. All the while I waited for her, I thought about my mother discovering Tony had bribed her father to stay away from her wedding and stay away from her. I recalled how her eyes would become sad and distant whenever she talked about Luke. How sad it was that she had been denied the opportunity to have one more talk with him so they could forgive each other.

Yet the fault wasn't solely Tony's, I thought. Luke had agreed to the terms. He had been willing to reject my mother to own his precious circus. When my mother discovered the truth, that fact must have occurred to her and made it even more painful to bear. I could understand why she would be furious. Since Luke was no longer alive, she had to turn all that fury solely on Tony.

However, when I pictured Tony the way he had

described himself—alone in this great house, regretting what he had done and unable to gain my mother's forgiveness, I couldn't help but pity him as well. Perhaps if Mother had seen him now, she would have softened. She was too compassionate and caring a person to turn her back on so troubled a soul.

No, I decided, I wouldn't demand to be taken from Farthinggale Manor. I was providing Tony with a way to work out his repentance. To leave would be to punish him even more, perhaps even to drive him to the same sort of fatal choice his brother Troy had made.

All these thoughts ran through my mind as Mrs. Broadfield kneaded my thighs and massaged my calf muscles. The stinging sensations returned even more sharply, but I didn't tell her. I would wait for the doctor, I thought.

She lifted and turned me this way and that. When I looked down, I saw her strong hands squeeze and rub my flesh until the pale white skin turned crimson, and when her fingers reached my buttocks when she had me turned on my stomach, I felt them . . . not accompanied by pain, either. I just felt them. The pressure was even annoying.

"I feel your fingers and there is no pain, Mrs. Broadfield."

"Really?" She continued, pressing even harder.

"Yes, isn't that important?"

"Could be. I'll put it in my report." She rubbed on and on.

"Isn't it enough yet?" I finally asked.

She snapped back as if I had slapped her, and she immediately pulled my nightgown down so it covered me to the tops of my ankles. Her face was red from the effort she had expended and her eyes were as small as a rodent's. Just at that moment we heard voices in the hallway.

Drake and Tony were approaching. I hurriedly covered myself and lay back to greet them. Drake beamed when he set eyes on me. I returned his smile, but mine was short and thin. Luke would have noticed something was bothering me, I thought. Drake looked right through the clues.

"Hi, Annie." He kissed my cheek. Tony remained back by the foot of the bed. "I came for your list. Should I have brought a truck?" He laughed and turned to Tony, who was completely restored to his usual distinguished self.

"I don't want that much, Drake. I'm not going to be here forever," I said. I saw Tony wince, but Drake nodded emphatically.

"Of course. Good thinking, positive thinking."

"I'll be downstairs," Tony said suddenly. "You two visit awhile."

"I won't be long," Drake responded. "Have to get under way."

"This is the list, Drake." I pulled it out from under one of my pillows. I had kept it there because every once in a while something else would occur to me and I didn't want to have to bother Mrs. Broadfield with endless requests for a pen and the paper.

"Mrs. Avery will help you find everything," I told him. He nodded, still studying the list.

"Both charm bracelets? That's all the jewelry you want?"

"I have no use for anything else, Drake. Where am I going?"

"Oh, you might get to the point where you dress up for something. I don't know. Whatever. If I see anything else I think you might want, I'll grab it," he said, folding the paper and shoving it into the inside pocket of his suit jacket. Finally he saw the troubled look in my eyes. "Something's wrong, isn't it, Annie?"

"Oh, Drake." I started to cry.

"Annie, oh Annie." He sat on the bed and embraced me as best he could. "What is it? Did you find out about Luke?"

"Luke?" I swallowed my lump quickly. "What about Luke? Drake . . . tell me." My heart began to pound.

"Well, I was going to tell you, just so you wouldn't worry about why he hasn't called or contacted you yet, but—"

"What!" A knot of terror formed in the pit of my stomach.

"Easy, Annie. Nothing bad has happened to him. After I saw you yesterday, I thought I would go to Harvard and find out what he's been doing. It took me a while to locate him. I found him in the dormitory lounge . . . head to head with a coed." He shifted his eyes away so I couldn't read the rest of his thoughts.

"What do you mean, Drake? I don't understand." I couldn't fight the faintness that took hold of me. It was hard to speak, but I didn't want Drake to see just how hard it was.

"He found a girlfriend, rather quickly, I know, and he was quite involved with her."

"A girlfriend? But didn't he ask about me?" I asked hopefully. It was almost a prayer.

"Oh yes, and then he promised to call Tony today. I asked him about it as we came up the stairway on the way up to you, but . . . Luke hasn't called yet. I suppose he will later. For a moment there," he added, looking toward the doorway, "I thought Tony might have sent someone to Harvard to locate Luke for you, and whoever went brought back the same information, which Tony then brought to you."

"No." I turned away. My heart felt like a chunk of cement. Luke, distracted by a new girl, forgot about me? I had lost Daddy and Mommy and now . . . now I was about to lose Luke, too? This couldn't be happening; it couldn't be true. If Luke was distracted, it was only because I was sick and away from him, I thought. Once I recuperated, regained my strength and returned, he would lose interest in this coed. No one he met could share with him the things I did. As soon as I walked into a room and he set eyes on me again, our lives would be as they were. I prayed they would. I was determined they would.

"I know what you're thinking, Annie, but you don't understand how exciting it can be for someone like Luke, who has been stuck in a one-horse town all his life, to suddenly come to a place like Harvard and meet different, far more sophisticated people. He got swept off his feet, just like anyone could. You can't blame him for it," Drake added.

I nodded. "I know. I just . . . just miss him." I couldn't tell Drake the way I really felt, and I didn't want him to see it in my eyes.

"Well, if he doesn't call or appear soon, I'll drag him here myself."

"Oh no, Drake. He must come here on his own, because he wants to, not because he has to. I won't be thought of as some obligation!" That would be the most terrible thing of all, I thought. I'd feel like some burden to him, instead of someone he loved and wanted to be with.

"Of course. I'm sorry," Drake said. He looked away.

"Poor Drake. I didn't mean to shout at you just now. I'm sorry." It seemed Drake was all that was left of my family now . . . Drake and Tony Tatterton.

"Oh, that's all right. But tell me now, Annie. Why did you look so troubled before, if it wasn't because of Luke?"

"Help me sit up, Drake," I said. He got my seat pillow and fixed it so I could be comfortable. Then he sat beside me on the bed again. "Drake, I forced Tony to tell me why he and Mommy had their falling out."

Drake nodded, his eyes unmoving, but a slight smile on his lips.

"I knew you would . . . somehow. Can't hold you down, Annie. You're too much like your mother. Well? What terrible skeleton did you drag out of the closets of Farthy?"

I told him all of it, trying to be fair to Tony by explaining his reasons as he had explained them to me. As I spoke, Drake's face grew gray. Shadows, deep and dark, settled around his eyes. When I was finished, he turned away and remained silent for a long moment.

"Of course," he began, "I don't remember my father all that well. I was only five when he and my mother were killed, but I remember I had this beautiful fire engine, a Tatterton Toy that Heaven had given me, and whenever my father saw me playing with it, he always looked sad.

" 'You know who gave you that?' he would ask.

" 'Heaven,' I'd say. Of course, I forgot who she was or what she looked like, but the name stuck with me because he would always reply, 'Yes, Heaven, your sister.' And then he'd smile. There's no question that Tony did a terrible thing, but you are right to point out that my father bears half of the blame for sacrificing his daughter so he could own a circus.

"I think the time has come to forgive Tony, Annie. I loved Heaven almost as much as you did, and I don't think she would hate us for it."

Hot tears burned down my cheeks. All I could do was nod. He wiped away my tears and hugged me.

"Now then," he said, standing up quickly. "I'd

better get on my way. I want to return by late tomorrow. I'll bring everything directly to you."

"Please give Mrs. Avery and Roland and Gerald my regards, and Drake . . . promise me you won't have any bad words with Aunt Fanny. Promise me, Drake."

"All right, I promise. I'll just pretend she's not there, if she is."

"And tell her it's all right for her to come to visit me at Farthy."

"Sure." He smirked.

"And you're not to say anything nasty to Luke."

"Aye aye, commander." He performed a mock salute.

"Please be careful, Drake."

"I will, Annie. We haven't got much more than each other anymore."

"Oh, Drake."

He hugged me and then he left. Although the doors were open, it was as if he had shut them and I was locked away. The silence that followed his footsteps was heavy and oppressive. Chilled, I pulled my blanket up around my neck and stared up at the high ceiling.

Luke with another girl, I thought, and even though I tried to keep the images away, I couldn't. I saw him with some beautiful college girl, sitting in the cafeteria, talking. I saw him walking hand in hand over the campus, and I saw him kiss her, hold her the way I had always dreamt he would hold me.

Everything was slipping away, everything I loved. All the world I had known and loved seemed consumed in fires of pain and tragedy. Everything, even my precious magnolia trees, were charred. I was like a small bird, exhausted from a long flight, searching desperately for a safe place on which to alight. But all the branches were burned.

I closed my eyes and dreamed of Daddy, his arms outstretched, waiting to receive me. But when he embraced me, his arms were made of air.

"No! No!" I screamed. I woke up screaming. Tony was at my side.

"I had a terrible nightmare," I said, expecting he would want me to describe it.

"It's understandable, Annie." He sat on my bed and leaned over to stroke my hair. "After all you've been through. But when you awaken, you will be here, safe with me.

"Anyway," he said, continuing to stroke my hair lovingly, "soon the world will be brighter and happier for you. I have great plans for you. There are so many wonderful things I want to do, changes I want to make. This place is going to come back to life and you will be the center of it. Like a princess," he added, and I couldn't help but think about Luke and our fantasies. The memory brought a smile to my face, a smile Tony assumed he had put there.

"See, you're feeling better already. Now," he added, leaning over to the night table to get one of my sedatives. "Mrs. Broadfield says you have to take one of these." He handed me the pill and poured me some water. I took it obediently. After he placed the glass back on the table, he leaned over to kiss me on the forehead. "Just close your eyes again and try to remain calm until sleep takes over." He stood up. "Sleep is a kind of medicine all to itself, you know," he explained, obviously speaking from personal experience. "Talk to you later. You all right now?"

"Yes, Tony."

"Good."

I watched him leave. Maybe it was a short time later, or maybe it was in the middle of the night—I couldn't tell anymore because the sedative had confused me and jumbled up my awareness of time and place—but whenever it was, I thought I opened my eyes and saw a dark, thin, shadowy figure in my doorway.

He approached my bed, but for some reason I wasn't afraid. I felt him stroke my hair gently and then lean over and kiss my forehead. It made me feel safe, and I closed my eyes. I didn't open them again until I was awoken by the sound of Dr. Malisoff's voice.

place—but wherever it was, I thought I opened my
eyes and saw a dark, thin, shadowy figure in my
doorway.

He approached my bed, but the force reason I
wasn't afraid, I felt bumsickeny just eerily and then
it ran over and kiss my forehead. It made me feel safe,
and I closed my eyes I didn't open them again until I
was awoken by the sound of Dr. Malisof's voice

FIFTEEN

Like Mommy

Good morning, Annie. How do you feel?" Dr.
Malisoff sat on the bed and Tony hovered a few
steps behind him, looking like an expectant father,
nervously rocking on his feet, his hands clasped
behind his back. Mrs. Broadfield rushed in from
the sitting room to bring the doctor a blood-pressure gauge. I struggled to sit up. I had slept deeply,
but I didn't feel refreshed, and my lower back was
stiff.

"A little tired," I confessed. Truly I felt exhausted,
wrung out, but I also wanted the doctor to allow a
phone and visitors.

"Uh-huh." He wrapped the blood-pressure cuff
around my arm. "Has she been eating well, Mrs.
Broadfield?" he asked without taking his doctor's eyes
off me. They looked like little microscopes turned on
my face.

"Not as well as I would like her to eat, no, Doctor,"
Mrs. Broadfield replied like one schoolgirl tattling on
another.

The doctor put on a face of reprimand and shook his head.

"I haven't had that much of an appetite yet," I offered in my defense.

"I know, but you've got to force yourself to keep up your strength for the fight . . . Are you relaxing, Annie? You don't look relaxed." I glanced quickly at Tony, who shifted his eyes away guiltily.

"I'm doing my best."

"She hasn't been having visitors and such, has she?" Dr. Malisoff asked Mrs. Broadfield.

"I've tried to keep her quiet," she said without really answering. Why did she take everything so personally? I wondered. Was she afraid she would be fired as quickly as Millie was?

"I see." The doctor examined my legs, tested my reflexes and feelings, looked into my eyes with a small lighted instrument, and then shook his head. "I want to see more progress the next time I visit, Annie. I want you to concentrate more on your recuperation."

"But I am!" I protested. "What else can I do? I have no telephone. All I can do is watch television and read. Only Tony and Drake and Rye Whiskey, the cook, have come to see me." I couldn't keep the shrill sound out of my voice.

"I realize you're in a highly emotional state," the doctor said softly, obviously trying to keep me calm, "but the reason you were brought to this house was so you would have a serene environment, conducive to improvement."

"But what have I done that I shouldn't?"

"It's mental attitude that we need now, Annie. The therapy, the medicine, none of it will work unless you want it to work. Think health; think about walking again, concentrate only on that and give Mrs. Broadfield one hundred percent cooperation, okay?"

I nodded, and he smiled, his reddish-brown mustache curling up at the corners. I didn't tell him about the pain and feeling I had experienced in my legs because there was something very important to be done before I could even think about myself.

"Doctor . . . " I lifted my upper body by pressing my hands down on the bed. "I want to be taken to my parents' grave site. I'm strong enough to go, and I can't concentrate on getting better until I do." I didn't mean to sound stubborn and petulant, but I believed it was true.

He eyed me thoughtfully a moment and then looked at Tony. I saw the way their eyes read each other's and saw the slight nod in the doctor's head.

"All right," he said. "One more day of rest and then Mr. Tatterton will make the arrangements, but I want you to be brought right back here and given a sedative," he said after glancing at Tony again.

"Thank you, Doctor."

"And try to eat. You'd be surprised at how much energy a healing body needs."

"I'll try."

"By this time next week, Annie, I want to see those toes moving and I want you giggling when I tickle your feet, understand?" He waved his long right forefinger at me like a parent chastising a child.

"Yes." I smiled and lay back. He nodded and then started out, Mrs. Broadfield and Tony flanking him as he left. I heard the three of them whispering about me outside the bedroom door. They were in conference so long, I thought they might be thinking of returning me to the hospital. Tony was the first to return. He came directly to the side of the bed and took my hand into his. Then he shook his head.

"I'm angry at myself," he explained. "I feel rather responsible for your poor checkup. I shouldn't have permitted you to talk me into telling you all those sad

226

and tragic stories in your parents' old suite yesterday."

"Don't blame yourself," I insisted, but now I was
afraid the three of them had changed their minds
about the service when they discussed me out in the
sitting room. "Tony, you will take me out to the
monument tomorrow?"

"The doctor has approved. Certainly. I'll make the
arrangements for the service right now."

"Will you invite Drake and Luke? I want them to be
there with me."

"I'll do my best. Drake should return from Winnerrow by dinner time tonight," he said, smiling.

"But Tony, you shouldn't have any trouble finding
Luke," I cried. How could he even suggest that? And
yet, what if Luke was busy with . . . with some new
friend? He would miss the call and the message or get
it far too late. I wanted him; I needed him. "Drake
found him without much trouble."

"I don't suppose there will be any problem," he
said. "I'll put my secretary right on it."

"Thank you, Tony. Thank you." He continued to
hold my hand even as I fell back against the pillow. I
closed my eyes. Even this little excitement made me
feel weak and tired. I guess they were right about
protecting me, I thought. I was thinking I would rest a
little more, but Mrs. Broadfield wasn't about to let me
sleep.

"Time I got her up and ready for breakfast," she
told Tony. He nodded and released my hand.

"I'll return early this afternoon. Have a good morning."

My morning was the same, except I forced myself to
eat every morsel of the breakfast. I didn't want Mrs.
Broadfield or anyone coming up with a reason why I
shouldn't go to my parents' monument the next day.
What if Tony contacted Luke and he was coming

and then it was all canceled? His trip here would be canceled. They would certainly forbid him to see me if I couldn't even attend my own parents' memorial service. The thought of losing an opportunity to finally set eyes on Luke put me in something of a panic. I had to calm myself down before Mrs. Broadfield took note.

After breakfast Mrs. Broadfield performed my morning therapy. I felt her fingers all over my legs, but I didn't say a word for fear that somehow she would use it against me to cancel the memorial service. Whatever pain I now had, I quickly swallowed, making my face as indifferent as possible, and then I spent the remainder of the morning lying in bed watching television. Sometime after lunch, a meal I again finished completely, Tony returned.

"Did you speak to Luke?" I asked him as he came through the doorway.

"No, but I left a message at his dorm. I'm sure he'll call later today, or perhaps he'll just show up at the service. An old friend of mine, Reverend Carter, will lead us in prayer. I've scheduled it for two o'clock."

"But Tony, you should have kept trying until you reached him! Maybe you can try again. Please, Tony!" I begged.

"I'll have someone try again, if I don't. Not to worry, my dear. Please, don't get upset over it."

"I won't," I promised.

Tony seemed surprisingly chipper, most likely because I hadn't decided to leave after his confession.

"You're probably worried about what to wear tomorrow, aren't you?" he asked, completely misreading my look of concern.

"What to wear?"

"You couldn't have a better selection from which to choose," he continued, and went to the closet. He slid open the door to reveal garment after garment.

"There is so much here; Heaven never got an opportunity to wear a lot of it. And the wonderful thing is, everything will fit you!

"Of course," he said, plucking a dress from the rack, "some things were her favorites. I remember she wore this to a funeral once." He held up a black cotton dress with long sleeves and a long skirt and then stroked it lovingly, as if he still saw her in it.

Then he turned to me, that faraway look in his eyes as he recalled a memory.

"Everyone stared at her, mesmerized, when she entered the church and walked down the aisle. Even Reverend Carter looked dazzled. I could see him wondering. Had an angel entered his church to attend the service?" Tony laughed and shook his head. "Just like her mother, black brought out her fairness." He smiled at me. "I'm sure it will do the same for you."

"I'm not worried about how I will look, Tony. I'm not doing this for other people."

"Oh, I know, but it does honor to your mother's and your grandmother's memories for you to wear something like this." He put the dress down on my bed and stepped back, his gaze hypnotically fixed on it. Then he considered me. "You know, Annie, if you dyed your hair silvery blond, you would be the image of your grandmother." He looked about quickly and settled on one of the pictures in the silver frames that was on the long vanity table. "Wait, I'll show you what I mean." He got the picture and brought it to me. "See?"

It was a photograph of my grandmother Leigh when she was about my age, and I did have to admit that the resemblance was strong, and would be even stronger had I the light hair, too.

"Won't you consider doing it? Just for a diversion, perhaps, to amuse yourself while you're so confined.

I'll get the best hairdresser around to come up here for you. What do you say?"

"Dye my hair silvery blond? Tony, you're not serious?"

"Absolutely. I couldn't be more serious. Imagine everyone's surprise when they come to visit you."

"I don't know." I nearly laughed, but then I looked at my grandmother's photograph. There was something fascinating about her face . . . her eyes, her nose, her chin were so much like Mother's and mine. Was this why Mommy had dyed her hair? I wondered.

"There are many pictures of your mother when she had light hair, too," Tony said, as if he knew what I was thinking. He brought me another photo in a silver frame. This one was of Mommy when she and Daddy had first arrived after their marriage. They were down at the private beach. I held the two photographs side by side.

"Interesting, isn't it?"

"Yes."

"When would you want the hairdresser?"

"Tony, I didn't say I wanted to have it done. I don't know."

"You see how beautiful your grandmother was in light hair, and your mother as well. What do you think?" His eyes burned with excitement.

"I don't know. Maybe."

"All this therapy and medicine and solitude can be very boring." He looked about. "Oh, let me do it," he pleaded. "Let me hire the hairdresser. You should feel pretty, like a beautiful young woman again and not like an invalid."

I smiled at his exuberance. It would be nice to feel pretty again. I looked down at the photographs. I imagined that having my mother's hair color when she was about my age would make me feel close to her again. She looked so happy there on the beach.

230

And my grandmother Leigh . . . there was something wildly beautiful about her. The light hair suited her complexion, but would it suit mine?

"Well? What do you think?" he pursued, hovering over me like someone on pins and needles.

"Oh, Tony, I really don't know. I've never thought about dying my hair another color. It could turn out horrible."

"If it doesn't suit you, I'll bring the hairdresser right back to restore your hair to what it is now."

"Maybe after the service, Tony. I don't want to dote on myself right now. Thank you." I handed the photographs back. He was disappointed but nodded with understanding.

"What about this dress?"

"Drake should be bringing me something appropriate. I included a black dress of my own on the list."

"Won't you at least try it on?"

I saw how much it meant to him and began to wonder myself how I might look in it.

"I will."

"I'll send Mrs. Broadfield right in to help you. After you have it on, call me," he added, rushing out before I could say another word. I hadn't meant I would try it on right this moment, but he looked as excited as a child on Christmas morning. I couldn't see denying him. A moment later Mrs. Broadfield appeared. She didn't look happy about it.

"It's not necessary to do this right now, Mrs. Broadfield, if you're busy with something."

"If I were, I wouldn't be here." She took the dress off the bed and looked at it a moment. Then she shrugged to herself and came around to help me sit up and slip off my nightgown. After she and I got the dress on me, she helped me into the wheelchair so I could see myself in the largest wall mirror.

Because I was seated, it was difficult to appreciate

231

what I looked like in this dress, but I did think it made me look older. I hadn't taken much care with my hair since the accident, and now that I put on something other than a nightgown, it made me more aware of how terrible I looked. My hair looked dirty, stringy, greasy. The black dress brought out the paleness in my face and the fatigue in my eyes. I nearly burst into tears seeing myself.

Mrs. Broadfield stood to the side, her arms folded, watching me like some bored saleswoman in a clothing store. Helping me on with a dress was obviously not part of what she considered to be her nursing duties. I didn't hear Tony reenter. He stood just inside the doorway, staring. After a moment I felt his eyes on me and turned toward him. His face was enraptured, twisted in that strange smile I had been seeing more and more of lately. Mrs. Broadfield said nothing. She simply left the room.

"Oh, Tony, I look so terrible. I didn't realize. My hair is disgusting. No one said anything, not Drake, not you, none of the servants."

"You're beautiful. You have a beauty that can't fade with time or illness. It's immortal. I knew that dress was right for you; I knew it. You'll wear it, won't you?"

"I don't know, Tony. I won't like myself in anything, so maybe it won't matter."

"Of course it will matter. I'm sure that your mother will be smiling down and thinking how beautiful her daughter has become."

"But my hair," I repeated, holding up a straggly clump and then dropping it with disgust.

"I told you . . . let me send for a hairdresser right away. Look how horrible you feel because of your appearance. I'm not a physician, but I know if we don't feel good about ourselves, we don't improve. In fact, we can get sicker and sicker."

How persistent he was, and yet what he was saying

made sense. Was I wrong to think of my own looks at a time like this? Then Tony said something that convinced me.

"Luke hasn't seen you since you were in the hospital. I'm sure he expects you to look somewhat improved."

Luke, I thought, surrounded now by pretty coeds, healthy, happy girls who can walk and laugh and do fun things with him. Maybe he had delayed coming to visit me because he couldn't stand to see me the way I was. I would surprise him; I would look stronger, better, and I would be better.

"All right, Tony, send for the hairdresser, but I'm not saying I'll permit him to dye my hair yet. I think I just want it washed and styled right now."

"Whatever you think." He stepped back. "How well that dress fits you. You will wear it, won't you? You should," he said, nodding, his eyes intense, "being it was your mother's."

Once again he said magic words.

"I'll wear it, Tony."

"Good. Well now, I've got things to do. That hairdresser will be here if I have to fetch him myself." He stepped closer to me. "Thank you, Annie, for giving me a chance after the things I told you. You're truly a sweet and wonderful person." He kissed me softly on the cheek. "Be back soon," he said and rushed out.

For a long moment I simply sat there staring at myself in the wall mirror. Back in Winnerrow Mommy had a few different black dresses, one very similar to this one, I thought. Maybe that was why, as I gazed into the mirror now, I felt as though her spirit merged with mine. I saw her eyes in my eyes, the smile around her lips become the smile around mine. It was like focusing a camera, bringing the lines of the image together so the picture would be clear and sharp.

My heart pounded with the pain that resulted from the realization she would never again come up beside me while I prepared to go out to a party or to school and put her hand on my shoulder, stroke my hair, give me some advice, or kiss my cheek. Wearing this dress and making myself look more like her only brought home that painful truth more vividly.

I wheeled myself away from the mirror and over to the vanity table to get a tissue. While I wiped my eyes, I looked at some of the other photographs. There was one particular picture that captured my attention. In it Mommy was posing in a silly way by the stables. Maybe Daddy took the picture; but what caught my eye was Tony in the background. He was gazing at her the same way he had just been gazing at me, with that same twisted smile.

I studied it for a few moments and then looked at some of the other photographs. One of my grandmother Leigh stood out. I brought it beside the one of my mother at the stables and realized what it was that made the two pictures so significant. My grandmother was at the stables, too, and she was taking a similarly silly poise and wearing the same riding outfit. When the two pictures were held side by side, my mother and her mother looked more like sisters.

Maybe that was what made Tony smile so. It should have made me smile, too, but it didn't.

"Did you want to take off that dress or wear it all day?" Mrs. Broadfield snapped. I turned about and saw her standing just in the doorway, her hands on her hips. If she was annoyed by Tony's orders, she shouldn't be taking it out on me, I thought. Aggressively, no longer willing to play humble and helpless, I held my head high and proud, flaring back.

"Of course not," I said. "I'll take it off and set it aside for tomorrow "

Her eyes widened with surprise at my tone of voice and she dropped her hands from her hips.

"Fine. It's time for your hydrotherapy, anyway." She went into the bathroom to prepare the hot water. This time when she lowered me into it, it seemed absolutely scalding. I cried out in pain, but she didn't seem concerned. I could see my skin turning crimson under the water. It took my breath away, and I tried to lift my body up and out, but she pressed my shoulders down, keeping me submerged in the scorching water.

"You've got to build up a tolerance to the heat," she explained after I complained again, and then she started up the jets that made the water bubble and toss about. Hot drops bounced up to my breasts and neck, some hitting my cheeks and stinging. She left me there, clinging to the sides while she went out to prepare some creams for my massage.

I looked down at my traitorous legs and feet and did as the doctor told me to do, think recuperation . . . recuperation . . . recuperation. I had to get myself out of this situation as fast as I could. I stared at my toes and thought about moving them. Suddenly, I saw my big toe twitch.

"Mrs. Broadfield!" She didn't come back, thinking I only wanted her to get me out of the hot tub. *"Mrs. Broadfield, come look!"* I demanded. After I called again, she returned.

"I told you. You have to—"

"No, no, it's my big toe. The big toe on my right foot moved." She looked down into the water.

"Move it again."

I tried, but nothing happened.

"It did move. I saw it. I did!"

She shook her head.

"What you saw was the wave in the water. It made it appear as if the toe moved."

"No, it did. I swear."

"Uh-huh. Very nice." She spun on her heel and went back to preparing my massage.

Feeling dejected, exhausted from the heat and the effort, I lay my head back and closed my eyes and waited for her to make up her mind I had had enough. Finally she returned and helped me out of the tub. My skin was as red as it would be had I fallen asleep on Virginia Beach in July and I was as limp as over-cooked spaghetti. She spread me out facedown on the towels on my bed. I closed my eyes as she worked her strong hands down my body, beginning behind my neck and moving in slow circles over my back and buttocks.

I opened them abruptly when I heard Tony's voice. My God, I thought, I'm stark naked on this bed! I tried to turn around to pull some of the toweling over me, but I couldn't move fast enough or enough of my body to do so, and Mrs. Broadfield did little to help.

"Sorry," he said. I just caught sight of him out of the corner of my right eye. "Just stopped by to tell you the hairdresser will be here at three. Sorry," he said again and left.

"Mrs. Broadfield, why didn't you close my door when you started this?" I demanded.

"That's the least of my concerns."

"Well, it's not the least of mine. I do have some modesty left, you know. Tony is a man."

"I know what Mr. Tatterton is, thank you. I'm sorry," she relented after a moment. "I'll be sure to close the door next time."

"Please do."

Even after she rubbed on the soothing cream and I put on my fresh nightgown, my skin tingled from the heat of that hot bath. It wasn't until I awoke from a brief nap that I felt any relief. Mrs. Broadfield brought me some juice and a little while later returned to tell me the hairdresser had arrived. She helped me back into my wheelchair just as Tony brought up the beautician, a tall, thin man with curly blond hair and eyebrows so light, they were practically invisible. He had very fair skin, but bright pink lips. I thought any woman would sell her soul for his soft green eyes.

Tony introduced him just as Renee and immediately added he was French. However, I had the impression he was of French background but born here in America. His accent seemed somewhat artificial, deliberate, something he might be affecting for his customers. After work he probably spoke like any other native American.

"Ah, mademoiselle." He stepped back and tilted his head first to the right and then to the left, nodding as he considered what had to be done with my hair. He reached forward and touched the strands, bouncing them in his palm and shaking his head. "Rich and *très* thick," he said, "but alas, neglected, *n'est-ce pas?*" He turned to Tony for confirmation. Tony nodded. "Do not worry, mademoiselle, Renece will work his magic. In a short time I shall make miracles, eh?"

"I just want it washed and set," I said.

"Pardonnez-moi?" He looked at Tony. "But I thought . . . the color."

"Renee's an expert, Annie. Get his opinion first."

"You would brighten your face *beaucoup,* mademoiselle," he said, stepping back to consider me again. "Not difficult." He nodded, convincing himself. "Just put yourself in my hands, mademoiselle." He held out his palms as if I could see something unusual in his soft, thin fingers.

I glanced at myself in the wall mirror on the right. Maybe I should turn myself over to this so-called beauty expert, I thought.

"Very well, do what you think has to be done."

"Très bien." He rubbed his hands together. Tony

was beaming. I closed my eyes and lay back in the chair as he wheeled me to the sink and his beauty expert began his work.

Looking into the mirror, I saw Mommy's face instead of my own. The change in hair color had done something magical, turned me into the face that gazed up at me from all those old pictures. It was as if the beautician had been some kind of conjurer, sending me back in time, doing what I knew Tony wished would happen—roll back years to the days when he was the happiest here at Farthy. There was a new look in my face. Renee had turned my hair silvery blond and had trimmed and set it so I looked just like Mommy had in that picture of her at the stables. In fact, Tony had given him the picture to work from before he left us.

I wondered how Luke would react. He had seen the old pictures of Mommy and he always told me he thought she was a dazzling beauty. Would he feel the same way when he first set eyes on me? Afterward, when we were alone, would he take my hand into his and whisper his true feelings. In my warm and loving imagination, I heard his words.

"Annie, when I first set eyes on you with your hair your mother's color, I knew that no matter how forbidden it was, I had to tell you my true feelings, let you know about my deep love for you. Oh, Annie, I can't deny it. I can't!"

I played those wished-for words over and over in my mind and then opened my eyes and gazed at myself in the mirror again. If changing my hair color could only do all that . . .

"Annie, is that you?" Drake came into the bedroom carrying two suitcases filled with my clothing and shoes. He put them down at the foot of the bed and stared at me, a half smile on his face. I put down the hand mirror and studied his face closely for his truthful reaction.

"Do I look silly?"

"No, not silly, just . . . different. You remind me of someone."

"My mother. When she first fetched you," I prompted.

"Yes." His eyes lit up with the realization. "Yes," he repeated excitedly. "Exactly. Hey, you look very good." As if he finally convinced himself I was still me, he jerked forward and came over to kiss me hello. "Really. I like it."

"I don't know. I feel . . . so different. Yet I can't believe Mommy was all that comfortable in this hair color. It's as if I'm pretending to be someone I'm not. Surely, she must have felt the same way."

Drake shrugged.

"She changed back soon after she and Logan returned to Winnerrow and bought Hasbrouck House. Maybe you're right."

"Tony has me convinced I'll feel more like a young woman again. I was getting depressed about myself. But enough about me. Tell me about your trip to Winnerrow. Who did you meet? What did the servants say? How was the house and Aunt Fanny?"

"Whoa . . . slow down." He laughed. I bit down on my lip to keep myself quiet and sat back impatiently. "Now, let's see . . . Winnerrow." He pretended he was trying to remember.

"Oh, don't tease me, Drake. You don't know how it's been being shut up like this."

His impish smile evaporated instantly and his eyes became soft and caring.

"Poor Annie. I am being cruel. I promise I will get myself back here more often to take you out and about. But, about Winnerrow. As soon as I entered the house the servants nearly ran me over rushing to find out about you. Mrs. Avery was in tears immediately, of course; even Roland looked on the verge of bawling. Gerald was the only one who kept a stiff upper lip, but that's because . . ."

"His upper lip is stiff," I recited along with him. It was a joke we made behind Gerald's back.

"Oh, I miss them . . . all of them."

"I saw some of your school friends at the drugstore. They were all anxious to hear about you, and all send their love."

"And Aunt Fanny? What about Aunt Fanny?"

"Well . . . " He shook his head. "She was weird. I found her sitting out back reading. Yes, reading. And she was dressed kind of conservatively in this long-sleeve, white cotton blouse and long, flowing skirt. She had her hair brushed down and pinned back. I actually didn't recognize her and asked Gerald who was that sitting on the gazebo."

"The gazebo!"

"Yes."

"Reading? What?"

"Get this—Emily Post. When I approached, she looked up and said, 'Oh, Drake, how wonderful ta see ya.' She held out her hand and wouldn't let go of mine until I kissed her on the cheek hello. I think it was the first time I ever kissed her. I actually had a half-intelligent conversation with her. Your mother and father's death has had a dramatic effect on her. She is determined to better herself, she says, to—how did she put it?—to be a credit to Heaven's memory. Can you imagine? I have to give her some points, though. The house was immaculate, and from what the servants told me, she hasn't been fooling around with any of her young boyfriends. In fact, she's been living like a nun."

"Did she ask about me?"

"Of course."

"Is she coming to see me?"

"She wanted to, but I was afraid to say anything until Tony tells me the doctor says it's all right."

"But she's my aunt. I can't be kept like a prisoner in solitary confinement!" I pleaded, perhaps too emphatically. Poor Drake looked absolutely devastated by my outburst. "I'm sorry, Drake. It's not your fault. You did only what you thought was right, I'm sure."

"It can't be much longer, anyway, Annie. You look so much better already. Now that I'm a little more used to it, I think that hairdo does suit you. When I first came through that door, I thought Tony had put some movie starlet in this room while I was gone."

"Oh, Drake."

"No, you look a lot better than you did when I left. I mean it."

"I hope you're right, Drake." I looked down and then remembered tomorrow's service. "Did you speak to Tony before you came up here? Did he tell you about the service?"

"Yes, of course. I'll be right at your side."

"And Luke? Has Luke called yet?" I asked hopefully.

"You mean, he still hasn't called?" Drake shook his head. "He told Fanny he was going to call. The selfish little—"

"Oh, Drake, I can't believe that of Luke. Please call him yourself. Tony called the dorm and left word and instructions about the service tomorrow, but be sure Luke gets the message, will you? Maybe someone at the dorm is pulling a prank on him and hiding his messages," I added desperately. What if what Drake was suggesting were true? People change when they leave home, I thought. Maybe all the pressures and hardships of his life in Winnerrow had finally taken hold and he had decided to throw off all connections with that life, including me!

Oh God no, I prayed. The world couldn't be that cruel.

"Sure. I'll try to get ahold of him later. Well," he said, getting up and going to the suitcases, "here are the things you wanted."

"I don't have a maid anymore to help put them away. Tony fired Millie."

"I heard. No problem. I'll hang everything up for you." He fixed a section in the closet for my things. "Look at all this. These things were all Heaven's?"

"And my grandmother Leigh's. Tony hasn't thrown out a thing."

"Some of it still looks new."

"I know. I'm wearing one of my mother's dresses tomorrow—that black one Florence Farthinggale left hanging in the corner."

"Florence Farthinggale?" He laughed. "That's very funny. I gather you two are not forming what we could call a warm patient-nurse relationship?"

"As long as I behave like a lump of clay, we get along fine," I said sarcastically, and he laughed again. "Anyway, that's the dress Tony chose."

"Don't say?" He gazed at it quickly and then finished hanging up my garments. After he was finished, he returned to the bed and sat beside me. He dug into his pockets and took out the two charm bracelets. "Here they are."

"Oh, thank you, Drake."

"Now how are you going to wear them, both on one wrist?"

"I'll alternate days. The days Luke comes, I'll wear his," I said and ran the tip of my fingers over it softly, lovingly, as though I were running them over Luke's cheek.

"Always the little diplomat." Drake smiled. "It's all right; I don't mind," he said, and then he fixed his eyes on me more intensely than ever. "When I look at you

242

now, I do see Heaven. I see the warm, loving face that was pressed against mine when I was small and afraid, lonely and lost. I see the love in those blue eyes that gave me comfort just when I needed comfort most in my life. I never told you how good I feel when I'm with you, Annie."

"I'll always be your friend, Drake. After all, I'm your niece." Reminding him of our relationship made him wince.

"I know." He leaned forward and kissed me on the cheek, lingering there the way Tony often did. Then he straightened up.

"Well, I better be going. I have to catch up on some business at the office so that I can take most of tomorrow off, too, now." He stood up.

"Drake, don't forget about Luke," I cried.

"Right. Oh, there was one more thing I brought," he said, reaching into his suit jacket's inside pocket. "I thought . . . somehow, for some reason, one day you might want to get dressed up here. Who knows, maybe Tony will throw a party for you after you've recuperated enough to leave . . . whatever. Anyway, I brought this along." He took out the black jewelry case that contained the diamond necklace and matching earrings that had belonged to my great-grandmother Jillian.

"Oh, Drake, you shouldn't have brought that. It's too valuable."

"So? This place isn't exactly open for grabs, and I knew how much this meant to you. Surely, just having it nearby will bring you some comfort, won't it?" he asked hopefully. I smiled and nodded.

"Yes, I suppose so. I'm sorry. Thank you for thinking of me, Drake. I know I sound selfish and unappreciative sometimes."

"Oh no, Annie, you are the most selfless person I know. When I think of you, I think of . . . of someone pure and beautiful, like brilliant candlelight." Once again he looked at me intensely. I could say nothing. His words brought a lump into my throat and sent my heart thumping. "Well," he finally said, putting the black jewelry case beside me on the bed, "I'd better get on the road. See you right after lunch tomorrow."

"Good night, Drake. And thank you for all you've done."

"Are you kidding, Annie. There's nothing I wouldn't do for you. Just remember that."

He blew me a kiss and then left, quickly assuming the gait of a busy executive with one crisis after another on his mind. I sat back on the pillow chair and looked down at the black jewelry case. Then I opened it and took out the diamond necklace. How it sparkled! The memory of my birthday rose up within me and I recalled Mommy's face when she held this necklace out to me. Her eyes were full of such pride and love.

I clutched the necklace to my bosom and thought I felt its warmth, a warmth handed down from her grandmother to her and from her to me. I didn't realize I was crying until the tears fell from my cheeks and splattered like warm drops of summer rain on my chest and bosom. Swallowing hard, I put the necklace back into the case and closed it. Drake was right. It was comforting to have it nearby.

I wiped my face with the back of my hand and looked at the two charm bracelets on the bed. Then I took the smaller but more precious one to me, and put it on my wrist. The sight of it made me smile.

What had Drake said . . . Aunt Fanny was on the gazebo? Luke's and my magical place? Those days seemed so long ago now, the fantasy days. Maybe if I were back there, if they put me on the gazebo, I would lean on Luke's arm and I would suddenly walk again. How the doctor would laugh if I suggested it, but I knew that sometimes a little make-believe can truly be magical. Luke believed it, and when two people believe so strongly in something, it could come true.

Luke. How I needed his comfort, his smile, his optimistic reassurance. More than that, I longed for his lips against my cheek and I remembered each and every time we had kissed, even when we were only small children.

As I thought of him, I embraced myself, imagining him beside me, his fingers twirling my hair, his eyes so close to mine as we gazed longingly at each other, tormented by our desire and our forbidden love at the same time.

Thinking about him this way warmed my body and made it feel alive again. Surely if visions of Luke loving me had such a wonderful effect, it couldn't be all bad, I reasoned. With Luke at my side, I would overcome this tragedy. Fate had placed those ever-present tall mountains in my path, but I would do as Luke always advised—I would go deliberately for the tall ones.

"Because, Annie," I heard him whisper, "the view is always better. Go for the tall ones." But now Luke seemed the tallest mountain of all.

I looked up at my empty room. I could hear people talking and moving about downstairs. Drake was saying good-bye to someone. A door was closed. A gust of wind whistled through some shutters. And then it was quiet again.

Oh, Luke, I thought, what could possibly be your reason for not moving heaven and earth to see me?

SIXTEEN

Crippled!

I have a wonderful surprise for you," Tony announced. By the way he was standing in the doorway, just off to the side, I thought the surprise would surely be Luke's appearance; but it was something else. "You're going to have to come out of your room to see it. It's time to start for the cemetery, anyway."

I turned to Mrs. Broadfield, who was folding the towels she used during my massages. Her face was blank and as unmoving as a mask. Yet, still I sensed that she knew what the surprise was.

"Come out?" He nodded, and I started to wheel myself toward the door. I was wearing my mother's black dress and the charm bracelet Luke had given me. Renee, the hairdresser, returned late in the morning to comb out my hair. Mrs. Broadfield had not reduced my morning therapy because of the service to be held at my parents' monument, but either she was right about my growing tolerance and strength or I was just determined not to be tired because of it.

Tony stepped back, indicating I should keep going. I glanced at Mrs. Broadfield to see if she would be coming along, too, but she continued to do her work in my room, appearing to be uninterested in anything else. Tony helped me turn to the left and start down the long corridor. Soon I saw Parson, the grounds worker who had set up my television set, and another man, also dressed in coveralls, standing at the top of the stairway. I looked back quizzically at Tony, who was now pushing me along with a Cheshire-cat grin on his face.

And then I saw his surprise.

He had had an elevator chair installed so I could wheel myself to the top of the stairway, slide into the chair, press a button, and have myself lowered slowly down the stairway to the first floor.

"Now it will be very easy to take you up and down the stairway," Tony said. "And very soon, I'm sure, you will be moving yourself from floor to floor. I'll have a second wheelchair waiting for you below."

I stared at the mechanical device for a moment. I knew Tony was disappointed in my reaction, but I couldn't help it. Things like this only confirmed my invalid state and suggested that my recuperation was a long way off.

"But Tony," I said, "soon I'll be walking myself! You've gone through this tremendous expense for nothing!"

"Oh, is that what you're worried about? No problem. This is a rental agreement. We use it as long as we need it and no longer. As for the second chair—I assure you, that's no major expense for me. Now," he added, slapping his hands together, "it's time for our first test flight, eh? That is, with you as the passenger.

247

I've already tried it and it held my weight well, so there won't be any problem with its holding you."

I looked back to see if Mrs. Broadfield was going to assist in this, but she still hadn't come out of my room. From my seated position in the wheelchair, the stairway looked awfully steep and long.

"Just roll yourself alongside the mechanical chair," Tony instructed, "lift the left arm of your chair and slide yourself into it. The idea is for you to be able to do this yourself."

Fear began to swell in me like a great dark symphony booming through my blood. I felt a cold sweat break out over the back of my neck. And I could feel myself falling, tumbling down that great marble staircase, crumpled at the bottom.

Parson and the man beside him watched me with concerned, sympathetic eyes. I smiled as bravely as I could and began to wheel myself alongside the mechanical chair. I struggled to loosen the arm of my chair. It seemed to stick a bit, but no one offered any help. I imagined this was all part of the test—to see if I could do it all myself. Finally I detached the arm and began pulling myself into the mechanical chair.

"Once you get securely in, miss," the man beside Parson said, "you strap yourself with this safety belt, same way you would in a car."

Just the mention of "car" sent my heart fluttering. My chest tightened so, I thought I wouldn't be able to breathe. Where was Mrs. Broadfield? Why wasn't this important enough for her to be right beside me?

"Oh, Tony, I don't know if I can do this," I wailed.

"Sure you can. Don't you want to be able to go downstairs and wheel yourself into my office? Eventually you'll be able to come to the dining room table for dinner and sit where your mother used to sit. And surely you want to go about the grounds."

"When you're ready, miss," the man said, "just press that red button on the right arm and it will begin to lower you. The black one will raise you."

"Go ahead," Tony cheered.

With trepidation I pressed the red button and closed my eyes. "Go for the tall ones," Luke was telling me in my mind. "You can do it, Annie. You and I are special. We overcome the hardest and greatest obstacles Fate puts before us. We do. Try harder. Make it work."

How I wished he were the one giving me the encouragement and holding my hand. With Luke beside me, I wouldn't be afraid and I would try anything if it could mean a return to full health and strength.

The chair jerked forward and began a slow descent down the stairway. The three men followed along closely as I traveled downward, the mechanism humming smoothly.

"Isn't it great?" Tony asked. I opened my eyes and nodded. The chair shook a little, but other than that, it did feel very secure, and it was nice moving down these stairs without being a burden to anyone.

"How does it know when to stop?"

"Oh, it's been adjusted for that, miss," the man said, and sure enough, as it reached the foot of the stairway, it came to a soft halt. Parson had brought my wheelchair along and set it up beside the mechanical chair.

Just at that moment Drake popped out of the entry from where he had been watching the entire event, cheering and clapping.

"Hooray for Spaceship Annie!"

"Drake Ormand Casteel, how could you hide down here instead of being with me when I needed support?" I complained.

"That was just it," Drake explained. "Tony wanted you to do this without anyone assisting, so you would become independent that much faster."

"You're two conspirators," I chastised playfully. Secretly I was very proud of myself and happy Tony had made me do most of it myself. I looked behind Drake. "But where is Luke? Is he hiding, too?"

Drake's face soured. He looked at Tony, whose face was as solid as granite, his eyes a cold, dark blue, like two sapphire stones.

"He went on some orientation picnic arranged for all the freshmen."

"Picnic?" I looked back at Tony. "But I thought you left a message about the service, Tony."

"I did, with whoever answered the phone at the dorm. At least, my secretary did. She said there was a lot of noise in the background and it sounded as if they were having a big party."

"Didn't you call him yesterday, Drake? After you left here?" I felt my heart sinking, an empty, hollow, cold cavern replacing its warm pocket. How could Luke not be here? How could he not have responded?

"I called early this morning, but they had all already left."

"I don't understand."

"Just a mix-up, probably," Drake said. "He never got the original message and left not knowing about the service."

"How could there be a mix-up? This isn't some freshman dance. Whoever took the message must know how serious it is. He wouldn't be so casual as to forget or misplace it. No one can be that callous."

"He's not here," Drake said softly.

"But he would want to be here!" I cried. "It's . . . it's a service for his father, too!" I felt myself losing control. All of it was closing in on me at once—the accident, my parent's deaths, my injuries, Luke's absence. I had the greatest urge to scream and scream and scream. "I don't understand!" I repeated in a shrill voice.

Both Tony and Drake looked stricken. The expressions on their faces forced me to get hold of myself. I didn't want to become hysterical and cause a postponement of the service. That was too important to me. Parson and the technician responsible for the mechanical chair quickly excused themselves and went out.

I pulled myself up stiffly in the wheelchair. "I'm all right." I wiped my eyes with the back of my hand. "I'm all right," I lied. "Luke will just have to make a special trip."

"Drake, why don't you wheel Annie to the front and wait there while I fetch Miles to bring the limo around." Tony patted my hand and rushed off. Drake wheeled me to the front door. Just as he opened it, Mrs. Broadfield came up beside me, appearing as quietly and as quickly as a ghost.

Drake moved me out and into the pool of sunshine that spilled over the portico and steps. The day did not reflect my sad and tragic mood. It was as though even Nature refused to pay attention to my feelings. Instead of dull-gray clouds, starch-white cotton-candy puffs scattered across the aqua sky. The breeze that brushed across my face and made some of my strands of hair dance over my forehead was gentle and warm. Everywhere I looked, birds fluttered and sang. The strong, fresh scent of newly mowed lawns perfumed the air.

All around me was life and happiness, not death and sadness. The sight of such a bright and wonderful day made me feel even more alone. No one could understand why, no one but Luke. If only he were here now, holding my hand. We would look at each other and he would nod knowingly. His fingers would entwine with mine, and I wouldn't feel as if the world were conspiring to make my pain even sharper. I'd feel able to fight back. The need and the desire to become a part of it all again would be overwhelming. More than anything, I would want to walk.

Desperately trying for that mood and strength, even without Luke's presence, I pressed my hands against the arms of the chair and willed my feet to press down on the footrests, but the muscles in my legs weren't cooperative. There was only a slight sensation traveling up through my calves and thighs. Disappointed, I sat back.

Miles drove the limo as close to the steps as he could. Tony and he stepped out just as the Reverend Carter appeared. He was a tall, lean man with sharp features and graying blond hair. Tony shook hands with him and spoke with him a moment and then the two of them, Miles following, came up the steps.

"This is my great-granddaughter Annie."

"God bless you, my dear," the reverend said after taking my hand into his. "You're a strong and courageous child."

"Thank you."

Tony signaled to Miles and Drake to carry me, chair and all, down the stairs to the car. I saw Rye Whiskey, dressed in an old black suit, standing by. His thin gray hair was slicked back and brushed flat over his head. His smile and his comforting and loving, soft eyes warmed my chilled heart.

We went through the great gate and turned right to the Tatterton family cemetery. As we drew closer and closer to the large marble monument, my heart ached, feeling like a small fist tightening and tightening until it could tighten no more. A small cry escaped from my throat. Drake took my hand and squeezed it tightly. When the car stopped, Drake opened the door and reached back in to guide me to the awaiting chair. He and Miles lifted me and placed me softly into it. Then Drake turned the chair and I came face-to-face with the tall stone that read:

STONEWALL

| LOGAN ROBERT | HEAVEN LEIGH |
| BELOVED HUSBAND | BELOVED WIFE |

I stared in awe, in disbelief, the reality of my parents' death never as vivid as it was at this moment, but my body did not soften and wither like some fragile flower. I was as hard and as cold as the very stone I faced.

The reverend walked up to the monument, he opened his Bible and began the service. When his words reached my ears, my brain channeled them off to some archive in the library of my memory. I saw his mouth moving and I saw him turn the pages, but I didn't hear a word.

Instead I heard the words I knew Mommy would utter if she could be beside me now.

"Annie," she would say, "you must get strong again. You can get strong again. You must not become some weak and dependent creature withering away in the shadows of Farthy. If you do, you will pale and die like some flower kept out of the sunlight."

"My Annie," Daddy would continue, "I wish we could be there beside you to give you the love and support we have given you all your life, but we can't. I know that you have it in you to stand on your own two feet once more, and once more carry on the work your mother and I began in Winnerrow."

"We're with you, Annie; we're part of you."

"Mommy," I whispered.

But I couldn't deny the reality of what all this meant. It meant the end of the world as I had known it. I had come here to say good-bye to Mommy and

Daddy, but I was saying good-bye to myself as a little girl, too. Good-bye to the tinkle of music boxes and the laughter of a family together, close, eager to see each other every day. Good-bye to hugs and kisses and words of encouragement. Good-bye to Mommy's comforting embrace whenever the world seemed hard or cruel or cold. Good-bye to Daddy's laughter ringing through the house and chasing away the worries that sometimes come into our lives.

Good-bye to Sunday dinners when we were all talking around the table. Good-bye to all the holidays, the gathering around the Christmas tree to open presents, the delicious Christmas dinner. Good-bye to Thanksgiving dinners with relatives and guests contentedly stuffed. Good-bye to singing around the piano and playing charades. Good-bye to looking for Easter eggs and munching on chocolate rabbits. Good-bye to Sunday walks and vacations on the seashore.

Good-bye to staying up New Year's Eve just to kiss Mommy and Daddy and wish each other a happy new year. Good-bye to all the reasons for all the holidays. Good-bye to all the presents and pretty gift wraps and ribbons and surprises. Good-bye to everything that made life delightful and exciting and warm.

I shook my head in disbelief. I was like a ghost of myself, empty, bereft of feeling, floating aimlessly. Even the reverend's final words seemed hollow, lost in the wind.

"Please join me in the psalm. "The Lord is my shepherd; I shall not want . . ."

I buried my face in my hands and felt Drake's hand on my shoulder. As soon as the psalm was completed and the reverend had closed his Bible, Drake turned my chair toward the limo. I fell back and closed my eyes.

"Let's get her upstairs and into her bed quickly,"

254

Tony muttered. The chair was pushed faster. Miles opened the door and he and Drake lifted me into the backseat. I was as limp as a wet tissue. I felt Tony slip in on the other side of me, and I felt the limo turned about.

I opened my eyes, intending to look back at the monument one more time as we left the cemetery, but something in the nearby forest caught my eye instead. It was a quick movement, a shadowy figure coming to life, stepping through the sunlight as it rushed back into the protective darkness of the woods.

It was he, the tall, lean figure I had seen from my window!

Like a guest everyone had forgotten to invite, he had appeared in the background to share the ceremony of mourning, quietly, unnoticed, and then he had disappeared so quickly. Indeed, no one but I seemed to have noticed.

I took a sedative and rested. I awoke late in the afternoon. The great house was so quiet, and the sedative had put me into so deep a sleep, it took me a few moments to realize where I was and what had happened. At first it all seemed like some dream, some long nightmare; but the sight of my waiting wheelchair and the medicines, towels, and lotions lined up on the long vanity table were evidence that this was, unfortunately, no dream.

When I gazed out the windows, I saw that the cottony clouds had flattened into a dark gray blanket, making the afternoon dismal and dark, a fitting aftermath to the morning's ceremony. I pulled myself up into a sitting position and poured myself some water from the blue plastic jug on the night table beside the bed. The stillness around me was puzzling Where was Mrs. Broadfield? Tony? Had Drake gone back to Boston?

I rang the little bell hung from one of the posts and waited. No one came. I rang again, this time a little longer and louder. Still no one came. Had they expected me to sleep longer? Most likely, I thought, but now I was hungry. I had slept through lunch and it was closing in on dinnertime.

"Mrs. Broadfield?" I called.

Strange that she wasn't just outside my door. She always came running on a moment's notice. The continued silence frustrated me. Confined to a bed, always dependent upon others . . . it made me angry. Driven by this frustration and anger, I leaned over and stretched out until I could grasp the arm of my wheelchair. I would show them all. Why was the chair left so far from my bed, anyway? I wondered. It was almost as if Mrs. Broadfield wanted me trapped.

I pulled the chair close to the bed and unfastened the right arm. I had never done this before, but I felt sure I could do it now. Sliding myself to the side of the bed, I had to pull my legs along like two long leaden weights.

I locked the chair wheels so it wouldn't move, took a deep breath, and pulled myself off the bed.

First I was on my left side on the chair; then I turned my body so I was on my back. After that I pushed down on the arms of the chair, lifting my uncooperative lower body slowly until I was in the sitting position. Buoyed by this success, I realized I could lift my legs by grabbing under my thighs. My feet dangled stupidly below. I swung them onto the footrests and finally sat back, exhausted. But I had done it! I was not as helpless as they would all make me think! I closed my eyes and waited for my thumping heart to calm.

Once again I listened for sounds from without, but heard only a deep silence. I inhaled deeply and released the wheels so I could move myself forward to the doorway. Once there, I paused and looked about the sitting room. There was no sign of Mrs. Broadfield, no open magazines or books, nothing.

I wheeled myself through the sitting room to the corridor. The air was cooler out there; the lights were still dim and the shadows long and dark. I started to turn left to head for the stairway, where I expected I would stop and call down, but I was tempted to explore on my own, to employ my newly realized mobility for adventure. Where was Tony's bedroom? I wondered. Wasn't it down this way? Maybe he was in it. Perhaps the morning's activities had tired him out as well. Using that as an excuse to quiet my frightened heart, I wheeled myself on. Every once in a while I paused to listen, but heard nothing.

I continued on until I reached an opened double doorway. I could see that the design of this suite was much like the one I was in. A single lamp was illuminated, but when I pushed ahead and entered, I saw no one.

"Tony? Anyone here?"

Whose suite was this? I wondered. It didn't look like it would be Tony's. There was something feminine about it. Then I caught the strong scent of jasmine. My curiosity was like a magnet, much stronger than caution, pulling me along, drawing me forward to the second entryway, the doorway of the bedroom.

I wheeled myself into it and stopped. On the chair before the white marble vanity table was draped an ivory float trimmed with peach lace. The table itself was crowded with powders and skin creams, lotions and bottle after bottle of perfume. What drew my attention quickly, however, was the blank oval of bare wall. The glass in the mirror that had once hung over this vanity table had been removed. Why?

When I turned to the left, I saw that the same was

true for the wall mirror and the mirror that had been on the closets. Both were only frames. Steeped in curiosity now, I wheeled farther in and saw the red satin shoes beside the king-size canopy bed, a bed almost the duplicate of mine. Over the bed had been laid a cherry-red crinoline party dress with puffed sleeves and a frilly collar. The quilt was turned down on the bed the way it would be had someone just gotten out of it.

Farther to the right I saw that the dresser drawers had been left open. It looked as though someone had come into the room and rifled through those drawers, searching madly for some precious hidden valuable. Undergarments and stockings dangled over the sides.

On top of the dressers and tables jewelry boxes lay open. I saw glittering necklaces, bejeweled earrings, diamond and emerald bracelets scattered everywhere randomly. I felt I was definitely intruding on someone and began to back myself out. Suddenly I had backed myself into a wall. But when I turned around, I looked into the hot eyes of Mrs. Broadfield.

Her face was blazing red. She looked as if she had been running at full speed. Her usually perfectly brushed-back hair had rebellious strands popping up like ruptured piano wires. Because I was seated so low and looking up at her, her nostrils seemed larger, bull-like. Her bosom heaved with her heavy breathing, rising and falling against her tight, aseptically white nurse's uniform. The buttons looked as if they would pop and she would explode right before my eyes. I actually began to wheel myself away, but she reached down and seized the arm of the chair, preventing any more movement.

"What do you think you are doing?" she demanded in a harsh, threatening voice.

"Doing?"

"I came into your room and discovered you weren't

in your bed, the wheelchair gone." She took a deep breath and pressed her hand against her lower throat. "I called for you, knew you weren't downstairs, and then began searching the corridor, never expecting you had gone down this way. I couldn't imagine . . . I thought for sure something had happened to you in one of the rooms."

"I'm fine."

"You don't belong down here," she said, getting behind my chair and wheeling me out quickly. "Mr. Tatterton specifically asked that no one come down here. He's going to blame it on me, think that I brought you," she said, coming out of the suite and looking carefully up and down the corridor before preceding any farther.

I thought she was being ridiculous, sneaking me back to my suite like this. "Tony surely wouldn't mind my coming down this side of the corridor," I exclaimed, but she didn't slow down. It was obvious she was petrified she would lose her position.

"If he finds out, I'll tell him it was all my doing, Mrs. Broadfield."

"That won't matter. I'm responsible for you. I step out just for a few moments to take a short walk and get some fresh air and look what happens. You wake up, drag yourself into the wheelchair, and go wandering off through the house."

"But why would Tony mind?"

"Maybe there are sections of this house that are no longer safe . . . weak floorboards or something. How would I know? He told me what he wanted. It was simple enough. Who would have thought you would do this? Oh dear." She turned into my suite quickly.

"I'll ask him when he comes in."

"Don't you dare mention it. Maybe he won't find out and it won't matter."

She stopped at my bed and stepped back, looking at me and shaking her head.

"There's someone else living here, isn't there? Who is it?"

"Someone else?"

"Beside Tony and the servants, you and me. That room's being used."

"There's no one I've seen. See, you're starting to imagine things, make up stories. Mr. Tatterton will be furious. Don't say any more about this," she warned, her eyes narrow and cold. "If I get in trouble because of this . . . both of us will suffer," she added, the tone of threat quite clear. "I'm not losing this job because a crippled girl violates rules."

Crippled girl! No one had ever put the label on me. Rage filled me until it spilled out my eyes in tears. The way she had pronounced "crippled," she had made it sound less than human.

I was not a crippled girl!

"I called for you," I asserted. "I was hungry, but there was no one here. Even after I got into the wheelchair, I called."

"I just took a short break. I was coming right back. If only you would be a little more patient."

"Patient!" I exclaimed. This time when my eyes met hers, I didn't shift them away. My rebellion rose like a giant fire. I glued my gaze to hers, the rage pouring out. She stepped back as if slapped. Her face became horribly animated, her mouth working as if to find the right shape to phrase words, her eyes growing large and then small. The veins in her temple became prominent in the light, the outline of their weblike shape pressing up against her thin, scaly skin. She took a few steps toward me.

"Yes, patient," she repeated disdainfully. "You've been brought up spoiled. I've had patients like you before—rich young girls who have been pampered

260

and given everything they've ever wanted whenever they've wanted it. They don't know what it is to sacrifice and struggle, to do without, to live through pain and hardship.

"But I'll tell you something," she continued, her face distorted in a mad smile, "rich, pampered, spoiled people are weak and they don't have the strength to fight adversity when it strikes, so they remain crippled . . . they're invalids, trapped by their own wealth and luxury, stupid blobs." She pressed her hands together and rubbed them vigorously, as vigorously as she would if she were out in the cold. "Clay to be molded, no longer able to mold themselves into anything. Oh, they're still soft and pretty, but they're like . . ." She looked over at the dresser. "Like silk lingerie, delightful to touch and wear and then put away."

"I'm not like that. I'm not!" I cried.

She smiled again, this time as if she were speaking to a complete idiot.

"You're not? Then why can't you listen to my orders and do what I tell you when I tell you to do it, instead of fighting me every inch of the way?"

"I do listen. I'm just . . ." The words caught in my throat. I thought I would choke on them.

"Yes?"

"Lonely. I've lost my parents, I've lost my friends, and I'm . . . I'm . . ." She nodded, encouraging me to say it. I didn't want to say it. I wouldn't.

"Crippled?"

"NO!"

"Yes, you are! And you'll remain crippled unless you listen to what I tell you. Is that what you want?"

"You're not God!" I snapped. I couldn't help my frustration.

"No, I never said I was God." Her calm, profession-al tone only infuriated me more. "But I am a trained nurse, trained to treat people like yourself, and what good will all this training be if the patient is stubborn and spoiled and refuses to follow orders?

"You think I'm being cruel? Perhaps it seems that way, but if I am, I'm being cruel only to be kind. You didn't listen to what I told you . . . rich, pampered young girls, such as yourself, are weak; they have no grit when it comes to hardship. You have to toughen up, deal with your loneliness, form a crust around yourself . . . a scab over your wounds so you can fight, otherwise you'll remain soft and the ugly thing that has made you an invalid will maintain its grip on you. Is that what you want to happen?" she asked. My heart was pounding because she sounded so right. I wasn't trapped by my physical problems; I was trapped by her words.

"I told you," I said, lowering my head in defeat, "I was hungry and felt deserted. I heard no one and no one answered my calls . . . not Tony, not Drake, and not you."

"All right, I'll go down and see if your meal is ready yet."

"If Drake is still here, send him up," I pleaded.

"He's not; he had to return to Boston."

"Where is Tony, then?"

"I don't know. I have enough trouble looking after you," she muttered, and left the suite.

I sat there for a few moments staring into empty space, into the wake of her cold presence. She might be a good nurse, even a great nurse, I thought, but I didn't like her. Despite all that Tony had done for me—the doctors, the machinery and the private care, I wished I could leave here. Maybe my aunt Fanny was right; maybe I was better off recuperating among people I loved, people who loved me.

I had to admit that I jumped at the opportunity to come to Farthy not only because I had always had a secret desire to come here, but for the same reason Drake told me he wasn't anxious to return to Hasbrouck House and Winnerrow. I didn't have the courage to go back there and look at my parents' room, see their clothing and their possessions, awaken every morning expecting to hear Daddy's footsteps and warm "Good morning, princess." I knew I would continually look up in anticipation of Mommy coming in to talk to me about this or that.

No, coming to Farthy had postponed the inevitable reality I would have to face. But now I wondered if I had made the right decision. Perhaps with Aunt Fanny there, keeping me amused in her inimitable way—gossiping about the rich people of Winnerrow, laughing about the way they treated her—I might be better off, even without all the special equipment and private nursing care.

I wished Luke would have come to see me by now so he and I could have discussed it. It was no use talking to Drake about it. He was so infatuated with Tony and the business that he was blind to any of the failings and problems in Farthy. Now he was almost as blind as Tony was even when it came to the rundown sections of Farthinggale.

I had to contact Luke, I thought. I must see him. I must!

I wheeled myself to the desk and found some more stationery. Then I wrote Luke another letter, and this time allowed myself to sound desperate.

Dear Luke,

It seems one confusing thing after another has happened to keep you from paying me a visit here at Farthy. Messages are not delivered or perhaps left confusing.

I need to see you immediately. A great deal has happened since my arrival at Farthy. I think I am somewhat stronger, but I haven't made any dramatic progress with my legs yet, despite the therapy.

The truth is I'm not sure I should remain here much longer and I want to talk with you about it. Please come now. You don't need special permission. Come the day you receive this.

Love,
Annie

I put it into an envelope, sealing it immediately. Then I addressed it the same way I had addressed the first letter I wrote him, the one Millie Thomas never gave Tony.

"Do you want to remain in your wheelchair to eat or return to bed?" Mrs. Broadfield asked as soon as she returned with my tray of food.

"I'll remain in the wheelchair."

She put the tray down to fetch the small table that went over the arms, fit it into place, and brought me the tray. I lifted the silver cover and looked at a breast of plain boiled chicken, a portion of green peas and carrots, and a slice of buttered white bread. It looked like hospital food.

"Rye Whiskey prepared this?"

"I had his helper prepare it, following my specific instructions."

"It looks . . . blah."

"I thought you were hungry."

"I am, but I was expecting something different . . . something Rye made. Everything he makes is special."

"He's been using too much spice and making your food too exotic."

"But I like it; I eat everything now, and that's what Dr. Malisoff wanted, isn't it?" I protested.

"He also wants you to eat things that are easy to digest. Considering your condition—"

I slammed down the lid over the plate. Something proud sprang into my spine. I could put ice into my words, too, I thought. I sat back, crossing my arms over my chest.

"I want something Rye makes. I won't eat this."

She stared down at me. I knew she was burning with anger, but she kept her eyes clear, calm, and unreadable. There was even a small, tight smile around her lips.

"Very well." She took the tray. "Maybe you're not as hungry as you think."

"I am hungry. Tell Rye to make me something."

"Something was made for you; you don't want it," she said as if stating the obvious, simple fact.

"I may be crippled, but I still can enjoy food. Ask Tony to come here, please," I instructed.

"You don't realize how you're acting, Annie. I'm just trying to do what I know is best for you."

"I have had no trouble digesting anything Rye has made so far."

"All right," she said, relenting. "If you have to have something he makes, I'll ask him to fix the chicken."

"And I want him to fix the vegetables and potatoes, too. And I want some of his homemade bread."

"Don't complain later when you have stomach problems," she said before leaving. She just had to have the last word. But I saw how to get her to do what I wanted—just ask for Tony.

Tony arrived before Mrs. Broadfield returned with my new food.

"Well now, how are you feeling?"

"Tired, but hungry. I'm waiting for Mrs. Broadfield to return with something Rye Whiskey makes. I don't want to be troublesome, but I didn't like what she had brought me." I told him because I thought she would complain to him about me later and give only her side of the story.

"Don't you worry about that," he soothed. "You're no trouble. I'm sure Rye wouldn't mind cooking around the clock for you."

"No, I know he won't mind."

"You sound irritable."

I didn't respond for a few moments, and then I turned to him abruptly.

"Tony, I know Mrs. Broadfield is a professional and I'm lucky to have a nurse who has experience with my problems and who is a therapist as well, but she can be very trying."

"I'll speak to her," he said. His eyes were soft and sympathetic, and I trusted he knew just what I meant. "My main concern is that you be happy, Annie. Everything else comes second. You know that, don't you?"

"Yes, Tony. I do appreciate what you have been doing." I felt myself calm down. Then I remembered the letter in my lap.

"Tony, I have written another letter to Luke. Would you please see that it is delivered to him . . . special delivery, so he gets it immediately."

"Of course."

He took it from me and put it into his suit jacket quickly.

"Let me go down and look into your food. Can't have you going hungry long in my house."

"It's all right now. I can wait."

"I'll just look into it anyway. And I'll speak to Mrs. Broadfield."

"I don't mean to make extra trouble."

"Nonsense. I told you. You come first. It's the way I want it," he assured me, and pivoted on his heel.

"Oh, Tony . . ."

"Yes?" He turned back at the door.

"Is there someone else here? A woman?"

"A woman? You mean besides Mrs. Broadfield?" His blue eyes narrowed.

"Yes. I wheeled myself out before and wandered into another suite, just like this one, and—"

"Oh." He took a few steps back. "You mean you went to Jillian's suite."

"Jillian's?" But Jillian had been dead so long, I thought. That suite looked like it was being used today.

"Yes. I must have left the door open. I usually don't like anyone going in there," he said, his tone harder and sterner than it had ever been.

"I'm sorry. I—"

"That's all right," he said quickly, "no harm done. I've kept the room just the way it was the day she died. It's always been hard facing the fact that she's gone."

"Why are all the mirrors gone?"

"That was part of her madness toward the end. Anyway, there's no one else here," he said quickly. Then he forced a laugh. "Don't tell me you, too, are seeing Rye's ghosts." He shook his head and strutted off.

Another room kept like a museum? Did Tony move from one moment in the past to another, keeping his memories vivid by keeping up the illusion of Jillian still being here? I could understand why a lonely man might hold onto mementoes, pictures, letters, things that had a special and loving meaning for him, but to keep her room the way it had been the very day she died . . . that was eerie. A chill passed through me and for the first time I wondered if it wasn't time for me to demand I be returned to Winnerrow.

Shortly afterward, Mrs. Broadfield returned with a new tray of food. This time she had brought me some of Rye's famous fried chicken, his special whipped potatoes, and steamed vegetables that smelled fresh and delicious. I was so hungry and everything looked so good, I gobbled my food.

Mrs. Broadfield stood back, her face expressionless but her eyes cold. It was as if she wore a mask and only her eyes peeped through this granite face. She went into the sitting room and returned soon after I had completed my meal.

"It was delicious," I said.

"Do you want me to help you back into bed?"

"No, I think I'll remain sitting up in the chair and watch television."

She took the tray and left. I took the remote control and turned on the television set. I settled on a movie I had never seen and sat back, but what seemed to be only minutes later a sharp pain stabbed across my abdomen. I groaned and pressed my palms against my belly. The pain ceased and I sat back, taking deep breaths; but then it came again, this time with a great deal more ferocity, tearing up and down my stomach and sending pain into my chest.

I heard my stomach bubble. I knew that I was going to have an accident any moment.

"Mrs. Broadfield!" I called. *"Mrs. Broadfield!"* I screamed. But she didn't respond. I started to wheel myself toward the doorway. *"Mrs. Broadfield!"*

It was happening. My body was rebelling.

"Oh no. *Mrs. Broadfield!"*

By the time she arrived, I was doubled up in the wheelchair and a mess.

She stood in the doorway, her hands on her hips, a sharp, cold smile of self-satisfaction carved on her stone face.

"Don't say I didn't tell you so," she said, shaking her head.

Bent over in the chair, I could only moan and plead for her to help me.

that I correct myself as soon as I heard Tony. He had heard the commotion and had come running to my aid.

"What's wrong?" he called from the sitting room.

"Close the entrance door," I pleaded.

Mrs. Broadfield smirked.

"Just sit there and relax," she commanded and left the bathroom, closing the door firmly behind her.

SEVENTEEN

Mrs. Broadfield's Revenge

Mrs. Broadfield wheeled me into the bathroom quickly. She began to fill the tub, and then she stripped me down, peeling the clothing off me roughly. I felt like a ripe banana in the hands of a starving monkey. If she could have torn off my skin, I think she would have done it. All the while she said nothing, but I could read the repeated "I told you so's" in her furious eyes. I moaned, still clutching my stomach.

"It feels like someone's in there lighting matches," I cried, but my complaints fell on deaf ears. She wiped me down with some towels and then, pulling me up and tugging me out of the wheelchair, she literally dumped me into the hot water. She was very powerful for a woman her size.

As soon as I was submerged, she turned off the faucet and I slipped lower and lower until the water was up to my neck. Although it was as hot as ever, it seemed to bring some relief. I closed my eyes and lay back, still whimpering softly.

But I opened my eyes as soon as I heard Tony. He had heard the commotion and had come running to my aid.

"What's wrong?" he called from the sitting room.

"Close the bathroom door!" I pleaded.

Mrs. Broadfield smirked.

"Just sit there and soak," she commanded and left the bathroom, closing the door firmly behind her. Even so, I overheard their conversation.

"Has something happened to Annie, Mrs. Broadfield?"

"I pleaded with her not to eat those spicy, exotic meals your chef often makes. I even had the other cook prepare something proper and nutritious, but she was stubborn and insisted on having your chef's food, so I had to go back and have him prepare it."

"I know, but—"

"Her stomach is sensitive, as is most of her body. I tried to explain, but she is in a rush to recuperate, and like most teenagers, won't listen to older people who have experience."

"Should I send for the doctor?" he asked anxiously.

"No, I can handle it. She will be uncomfortable for a while, but there is no need to send for the doctor."

"Is there anything I can do?" God bless Tony, I thought. He sounded so concerned, his voice full of worry and sympathy in contrast to Mrs. Broadfield's stern, correct tones.

"No, I'll get her cleaned up, medicated, and comfortable. By morning she should be better, but her stomach will be even more sensitive. What you can do is speak to that chef and tell him to prepare food exactly as I instruct him from now on."

"I will."

I heard Tony leave, and moments later Mrs. Broadfield returned to the bathroom. She loomed over me. My tears mingled with the droplets of steam that ran down my reddened cheeks. Suddenly her stone face softened and, like a wax bust a little too close to heat, her lips dipped, the corners of her mouth widened, her puffy cheeks drooped, and her eyes watered with sympathy.

"You poor child. If only you would have listened . . . to have such unnecessary pain on top of the agony already wreaked upon your tormented body."

She knelt down beside me and took a washcloth to my face to wipe away my tears.

"Just close your eyes and relax a little longer. I'll have you up and out of here in moments. We'll dry you off, dress you in a clean, crisp nightgown, and give you something to relieve the abdominal cramps. Then you'll sleep like a baby."

"I don't understand . . . nothing I ate before did this to me."

She lowered the washcloth to my neck and shoulders, wiping my skin in small, soft circles as lovingly as would one polishing fine china.

"You're in my hands now. Let me do my work and you'll recuperate as you should, when you should, Annie. Will you let me do what I am being paid to do?"

I nodded, my eyes closed now. The pain had eased some, although my stomach was still bubbling and threatening. Mrs. Broadfield ran her fingers down between my breasts and pressed the palm of her hand against my abdomen. When I opened my eyes, I saw her face was so close to mine I could read the pores in her skin, see the little hairs in her nostrils and the cracks in her lips.

"It's still very active in there," she whispered. She turned her eyes on mine, but she had a faraway look.

"Can I come out of the water now?"

"What? Oh . . . yes, yes." She stood up quickly and reached for the towels. Then she helped me out of the tub and wiped my body dry. After I put on the new nightgown, she assisted my return to bed and gave me two spoonfuls of a gray, chalky liquid. Moments later the bubbling in my stomach ended and she then gave me a sleeping pill.

I did as I was told . . . closed my eyes and fell asleep, eager for the relief sleep would bring. Before I drifted off, I opened my eyes once and saw her standing beside me, looking down at me like a cat who had trapped its mouse in a corner and hovered confidently above its prey, now enjoying the torment it could lay upon its weaker and pathetic counterpart.

Tomorrow I would feel better, I thought, and to-morrow Luke would receive my letter and would come to me. I had a dream about him. In it he was a knight on a white horse. He came galloping through the tall gates of Farthy and came charging into the mansion, rushing up the stairs to my room. He threw open the doors and came to my bed, where he quickly embraced me. I was so happy to see him, I put all restraint aside and kissed him fully on the lips. My nightgown slipped off my shoulders and he pressed his lips to my naked breasts, closing his eyes and inhaling as if I were a rose.

"Oh, Luke," I moaned, "how I've waited for you, how I've longed for you."

"My Annie." He caressed me gently, making my body sing with every kiss, until the tingles reached my legs and filled them with renewed strength and life. "I must take you away from here so we can be free to be lovers forever and ever."

He scooped me into his arms and carried me out and down the stairs. I was still half naked, but I didn't care. He put me on his horse and we rode off, away from Farthy. I looked back only once in the dream, and when I did, I saw Tony in a window watching, his face torn by sadness. Only there was also a dark, shadowy figure standing behind him. I couldn't see his face, but I felt sad about leaving him. I reached back, as if calling to him, and then I awoke.

All the next morning and part of the afternoon, I remained in bed. Mrs. Broadfield decided we would have to skip my therapy for one day. She had Rye Whiskey prepare hot oatmeal for breakfast and allowed me very sweet tea and toast and jelly the rest of the day. Toward mid-afternoon I felt strong enough to get into my wheelchair. A little after two o'clock Rye appeared, still dressed in his apron. Mrs. Broadfield had gone for a walk.

He entered, looking timid, remorseful. I knew immediately that he felt responsible for what had happened to me.

"How ya feelin', Miss Annie?"

"Much better, Rye. Now don't you go blaming yourself. There was no way for you to know what would and wouldn't disturb my digestion. Nothing you made had disturbed it before," I pointed out, widening my eyes for emphasis. He nodded thoughtfully. I could see there was something on his mind.

"Dat's what I was thinkin', Miss Annie. I didn't put nothin' inta the meal I hadn't put in befo'."

"It was my fault," I stressed. "I shouldn't have sent Mrs. Broadfield back with the food your helper had prepared."

"I'll say. She come rushin' inta dat kitchen, flames in her hair, and slaps the tray down. I jumped a mile. Den she says, fix your special chicken, vegetables and potatas. I was doin' it anyway for Mr. Tatterton, so I said, it's all ready, ma'am. She grunts and I dished out de platter."

"Then what happened?"

"Nothin'. I give it to her to take back, 'cause we ain't got the maid no more, an' she takes the tray.

Only I forgots the bread, so I come after her. I catched her because she stopped in the dining room to add in the medicine and—"

"Medicine? What medicine?"

Rye shrugged. "Medicine, she told me. To help you digest the food."

"I never had that before."

"I gives her the bread and she goes up ta yer room and next thing I know, Mr. Tatterton's rushing about, frantic because the food made ya so sick. He come in ta see me 'bout it and I said, yessir, I'll listen to whatever the nurse tells me. Dat was dat. But ya feelin' better now?"

"Yes, Rye. You're sure she put medicine in my food?"

"In de potatoes. She was mixing it up when I comes out of the kitchen. Hope it didn't ruin the taste, I thought, but I was too scared ta say dat ta her. She must be a good nurse; she can scare the sickness right outta ya."

"If she wants . . ." I said knowingly. That was no medicine. She was taking revenge on me for insisting on the food, for defying her. My God, I thought, I'm in the hands of a sadistic, vengeful, hateful person. All this pain and embarrassment was her doing! "Or maybe she puts the sickness into you, too," I added, nodding knowingly. Rye understood.

"Miss Annie . . ." He turned and looked at the empty doorway to be sure no one was coming. "Maybe ya better already. Maybe it be best ya go on home now."

"What?" I smiled with confusion. "You want me to go home?"

"I better gets back to ma kitchen. Glad ya feelin' better, Miss Annie." He hurried out before I could ask him another question, but there was no doubt in

274

my mind that he knew more, much more, about what was going on at Farthy.

Tony didn't appear until dinner time. I was given the meal I had originally sent back: a breast of boiled chicken, peas and carrots, and bland mashed potatoes. Mrs. Broadfield smiled widely as she brought in the tray and placed it on my chair table. She stood nearby and watched me eat, just to be sure I could take in solid food again, she said.

"Did you put anything in this to help my digestion?" I asked. Her smile evaporated.

"What? Like what?"

"I don't know . . . like what you put in my food when you brought me my dinner the second time last night," I said, my eyes narrowing on her.

"What? Who told you such a thing?" She didn't look angry; she looked amused, as if she were talking to a complete idiot. The tight, cynical smile around her lips infuriated me.

"Rye told me," I spit back at her. "He came up to see how I was doing and he told me he saw you putting in what you told him was medicine after you took the tray out of the kitchen."

"What a story." She laughed; a thin, chilling laugh. "Why would he make up such a thing? It's ridiculous to suggest it."

"You did it," I said accusingly.

"My dear girl, he's merely trying to cover up his own guilt for what happened to you. The first day we arrived here, I went to see him and specifically told him he must eliminate spicy foods from your diet. You'll remember I told him not to give you heavy sweet things, but he sent up that chocolate cake anyway. He's either stubborn or stupid. I'm sure Mr. Tatterton was quite upset with him and might even have fired him."

"Fire Rye?" It was my turn to laugh and make her feel ridiculous. "You don't realize how long they've been together. Rye's family here; he'll be here until the day he dies. And as for him feeling guilty, that's even more ridiculous. Rye is a wonderful cook. People don't get sick from the food he makes," I continued, challenging her, my eyes burning through her. She shook her head and looked away. That confirmed my suspicions.

"Nevertheless, Mr. Tatterton was upset with him. Now why don't you finish your food before it gets cold. I'd like it to be warm when it hits your stomach." She spun on her heel and left the room.

Soon after, Tony arrived.

"How are you doing, Annie? I called Mrs. Broadfield twice today and she said you were coming along fine."

"She's been lying to you," I snapped. I was determined this would all come to an end or I would leave immediately.

"What? Lying?"

"I didn't get sick from any spicy food, Tony. The food wasn't overly spiced, it was poisoned!" I declared. He stared at me a moment, his eyes widening.

"Poisoned? Do you realize what you're saying? Maybe you're just—"

"No, Tony, listen. If you really care for me, listen," I said. That got to him. He came closer. "Mrs. Broadfield is a competent nurse, technically competent, but she's not a nice person and she hates wealthy people. She thinks wealthy people, especially young wealthy people, are spoiled rotten and weak. You should see her face when she talks about it—she becomes even uglier, ghastly, hideous, monstrous."

"I had no idea," he said in amazement.

"Yes, and she can't stand being challenged. Why,

276

even if I ask a question about what she's doing, she becomes enraged. When I demanded Rye's tasty food and challenged her command, she made up her mind to teach me a lesson. Rye was just here to apologize, and he told me she had taken his food and put something in it, claiming it was medicine, but I don't get any medicine in my food, Tony. You know that. She brought about this painful and embarrassing scene just to teach me a lesson," I repeated, my rage and fury bright, my face hot with anger.

He nodded. "I see. Well then, I think it's time we terminated her services, don't you?"

"Yes, Tony. I won't stay here another day with that woman."

"Don't you worry about it. You won't have to. I'm going to pack her off tonight. We'll spend a little more time finding a suitable replacement, but I'm sure we will very quickly," he added with confidence.

"Thank you, Tony. I didn't want to make trouble, but—"

"Nonsense. If you're not happy and comfortable with your nurse, you won't improve. And I certainly don't want someone as sadistic as this woman seems to be. Anyway," he said, "put all that behind you now. I'll handle it. Let's turn our attention to other, brighter and more cheerful things." He looked around. "I know just what else is wrong. You're sitting and lying around doting on your illness too much. Look at this room . . . it's a duplication of a hospital room . . . wheelchairs, walkers, medicines, special trays and basins . . . depressing," he said, shaking his head. "But I've got just the magical medicine for you." His blue eyes twinkled with glee like the eyes of a mischievous little boy.

"Magical medicine! What is it?"

He held his hand up to indicate I should be patient.

Then he went out of the suite. A moment later Parson appeared, carrying a long carton. He put it down by the window and turned to Tony.

"You want it here, Mr. Tatterton?"

"Exactly."

"What is that?"

"You'll see," he said and took my now empty tray off my wheelchair. He put it on the dresser and pulled my wheelchair back to the bed so he could sit beside me on the bed and both of us could watch Parson unpack whatever was in the carton. Moments later I realized what it was—an artist's easel. Parson assembled it quickly and adjusted it so I could paint from a sitting position.

"Oh, Tony, an easel! How wonderful," I cried.

"It's the best one money can buy," Tony announced proudly.

"Oh, Tony, thank you, but—"

"No buts. You've got to get back into the swing of things. That's what everyone I've spoken to about you tells me." He nodded to Parson, who left and returned with two more cartons, one filled with artist's supplies and one with paper. Tony set up a sheet on the easel immediately.

"I don't know much about the rest of this stuff. I simply gave orders to my purchasing agent to go out and buy everything a budding young artist requires. There's even a beret in here somewhere." He sifted through the carton until he found it, a black beret, and put it on me. I laughed.

"See? I've already got you smiling and laughing." Then he came over and put the hat on me. "Black is your color, Annie." He turned me toward a mirror so I could see myself. "Feeling inspired already?"

I was. Just the sight of myself in that beret brought back the dreams I had almost forgotten. Art filled my

278

life with an inner joy and meaning nothing else could. I hadn't realized how much I had missed it. The accident and the aftermath had separated me from all the people and things I loved, especially my artwork. Maybe that was another but more significant reason why I had felt like half a person up until now. I was so afraid that all the sadness and the tragedy had made me incapable of calling up the innermost feelings and inspiration that could be transformed into something beautiful. What if I lifted the brush to the canvas and saw only a blank, stark-white field forever and ever?

"I don't know, Tony."

"Well, you'll try, won't you? You'll at least try. Promise?"

I hesitated, looking at him hopefully.

"Well? Do you promise?"

"I'll try, Tony. I promise."

"Well now." He clapped his hands. "I'll just leave you to your work, then. In a day or so I expect to see something magnificent."

"Don't expect too much, Tony. I was never really that good anyway and—"

"You're much too modest. Drake has told me. He even brought back one of your paintings."

"He did!" I exclaimed.

"It's hanging in my office downstairs."

"He didn't tell me he did that. Which painting?"

"The one with the little sparrow on the magnolia tree. I love it. I hope you don't mind his bringing it to me."

"It's not that I mind . . . but he should have told me. He should have asked," I said, gently chastising, even though I felt flattered and happy about Drake's appreciation of my artwork.

"Well, I asked him to bring one and he was just

279

trying to please me. Don't be too hard on him," Tony pleaded.

"All right, Tony. I won't." He smiled and started to leave the room. "Tony," I called.

"Yes?"

"If Luke doesn't call by seven o'clock, I want you to have me taken to a phone to call him. I can't understand his failure to come or to respond to our letters and calls. Something must be wrong."

"If something is wrong, Annie, you should be shielded from it awhile longer. I'll tell you what—I'll call him myself if he doesn't call."

"But you just said you won't tell me if something is wrong."

"I'll tell you. I promise."

"Tony, I want a phone installed here. I can't stand the isolation. Please ask the doctor to permit it."

Tony seemed pained by my use of the word "isolation," but I couldn't help it. That was how I felt. He grimaced.

"It's not that you're not doing everything you can for me, Tony. And I do appreciate it, really I do, but I miss my friends and the life I had before. I'm a young woman who was about to start the most exciting part of her life. I can't help being lonely, even though you and Drake have paid as much attention to me as you can. Please, speak to the doctor," I begged.

His face softened. "Certainly. I'm sure he'll agree. You're on your way toward a full recuperation. I'm positive. Paint, eat well, rest, and you'll be on your feet sooner than you think."

"Come right up after you call Luke." He nodded and left.

I sat there quietly for a moment, thinking about all that had happened. Perhaps Tony was right . . . I shouldn't dote on my illness and these sad thoughts any longer. He had promised to get rid of Mrs.

Broadfield immediately. But even with a thoughtful, compassionate nurse, I would still feel entrapped.

Tony could surround me with the most expensive equipment and bring me one thing after another: televisions, stereos, whatever, and I still wouldn't be content. I missed my own room, the scent of my linens and pillow, the fluffy feel of my feathered quilts. I missed my own dresses and shoes and combs.

I missed giggling on the phone with girlfriends, listening to music alone or with friends at the luncheonette. I missed parties and dancing and laughing with people my age. I missed the simplest things and the most complicated things. I missed seeing flowers blossom in our front yard or watching Mommy crochet quietly in the living room. I missed Daddy reading the newspaper, turning those big pages thoughtfully, and occasionally looking over them to wink at me.

Most of all I missed Luke. I missed the sight of him coming down the street or watching him without his being aware as he sat outside on the gazebo waiting for me. I missed our nightly talks on the phone.

Once upon a time, hardly a day passed that we didn't see each other or speak to each other, and now he seemed thousands of miles away, a lifetime away, distracted by his own private world, perhaps. It tore my heart to shreds just thinking about it. But Tony was right. I shouldn't dote on my condition. The only way to be with Luke was to get hold of myself and make myself well again.

I should begin to return to my former self as much as possible, and one way to start that return was to paint again. I wheeled myself to the easel and looked into the carton of supplies. Slowly, I unpacked the things I would need to begin.

But what would I paint? I wondered. As if in

answer, the window drew me to it and I gazed out
toward the Tatterton family cemetery. I took out the
pencil and began to sketch, working as if one of Rye
Whiskey's spirits had taken hold of my arm and
guided my fingers across the blank white sheet. And
as I drew, the tears began to come.

Just like any other time when I started a painting, I
soon lost myself in my work. It was truly as though I
had shrunk and become a tiny figure in the sketch,
moving over the scene, directing my larger self to
draw this and fix that. The world around me faded
away; I lost track of time and even place. I didn't even
hear Tony return, and I had no idea how long he was
standing just behind me, watching me work. I jumped
when I realized he was there.

"Sorry. Didn't mean to startle you, but I didn't
want to disturb you and ruin your mood. I know how
you artists need your concentration. Jillian's just like
that. I mean, she was just like that whenever she drew
or painted something. I could be standing there for
hours and hours and she wouldn't take the slightest
note of it. It always amazed me—fascinated me, I
should say—and I find you just as fascinating when
you work, Annie," he added. He said it so intensely, I
couldn't help but blush.

He smiled and then remembered why he had come.
"Oh. I wondered if you were going to need your
sleeping pill. Before she left in a huff, Mrs. Broadfield
left some instructions. If she hadn't, I would have
reported her and she would have never gotten another
job."

"No, I think I'll fall asleep without any help tonight,
Tony. Thank you."

"Fine. I'll just let you work awhile longer and then
stop by to see if you need any assistance getting

yourself to bed." He flashed a smile and started to leave.

"Oh, Tony," I called. He turned back. "What happened when you phoned Luke?"

"Oh, I haven't gotten to that yet, Annie. I dealt with Mrs. Broadfield first. I'm sure you understand. I'll try to reach him right now," he said, and left. I went back to my work.

Hours later I fell back in my chair, mentally exhausted. I had really been like one in a daze, because when I looked at my work now, it was as though someone else had done it and left it there before me.

I had drawn a window frame to serve as the frame for the picture. The monument loomed large at the center of the picture, the other tombstones barely sketched in around it. There was a figure kneeling before the large stone. It wasn't Tony and it wasn't me; it was the dark, mysterious man I had seen before. His face was blank, but he was tall and lean.

I looked at my palette and thought about the colors I would use. It seemed to me the painting should be all grays and blacks; they fit the mood. I decided to put off painting until the morning, when I might be in a lighter and happier mood. When I turned from the window, I saw the charm bracelet Luke had given me. Mrs. Broadfield had taken it off quickly when she stripped me down after my stomach problems. Now it lay on the night table by the bed. It was well after eight P.M., so Tony would have called him by now. Why hadn't he come up to report on the call as he had promised he would? Did this mean Luke was still unreachable or had made some other excuses for not coming to visit me?

I sat back in my chair and took deep breaths to calm my pounding heart, which seemed more like a military drum being thumped in the middle of a battle. How I wished I could find things out for myself.

I wasn't feeling sorry for myself as much as I was feeling angry, and something told me that was good, that was the beginning of a fight to return to health and strength. Frustration turned my hands into fists and tightened my spine like a rope being pulled firmly from both ends. None of this was going to change when Mrs. Broadfield's replacement arrived, no matter how nice she was.

I would still have to get up when others wanted me to get up, eat when others wanted me to eat and what they wanted me to eat, take therapy when someone said it was time, nap at her command, dress, wash, go to the bathroom when she decided I should, and speak to people when she wanted me to speak to people. I've become a puppet, and my nurses, my doctors, even Tony, have become the puppeteers, I thought.

"No!" I screamed to an empty room. I felt my anger and frustration flowing down my body, warming the blood that ran through my rebellious legs. Suddenly there was a twinge; something electric shot through my lower spine. At first it was like a pinprick on the backs of my thighs, then it became a tingling along my ankles and into the tips of my toes. I willed my feet to press against the pads of the chair.

I felt the pressure against the soles of my feet. I felt tension in my legs, wobbly and weak, but nevertheless, tension. This time when I made an effort to rise out of the chair, I wasn't depending entirely on my arm strength. My legs were aiding. I was getting a response to my mental commands. It was working! I was doing it! Doing it! . . . My entire body trembled, but I felt it . . . I could work myself into an unsteady standing position. I was making it happen, doing what I had taken for granted most of my life, but achieving what now was a major accomplishment! My heart pounded with anticipation and happiness. My body was responding!

It seemed to take hours instead of moments, but I was rising out of the chair, guiding myself by holding the arms as I began to stand. Just as I reached the full upright position, my legs shaking like toothpicks asked to hold a weight far too heavy for them, Tony came in. He stopped and looked at me in amazement.

"Tony . . . I just tried and it happened! My legs are working, Tony! Really beginning to work! But it feels so funny, like I'm standing on air." I wobbled when I laughed.

"Easy," he said, stepping forward slowly and holding his hands out as though he were speaking to a potential suicide victim out on a window ledge. "Don't try to walk yet. You don't want to break any bones."

He didn't look as happy and as excited by it all as I had expected he would. If anything, he looked annoyed. Why wasn't he as happy as I was? It was happening, what we had all hoped would happen was happening!

"I'm going to get better! I am!" I emphasized, in an attempt to evoke some excitement in him. But he didn't change expression.

"Of course you are," Tony said calmly. "But don't rush things now. Take it easy. You'd better sit down again," he said.

"But I don't feel tired yet, and it feels so good to be standing on my own two feet! Oh, Tony, it feels so good . . . so wonderful to do a simple thing like stand up! I wish Drake could have been here to see; I wish Luke . . . what about Luke? You called him, didn't you?"

"Yes, I called him," Tony said.

"Oh, I'll stand for him! You'll tell me exactly when he's coming up and I'll stand just as he comes through that door and—"

"He can't come tomorrow," Tony declared flatly. "He has some sort of entrance exam to take."

The excitement that had blown me up so, seeped out as if I were a leaking balloon. I could feel my newfound strength weakening, my pounding, stronger heart softening, that hateful shadow falling over it again.

"What? But that can't possibly take him all day."

"It's just not convenient. Maybe the day after or on the weekend. He wasn't sure."

"Wasn't sure? Luke said he wasn't sure?"

Suddenly my legs became like jelly. Without warning they lost all their firmness. I screamed. Tony lunged forward, unfortunately not reaching me in time to prevent me from crashing to the floor.

286

EIGHTEEN

Rebellion

The first thing I thought after I regained consciousness was I was wearing a different nightgown, one of the silk ones Tony had brought me at the hospital. That meant he had changed me before the doctor's arrival. But why? Had I torn it when I fell unconscious? It was embarrassing to realize he had taken off my nightgown and dressed me while I was unconscious. He was much older, a great-grandfather, but still . . . he was a man!

Before I could ask him about it, he and Dr. Malisoff rushed into my room. My thoughts cleared and I remembered my physical accomplishments. It was happening—I was really recovering! Despite my collapse, I knew it was true. There was an end in sight to this existence as an invalid. My heart was cheered. Soon I would once again walk unaided, never again to be dependent upon nurses and doctors, medicines and equipment.

I waited patiently but excitedly as Dr. Malisoff

completed his examination of me—testing my reflexes. Tony waited near the door.

As I lay there in bed, I again felt an awakening in my lower limbs and knew something significant had begun to happen. And even though the doctor wore his expressionless, analytical face, I could see something new in his eyes when he gazed down at me.

"Well?" I asked anxiously. Tony stepped forward to hear what he would say. "Am I improving?"

"Yes," he said, "your legs are coming back; your reflexes are stronger."

"Oh, thank God! Thank God! Thank God!" I chanted. I looked at Tony, but he seemed troubled. The doctor decided to have a quick consultation with him. I waited again as they spoke in the sitting room. Why they had to do it beyond my hearing, I couldn't understand. The only thing I could think was, he didn't want me to get too excited. When they returned, they both looked happier.

"Annie," the doctor said, "you are definitely on the way to a complete recovery; however, it is very important, especially now, that you don't rush things and cause a setback."

"Oh, I won't."

"What you must do is follow my orders to the letter, okay?" I nodded. He could have told me to cut all the grass at Farthy with a pair of scissors and I would have agreed. "The reason you collapsed after you stood up is you are still physically exhausted. We want to build your strength for the battle ahead, now that your legs are returning. I am going to adjust your therapy. I have given Mr. Tatterton some simple instructions to follow. In any case, I will return the day after tomorrow and examine you again."

"Can't I begin to use the walker in the morning? I want to try to stand and walk as soon as I get up."

Dr. Malisoff looked at Tony and then squeezed his

chin with his thumb and forefinger as he considered me.

"Annie, I've described the stages of your recuperation to Mr. Tatterton in great detail. Don't do anything without asking his permission first, okay?"

"Yes, but—"

"No buts. Buts create complications," he added, smiling. "Can I depend on you?" I shifted my eyes away, unable to hide the sad expression on my face. "Now, now, you should be happy. You're on your way." He patted my hand and started out. Tony shook his hand and then remained behind. He looked down at me with sad blue eyes.

"After you passed out, I was sure we would have to bring you back to the hospital. Now we have good news, but you don't look happy."

"I'm just anxious to get back to normal, Tony."

"Of course." He stood thoughtfully a moment and then suddenly brightened as something came to mind. "But I have another surprise for you, and now that there is this definite degree of improvement, I'm even more excited about it."

"What have you done?" He did look excited—his eyes young and soft blue again, his face flushed.

"Since we put in the chair elevator for you to go up and down the stairway, I decided to have a ramp built in front of the main entrance this afternoon. You can wheel yourself to the stairway, go down, and wheel yourself to the front. Then you can wheel down the ramp and go along the sidewalks and paths to enjoy the grounds around Farthy. Of course, the first few times, I will take you, but in time—"

"In time I will walk out on my own, Tony." I was sorry I had said it so quickly and so sharply. He looked dejected, like a little boy who had been turned down, but I couldn't help it. My progress had filled me with such hope, and now Tony and the doctor

289

were telling me it would be a much longer wait than I had anticipated. I was still going to be confined to a wheelchair.

"Of course. I didn't mean to—"

"But I do appreciate what you have done, Tony. I can't wait to go out and around Farthy. Thank you, Tony. Thank you for everything, because I am sure without you I wouldn't be recovering so soon."

His face brightened again.

"I'm glad you feel that way, Annie. Oh," he said, looking over at the easel, "I see you have made progress on your painting. How wonderful." I studied his face as he turned a sharp, penetrating gaze on my work. His smile melted slowly, and with it went all that had made his expression bright and young. Then he looked out the window as if he could see through the darkness. He continued gazing as if he saw through the inky night. I didn't know what to say.

"It's just a drawing right now."

"Yes." When he turned back to me, his blue eyes looked troubled. He folded his brow and curled his lips inward like someone under great mental strain. "It's good, but I was hoping to see you paint the gardens and hedges, the little walkways and small, sparkling fountains."

"But Tony, the fountains aren't running. They're stuffed with autumn leaves. And the gardens need pruning. Whatever flowers there are, are being choked by weeds. Some of the hedges are trim, but even they need more work." He stared ahead, his eyes unblinking. I didn't think he heard a word I said.

"When the sun is out, the grounds glitter." He smiled. "Jillian says it's as if some giant stood on the roof and cast jewels over the lawns. She's an artist, so she has an artist's eye and imagination. She paints only pretty, pleasant things, happy things, things that make her feel young and alive. That's why she started with illustrations for children's books."

"Jillian . . . you mean, my great-grandmother Jillian? But she's dead. Tony?" He was just staring at me again, that faraway look in his eyes. I felt myself tremble. Was something more happening to him? Were his journeys back to the past becoming more frequent, and to the point where he was having trouble returning to the present?

"What? Oh, I meant, Jillian used to say." He laughed, a short, dry laugh and looked at my easel again. "It's just when I see artwork, art supplies, I think of her and vividly remember those early days. Oh well, after you're up and about, you'll set yourself up down there in the gardens and paint and paint until you wear the brushes down to nothing.

"I'm not surprised you chose a sad scene, closed up in this room the way you are. An artist needs space, to roam, to breathe. Only Troy could lock himself up and create one beautiful thing after another. They were already alive in his mind, I suppose."

"I'd like to see more of Troy's work."

"Oh, you will. When you come downstairs, we'll go to my office and look at all the models on the shelves. He created each and every one, down to the smallest detail."

"Maybe I'll come down tomorrow," I said hopefully.

"Yes. We'll arrange your first outing. Isn't this wonderful—to have you moving through the corridors of Farthinggale Manor once again!"

"Once again?"

He clapped his hands together. Everything he was saying seemed mixed up. Perhaps it was just the excitement of my impending recovery, I thought. I had to keep reminding myself—Tony was no youngster. Having all this thrust upon him after so many years of living in relative solitude had to be mind boggling.

"Now, I should let you get your rest."

"I'm too excited to sleep." I was reminded about my nightgown. "But Tony, why am I wearing a different nightgown from what I was wearing before I collapsed?"

"Different nightgown?" His smile became a smile of confusion. "I don't understand."

"I wasn't wearing this one before. You changed me, didn't you?"

He shook his head.

"You're probably just confused. You always wore that nightgown. It's your favorite. You've often told me so."

"I . . . I did?" He had me wondering myself, now. I shook my head. It didn't seem all that important anyway.

"Maybe I should give you something to help you sleep. The doctor left instructions to continue your sedatives."

"I hate sleeping pills. They give me nightmares," I cried.

"Now Annie, you've got to continue to do the things that have helped you reach this point of recovery, don't you?" he said in a soothing voice. "The doctor thinks you should, and after all, that's what we're paying him for—his medical knowledge. I'll be right back."

Moments later he returned with the pill and a glass of water. Reluctantly, I took it and swallowed it. Then I fell back against the pillow. He fixed my blanket and turned down the lights. Then he returned to my bedside and took my hand.

"Comfortable?" he asked.

"Yes." My voice sounded so small. I wished so much that it was my daddy's hand I was holding.

"That's good; that's the way it will be from now on," Tony said. "I'll always be here for you. Just call. I'll listen for your call, Annie, and I'll come as quickly as I can."

"But you can't devote all your time to me, Tony. You have a business to run," I declared.

"Oh, I don't worry about my business. It runs itself, and I have competent people in charge, including Drake now. Don't you ever think you're a burden for me," he added, patting my hand.

"Are you going to get a new nurse tomorrow?"

"I'll call the agency first thing in the morning," he assured me. "Sleep well." He knelt down and kissed my cheek, this time his lips lingering much longer against my skin, his hand pressed firmly over my shoulder as if he never wanted to let go. "Good night."

"Good night, Tony," I said, and watched him walk slowly out of the room, moving like one of Rye Whiskey's ghosts, turning off the lights as he went, the darkness dropping behind him.

Even with the sleeping pill, I was too excited to fall asleep quickly. Every once in a while I would try to move my toes and feel the tingle in my feet and the sensation of them moving against the blanket. I imagined I was not unlike a newborn baby discovering her limbs, discovering her own body. Each tiny movement, each feeling, brought new wonder. Oh, how I wished I had someone who was close, someone very close to share this physical comeback with me! How wonderful it would be if Luke were here when I stood up! He would embrace me and hold me against him, kiss me and stroke my hair. I smiled to myself imagining it, hearing him whisper in my ear as he ran his fingers along my shoulders. It made me tingle just to imagine it. Oh, Luke, I cried, am I being horribly sinful thinking these thoughts?

Finally the sleeping pill Tony gave me took effect. I felt myself growing more and more groggy, my eyelids growing heavier and heavier, until it was hard to keep them open. I closed them and the next thing I knew, there was sunlight on my face and Tony was opening the curtains. He was still in his robe and slippers, but he had already shaved. The room reeked of his after-shave lotion.

My first fearful thought was I had dreamt everything—the sensations in my legs and feet, my effort to stand, and my actual standing. But I concentrated on moving my feet, and lo and behold, this time my leg folded inward.

"Tony!" I cried. He spun around as if I had poked him in the back of his neck. "My legs . . . they're easier to move and they feel so much better."

He nodded quickly and continued to open curtains and move about the room, getting things ready for me to be helped out of bed, washed and dressed.

"You should wear this today, Annie," he said, taking one of Mommy's old dresses from the closet. He held it up admiringly. "You look great in it."

"I never wore that, Tony."

"Then you should. You'll look great in it. Take my word for it."

It was a light blue cotton dress with ruffled sleeves, a wide, embroidered collar, and an ankle-length hem. I thought it was quite inappropriate. It was more like a dress to wear to an afternoon tea party than a dress to wear while confined to a room.

"I can pick out my own clothing, Tony. Don't worry," I said. I was sure I didn't need as much help as usual this morning. To prove it I sat up and carefully brought my legs out from under the blanket, dangling them over the edge.

"What are you doing?" he cried excitedly.

"Getting up. See, I can do this myself now!"

"Didn't you listen to anything the doctor said last night? Wait for me," he commanded. "If you try to stand and you fall, you could break a bone. Do you want to be laid up with a cast for six weeks on top of everything else?"

His words filled me with terror.

"All right, Tony. I'm waiting."

He put the dress down on the foot of the bed and came around to me with the wheelchair. I lowered myself until my feet reached the floor, but when I went to put real pressure on my legs, he seized me under my arms and lowered me into the chair.

"I think I could have done that myself, Tony."

"I can't take any chances with you, Annie. The doctor would blame it on me if something happened to set you back."

"It seems to me I should be strengthening myself, working on building myself up."

"In time," he instructed. "In time. Don't rush things," he warned. "Now, about this dress—"

"I'll pick something out myself, Tony, after I wash up."

"I'll help you," he said, taking hold of the wheelchair and turning it toward the bathroom before I could move it myself.

"But Tony—"

"Remember what the doctor said about buts," he said. He turned the chair toward the bathtub and brought me face-to-face with it. Then he started running the water.

"Tony, I can't let you do all this," I protested.

"Nonsense. I feel terribly responsible for what

295

happened with Mrs. Broadfield. I hired her. The least I could do until she is replaced is provide the service you need and deserve. Just think of me as a male nurse," he added cheerfully. "How about some bubble bath?" He shook some pink powder into the water, then went out to get a washcloth and some towels.

"Tony," I said as softly as I could when he returned, "I'm a grown woman now. I need my privacy."

"You mustn't worry about those things now," he said. "And anyway, this is all as the doctor instructed."

I didn't know how to reply. He turned off the water in the tub and smiled down at me.

"Time to go in," he said. I looked at the water and up at him. His gray hair was brushed back neatly and his eyes were soft, loving. "Once you're in, I'll let you wash yourself," he offered. "I just want to be sure you don't slip and bang yourself against the tub."

With great reluctance, I lifted my nightgown over my body. He took it from me and brought his hands under my arms. Inevitably, his fingers touched the sides of my naked breasts. I gasped. No one but my parents and doctors and nurses had ever seen me naked before, much less touched me. But Tony didn't seem to notice what he had done. He brought his arm under my legs and lifted me into the water, lowering me slowly, until bubbles hid my nudity. I felt terribly helpless, more like an infant than an invalid.

"There," he said. "See how easy it was? Here," he added, offering me the washcloth. "I'll just go out and straighten up the bed while you bathe."

About ten minutes later he returned.

"How are you doing?"

"Fine."

"Want me to scrub your back? I'm an expert at that. I used to do it for your grandmother and your mother."

"Really?" I couldn't imagine Mommy permitting him to do so.

"Absolute expert," he said and took the cloth from my hands, positioning himself on the rear of the tub. I leaned forward as he brought the cloth to my neck. "You have the same smooth, graceful neck, Annie," he said, moving the cloth down to my shoulders gently. "And the same dainty, feminine shoulders, shoulders that can tease and torment the strongest men."

I felt the way he used the washcloth to trace the lines in my shoulders, around, over my collarbone, and back behind my neck again. Moments later I also felt his breath against me, and when I gazed at the mirror across from us, saw that his eyes were closed and he was holding his head as though he were inhaling me. A chill of terror rushed through me.

"Tony," I said, putting my hand over his and the washcloth, "I can finish up now. Thank you."

"What? Oh yes, yes." He stood up quickly. "I'll lay a towel over your wheelchair seat," he said, and did it. "Are you finished?"

"Yes, but you're going to get all wet."

"Don't worry about me. I've been all wet before," he kidded, and reached into the water to scoop his arms under me again. Then he lifted me gingerly out of the tub and set me down on the chair. Quickly, I wrapped the towels about myself. Tony seized another towel and began wiping my legs.

"I can do that, Tony."

"Nonsense. Why exhaust yourself when I'm around to help?" He went on, massaging my calves and working his way up over my knees, wiping my skin with an artist's care. He squatted and raised his eyes slowly to confront my gaze. "When I see you here like this, I can think only of your grandmother Leigh."

"Why do you say that, Tony?"

"The way you look—young, innocent, so soft, and your hair . . ."

I was beginning to regret agreeing to the change of color. Perhaps because of it, Tony often didn't see *me* when he looked at me.

"I'd better get dressed, Tony," I said.

"Yes, of course." He stood up and wheeled me out of the bathroom to the bed, where he had laid out the blue cotton dress. "I'll help you," he said, and moved quickly to get me a pair of panties and a bra. He squatted before me again.

"I can do this, Tony." I reached for my panties, but he simply lifted my feet and slipped the undergarment over my ankles, moving it up my legs slowly, his gaze fixed, his fingers never touching my skin. When he reached my thighs, he stopped and came around behind me. There was no stopping him. Using his forearms, he lifted me just enough to pull the panties into place. I closed my eyes to deny what was happening. He started to unwrap the towel.

"Tony, please, let me do this."

"I'll just assist," he insisted, and brought my bra around. I shoved my arms through quickly, but when I started to fasten it, his hands moved over mine and quickly took over. "And now for the finish," he announced, and came around to the front with the dress.

"Tony, I don't think this dress—"

"Just lift your arms. It'll be easy."

Reluctantly, realizing it was the easiest way to bring all this to an end, I lifted my arms and let him bring the dress down over my head. He lifted and adjusted my body so he could pull the dress on completely, and then he stood back.

"See? Nothing to any of it. I'll be here every morning to help you, Annie."

"Every morning? But surely we'll have another nurse by tomorrow."

"I hope so, but I'm going to be a great deal more careful about whom I hire now. We don't want another Mrs. Broadfield, do we?" He smiled and then clapped his hands. "Now let me see about your breakfast," he added, and hurried out of the room, energized by all he had done and all he had to do.

In minutes he reappeared carrying my breakfast tray.

"I hope you're hungry this morning," he said, stepping back.

"Yes. I'm famished." I hoped that was another sign of my recovery.

"I'll just get dressed while you eat," he finally said, and left.

When he returned, he looked quite untidy, much like the way he had appeared in Drake's letter—his hair disheveled, his tie loose, and the tie itself stained. His suit jacket and pants were quite creased. It was as though he had put on an old set of clothes.

"Good morning," he said, as if this were the first time he had seen me this morning. I just stared in amazement, but he didn't seem to notice. He didn't look at me long. Instead he stood rocking on his feet, peering out the window, his hands behind his back. He ran his tongue over his lips, popped his cheeks in and out and nodded. Once again I had the sense he was moving in and out of reality, traveling back and forth between the past and the present. Truly he was beginning to alarm me.

"I feel a lot stronger this morning, Tony," I said, eager to get things back on track so I could contact Luke. "Maybe you will take me on my outing after all."

He spoke, but it wasn't in response to what I was

saying. He acted like a man hearing another conversation.

"I promise you," he began, "I'll give you a home and all that goes with it. . . ."

"Home? I don't understand, Tony. I have a home . . ."

"From what I already know about you, you adapt quickly. I suspect in the long run you will soon be more Bostonian than I myself am, and I was born here." He started to laugh, but stopped, his face hardening as his lips curled. "But I want no hillbilly relatives of yours showing up, not ever. . . ."

"Hillbilly relatives?" I hope he didn't mean Luke. "What are you saying, Tony? You're frightening me."

He blinked quickly, as though he were waking up from a dream right before my eyes. Then he shook his head.

"Tony? Are you all right?"

"What? Oh yes. I'm sorry . . . I was in deep thought. Well, I must get downstairs and tend to a few business matters," he said. "Ryse will be up to take care of your tray," he added, and rushed out of the room.

My heart was pounding. What was wrong with him this morning? Was he having some kind of reaction to what he had done, helping to bathe and to dress me? I was happy when Rye Whiskey appeared, although he didn't look his happy self.

"How are ya this mornin', Miss Annie?"

"I'm feeling a great deal stronger, Rye, thank you." He took the tray and looked like he was going to rush out of the room, too. "Is everything all right with Mr. Tatterton, Rye?"

"He looks all right. He's workin' in his office."

"He said the strangest things to me just before, and for a few moments he acted as though he didn't even know it was me."

"Maybe he was jes' havin' a dream," he said. "When peoples gets to be his age, they're often confused when they first gets up in the mornin'."

"He had already been up some time. And as for age, you're older than Tony, Rye, and you don't get confused in the morning, do you?"

"Yes, ma'am, sometimes I does. 'Specially after last night." I stared at him.

"Last night? Why?" He seemed reluctant to speak. "What's wrong, Rye? Please tell me."

"Old Rye don't speak outa turn, Miss Annie, but are ya stayin' much longer?"

"Not much. I'm getting better quickly."

"Dat's good. The old ghosts been riled up somethin' terrible. I heard them wanderin' about all night last night."

"Oh. The old ghosts?" I smiled.

"Jes' the same, Miss Annie, I hopes you get better fast and gets back to your own home now. Not that old Rye don't want'cha here. You brings back the best memories ta me. I jes' don't want ya haunted none."

"Well, I'll keep my eyes open, Rye." He nodded. I couldn't make him laugh about it. Ghosts and spirits were things he took seriously. He nodded and left with the tray.

To get my mind off these things, I went back to my painting. Perhaps because of my regained strength and new hopeful outlook about myself, I felt like adding color to the work. I concentrated on the trees and foliage in the monument's background and then I found the brightest green for the grass. I made the sky azure blue instead of storm gray. I worked on everything in the picture except the man at the monument.

Sometime, just after lunch, Drake arrived. He came charging into the room like a man hurrying to catch a train and quickly kissed me on the cheek. Ever since he had started working for Tony, he had taken on this frantic pace. It was as if his whole life were fixed on a schedule. I sensed that he had planned out just how much time he would spend with me, and when the gold watch Tony had recently given him announced the hour, he would leave no matter what. Drake seemed so changed, so much more a stranger. I could only hope it wasn't true of Luke as well, that when he finally arrived, I wouldn't find him radically different. That was my biggest fear.

Apparently, no one had told Drake about my improvement.

"You mean no one told you all that has happened? Mrs. Broadfield practically poisoning me to get her way, Tony firing her, my recovery!" I cried in astonishment.

"Well, I haven't seen Tony yet. I just rushed right in and up here. But you tell me. What did the nurse do?"

I described it all quickly. Drake sat back, shaking his head.

"I was never crazy about her, but she came so highly recommended. It just shows you how hard it is to find competent good people out there. I'm finding the same thing in business. I'm doing some hiring, too, you know." He paused and stared at me a moment. Then he smiled. "You do look different, excited, stronger. Now what's this about a recovery?"

"I stood up . . . on my own!" I cried, impatient with his complacency.

"When?" He looked skeptical.

"Last night. I can do it now, but the doctor and Tony are telling me I have to go slowly. Oh, Drake, I don't want to go slowly. I'm so anxious to walk out of here."

He nodded thoughtfully, gazing at me with his eyes narrow and sharp, just the way Tony often did.

"I'm sure what they are telling you, they are telling you for your own good, Annie."

"But it doesn't seem right," I insisted. "I know I can stand. I should be doing it more often, getting my legs used to it again, building their strength. And I should be using that walker," I said, pointing to it in the corner. "What's the point of having it if I don't use it?"

He shrugged.

"It's probably something that has to be done at a certain point or . . . it'll do more harm than good. I don't know, Annie. I'm not going to be a doctor."

"Luke is," I said. He winced as though I had slapped him, but I couldn't help my feelings. "I wish he was here. I don't understand why he's not here," I said and folded my arms across my chest.

"I've left messages."

"He's not getting them." I pouted.

"All of them?"

"It's not like him," I contended.

"People change, especially when they go off to college. I think I told you that."

"Not Luke," I insisted. "Drake, do you care about me? Really care about me?"

"Of course. How could you even ask such a question?"

"Then I want you to wheel me out of here. I'll go downstairs on my chair elevator and you will wheel me to the nearest telephone. I want to call Luke myself now. Tony promised to have a phone installed in this room, but he hasn't done it yet, and I have real doubts that he has made any real attempt to contact Luke for me."

"Why? If he said he tried . . . and if he promised to get you a phone—"

"No, no, he forgets what he says and what he promises. You don't see him the way I do, Drake. I think Tony is somewhat senile, and he's getting worse and worse each passing day."

"What? Now, I've been working with—"

"Listen to me, Drake. Sometimes, when he speaks to me, he gets everything confused . . . talking about my mother, my grandmother, my great-grandmother. He forgets who's dead and who isn't. I'm sorry now that I let him and his beautician talk me into dying my hair this color. It's adding to his confusion." Now that I was telling Drake everything, it all seemed more serious to me than it had been before.

He smiled and shook his head. "Annie, you're the one who's beginning to sound senile."

"No, Drake. There are odd things going on . . . the way he keeps Mommy and Daddy's old suite, and my great-grandmother Jillian's suite . . . as if everyone's still alive. Even Rye Whiskey thinks things are weird. Of course, he talks about ghosts wandering the halls, but he knows things. He wants me to go home!" I exclaimed. All this time, I realized, I was feeling sorry for Tony. I was trying to understand why he was like he was and I was making excuses for it. But now that I listed everything, I realized I should be feeling more sorry for myself. I could be trapped in the home of a madman, not just someone who went into memory lapses from time to time.

"Rye wants you to leave?" Drake shook his head. "Now there's someone senile."

"And Tony keeps Jillian's room like a museum," I continued, feeling desperate for Drake to understand my worries. "He doesn't let anyone in there. It's . . . weird. You should have seen him a short while ago, mumbling about not permitting my hillbilly relatives to come live here . . ." I shook my head. "Do you know all the glass has been taken out of the mirrors in Jillian's room and—"

"Hold on a minute, my head is spinning." He sat back. "Get you downstairs to call Luke, Tony's turned a suite into a museum suite, Tony's confused, you wish you hadn't dyed your hair . . . could this all be because of some medicine you're taking?"

"Drake, aren't you listening to me?" He just stared. "I'm beginning to feel afraid. I want to be cooperative and do what everyone thinks I should, but I can't help wondering what Tony's going to do next."

"Tony?" he said, still disbelieving. "I never met anyone as kind, as loving, as devoted to us as Tony."

"Wheel me out," I demanded. "Now."

"Let me talk to your doctor."

"No," I said quickly, a new possibility coming to mind. "He's under Tony's employ. He does what makes Tony happy." The real possibility of that drove a sword of cold terror through my heart. "My God . . . what if . . ." I looked around the room, frantic now.

"Even the doctor is no good? Annie, you should hear yourself. You're just overwrought because of all you've gone through . . . the accident, your crippled state . . . the service at the tomb . . . I understand how you feel, but you really do have one of the best doctors and you are getting the best possible care here. I'm sure you'll have a new nurse by the end of the day and—"

"Oh, what's the use?" I said, lowering my head. He couldn't see what was going on here, or . . . I raised my head and looked at him. Or he didn't want to see because he was so happy about the new executive position Tony had given him. He was in love with his own power and authority. In a real sense, Tony had done something he had done before—he had bought Drake. "You just won't listen. I thought I could depend on you. With my parents gone, you and Luke and Aunt Fanny . . ."

I felt sick inside, sick and alone. My heart felt hollow, an echo chamber filled with my empty cries, cries that would be heard by no one because the people who had once really loved me were dead. Even Luke seemed dead to me now.

"Look," he said, reaching out to take my hands quickly, "I'm on my way to New York. I've got a rather big project all on my own to run. I'll be gone a few days and then I'll come right back here, and if you still feel the same way about all this, I'll take you back to Winnerrow myself."

"Will you? Promise?" Somehow, I didn't hold much hope for that.

"Of course. I'll simply take charge of your recovery myself, get our own doctors, our own nurses—"

"Oh, Drake, I wish you could do that now."

"Just give it a few more days, Annie. You might be jumping the gun here, and we could set you back by starting all over again. You've got to be sure it's the right decision, but . . . if you are, I promise to help you."

He kissed me softly on the cheek and held me to him, and then he jumped up as if a buzzer had gone off in his businessman's head.

"I've got a plane to catch."

"But Drake, I thought you would at least take me downstairs to call Luke."

"There's really no point in calling him and calling him. He'll come when he wants to come."

"Drake, please," I begged, really begged to make him understand how important this was to me.

He gazed down at me a moment and then nodded.

"I'll speak to Tony on the way out. He's sure to do it."

"But Drake—"

"Keep your chin up, Annie. Everything will be all right. You'll see. At least you've gone back to your painting," he said, pointing to the easel. He didn't even go over to look at my work. He smiled quickly, like some automated functionary, and waved as he

306

backed quickly out of the room, obviously afraid I was going to insist on something that might bring him into a conflict with Tony. I was so disappointed in him, Drake, the uncle who had been more like a big brother to me, now acting more like some stranger.

In a moment he was gone and I was left with the silence that made me more aware of my helplessness. I was alone once more, trapped like a wounded animal in a gilded cage.

More determined than ever, I wheeled myself to the door and opened it. Then I wheeled myself through the sitting room and opened the outside door. I wheeled down the corridor toward the stairway. Looking down, I saw there was no one below, but my second wheelchair was just where Tony had promised it would be—next to the foot of the stairway. I unfastened and lifted up the chair arm so I could pull myself into the elevator chair just the way Tony and the technician had shown me. Securely in it, the belt fastened, I pressed the down button and began to descend. My heart was pounding, but I was determined to be rebellious, determined to end this state of imprisonment.

The chair came to a halt at the bottom of the stairway and I worked my way into the wheelchair that waited. Encouraged by my success so far, I began to wheel myself over the carpeted corridor toward Tony's office.

The office door was slightly open. I paused, heard nothing from within, but pushed on anyway. A single small reading lamp was on at the desk, but other than that, the room was relatively dark, the closed curtains locking out the afternoon sunlight. I looked around. There was no one there. Where had Tony gone? I sat back in my chair, frustrated. Then my eyes settled on the phone on Tony's desk.

Finally, an opportunity to speak with Luke myself! I wheeled myself to the desk. It wasn't until I picked up the receiver that I realized I had no idea how to reach him. I had no number. What was the name of the dormitory he was living in? Drake had never told me.

I dialed information and asked for Harvard. The operator, annoyed with my lack of specifics, began reading off a list of possible offices. When she mentioned the housing administration, I stopped her. A tape-recorded voice came on and recited a number. I called and explained what I wanted as soon as someone answered. The secretary was very kind. She told me most of the students hadn't gotten their phones hooked up in their rooms yet, but she gave me the number of the phone on Luke's dorm floor. I thanked her and dialed again.

A young man answered. He sounded like a Bostonian, a younger version of Tony.

"I need to speak with Luke Casteel. This is his cousin Annie. It's urgent."

"Wait one moment, please."

I waited, watching the office doorway, expecting Tony to arrive any moment. I couldn't help feeling that I was doing something he would disapprove of. I hated the idea that a mere phone call seemed so adventurous.

"Miss?"

"Yes?"

"Luke Casteel is in class now. His roommate said he would tell him you called."

"Oh, but . . . please, tell him more. Please," I begged.

"Why, of course. What would you like me to tell him?"

"Tell him . . . tell him I need him desperately, and no matter what anyone says, he should come to Farthy immediately."

"Farthy?"

"Yes, he'll understand. Make sure you say immediately. It's very, very important."

"And this is Annie?"

"Yes."

"Okay, I'll give the message to his roommate, who will most assuredly give it to him."

"Thank you."

"You're very welcome."

I cradled the phone. My heart had started to pound again, thumping so hard I thought it would burst out of my chest. The excitement gave me a cold flush. I felt the beads of sweat that had broken out on the back of my neck.

I straightened up in my chair and caught my breath, forcing myself to calm down. Where was Tony? He had told me he was coming down here to do business in his office. Maybe he had gone to get a new nurse. I wheeled myself out to the corridor again and listened. The house was so quiet.

I went to the front door and opened it. Sunlight burst in upon me like a wave of warm water. I blinked and then closed my eyes and lay back as if I were on a beach. How wonderful to feel the fresh air and the warmth after having been locked in a room so long! It filled me with strength and hope. My heart grew stronger, and as the blood pulsated more quickly around my body, my limbs felt whole and well again.

I sat up and rolled my chair forward and out onto the portico, and there it was, just as Tony had described: a wooden ramp. But it looked so steep. Dare I try to wheel myself down it? What would happen when I wanted to wheel myself back up? I wondered.

Fear gripped me. I had gone too far, I thought. Now I was doing too much. But as I remained there in the opened doorway staring at the ramp, I thought of Luke. I could hear him telling me, "Go for the tall ones." What was I going to do now . . . turn back and retreat to my room, beaten down?

I was strong enough, I told myself. My body wasn't going to disappoint me. Slowly, I wheeled myself to the ramp. How my heart was pounding! But I refused to be defeated. I had to do it.

The wheels went up. I tottered at the top of the ramp and then . . . I began to descend. My arms were barely strong enough to keep the wheels from spinning on their own. It did take more effort than I had anticipated to keep the chair straight and in control, but I reached the bottom and spilled off onto the walkway. I had done it!

I had done all this and still felt able to go on.

I looked down to my right, but the sounds of someone talking turned me to the left. Most likely Tony was out there overseeing some work, I thought, and I began to wheel down the walkway to my left. The pitted stone made it difficult at times, but I found a smooth rhythm and took myself a good five hundred feet from the front of Farthy before pausing.

I saw a handyman down by the pool. He carried what looked like a lounge chair into the storage building. There was no one else around. For a few moments I stared at the large gazebo and thought about Luke. At least I felt sure now he would get my message. He would understand how important it was for him to come, how desperate I had been. Perhaps he had felt I had deserted him because he hadn't heard directly from me for so long. Perhaps I had been wrong, horribly wrong, to think bad thoughts about him, to accept Drake's assertion that Luke had changed just because he was at college and meeting new people, especially new girls. He would come here immediately, I knew he would.

How I wished I was gazing upon my own gazebo in

Winnerrow now. How I wished Luke were already here, waiting for me.

Behind this gazebo and farther off to the left was the maze. Seeing it from a seated position in my wheelchair, I recalled what Drake had said about it looking so large because he was so small that first time he had seen it. It did look large, formidable, mysterious; yet I couldn't help being drawn to it, wanting to wander through it, just as I imagined my mother and her mother must have done.

"Would you like to go in there?" a voice asked. I nearly jumped out of my wheelchair. I struggled to turn to the right so I could see who was suddenly behind me. It took me a few moments, for he didn't help me. But finally, by backing up and turning and backing up again, I got myself around. At first I saw no one and thought I had imagined someone speaking.

Then he stepped out from behind a tall hedge.

Shadows still draped his face, but I knew immediately I was looking up at the mysterious man who had knelt alone at my parents' monument. It was as if he had stepped out of my paintings and drawings, stepped out of my imagination and now stood before me in the real world.

311

NINETEEN

The Other Side of the Maze

Who are you?" I gazed up at him in fascination. He had stepped out of the shadows and stood before me with his hands in his pants pockets. Although he was tall and lean, his shoulders were broad. He had unruly copper-brown hair that was graying along his temples, long hair that curled up at the ends, just brushing the white collar of his thin artist's smock with very full sleeves.

I thought he had very fine facial features, not pretty-boy fine; more like the features carved on the face of a Greek statue. He tilted his head a bit to the side and one of his dark, thick eyebrows lifted as he considered me. He was looking at me so intensely that I became very self-conscious. Something he saw in me was affecting him, moving him. His eyes grew small, like Tony's eyes when they took on that faraway look just before he would babble and confuse past and present. Why didn't he speak? I began to tremble, naturally feeling threatened by his unwillingness even to say hello. I looked toward the house, but no one had followed me out; no one knew I was here.

When I turned back to him, I saw that his lips curved into a smile, and there was something in that smile and in those dark brown eyes that made me feel warm and safe.

"You don't have to tell me who you are," he said, his voice soft, soothing, almost loving. "You are Heaven's daughter. Although, you look more like Leigh with that hair color. Tell me, is it your natural color or did you dye it as your mother once did?"

"Who are you?" I demanded more emphatically now. I saw in his eyes that he was thinking, deciding whether to continue to speak to me or just to rush off. Something he couldn't overcome kept him at my side.

"Me? I'm . . . Brothers. Timothy Brothers."

"But who are you? I mean, how do you know my mother and her mother? And how did you know she once dyed her hair?"

"I work for Mr. Tatterton."

I sat back. He certainly didn't look like one of the handymen, and Rye had told me there was no one with this man's description working on the grounds. Of course, Rye could be forgetful, too, I thought, but I didn't think this man did hard labor. There was a softness about him, a gentleness that suggested a contemplative nature.

"Oh? And what do you do for Mr. Tatterton?"

"I . . . create toys."

"Create toys?"

"Don't look so surprised, Annie. Someone has to do it."

"How did you know my name?" I asked with surprise.

"Oh, by now everyone knows your name. Mr. Tatterton talks so much about you."

I continued to gaze into his eyes. I sensed that there was a lot more mystery to this man than he was willing to reveal.

"And what were you doing here in the hedges, or is that where you create toys?"

He threw his head back and laughed.

"Hardly, no. I was taking a walk when I saw you coming down the walkway."

"Where do you live? Farthy, too?"

"No. I live on the other side of the maze. That's where I create the toys."

"The other side of the maze? Isn't that where . . . isn't there a cottage there?" I asked quickly.

"Oh, you know about the cottage?" I nodded. "Because your mother told you about it?"

"No. She didn't tell me very much about Farthy; she never liked to talk about it."

He nodded slowly, his face turning sad. He shifted his eyes away, gazing toward the Tatterton family cemetery. There was something in the way he held his shoulders that reminded me of myself whenever I was feeling melancholy. After a moment he took his right hand out of his pocket and brushed back his hair. His fingers looked long, sensitive, strong, the fingers of an artist. They were quite similar to my own. Perhaps certain people were born to be artistic, I thought.

"I'm very sorry about what happened to your parents," he said, almost under his breath. He didn't look at me when he spoke.

"Thank you."

"So?" He looked up quickly. "You know about the maze, too, I take it. I couldn't help but notice how you were looking at it."

"It looks so mysterious."

"Like anything, it is for those who don't know it. Would you like to go through it?"

"Through it? You mean . . . to the other side?"

"Why not?" He looked up at the blue sky streaked here and there with strokes of long thin clouds. "It's a nice day for a walk. I'd be glad to wheel you about."

I hesitated to say yes, even though I was most eager to experience the maze and certainly wanted to see the cottage, for despite Mr. Brothers's pleasant and friendly way, he was still a complete stranger. What would everyone say to my going off with him like this? I wondered. On the other hand, he did work for Tony, and Tony was going to be upset that I had left the house, anyway. I might as well add a side trip, especially this side trip.

"All right," I said. He saw the way I was looking around furtively.

"Mr. Tatterton doesn't know you are out here?"

"No, but I don't care," I said defiantly.

"You've inherited your mother's spirit, I see." He came around my chair and took hold of the handles.

"You knew her well?"

"Yes. I knew her well. She was about your age when I met her, too."

"You mean you've been working for Tony all this time? Making toys?"

"Yes." He was behind me now, pushing the chair along, so I couldn't see his face, but his voice had grown even softer.

"But I thought his brother Troy was the one who designed all the toys then."

"Oh, he was. I'm just making replicas of his designs. He taught me everything I know."

"I see." I sensed he wasn't being quite truthful. "Did you work in the cottage, too? Or did you work in a factory?"

"Both."

"Where did you meet my mother?" We were getting closer and closer to the entrance to the maze, and I thought I would talk to cloak my fear.

"Here and there." He stopped pushing me. He seemed to sense the anxiety in me. "Are you sure you want to go on?"

I didn't answer immediately. The hedges were so high and thick, the pathways through the maze were dark and looked so deep. What if this man didn't really know his way and we got lost?

"You're sure you can go in and find your way out?" He laughed.

"Blindfolded. Maybe one day I'll do it just to show you I can. But if you're afraid . . ."

"No, no, I want to go on," I said, forcing myself to be brave.

"Very well, then. Here we go," he said, and pushed me forward into the great English maze. I was actually going into it! Something that had been a fantasy for much of my life was about to happen! Once again I longed for Luke to be with me. I sat back, holding my breath, and soon we were walled up in a castle of shiny green ivy.

It was pretty in the maze, the hedges growing as tall as ten feet and making precise right-angle turns. Of course, like most of the greenery about Farthy, it needed trimming and care. But it was dark and green and soothing in there, and I felt the tension of the day, the worry, the fear, the struggle ease away from me.

"What do you think so far?" he asked as soon as we had made our first turn and gone in deeper.

"It's so quiet. I can barely hear the garden birds chirping."

"Yes, the peaceful serenity is what I love about the maze."

I looked up. Even the plaintive shrieks of the sea gulls flying overhead seemed muffled, faraway. He paused as we made another turn.

"Are you seated too low to see the roof of Farthy?"

"No, I can just make it out above the hedge. It looks so far off already."

"In the maze you can pretend you're on a different world. I often do," he confessed. "Do you like to pretend, to live in fantasy from time to time?"

"Yes, very much. Luke and I often did that, and if we were both home now, we probably still would, even though we would seem too old for it."

"Luke?"

"My . . . cousin . . . my aunt Fanny's son Luke Junior."

"Oh, yes . . . your aunt Fanny. I had forgotten about her."

"You knew her, too!"

"I knew of her," he said.

He knew more than he was saying. I could tell. Who was this man? Had I been too adventurous to accept his invitation so quickly? We were heading deeper and deeper into the great maze. I wrapped my arms about myself protectively. Part of me wanted to go right back to the house, but a stronger part of me wanted to see the cottage, wanted to know more about this mysterious, fascinating man.

"Are you cold? It does get quite cool in here."

"I'm okay. Is it going to be much longer?"

"Only a few minutes more. We take this turn and then that and then go straight into another turn and another and then we'll be on the other side."

"I can see how someone could easily get lost."

"People do. Your mother once did."

"She did? She never told me about it."

He laughed.

"The first time I saw her. She couldn't find her way back."

"Please tell me about that," I begged. "She was so reluctant to talk about her days at Farthy."

317

"It was the first time she had gone into the maze. I was working in the cottage—making little suits of armor for tiny knights, I think—when suddenly she appeared at the door. She looked innocent and lost, almost like an angel who had stepped out of the mist . . . so beautiful and so full of determination. It was very foggy that day and had grown dark quickly She was afraid she wouldn't find her way back."

"Was Troy there, too?"

"Yes, he was."

"Well, what happened next?" I asked, impatien† with his dramatic pauses.

"Oh, we calmed her down. Gave her something to eat, as I recall, and then directed her back through the maze."

"It's funny to think of my mother as a young girl.'

"She was a very beautiful young lady, much like yourself."

"I'm not feeling particularly beautiful these days. though."

"You will. I'm sure. Well, here we are, one more turn." We went around a corner and emerged from the maze.

Before us lay a path of pale flagstone lined with tall pines. Directly ahead was the small stone cottage with a red slate roof crouched low amidst the pine trees. I couldn't keep the small cry from escaping through my lips.

It was Mommy's toy cottage, the one she had given me on my eighteenth birthday. The Tatterton replica was exact. How eerie, I thought. It was as if I had just stepped into a fantasy world, truly a toy world where people lived their dreams.

Oh, I thought, if only Luke were here. He would see that all our make-believe could come true. Those two toy figures in the toy cottage really would be us

There was the knee-high picket fence, not meant to keep anything out, winding its crooked way around the cottage, giving support to climbing roses just the way they were in the replica.

Unlike the rest of Farthy, the grounds around the cottage were well cared for, maintained with a loving hand . . . grass rich and trim, the fence whitewashed, the walk clean and smooth, the windows glistening.

"Well . . . there's the cottage."

"Oh, it belongs in a picture book. How I wish I could come here to paint it!" I exclaimed.

"You paint?"

"Oh yes. Painting is my passion. I'm even doing it now while I recuperate. I want to study art and work on my talent forever and ever," I added hopefully.

"Of course. Of course," he repeated, once again sounding distant, lost in his own memories. "Well, then maybe you will paint it someday. Why not?"

"Can we go inside?" I asked.

"Certainly, but won't they be missing you back at Farthy by now?"

"I don't care. I feel like a prisoner in there, anyway. Please, take me into the cottage."

He pushed me forward down the path of flagstone to the front door, opened it and then wheeled me in. There were Tatterton Toys everywhere, on shelves and on the mantel above the fireplace, and at least a half-dozen antique clocks, all on time. As if to punctuate this realization, the grandfather clock in the corner struck the hour and the light blue music-box clock that was shaped like the cottage itself opened its front door. The tiny family within emerged and then retreated to a sweet, haunting melody, a melody that was familiar.

It was the same melody that played whenever the roof of the toy cottage back at Winnerrow was lifted:

Chopin's nocturne. We looked at one another as the melody came to an end.

"My mother had a toy cottage that looked exactly like this cottage, with the hedges and the pine trees, and it played the same tune. She gave it to me on my eighteenth birthday. It is as old as I am and it still works. Someone sent it to her right after I was born."

"Yes," he said. He could barely utter the word. He looked frightened, his eyes a little wider. Then his expression changed and he looked very sad, his head tilted as he went into deep thought for a moment. Suddenly he realized I was staring, and smiled.

I turned away quickly and continued to inspect the cottage. It was quaint, cozy, and warm, as I imagined a gardener's cottage might be. Although the furniture was old, none of it looked worn. Shelves, floors, curtains—everything looked neat and clean, looked like it belonged in the home of a meticulous person. There were really only two rooms, and in the living room right before the fireplace was a long table, covered with tiny pieces of metal, tools, and what was an unfinished toy medieval village. The church with its spiral roof and stained-glass windows was completed. There was even a priest standing in the doorway waving hello to his approaching parishioners. There were shops and fine stone houses and the huts of the poorer folk. Some tiny wagons drawn by horses were only partially completed, as were some of the buildings and walkways.

"I have some ice tea, if you'd like."

"Yes, please." I wheeled myself into the living room to look more closely at the Tatterton Toy village.

"That one's taking me a lot longer because I keep adding something here and there," he explained.

"It's so beautiful, so lifelike! I love it. Look at how you've captured the expressions on their faces. No two are the same." I looked up and caught him gazing intently at me, a soft and wonderful smile on his face. He realized how he was staring.

"Oh . . . the tea. One moment," he said, and went into the kitchen. I sat back and looked around the cottage.

"Here you go," he said, coming over quickly to hand the ice tea to me. I took it but didn't drink it. He tried to avoid my eyes, and turned away to busy himself putting tools back in their little niches on the wall.

"You're the man I saw from the window of my room," I declared.

"Oh?"

"I saw you at my parents' monument, didn't I?"

"I stopped there once, yes."

"More than once," I insisted.

"Maybe more than once." He flashed a smile and sat on the wooden rocker beside the fireplace. He put his hands behind his head, his long slender legs stretched out, and looked up at the ceiling. Now that I studied his profile, I saw that he was quite good-looking in a special way. He radiated a sensitivity that reminded me of Luke when Luke was his most loving, most intense and poetic self.

"My walks are my only form of exercise these days. I wander all about the grounds."

"You were at the service, too. I saw you," I said pointedly. "Why couldn't you come out of the woods and stand beside the other mourners?"

"Oh . . . I'm just shy. So," he said, anxious to change the topic, "how is your recuperation coming along?"

"But why wouldn't you want to be seen there? Are you afraid of Tony?"

"No." He smiled.

"I can't understand why you keep yourself so . . . so hidden, then."

"It's just my way. I suppose there's something peculiar about all of us if we care to look closely. I'm the type who likes being by himself."

"But why?" I pursued.

"Why?" He laughed. "You do hang on once something bothers you, don't you? Just like your mother."

"I don't understand how you know so much about her if you like to keep to yourself all the time."

He laughed again.

"I can see where I'm going to have to keep my life's secrets well undercover when you're around. I like to keep to myself," he said quietly, "but I did like to be with your mother and I do talk to people, just like I'm talking with you right now. Now, tell me about your recovery."

"Yesterday I stood up by myself for the first time since the accident."

"How wonderful!"

"But the doctor and Tony think I should go slowly. No one tried to get me to stand up today, and I have yet to use the walker. They keep insisting I take naps and sleeping pills and remained locked away from people. This is the first time I've been out of the house since, and I've been here nearly a week! I can't even call anyone and talk. I have no phone!" I cried.

"Oh?"

"I haven't seen my cousin Luke since I left the hospital, which is six days now. I sent him messages through Tony and Drake."

"Drake?"

"My mother's half brother."

"Oh yes, Luke Senior's son."

"You seem to know a lot about my family for a worker . . . an assistant at that," I said suspiciously.

"I'm just a good listener when people talk around me."

"What a remarkable memory for details you have.'

I narrowed my eyes to show him I thought there was a lot more he wasn't telling me.

He smiled, a boyish smile.

"And what happened to Luke?"

"He hasn't called or come. I wheeled myself into Tony's office and called Luke's dorm at Harvard and left a message for him with his roommate before I came outside."

"I see. Well, I'm sure he'll soon pay you a visit, then."

"I don't know. Everyone's different . . . Drake is . . . in love with being a businessman, working for Tony, and Luke would never ignore me before. We've grown up together and we have always been very close. I've told him things other girls would never dare tell another boy, and he's told me things boys would never dare tell girls. Because we're special to each other," I emphasized. He nodded thoughtfully. "We're more than just cousins." I paused. For some reason I felt I could share the family secrets with this man. I sensed his sincerity and I felt so comfortable in his presence. It was as if I had known him all my life. Complete strangers in Winnerrow knew about Luke. Why not him? I thought. "Luke and I have the same father," I finally blurted.

"I see," he said, but he showed no surprise at the revelation.

"You don't see. No one could see how hard it is, how hard it has been," I cried. "Especially for Luke. He's had so many, many obstacles to overcome, mountains to climb. People can be very cruel sometimes, especially in small towns like Winnerrow. They won't let you forget the sins of your . . ."

"Sins of your fathers?" he offered.

"Yes."

"Luke must have grown into a very extraordinary young man for you to care so much for him."

323

"Oh, he did. He's so bright. He was the class valedictorian! And he's thoughtful and polite. Everyone who's fair loves Luke and respects him, too! Mommy loved him. It was hard for her, but she cared just as much for him as she would have had he been her own son," I declared firmly.

"Tell me about your hair. When did you dye it? You did dye it?"

"Yes."

"When?"

"A few days ago, Tony brought a beautician to Farthy and talked me into doing it. He thought looking brighter would make me feel better about myself."

"Tony had you do this?" I saw the concern in his face.

"Yes. Why do you ask?"

"How has Tony . . . Mr. Tatterton, been these days? I haven't seen him for a while."

"Strange. He's forgetful and he confuses things."

"Confuses? Like what?"

"He often mixes me up with my mother, my grandmother . . . even my great-grandmother Jillian."

"How do you mean?" He leaned forward in his chair, his graceful hands clasped together, his arms resting on his knees.

"He talks to me as though he's talking to one of them, mentioning things I wouldn't know or remember."

He gazed at me, that look of concern firmly planted in his face. "How long will you remain here at Farthy?"

"The intention was for me to remain until I was fully recuperated, but I told Drake today that I want to go home and recuperate there." All the pent-up feelings of being imprisoned, of having been tormented by a cruel nurse, and now living with Tony, who moved from one world to another, flooded over me. "I do!"

"Then you should go. If you're not happy here, if you're not comfortable, you'd better go," he said, but so intensely, his eyes so determined, that I suddenly felt very frightened.

"Who are you . . . really? You know too much about this family to be a mere employee."

He sat back again and gazed at me for a long moment. My heart was pounding now, for I knew I was right.

"If I tell you, will you keep the knowledge locked away, for it is very important to me that few, if any, people know. I am happy here living an anonymous life, protected by the maze. My solitude is very precious and important to me. I am happy living with my memories and my work, which, as you can see, can take up a great deal of my time." He paused and said, very sadly, "It's the life I've chosen for myself. I didn't think I would live this long, anyway."

"Why not? You're not very old."

"No, I'm not very old, but when I was younger, I was sickly and I had dreams I would die very young . . . I wouldn't live past thirty. But I did. Death refused to claim me. I don't question why; I go on, doing what I do, living this quiet life, content with what I have. In a way I've made peace with myself, with all my fears and sorrows. My past is like an old wound that's healed; I don't want to do anything to open it up again." He fixed his eyes on me, his soft, warm eyes, which urged me to trust him.

"So . . . can you keep a secret as important as this one?"

"Oh yes," I assured him.

"I think you can. I don't know why I should feel this way, but I trust you . . . just as I would trust . . . my own daughter, had I gotten married and had a daughter."

"My mother always taught me to respect what is precious to other people, even though the same things may not be precious to me."

"She would tell you that."

"There, you see. You knew her too well to be a mere employee."

He smiled.

"I should have remained in the shadows, Annie. I should have known you would see the truth."

"What is the truth?" I waited, holding my breath.

"I am not Troy Tatterton's assistant; I am Troy Tatterton."

Strange how Troy's revelation didn't shock me as much as it should have, for everyone had told me of his death and spoke of him as long gone. Yet it was as if I had somehow always known.

"When Rye Whiskey sees you, he probably thinks he's seeing one of his spirits," I said.

"Rye." He smiled. "I'm not sure what he thinks, but I suppose you're right."

"But now that you have told me the truth about who you are, will you tell me why you have let everyone believe you are dead and gone?" I asked.

"Has anyone ever told you the circumstances of my supposed passing?" He eyed me carefully after he asked.

"I've learned a little here and there; I learned the most from Rye Whiskey, but I don't know how much of what Rye tells me is true and how much is in his vivid imagination. I know you rode a horse—Jillian's horse—into the sea and were never seen or heard from again."

"Yes, that part is so."

"How did such a thing happen?"

There was a smile around his eyes again.

"When you ask like that—so passionately—you remind me so much of your mother when she was your age. I think you are just as attentive a listener. Will you listen?" he asked, sitting back again.

I nodded, somehow scared by his new, serious tone of voice.

"What I told you was true: I was a sickly, melancholy child and teenager. All my young life I was depressed by heavy, sad thoughts. My brother Tony, who was more like a father to me, tried his best to get me to change, to be more hopeful and optimistic, but it was as if a gray cloud had been planted over my head when I was born and it grew wider and wider and wider until one day, when I looked up, all I could see was an overcast sky, no matter how bright and blue a day it was.

"Can you understand that?"

I shook my head because I couldn't. I couldn't understand how anyone could go on living his life forever under overcast skies. Sunlight was so important; it was important to flowers and trees and grass and birds, and especially to young children who needed to bathe in its loving warmth. How else would anything grow? He anticipated my thought.

"I couldn't grow into a healthy young man, not with these doomsday thoughts hanging over my head all the time. The worse I became, the more concerned Tony became and the more time and energy he devoted to me. His wife Jillian was a self-centered woman who was in love with only her own image in the mirror and expected everyone around her to be so enamored. You can't imagine how jealous she was of anyone or anything that would pull Tony's attention from her, even for a moment.

"So, eventually I moved into this cottage to live and to work on the Tatterton Toys. It was a very lonely existence; most anyone would have gone mad, I know, but I wasn't as lonely as you might think, for I made my toys my world, my tiny people my people, and imagined stories about their lives."

He shifted his eyes about the room, gazing at some of the toys, and laughed.

"Maybe I was mad. Who knows? It was a good madness, though. Anyway," he said, leaning forward again, "I was plagued by thoughts of my own death. Winter was an especially difficult time because the nights were so long, giving too much time for too many dreams to be born. I would try to hold back sleep until just before dawn. Sometimes, I succeeded. If I saw I couldn't, I would walk about outside and let the fresh cold air wash my dreary thoughts away. I would walk the trails between the pines, and when my brain was cleared, only then did I come back in here and try to sleep again."

"Why did you stay here during the winter? You were rich enough to go anywhere you wanted, weren't you?"

"Yes. I tried to escape. I spent winters in Florida, in Naples, the Riviera, all over the world. I traveled and traveled, searching for an avenue of escape, but my winter thoughts were like excess baggage, always with me. I couldn't shake them off, no matter what I did or where I went, so I returned defeated, unable to do anything but accept my fate.

"Along about that time, your mother came along. She was a flower planted in the desert . . . a cheerful, bright and beautiful person. I knew she had been through hard times already during her young life, but she seemed to be able to cling to that optimism and innocence that characterizes young people, that makes older people so envious.

"You have that same wonderful light in your eyes, Annie. I can see it. Even though some terrible, horrible things have happened to you and the people you love, that brightness is still there, burning like a large candle in a dark tunnel. Someone very lucky will be guided by your light out of the darkness of his own sad thoughts and will live happily in the warmth of your glow. I know it."

I couldn't help blushing. Few men had ever spoken to me this way.

"Thank you," I said. "But you haven't told me what drove you to ride a horse into the sea."

He sat back and tucked his hands behind his head again. I could see that was his favorite position. For a long moment he thought, his eyes fixed on the ceiling. I was patient, for I could sense how difficult it had to be for someone to explain why he had wanted to end his life. Finally, he sat forward again.

"Seeing your mother, seeing the brightness and the life, filled me with some hope for myself in those days, and for a while I was different. I even thought . . . believed it was possible for me to find someone like her and marry and raise children . . . a daughter much like yourself, perhaps.

"But my melancholy returned when I could find no one like her. I was depressing to most women, you see, for most didn't have the patience to deal with my temperament. One day, during a party that Tony had arranged to cheer me up, I decided I would turn the tables on Death . . . Death who had pursued me my entire life, Death who sat in the shadows smirking, waiting, haunting me with his dark, gray eyes, his patient posture . . . waiting for his opportunity. I decided to take the opportunity away. Instead of spending my life attempting to flee from what I knew would be his inevitable grasp, I charged forward at him and so surprised him with my action, he did not know how to react. I rode Jillian's wild horse into the sea, fully expecting to end my wretched existence.

"But as I said, Death was surprised and couldn't take me. I was cast back on the shore, alive. I had failed even at this.

"However, I realized I had given myself an opportunity to escape in a different way. I let everyone believe I had died. It enabled me to become someone else, to move about like a shadow and not be troubled by people who wanted to cheer me up. I only depressed them anyway, because when they failed, they had to contend with me in my gray, dark state of mind.

"This way I bothered no one and no one bothered me. But one day my brother discovered my existence. He had been mourning my death so hard anyway that I could no longer keep my life from him. We made a pact . . . I would live here, anonymously, and he would maintain the fiction of my death. After a number of years had passed, when most anyone who had known me had left or died, we told people I was a new artisan, creating toys in Troy's style.

"And so, no one bothers me and I can continue as I am, as I told you: working, living in my memories and my peaceful solitude.

"Now you know the truth and I am dependent upon your promise to keep it locked in your heart."

"I won't tell anyone, but I wish you would come back to the world on the other side of the maze. I wish, somehow, I could bring you back."

"How sweet you are sitting there in your wheelchair wishing you could help someone else."

We gazed at one another. There were tears locked in the corners of his eyes, for he knew that if he released them, my own tears would come bursting forth.

"Now," he said suddenly, clapping his hands together. "You say you stood on your own yesterday?"

"Yes."

"Well, you should be standing a little more every day, and you should be taking steps."

"That's what I thought, but the doctor said—"

"Doctors may know some things about the human body, but they often don't know enough about the human heart." He got up and stood about two feet in front of me, just far enough away for him to hold out his arms. "I want you to stand again, and this time, I want you to try to take a step toward me."

"Oh, I don't know . . . I . . ."

"Nonsense, Annie Stonewall. You get to your feet. You're Heaven's daughter, and Heaven would not sit there pitying herself, nor would she remain at the mercy of other people long."

He said magic words. I swallowed hard and bit down gently on my lower lip. Then I took hold of the arms of the chair and willed my feet to move from the footpads to the floor. Slowly, scraping along, they did so. Troy nodded encouragement. I closed my eyes and willed all the pressure I could down my legs.

"Make your feet one with the floor of the cottage," he whispered. "The soles of your feet are glued to that floor. Glued . . ."

I felt myself pushing. There was pressure there. My legs tightened, the wobbly muscles stretched, and I pushed down on the arms of the chair. Slowly, even better and smoother than yesterday, my body rose into a standing position. I opened my eyes. Troy smiled.

"Good. Now don't be afraid. Move your legs forward. Let go of the arms of the chair."

"I can't help being afraid. If I should fall . . ."

"You won't fall. I won't let you, Annie. Walk to me, walk to me," he chanted, holding his hands out just far enough away so that it would take one or two steps to reach him. "Walk to me . . . come to me, Annie."

Maybe it was that plea, something in the sound of his voice so similar to the voice in my own dreams calling me out of the darkness and into the light, that gave me the will and the strength to attempt it. Whatever it was, it was enough. I felt my trembling right leg move just a little bit forward, the foot barely lifting from the floor. My left leg followed suit.

It was a step! A step!

I took one more and then my body failed me. It softened with the effort and I felt myself falling. But I fell for only a moment because Troy's arms were around me, holding me securely to him.

"You did it! You did it, Annie! You're on your way back. Nothing can stop you now!"

I couldn't hold back my tears. I was crying a rainbow of happiness, colored blue and yellow, and a veil of sadness, colored gray. I cried because of my success and I cried because I was in the arms of someone who I now knew could be warm and loving, but who was trapped in a world of dark days.

He helped me to return to my chair and then stood back, gazing down at me as proudly as a parent who had seen his baby take her first steps.

"Thank you."

"It is I who should thank you, Annie. You made the clouds part enough for some sunlight to come into my world today. But," he said, looking at the grandfather clock, "I had better get you back. If, as you say, they don't know where you are, they must be frantic with worry by now."

All I could do was nod. I was feeling exhausted, and the prospect of lying in that big, comfortable bed upstairs in Farthy seemed surprisingly inviting.

"Will you come to see me?" I begged him. My days at Farthy seemed suddenly brighter with the prospect of Troy to help pass the hours.

"No. You'll come to see me . . . on your own, very soon, I'm sure."

"And after I leave Farthy and return to Winnerrow, will you pay me a visit?"

"I don't know, Annie. I don't leave the cottage very much these days."

He started to wheel me out. The afternoon sun had fallen considerably since we had come through the maze and entered the cottage. Now long shadows were painted over the little lawn and garden. The maze looked much darker and deeper.

"You're cold," Troy said. "Wait." He went back into the cottage and reappeared carrying a light eggshell-white cardigan sweater. I put it on quickly. "Better?"

"Yes, thank you."

This time when we entered the maze, I felt as if I were moving through some dark boundary between a happy world and a sad one. I longed to be turned around and go back to Troy's cottage. How quickly I had come to trust him and feel comfortable with him.

"Perhaps someday you'll let me help you take your first steps, Troy," I said.

"My first steps. How do you mean that, Annie?"

We rounded a corner.

"Your first steps into the bright warm world where you belong, the world you deserve."

"Oh. Well, maybe you already have. We're both cripples of a sort, I suppose."

"On the way to recovery," I assured him with a smile.

"Yes, on the way to recovery," he agreed.

"Both of us?" I insisted, raising my brows.

"Yes, both of us." He laughed. "I don't think I could remain depressed with you around. You wouldn't tolerate it long; your mother was the same way."

"You'll tell me more about what you remember about her when she was young . . . every time we talk?"

"I will."

"Then we must talk often," I insisted. "Promise?"

"I'll do the best I can."

There was no one outside the house when we emerged from the maze. I was positive they were looking for me by now, but I thought they just couldn't imagine me outside. Of course, they had found my chair by the elevator chair and knew I had come downstairs, but they were sure to be going through the bottom floor first.

"I'll help you up that ramp," Troy said. He pushed me forward and up until we reached the front door. "You're back!" He came around to the front of my chair. "Have a good night, Annie, and thank you. I'll have no nightmares tonight," he added, smiling down at me with a gentle warmth in his eyes.

"Nor will I."

"May I give you a good-bye kiss?"

"Yes, I'd like that."

He leaned down and kissed me softly on the cheek and then he was off. Almost before I could turn around, he was gone, absorbed by the shadows, as if he, too, were merely a phantom dream I'd conjured to wile away the long, lonely hours in Farthinggale Manor.

I opened the great door and wheeled myself into the house. I was halfway through the entryway and on my way to the elevator chair when Tony, accompanied by Parsons and another handyman, appeared.

"Here she is! Well, I'll be darned!" Parsons hollered.

"Where have you been?" Tony demanded. He looked very disheveled, his eyes wild.

"Outside . . . just outside," I said, trying to sound

334

casual, but the more casual I sounded, the angrier Tony became, his eyes brightening with surprising fire and rage.

"Outside? Don't you know what you have put us through, wandering about like this? We've been searching and searching. The whole house has been turned upside down, inside out. You told no one where you were going. I told you I would take you on your first outings. How could you do this on top of all that's happened?" he demanded.

"I wouldn't have done it if I thought I couldn't, but I was able to wheel myself about, and after I tell you all the rest, you'll understand," I replied, quite taken aback by his outburst. This was a side of him he had kept well hidden until now, I thought, the side of Tony Tatterton that made employees shake and servants jump, the ruthless executive who couldn't tolerate anyone going against his wishes and commands.

"Take her upstairs!" he bellowed before I could add another thing. "And don't use the elevator chair. I want her up there quickly! She looks exhausted."

Parsons and the handyman rushed forward at his order and took hold of my chair, wheeling me to the foot of the stairway and lifting me to carry me up the steps.

"Wait, Tony. I don't want to go up yet. I feel trapped in that room. I want to eat downstairs in the dining room tonight and I want to move about freely through this house. I have taken my first steps," I announced proudly.

"First steps? Where? You need your rest, your hot baths, your massages. You don't know what you're doing anymore. The doctor will be enraged. All your progress will be ruined."

"But Tony—"

"Just take her up," Tony repeated. "Quickly."

"Stop this. Put me down," I demanded. Parsons

and the handyman looked at Tony again, but what they saw in his face made them continue.

"Sorry, miss, but if Mr. Tatterton thinks this is best for you, we'd better do it."

"Oh, all right," I said, seeing how I was only putting the servants in a difficult position. "Do what he wants."

"Very good, miss." They lifted me easily and carried me up the stairs.

"You can put me down now," I said when we reached the upstairs floor. "I'll wheel myself to my room."

As I went through the outer door, I pulled it closed behind me. It slammed shut and then I sat in silence, confronting my bed, my walker, my medical facilities. It was all so depressing after being outside. I was determined to end this now. Luke was sure to get my message and come to visit.

And when he did, I would demand he take me home.

And I would leave this place, this house full of ghosts and haunting memories and painful times.

Luke and I had lost our fantasy world, perhaps, but we would have each other. It was that thought and that thought alone that made me determined to leave.

TWENTY

A Prisoner's Escape

Exhausted from my first outing, my efforts to walk, and Tony's dramatic outrage, I wheeled myself to the bed. Just as I lifted myself out of the chair and leaned over the bed, Tony came through the door.

"Annie, you should never, never close your door," he chastised. "How will I know when you need something? And look at you struggling to get back into bed. You should have realized I would be right up to help you." He pulled the wheelchair back and then swung my legs up and onto the bed.

"I can do it myself," I insisted.

"Oh, Annie. You're just like Heaven—stubborn. The two of you could rile up a preacher."

"The two of us?" I swung around. "Mommy's dead . . . dead!" I screamed. I was so tired and so mentally exhausted, I had no tolerance for his confusions.

"I know that, Annie," he said softly, closing and opening his eyes. "I'm sorry, sorry I had to be so

337

rough with you downstairs, but you did a very bad thing, and I was just overwhelmed by it all."

"It's all right, Tony. All right," I said, not wishing to prolong any discussion. I wanted only to get myself into bed, rest, eat my dinner, sleep, and wait for Luke's arrival.

"No, it's not all right, but I'll make it up to you. I promise. You'll see. There are so many things I want to do for you now, Annie, things I will do, things I could have done for Heaven if only she would have let me."

"Okay," I said. I closed my eyes and then felt his hand on my forehead.

"Poor Annie . . . my poor, poor Annie." He stroked my hair affectionately, and when I looked into his eyes, I saw the warm concern again. He was just too complex, too confusing for me. I just couldn't deal with him on top of everything else anymore. All I wanted was to leave here.

Suddenly the light in his eyes changed.

"This sweater you're wearing. Where did you get it?" he demanded.

I didn't want to get Troy into any trouble, but I couldn't lie about it. Tony had gone through my wardrobe after Drake had brought everything, and he knew what clothing was hanging in the closets here and what was in the dresser drawers.

"Someone gave it to me," I said.

"Someone? Who?"

"A very nice man who lives in the cottage on the other side of the maze," I replied, deciding to pretend I didn't know who Troy really was.

"The other side of the maze? You went through the maze?"

"I'm tired, Tony. Very tired. Please. I don't want to talk anymore. I just want to sleep."

"Yes, yes. I'll help you undress," he said, reaching down to help remove the sweater.

"No! I can do it all myself. I want my privacy. Just leave me be!" I demanded. He pulled back as if I had slapped him across the face.

"Of course," he mumbled. "Of course. I'll let you rest and then see to your dinner."

"Thank you." I didn't move, to show him I wouldn't do anything until he had left. He understood, nodded, still looking stunned, and then turned and left the room.

I was quite a bit more tired than I had anticipated, and the effort to undress and get myself into my nightgown was exhausting. It seemed to take forever, too. By the time I had pulled myself under the cover and lowered my head to the pillow, I was drained. In moments I was asleep.

I woke abruptly. It took me a few moments to acclimate myself again, and when I looked at the clock by the side of the bed, I realized I had slept into the middle of the night. The house was as quiet as a funeral parlor; my curtains had been drawn closed, and only that small, weak lamp in the sitting room was on, casting long, thin pale-yellow shadows over the walls.

My stomach churned and growled, complaining because I had slept right through supper. I pulled myself into a sitting position. Why hadn't Tony woken me to eat? Rye had not come in and left a tray of food here, either.

"Tony?" I called. There was no answer, nor did I hear him stirring about in the sitting room. "Tony?" I raised my voice and waited again, but still there was no response. *"Tony!"* I screamed.

I expected he would come charging in after that outburst to chastise me for sleeping through supper, blaming it on my excursion over the grounds of Farthy. But he didn't come. All remained quiet, still.

I reached over to turn on the lamp on the night table, deciding that I would get up and out of bed, wheel myself into the corridor to see what was going on and why no one would respond. But after I turned on the light and illuminated the room, I was shocked to discover that my wheelchair was gone. And so was my walker! I was really trapped in my bed.

"You can't do this, Tony," I muttered. "You can't keep me a prisoner here any longer. I'm going to leave. *Do you hear me? I'm going to leave in the morning!*"

There was no response. I fell back against the pillow, exhausted and overwhelmed once more. I must have dozed off again, because a movement near the bed made my eyes snap open and my heart thump. Grinding my fists over my eyes, I tried wiping the sleep away. Tony must have returned to my room after I had fallen asleep and turned off my lamp. Even the light from the sitting room seemed dimmer. I could barely make out his silhouette at the foot of the bed, but I recognized his shadowy figure.

"Tony? What are you doing? Why are you moving about in the darkness, and why did you take away my wheelchair and my walker?" I demanded. He didn't respond. He simply stood there, gazing through the darkness at me. "Tony!" I exclaimed, my voice more shrill. "Why don't you answer me? Why are you standing there staring at me like that? You're frightening me!" There was a long moment's pause before he finally did respond.

"Don't be afraid, Leigh," he said in a loud whisper.

"What?"

"You shouldn't be afraid. I'm not here to hurt you." He spoke as if he were speaking to a little girl who might be frightened by his sudden appearance.

"Tony, what are you saying?"

"I'm saying I do love you; I do want you. I do need you, Leigh." His voice was a hoarse, throaty whisper.

"Leigh? I'm not Leigh. I'm Annie. Tony, what's wrong with you. Please . . . get me Rye. I want to speak to Rye. I'm hungry," I said, nervous and frightened now. "I slept through supper and I'm hungry. I'm sure Rye will be happy to get up and prepare something for me," I babbled, hoping to snap him out of his dream. He sounded and looked like a man who was sleepwalking. "Go wake him. Please."

"She's asleep. She won't know anything," he said, moving around the side of my bed.

"She? Who's asleep?" My heart was pounding harder and harder. I felt as if my lungs were collapsing. It was so hard to catch my breath. My face felt hot, my neck on fire, and my mouth had become terribly dry. I couldn't swallow.

"Not that it matters. She doesn't know what I do at night or where I go. She doesn't even care anymore. She has her own interests, her own friends." He laughed. "She has herself. She's always had herself and that's always been enough for her, but it's not enough for me, Leigh. You were right." He reached out for my hand. I pulled it back and moved as quickly as I could to the other side of the bed, but the newfound strength I had found in my lower body during the day seemed gone. Fear and shock drove all my energy away. I was beginning to feel numb all over and not just in my legs. I had to bring him to his senses; I had to.

"Tony, I'm not Leigh. I'm Annie! *Annie!*"

For a long moment he didn't move or say anything and I thought I had gotten through to him, but then he untied his bathrobe and let it drop to the floor. In the dim light spilling in from the sitting room, I could see that he was completely naked.

Oh no! I thought. He's in a dream, moving through

341

a fantasy, and there's no one here to help me, not even that horrible nurse. I was going to shout for Rye, but then I wondered if I would cause Tony to become violent or even more crazed, and Rye slept in the servants' quarters, so far away, anyway, there was probably no chance he would hear me. My only hope was to talk Tony back to sanity.

"Tony, it's not Leigh; it's not Heaven. It's Annie, Annie. You're making a mistake, a terrible mistake."

"I think I loved you from the moment I set eyes on you," he replied. "Jillian's beautiful. She will always be beautiful, but beautiful like a butterfly. If you touch her, she won't be able to fly and she will fade and die. That kind of beauty belongs locked up in a glass case, to be seen, appreciated, but never loved and experienced like your beauty, Leigh. Jillian's a picture to hang on the wall; you're a woman, a real woman," he added, his voice full of sensuous meaning.

He sat on the bed and reached out for me. I cringed.

"TONY! You're my great-grandmother's husband. I'm Annie, Heaven's daughter, Annie. You don't realize what you're doing. Please, get off my bed and go. Please," I pleaded, but my pleas fell on deaf ears, ears unable to hear anything but the sounds and words spoken in his imagination.

"Oh, Leigh . . . Leigh, my darling Leigh." His hand groped about until he found my left wrist and began to pull me toward him. I tried to resist, but I was so weak and so tired, I could barely put up a struggle. I was sure he was taking that as a form of encouragement. "We'll make love through the night, just as we did before, and if you want, you can call me Daddy."

Call him Daddy? What horrible thing was he suggesting?

Tony's hand was on my shoulder and he was lowering his face toward mine, bringing his lips to mine. I pulled my head back, but his other hand was on my waist, gripping it tightly. Without the full strength of my lower body, I was at a great disadvantage.

"TONY! STOP! STOP!"

His hand moved up my waist to my breasts and he moaned with pleasure.

"Oh, my Leigh, my Leigh."

I broke free of his grip on my left wrist and swung down at his left hand, catching him on the forearm and driving his fingers from my bosom. The blow shocked him.

"TONY! STOP! I'M ANNIE! AND YOU ARE DOING A TERRIBLE THING, A THING YOU WILL REGRET FOREVER!"

My words finally found their target. He froze in a sitting position. To dramatize my resistance, I leaned forward and pushed on his chest with both my hands, driving him back. The effort took all my strength and I collapsed against the pillow.

"What?" he said, as if he heard voices I couldn't hear. "What?"

"Go away," I pleaded in a strained voice. "Go away. Leave me alone."

"What?" He turned and stared into the darkest shadows of the room. Was he imagining someone there? Were one of Rye Whiskey's ghosts calling to him? Perhaps it was the ghost of my great-grandmother, or even the ghost of my grandmother demanding he leave me be. "Oh, my God," he said to himself. "Oh, my God."

He stood up and looked back at me. I waited, my heart pounding. What was going through that twisted and tormented mind? Was he returning to reality or was he taking some other channel through the maze of his madness to find himself on my bed again?

"I'm . . . I'm sorry," he whispered. "Oh, I'm so sorry . . ." He knelt down and scooped up his robe.

Then he quickly put it on, tying the belt snugly. I watched without speaking, afraid that the sound of my voice might set him back. "I . . . I've got to . . . to go," he said. "Good night."

I held my breath and barely turned my head as he moved away from the bed and out the door. In a moment he was gone, but my heart didn't stop its racing. I was terrified he would return, and I was just too weak and too overwhelmed to struggle out of bed and crawl out of the suite.

I was sweating so much my nightgown stuck to my skin. I had to get out of this place. I had to convince Drake or Luke or someone to take me away immediately. But Drake was in New York. And what if Luke didn't come? Panicked, desperate, my mind raced like a caged bird. Rye Whiskey! I must get him to help me! Or Troy! Or Parsons! Anybody! Please somebody help me get away from this madman! What had he done to my grandmother to make her run away? I could barely stand to think about it. The only thing that comforted me was the realization that it would soon be morning. I embraced myself as tightly as I could, the way Mommy would hold me to her whenever I had a bad dream and she came to my bed. And this was more than a bad dream. This was a living nightmare. I was afraid to fall asleep again, afraid that I would awaken once more to Tony naked at my side, but my eyelids grew heavy and I slipped into an exhausted slumber.

"Good morning," Tony sang cheerfully. My eyelids fluttered open and I saw him opening the curtains wide. The bright sunlight turned away each and every shadow. He raised the windows to permit more air, and the curtains began a happy little jig over the windowsill. I didn't lift my head from the pillow. Instead, I lay there silently, watching him move about the room. He was dressed in a clean, light blue silk robe and looked unbelievably chipper. Was he pretending so I would think that none of what happened last night really happened?

"I'll have your breakfast in a jiffy," he said.

"Being nice to me this morning isn't going to help, Tony. I haven't forgotten last night."

"Last night?" He turned, smiling. "Oh . . . last night. You mean when I yelled at you downstairs. I've already explained and apologized for that, Annie. You shouldn't hold grudges. All of us make mistakes."

"I'm not talking about that. I'm talking about when you came to my room in the middle of the night," I snapped. I no longer felt any compassion for him. He had to bear responsibility for what he was doing, and one way or another, I was determined to leave the house today.

"What? You had another dream? You poor child. What you are going through." He shook his head, pressing his lips together like a concerned grandfather. "Oh well, once we get something substantial in your stomach—"

"I want my wheelchair. I'm going downstairs to the phone."

"Wheelchair? Oh no, Annie, not today. You need at least one day's complete rest after what you've gone through. I'll bring your breakfast to you in bed today. Won't that be nice?"

"I WANT MY WHEELCHAIR!" I demanded in the strongest voice I had ever turned on him. He stared at me a moment and then started to walk away as if he didn't hear me.

"TONY!"

He didn't turn back, and this time when he left my room, he closed the door.

"YOU CAN'T KEEP ME LIKE A PRISONER!"

I got myself into a sitting position and slowly brought my legs over the side of the bed. I did feel weak and tired, but my determination was strong. I would leave the room, even if I had to crawl out. I had to get help, get to Rye. I was sure he would help me.

I started to lower my feet toward the floor when Tony came bursting back in again, carrying my breakfast tray.

"Oh no, Annie. You want to sit up with your back to the headboard so I can put the bed table over your legs."

He put the tray down on the night table and took hold of my upper arms, pushing me back and turning me. My feeble resistance had no effect.

"Please," I cried. "Please. Let me up."

"After you eat and rest, I'll see how you are, Annie. That's a promise." He smiled as though we were the best of friends and began to set up my bed table. Then he put my breakfast tray on it and stepped back, the corners of his mouth drawn up in a clownish grin.

He was mad, I thought. Something had definitely snapped in him last night. There was no point in trying to reach him.

I gazed down at the tray. There was a glass of orange juice and some hot oatmeal with what looked to be honey spread over it. There was the usual dry toast and a glass of low-fat milk. Rye hadn't prepared this breakfast. Tony must have gotten up early and done it all himself. With him standing over me as he was, I thought I might just as well eat and get some energy in my body. I drank the juice and spooned in some of the oatmeal. The toast tasted like a piece of cardboard, but I washed it down with gulps of milk. He nodded, his face locked in a maddening smile.

After I finished and sat back, he lifted the tray and then removed the table.

"There now," he said, "that should make you feel so much better. It does, doesn't it? Now, do you want me to rub in some body oils?" he asked.

346

"No," I said as emphatically as I could.

"No? You mean no because you feel much better?"

"Yes," I said through my tears. "Please, please, get me my wheelchair."

"After your morning nap, we'll see," he said. He went to the dresser and took out a new red nightgown, another of the ones he had brought to me at the Boston Memorial Hospital. "You should put on a fresh nightgown. I think this one suits you, don't you? I always liked scarlet on you." He brought it to the bed. I sat there with the covers pulled tightly to my neck. "Come on, now. A fresh nightgown will make you feel so much better."

I didn't think he would leave me alone until I had put on the red gown, so I took it from him. He stood back to watch me take off the one I was wearing and slip this one over my body. I did it all as quickly as I could.

"Now, doesn't that feel good?"

"Yes," I said, giving him what he wanted. I was even more frightened because instead of feeling awake and energetic as I had hoped I would feel after eating the breakfast, I felt drowsy and tired again. His voice sounded faraway.

"I want . . . want . . ."

"You want to sleep. I know. I expected it. A nice rest." He pulled the blanket up and around me, tucking it in tightly like a straightjacket.

"No . . . I . . ."

"Sleep, Annie. Sleep, and you will feel so much better when I return. All those ridiculous nightmares will be gone when you wake up again."

I tried to speak, but I couldn't form the words. My lips felt sewn shut. In moments I was asleep again, my last conscious thought being he had put a sedative in the breakfast.

The next time I awoke, I was very disoriented. I had

no idea what time of day it was. Slowly, in what seemed more like hours than minutes, I managed to get the tightly tucked blanket off me and pulled myself up on the pillow. I lay back, breathing hard, my heart racing.

I saw that it was nearly twelve. My bedroom door was still shut, but the windows were open and a cool, refreshing sea breeze drifted in. I turned to it, longing to get myself outside again, and suddenly, very faintly at first, but stronger and stronger as I focused on it, I heard a familiar voice. It came from below . . . at the front of the house.

"Luke!"

I heard Tony's voice as well.

Concentrating as hard as I could and directing all my strength into my legs, I swung myself over the side of the bed, but my legs gave me no support. Whatever vitality had been reborn in them was gone. Something Tony had given me sent my renewed vigor back into hibernation.

"Luke!" I screamed. My voice echoed in the empty room, the sound shut up with me. I let myself fall to the floor, collapsing like a dress that had slipped off a hanger in a closet. I twisted myself around and began a slow struggle toward the window, pulling and tugging the best I could, encouraged by the continued sounds of Luke's voice. I began to make out some words.

"But she insisted I come," he pleaded.

"She's not ready for visitors."

"Why did she call?"

"She didn't; she couldn't have. It must have been a mistake."

"I've driven all this way. Couldn't I see her for just a few moments?" he implored.

"The doctors advise against it."

"Why?"

"Young man, I don't have all day to spend explaining medical procedures to you. It's time for Annie's therapy session, anyway, and she can't have visitors during that time."

"All right, I'll wait out here."

"You are stubborn."

I was only a foot or so from the windowsill. I pressed down to lift my body and reached up as quickly as I could to take hold of it, but I missed and fell forward, smacking my head against the wall. For a moment I was too stunned to do anything but lay there.

"All right, I'll leave, but will you tell her I came?" Resignation sounded in his voice.

"Of course."

"No," I muttered. "No . . . no . . ."

I reached up again, this time getting hold of the sill, and pulled myself toward the open window.

"Thank you."

I heard the front door close. He was leaving; Luke was leaving! Tony had driven him away! My hope! Luke . . . I was on my knees, and using both hands, pulled myself up until my face was level with the window.

"LUKE!" I screamed with all my might. "LUKE! DON'T GO. LUKE, COME UP AND GET ME. LUKE . . ." I screamed and screamed until my face felt it would burst from the effort and my arms weakened too much to hold me up. Just before I fell back to the floor, I thought I caught a glimpse of Troy standing at the edge of the maze, looking up. But maybe it was something I had only wished to see.

I lay there, the side of my face to the carpet, my body crunched up, crying and moaning for Luke. It was the way Tony found me.

"Oh, poor Annie," he said. "You fell out of bed. I just knew something like this might happen. It's my fault. I should have fastened the side guards to the bed."

"YOU MONSTER!" I screamed. "How could you send him away? You know how long I have been waiting for him to visit me. You know how important it is to me. How could you do it? How could you be so cruel? I don't care what's wrong with you or how sad and tragic your life has been. That was vicious, terribly vicious! I hate you for this! Go get him. Make him come back. MAKE HIM COME BACK!"

He ignored my outburst as if I were the mad one and he the sane one.

My body shuddered with sobs as he put his hands under my arms and lifted me from the floor. He carried me back to the bed and got me under the blanket, tucking it tightly around me once more. Then he stepped back to catch his breath.

"You shouldn't do this to yourself, Annie. You'll only make yourself sicker and sicker. Try to rest. You know I want only the best for you, only the best for my little Annie."

"I'm not your little Annie. I want Luke to come back," I muttered. "Luke will be back . . . he'll be back."

"Of course. You'll get better and he'll return. If you'll only listen to me, I'll have you up and around before you know it. Now, what was I thinking about? Oh yes, the side guards for the bed."

He went off and returned with them. I lay there helplessly as he fastened them to the bed and pulled them up, caging me like some poor animal.

"There. Now we needn't worry about your falling out of bed again. Feeling safe?"

I turned away, closed my eyes and waited for him to leave the room. After I saw he was gone, I closed my eyes again and imagined I was on the gazebo in Winnerrow. I wished and wished and wished. Oh,

Luke, be there for me. Hear me across distance and time and understand how terrible this is and how much I need you to take me from here.

Farthy is not the paradise, the magic castle we thought it would be. It is a terrible prison, dark and dangerous and full of twisted despair. I should have listened to my mother . . . she knew . . . she knew.

At first I thought I was still dreaming because when I opened my eyes, I heard the voices. I glanced at the clock and saw that it was nearly seven P.M. I had slept through the day. The voices grew louder. They were coming down the corridor toward my suite.

Moments later my bedroom door was thrust open and standing there before me were my aunt Fanny and . . . thank God . . . Luke.

"Why, she looks like a baby in a crib," Fanny drawled in her shrill voice. "And look, jist look at that . . . her hair is a different color. It's like Heaven's hair useta be."

"Annie!"

I lifted my hand and Luke rushed to the bed to reach over the side guards to grasp it. As soon as our fingers touched, I began to cry.

"Don't cry, Annie. We're here."

They were here, really here? I feasted my eyes on them the way someone lost on a deserted island might feast her eyes on her rescuers, half in disbelief, half in overwhelming joy. It was as if a wonderful light had come into this dreary suite, as if bars had been lifted from windows and locks unfastened. My Winnerrow world came rushing through the door, flooding me with a torrent of memories and wonderful feelings. Nightmares retreated. I could escape this madness. My heart burst with joy. Luke hadn't forgotten me, hadn't deserted me. He had heard my call. Our love was so strong it would overwhelm everything in its way. Instantly, I felt my strength return. I was like a flower that had been shut up in a dark corner and never watered. Just before it wilted forever, the prison had been torn away, the light had been permitted to caress it, and loving rain had revived it. It would bloom again. I would bloom again. Luke and I would be together once more.

"Oh, Luke, please . . . take me home."

"We will, Annie."

Tony rushed up behind Aunt Fanny.

"Are you satisfied now? Can't you see how sick she is?" he screamed.

"No, Luke. No. I'm not sick . . . he's making me sick. He puts medicine in my food that makes me weak. Don't believe him."

"Jist as I thought . . . jist as that man said." Aunt Fanny drew closer to my bed, her face creased with concern.

"What man, Luke?"

"Some man called my mother and told her to get me and get over here as soon as possible to get you out and home."

"Troy!" I exclaimed. Who else could it be?

"What's that?" Luke questioned.

"Nothing . . . thank God you came back."

"We'll git ya outta here in a jiffy, Annie honey."

"You can't take her out of here without talking to the doctor. She's an invalid; she needs special care, special medicine." Tony was red as a beet, agitated and grasping for control. His eyes were big and his hair on end. He looked like someone who had just gone through a terrible electric shock.

"Don't listen to him, Aunt Fanny," I pleaded.

"You could give her a terrible relapse . . . maybe even cause her death."

Aunt Fanny turned slowly and lowered her hands to

her hips. Her shoulders rose. She looked like a hawk about to pounce on a mouse.

"Seems ta me yer the one who might give this child a relapse. Look at her. She's pale and peaked, shut up in this"—she sniffed—"sickly-sweet smellin' tomb. This place is jist what I thought it would be."

"I'm going to . . . to call the doctor."

"Call him. What kinda doctor is he anyway? Look at what this place looks like. What's he, blind or stupid or jist not as smart as these fancy doctors claim ta be? How could he leave ma niece in this place? It's a big dump. Smells damp and rotten."

"I won't stand here and take this kind of abuse," Tony asserted, his Tatterton pride and arrogance glowing in his face. He left the suite, but I didn't expect he would go far away.

Aunt Fanny turned her attention back to me.

"Don'cha worry none now, Annie. Ya goin' home with us. Luke, lower them there bars so she kin get herself off the bed. I'll find a suitcase and round up her things."

"What's mine is on the right side of that closet, Aunt Fanny. It's not much. The suitcase is on the floor there."

Luke squeezed my hand. "I'm so glad to see you."

"You can't imagine how glad I am to see you, Luke. Why didn't you come before this?"

"I tried. I called Tony Tatterton and he kept putting me off, telling me the doctor didn't want you to have visitors."

"And Drake?"

"Drake said the same things. They wanted me to wait awhile longer."

"Even after you received my letter?"

"Letter? I didn't receive any letter, Annie."

"He never sent it. I should have known. All that

stuff about your tests and fraternities and friends . . .
girlfriends." I felt so terrible now, so guilty for sus-
pecting Luke of changing into someone selfish and
conceited. How could I have doubted him? I should
have known. I had been a prisoner here from the start,
and from the start Tony had deceived me. It made me
feel sick to know he had lied to me in such an ugly
way.

"What girlfriends?"

"Are ya two goin' ta jist keep on jawin' or are we
goin' home ta Winnerrow?"

"We're going home, Ma."

"Then do as I say and get them bars lowered."

Luke lowered the side bars while Aunt Fanny
packed my things and put out clothes for me to wear.

"Ya go on down with this suitcase, Luke, while I get
Annie dressed."

"Please bring my wheelchair back, Luke. There's
one up here and one downstairs."

"And don't stop fer nothin' or no one nuther,"
Fanny commanded.

"Right, boss," Luke said and gave Aunt Fanny a
mock salute. It felt so good to smile and laugh again.

"Oh, go on wit' ya. Ever see such a boy . . . s'cuse
me, young man?"

"He's a wonderful young man. Oh, Aunt Fanny . . .
I'm so glad you came. I never was so happy to see
you."

"Betcha was. Don't talk about it all now. Let's git
on outta here. What do I hafta do ta help?"

"Yesterday I would have done it all myself, Aunt
Fanny, but I'm feeling tired and weak, so just give me
a hand with my undergarments. I promise, I'm not
going to be a burden to you back at Winnerrow."

"Oh, ya poor child," she said, her eyes softening,
even glazing over with tears. I never had realized how

warm and loving Aunt Fanny could be. "Ya think I care. Be all the burden ya hafta be and don't worry yerself about it. We're family, no matter what anyone says."

"What do you mean, Aunt Fanny?"

"I don't mean nothin'. Let me get yer clothes on ya."

She helped me dress, and Luke returned with the wheelchair. He lifted me out of the bed as if I were a precious baby and slowly lowered me into the chair. It felt good and secure being in his arms. Then he began to wheel me out of the room.

I looked back at the canopy bed, the vanity table and dressers, the bedroom that was supposed to be a warm and wonderful place for me, my mother's old room.

How sad it was that this suite had been turned into a room filled with nightmares. The bed had become my cage, the bathroom and hot tub my torture chamber. I truly felt like one escaping a prison. All the magic and wonder of Farthy was just something Luke and I had imagined, a child's dream. Reality was much harder and crueler.

I saw the same disappointment in Luke's face when I looked back at him as we moved down the corridor. He saw the cobwebs, the dead chandelier bulbs, the faded carpet, scuffed walls, and the old faded curtains over the large windows, keeping the hallways dark and dank.

I directed Luke to take me to the elevator chair.

"It will make it all easier."

"Now Annie, ya sure ya know how ta work that damn thing? I sure don't want any accidents occurrin' here and give that Tony Tatterton a chance ta come after us with I told ya so's."

"It's easy, Aunt Fanny."

I slid over into the seat and strapped myself in firmly. Then I pressed the down button and the chair began its descent.

"Well, I'll be darned. Look it, Luke. We're goin' ta hafta git one for Hasbrouck House right quick."

"Company name's right on the chair," Luke said. He took a pen out of his top pocket and jotted it down. Luke was always prepared, always the student.

"How has college been, Luke?"

"It's been okay, Annie," he said, walking along with me as the chair moved down the stairway. "But I've made a new decision."

"Oh?"

"I'm withdrawing from summer school. I don't need to start yet, anyway."

"Withdrawing? Why?"

"To spend the rest of the summer home with you, helping you to recuperate," he said, smiling.

"Oh, Luke, you shouldn't." The chair came to a halt at the bottom and I slid over into the awaiting wheelchair.

"There's no sense arguing about it, Annie. My mind's made up," he said with a stern, determined air.

I knew it was selfish of me, but I was happy, thrilled that he had made that decision.

"And what does Aunt Fanny have to say about it?"

"She's happy I'm going to be around awhile longer. My mother's different, Annie. You'll see. The tragedy has turned her into a responsible person. I'm really proud of her."

"I'm glad, Luke."

"Miss Annie," someone called, and we paused at the front door. It was Rye Whiskey coming from the kitchen.

"Rye. It's Rye Whiskey, Luke. The cook."

"Y'all goin' home, Miss Annie?"

"Yes, Rye. This is my aunt Fanny and my cousin Luke. They've come to fetch me."

"Tha's good, Miss Annie," he said without hesitation. Aunt Fanny nodded because someone else confirmed her suspicions and decisions. "I wasn't able ta make ya anythin' special no ways with that nurse hoverin' over my shoulder while she was here, and now . . ."

"I know, Rye. I'm sorry."

"Tha's all right. Y'all come back when yer fixed up agin, and I'll make ya the best meal this side of paradise."

"I'll take you up on that, Rye."

His face grew serious again.

"Them spirits didn't stay away neither, did they, Miss Annie?"

"I guess not, Rye."

He nodded and looked at Aunt Fanny.

"What's he been drinkin'? Lawd, what a place."

"Only drinks to prevent snakebite, miss."

"Is that so?"

Rye's eyes twinkled.

"Yes, ma'am, and it works cause I never been bit."

"Let's go, Luke," Aunt Fanny said and nodded toward the front door. Luke opened it, but just as he came back to push me out, we heard Tony's scream.

All of us turn to look up the stairway. He was standing at the top, holding his fist high.

"You take that girl out of this house and you're responsible for whatever happens. I've already called her doctor. He's enraged."

"Well, you jist tell him ta go see a doctor himself, then," Aunt Fanny said, and chuckled at her own reply. Without further hesitation, she waved Luke forward and he started to wheel me out of the house.

"Stop!" Tony shouted. He came charging down the stairway.

"That man's loco," Aunt Fanny muttered.

"Stop," he repeated, approaching us. "You can't take her from here. She's mine."

"Yours?" Aunt Fanny started to laugh disdainfully.

"She is mine! She is!" He took a deep breath and made a desperate confession. "She's really my granddaughter, not my step-granddaughter. It's part of why your mother ran from here," he said, directing himself to me, "when she found out . . ."

"Found out what, Tony?" I turned my chair around to face him.

"Found out that Leigh and I . . . her mother and I . . . Heaven was my daughter, not Luke's."

"Good Gawd," Aunt Fanny said, stepping back.

"It's true. I'm ashamed of what I did, but not ashamed to have you as my real granddaughter, Annie. And you are. Don't you see? You belong here with me, with your real grandfather," he pleaded.

I stared up at him. Now what had happened last night made sense. No wonder he had called me Leigh when he came to my bed. He was reliving his affair with her, an affair he had in this house while she was only a girl!

"And so what happened last night really happened before," I concluded aloud.

"What happened last night?" Aunt Fanny asked, coming forward.

"I'm sorry for what happened last night, Annie. I got confused."

"Confused?" All the times that he had kissed me, touched me, yesterday when he bathed me and I saw him behind me, his lips nearly on my neck . . . all of it came back, and suddenly all of it was ugly, lustful. I felt nauseated. I could barely think, I felt so defiled, so

358

humiliated. My mind was an echo chamber of screams and shouts. *"You're disgusting,"* I screamed. "No wonder Mommy ran from this house and wanted nothing more to do with you." Then a horrible realization occurred to me. He seemed to anticipate what I was about to say. I could see it in his eyes, in the way he widened them and stepped back. "Did you get confused with my mother, too? Was that the real reason she left you and Farthy?"

"No, I . . . it wasn't my fault." He looked to Luke and Fanny in hope that they would somehow come to his rescue, but they were gaping at him with the same look of horror and disgust. "You can't hate me. I can't live through all that again, Annie. Please, forgive me. I didn't mean . . ."

"Didn't mean? Didn't mean what? To get my grandmother pregnant? So that's why she left Farthy and her mother. You drove her away, just as you drove Mommy away and just as you have driven me away." My words pounded like nails into a coffin. He turned white and shook his head. "You wanted to possess me like . . . like . . . like that portrait of Mommy on the wall," I said, nodding. "That's why you lied when you told me you had called Luke. You never called him, never mailed the letter. You wanted to imprison me here!"

"I only did what I did because I love you and need you. You are the true heir of Farthinggale and all that goes with it. You belong here. I won't let you go," he yelled.

"Oh yes you will," Luke said, stepping between us. My Luke, my gallant prince coming to my rescue, fighting off the evil wizard of our fantasies. Fate had made it all true.

Tony stopped his approach as Luke stared him down.

359

"Let's get outta here, Luke honey," Aunt Fanny said, and Luke took hold of my chair again, turning me toward the door.

"Annie," Tony called, "please . . ."

Aunt Fanny opened the door and Luke pushed me out.

"ANNIE!" Tony bellowed. "ANNIE! HEAVEN! OH, HEAVEN, NO . . ."

Fanny shut the door behind us to close off his horrible cry. I put my hands over my ears. Luke used the ramp to get me to the awaiting car.

"You kin sit up front if ya want to, Annie."

"I want to," I said.

Luke opened the door and then lifted me from the chair. I rested my head against his chest as he put me ever so gently onto the seat.

"Might as well take this wheelchair along, Luke. No sense in lettin' it rot away with everythin' else here."

Luke folded it and placed it in the car trunk. Aunt Fanny got into the backseat and Luke got behind the steering wheel.

Luke headed the car down the driveway.

"Luke, Aunt Fanny, before we go, I'd like to stop at the monument. Please."

"Of course, Annie."

Luke made the turn and drove to the Tatterton family cemetery. He brought the car as close to the monument as he could and I looked out my window. Night had fallen, but the moon cast enough of its yellow illumination over the cemetery for me to see.

"Good-bye for now, Mommy and Daddy. Rest in peace. Someday soon I'll return and walk to your monument."

"You surely will," Aunt Fanny said, and patted me on the shoulder.

Luke squeezed my hand. I turned to him to soak in the warmth and the love in his smile.

"Let's go home, Luke," I said.

As we pulled away I looked back and caught sight of Troy Tatterton stepping out of the forest from where I was certain he had observed my entire departure.

He lifted his hand gently to wave. I waved back.

"Who ya wavin' at, Annie?"

"No one, Aunt Fanny . . . no one."

Part

3

Part

3

TWENTY-ONE

Homecoming

I was too excited to sleep on the airplane. Luke and I sat beside each other near a window, and Aunt Fanny sat in front of us. I was so happy to see Luke, I couldn't take my eyes off him, and from the way he was looking at me, I knew he felt the same way.

"Pinch me and tell me this isn't a dream, Luke. Tell me you're really with me again."

"It's no dream," he said, smiling.

"I dreamt it so often and so hard that it still seems that way to me," I confessed. For the first time that I could remember, when I expressed my need and love for him, I didn't blush, nor did he look away. Our eyes fixed on each other. He put his hand over mine and squeezed it gently. Everything in me cried out for him, urged me to say more. I wanted him to embrace me, to hold me tenderly and kiss me.

"Annie, I worried about you day and night. I couldn't concentrate on anything in college. Everyone was trying to get me to go to parties, to meet people, but my heart was too heavy to appreciate or enjoy anything. I spent a lot of time in my dormitory room composing letters to you."

"Letters I never got!" It filled me with such anger. If only I had received his letters, my dark and desperate days would have been bright and hopeful.

"I know that now, but I couldn't understand why you weren't trying to reach me, weren't calling or sending messages somehow. I thought . . ." He looked down.

"What did you think, Luke? Please, tell me," I begged.

"I thought that once you entered the rich world at Farthy, you had forgotten about me, that Tony had surrounded you with so many distractions, brought so many new people for you to meet, that I wasn't important to you any longer. I'm sorry, Annie; I'm sorry I had those thoughts," he apologized.

My heart swelled to know he felt the same way I did.

"Oh no, Luke. I can understand why you thought them, for I thought them of you as well," I admitted eagerly.

"You did?" I nodded, and he smiled. "Then you cared, really cared?"

"Oh, Luke, you can't imagine how much I missed you, missed hearing your voice. I replayed it over and over in my mind, remembering the nice things you said to me in the past. Just thinking about you and the things you have done in your life despite all obstacles gave me hope and encouragement." I smiled. "I went directly for those tall mountains."

"I'm so happy I was some help to you even though I wasn't there beside you."

"Well, you were, and I dreamt and dreamt of us on the gazebo again."

"Me, too," he said, a slight blush coloring his cheeks. I knew it was harder for him to make these revelations than it was for me. Other men might think him soft, even immature. "While I was alone there in my dormitory room, I would imagine us together again the way we were on our eighteenth birthday. I wished we could be frozen into that day forever and forever. Oh, Annie," he said, his hand more firmly around mine, "I don't know how I am going to ever leave you again."

"I don't want you, too, Luke," I whispered. We were so close now, our lips nearly grazed each other's. Aunt Fanny laughed at something she was reading in a magazine and we sat back again. Luke looked out the window and I let my head fall back against the seat and closed my eyes. Luke didn't let go of my hand, and I felt safe, secure, protected and sheltered once again.

I was excited when the plane finally landed, but after we got into Aunt Fanny's car at the airport in Virginia, I fell asleep and slept most of the way back to Winnerrow. By the time I opened my eyes, we were in the hill country, steadily climbing, winding around and around. There was no fast expressway to take us up into the Willies. Soon the gasoline stations became more widely spaced. The grand new sprawling motels were replaced by little cabins tucked away in shadowy dense woods. Shoddy, unpainted little buildings heralded yet another country town off the beaten track, until those, too, were left behind.

Aunt Fanny had fallen asleep in the rear seat. We had soft music on the radio. Luke had to keep his eyes on the road ahead, but he wore a smile of contentment. He looked so much more mature to me. The tragedy had aged and changed us both, I thought, even in ways we were yet to discover.

Seeing the familiar countryside filled me with a warm and secure feeling. I wondered if Mommy had felt the same way when she had fled Farthy with

Drake because of the things Tony Tatterton had done. The world outside of the Willies and Winnerrow must have looked as hard and as cold and as cruel to her as it now did to me.

"Almost there," Luke announced softly. "We're almost back in our world, Annie."

"Oh, Luke, we thought escaping it, going to a fantasy place, would be more wonderful, but nothing is more wonderful than home, is it?" I asked him.

"Not as long as you're part of it, Annie," he said, and reached over to take my hand. When our fingers touched, they entwined tightly, for neither of us wanted to let go. My heart pounded with happiness.

He saw the look on my face, and his face suddenly became very serious. He sensed how deep my feelings were, and I saw that his were just as deep. It troubled him, I knew, because we were both surrendering to how we felt rather than paying heed to who we were.

"I can't wait to see Hasbrouck House," I whispered.

"Soon, soon."

Mile by mile I was growing more and more impatient, more excited. Finally we came upon the broad green fields on the outskirts of Winnerrow, neat farms with fields of corn soon to be harvested. The little farmhouses were all lit up, the families living within them gathered together in the warm glow of lamps. I nearly squealed with delight when I saw the lights of the shacks of the coal miners dotting the hills. They looked like stars that had fallen but had kept their brightness.

And then we entered Winnerrow proper and drove onto Main Street. To the very end we went, passing all the pastel homes of the richest, backed by the lesser homes of the middle class, the ones who worked in the mines, holding down overseer or manager positions.

I closed my eyes when we turned down the street that led to Hasbrouck House. In moments I would be home, but it would be a different home without Mommy and Daddy. I knew that when we pulled into the driveway neither Mommy nor Daddy would be there to greet us . . . no smiles, no warm kisses, no hugs and loving welcomes. The reality washed over me like a giant, powerful wave in the ocean. I couldn't escape from it or hold it back. My mother and father were dead and buried back at Farthy. I was still an invalid. None of it had been a dream.

"Well, thank Gawd we're here," Aunt Fanny drawled as we drove up to the house. "Beep yer horn, Luke, so the servants know."

"Annie doesn't have that much, Ma."

"Jist beep the horn."

She got out quickly and came around to open my door. I just sat there looking up at the house, at the tall white pillars and large windows. I inhaled the scent of the magnolias and for a moment I felt like a little girl again, being brought home from one of our family vacations at the beach, and just as they did then, the servants gathered together and came out the front door to greet us.

Mrs. Avery was all tears, her frilly silk handkerchief, the one I had bought her on one of her birthdays, looking damp and wilted. She waved it like a flag of welcome as she walked down the steps and to the car as quickly as her arthritic limbs would permit.

"Oh, Annie. Welcome home, dear." Aunt Fanny stepped back so she could lean in to hug and kiss me.

"Hello, Mrs. Avery."

"Your room is all ready . . . cleaned and polished and aired out nice and proper."

"Thank you."

I turned toward the house to see George sauntering down the steps, moving faster and showing more emotion on his face than I could ever remember. His steel-rod-perfect posture was somewhat relaxed and the smile that usually died three quarters of its way across his lips now drew the corners of his mouth up so high he looked like a cat.

"Welcome home, Annie." He extended his arm stiffly, but his long, thin fingers curled lovingly around mine when I took his hand.

"Thank you, George. It's good to see you."

Roland was at the door, a clean, bright, starched apron around his waist. He was carrying a vanilla sheet cake in his hands and brought it to the car to show me. The top of it read, WELCOME HOME ANNIE, GOD BLESS.

"Roland, that was so kind of you!"

"Jist somethin' ta keep my mind occupied, Miss Annie. Welcome."

"Thank you, Roland."

Luke had my chair unfolded and waiting. The servants stepped back and watched as he reached in to scoop me up and out and into the chair. His face was so tight and serious, but when our eyes met, he smiled. It felt so good to be in his arms. I saw how proud he was about the firm way he held me. He was still my prince and I was still his princess.

"You're getting good at this, Luke Casteel," I whispered.

"Just a natural, I guess." He flashed a smile, his dark sapphire eyes brightening impishly, just the way Daddy's used to.

"I'll get the bags," George said quickly as Luke started me toward the house. Roland handed the cake to Mrs. Avery and he helped Luke lift me up the steps.

"Maybe we need one of them ramps, too," Aunt Fanny thought aloud.

"No, Aunt Fanny. I'm going to be walking again before we could even get it built."

"Tha's sure the way ta think, Miss Annie," Roland said.

He and Luke brought me directly to my room. Never before did it look so wonderful and comfortable and warm to me. Tears of happiness ran over my cheeks. I was home, really home. I would sleep in my own bed, be surrounded by my own things. For a moment it was as if all that had happened had indeed been only a dream. That was the power of my room.

But then my gaze went to the toy cottage and I thought about Troy. It was as if I had grown gigantic and I was looking back at where I had been. I had so much to thank him for. In his own way, he had rescued me, too.

"Oh, Luke, it looks so wonderful. I'll never take it for granted again."

I gazed about hungrily, feasting my eyes on all my things. There were my pictures and art materials, organized as neatly as the day I had left them. The unfinished painting of Farthy I had begun shortly before the tragic accident was still on the easel. How wrong I had been about it, I thought. The colors were too bright, the world around it too soft and inviting. It was truly a picture drawn from a fantasy. No wonder Mommy wanted me to paint other things. She knew I was living in a dream world, and sometimes, living in dreams can be dangerous and tragic.

The only thing that was truly accurate in the picture was Luke. There was nothing imaginary about the way he looked, but more important, I had put him where I most needed him—with me, coming for me, bringing me home.

"I was all wrong about Farthy, Luke," I said. "My pictures were pure fantasy."

"Don't blame yourself for wanting it to be more, Annie. If we don't permit ourselves to have dreams, the world can be awfully dreary. Maybe now we'll be more satisfied with what we have and who we are," he added.

"Oh, Luke, I hope so."

The commotion around us drove away regrets and dark thoughts. George brought in my things and Mrs. Avery turned down the bed. Everyone was chattering at once. Their excitement was infectious.

"I will help Annie by myself now, ladies and gentlemen," Aunt Fanny announced.

"Yes, ma'am," Roland said, and everyone left obediently. I saw from the way they responded that Aunt Fanny had indeed taken over here.

"I'll look in on you later, Annie. Is there anything you want me to bring back?" Luke asked.

"Nothing right now, Luke. Just yourself."

"No problem with that. Matter of fact, you'll probably get tired of seeing me. I'll be like old wallpaper."

"I can't imagine that." I squeezed his hand. He held his face close to mine and I thought he was going to kiss my cheek, but Aunt Fanny spoke up before he made up his mind to do so.

"Well, if ya goin', Luke, go! We have work ta do."

"Sorry. Bye, Annie."

"I'll call Doc Williams so he kin come right ova as soon as possible in the mornin' and check ya out and tell us what we gotta do from here on in."

"And see if you can get the hairdresser up here tomorrow, Aunt Fanny. I want to get my hair back to the way it was as quickly as I can."

Aunt Fanny nodded.

"But tell me, Annie, what made ya do such a thing?"

"Tony talked me into it, convinced me it would make me feel more like a pretty young woman again. He kept talking about Mommy and how she had done it, and he had pictures of her with silvery blond hair. I missed her so that I suppose I was trying to get her back by looking like her, but I didn't know the sick reasons Tony had for wanting me to do it. He was trying to get me to look like my mother and like my grandmother Leigh. You were there; you heard why."

Aunt Fanny's eyes narrowed thoughtfully.

"I used ta hate Heaven fer not bringin' me ta Farthy ta live with her. I used ta think, here she is surrounded by all them sugar daddies and all that glitter and wealth, but now I understand what she went through. In some ways it musta been harder fer her there than it was in the Willies.

"I neva realized the real reason she was runnin' all about tryin' to reunite the family," Aunt Fanny continued. "She needed her family more'n I did, even though she was surrounded by all them rich things. She was also surrounded by crazy loons, too. That grandmother all shut up in her own madness. Tony Tatterton . . . who knows what else went on there. And we left ya in their hands . . ." She shook her head.

"It's not your fault, Aunt Fanny. Who could have known? I had the best doctors. Tony was buying everything I needed, including a special nurse. Only she turned out to be horrible."

I described some of what had happened. Aunt Fanny listened, shaking her head and pressing her lips together every once in a while.

"I wished she was here now. I'd wring her neck somethin' terrible."

"Aunt Fanny, you didn't seem all that surprised when Tony announced he was Mommy's real father. How did you know?"

"Shortly before ma brotha Tom got hisself mauled ta death by a tiger in the circus, he wrote me a letta, tellin' me 'bout this conversation he and ma pa Luke had. Tom was all hot and bothered 'cause he found out that Heaven wasn't really Luke's daughter. He and Heaven was so close, ya see, it bothered him somethin' awful to learn this and he had to tell someone. Anyway, it seems that by the time ma daddy married yer grandma Leigh, she was already pregnant with Tony's baby. Luke told Tom that Leigh said Tony raped her . . . more'n once, maybe. Anyhow, that was why she done run away from that castle and all that money and ended up livin' in the Willies with Pa. She died during the birthin', so none of us knowed her. Heaven always used ta think Luke hated her 'cause his angel Leigh died givin' birth ta her, understand? I guess there was a lot more ta it, especially when ya consider Luke knew Heaven wasn't his'n."

"So Tony is my real grandfather, and he didn't just say those things at the end to get me to stay," I concluded, the words now falling with greater weight on my ears.

"It looks that way, Annie," she said, and then misread the troubled look on my face. "Now jist becuz he's loose in the head don't mean ya goin' be, Annie."

"No, I wasn't thinking about that, Aunt Fanny. I was thinking about Mommy and how hard it must have been for her to discover all this, too. She never let anyone know, though, did she? And neither did you."

"No. I neva told nobody 'cept that no account lawya I had during the custody hearin'. It didn't come out 'cause me and yer ma made a deal. We bought and sold Drake betwixt us jist like we was bought and sold." She looked down, ashamed.

"Whatever you did in the past is over and finished, Aunt Fanny. You've more than made up for it now."

"Why, do ya mean that, Annie darlin'?" I nodded. "Even havin' Luke Junior with ya pa?"

"We'll all make the best of what we are and what we have."

"Well, ain't ya a wonderful young lady." Her face turned sad. "But now ya know I ain't really ya aunt."

"Oh no, Aunt Fanny. You will always be my aunt. I don't care what the blood relationships are."

"Well, I love ya jist as much as I could even if ya was blood related, Annie. I love ya more; I love ya like a daughter, an' Luke and ya are still half brotha, half sista."

"Yes," I said, and looked off through my window at the roof of the gazebo below. I couldn't help thinking about how much had changed since the accident. My mother hadn't really been a Casteel, even though she had been brought up as one, had lived in that shack and had thought Toby and Annie Casteel were her true grandparents. Even though these revelations were painful and disturbing for me now, I couldn't even begin to imagine what the effect must have been on my mother when she finally learned the truth. It was like losing her whole family in an instant and suddenly being adopted by strangers.

And then suddenly to be cast as a Tatterton and have to live in that mansion filled with memories that had made her true father jealous and disturbed. No wonder she fled from it with little Drake in her arms. Drake! He was not really my uncle, but surely he didn't know, and wouldn't unless Tony babbled the truth to him one day in a fit of madness. I was not eager to tell him. The pain of this revelation must remain enclosed within my heart, I thought.

I realized I had lost not only my parents, I had also lost my heritage, one of the important things that had linked me with Luke. We no longer shared a past filled with rich stories about life in the Willies, stories about our great-grandfather Toby. I had no past now because mine was linked to Tony Tatterton and I didn't want that link; I didn't want to remember anything he had told me about his father and grandfather.

I was truly about to start a new life and be someone different. Who would I be? How would it change the way Luke and I were with each other? The future was so unclear, and more frightening than ever. I had been dropped into a different sort of maze, and I had no idea how long I would wander about trying to find my way through it. I longed for someone like Troy, someone to take my hand and to guide me. Aunt Fanny was more wonderful than I had ever imagined she could be, but even she was overwhelmed by all that had happened.

I couldn't call for Daddy or go to Mommy. And Drake was so infatuated with Tony Tatterton and his position in Tony's enterprises, he was no longer as dependable as he used to be. I had lost the uncle who had been more of a big brother to me, lost him to the glitter of wealth and power. At this moment Tony seemed like the Devil and Drake like one of his victims.

My only bright and hopeful thoughts came when I thought about Luke. I would tell him how I felt and what my fears were. But would I be too much for him? Would he be overwhelmed by the responsibility of being a comfort and support to someone who was so desperate and alone? I had become much more than he had bargained for; that was certain.

Aunt Fanny helped me change into a nightgown and get into my bed . . . my own downy-soft bed with lilac-scented sheets. Mrs. Avery returned to put away my things and then fluttered about straightening this and dusting that until Aunt Fanny told her to let me get some rest.

"Luke and I will pick up some of the things ya'll need, like one of them fancy bed tables."

"And a walker. I want to start tomorrow morning."

"Right. Okay, darlin', welcome home where ya belong." She kissed me on the forehead and turned to leave.

"Aunt Fanny."

"Yes."

"Thank you, Aunt Fanny, for bringing me home."

She shook her head, her eyes gleaming with tears, and quickly left my room.

I stared at my bedroom doorway half in expectation, half in vain hope. If only Mommy would come through that door once more. If only she and I could have one of our talks again. How I needed her, needed her wisdom and her comfort. Perhaps, if I closed my eyes and wished real hard, I would hear her footsteps in the hall, her soft, warm laugh and then see her come bursting through my doorway.

She would throw open my windows and raise the shades. "Rise and shine, be happy to be alive and well. Don't waste a moment, for every moment is precious, Annie. Every moment is a gift, and you don't want to appear ungrateful, do you?"

"Oh, Mother, I'm still crippled. My legs are like old, water-soaked logs."

"Nonsense," I heard her say. "Life is what you make it. Now you tell those legs of yours they've had a long enough vacation. It's time to go back to work, understand."

Was that the sound of my laughter? I felt her hands on my legs, moving over them, magically restoring their strength.

"All right," she said, rising from the bed. Then she was drifting away, becoming a shadow. "Mommy? Mom . . . *Mommy!*" She was gone, and the sun was blocked by a large, dark cloud. My room was gray and dismal; there were shadows everywhere. *"Mommy!"*

"Annie?"

"What . . . who . . . Luke?"

He was standing at the side of my bed.

"Are you all right? I heard you scream."

"Oh Luke . . . please, hold me, hold me," I cried.

Quickly he sat on my bed and embraced me. I buried my face in his chest and sobbed while he stroked my hair gently and whispered, "It's all right. I'm here. It's all right."

Then I felt his lips on my forehead. His kisses of comfort brought a tingling to my breasts as I felt his warm breath on my cheeks. His heartbeat thumped against mine.

"I guess I had a bad dream," I said, a little embarrassed now. "And when I woke up, I thought Mrs. Broadfield was standing there. She was so mean to me, Luke. She would force me into baths of scalding water. My skin would turn as red as a rose in full bloom and take hours to cool down."

He touched my neck and nodded.

"My poor Annie. How you suffered, and I wasn't there to help you. I hate myself for being so stupid."

"It wasn't your fault, Luke. You didn't know."

We were still holding onto one another, neither wanting to let go. Finally he lowered me back to my pillow. He sat there, looking down at me.

"Annie, I—"

I touched his lips and he kissed my fingers. It made my body sing and come to life.

"I'd better get back to bed," he said.

"Wait. Stay with me a little longer. Stay with me until I fall asleep again. Please."

"I will. Close your eyes."

I did. He brought my blanket back over my bosom

and smoothed it out under my neck. I felt his fingers travel over my face and down the sides of my hair.

"Luke—"

"Just sleep, Annie. I'm here."

Sleep finally came again, this time soothing and restful. And when I awoke with the sunlight peeping through my window, I found Luke asleep at my feet, curled up like a little boy. For a moment I forgot what had brought him to my bedside. As soon as I moved, his eyelids trembled and he opened them and gazed up at me. The realization that he was in my bed struck him like a pail of ice water. He sat up quickly.

"Annie!" He looked about.

"Those are very cute pajamas, Luke."

"What? Oh . . . I must have fallen asleep. I'm sorry." He got up quickly.

"It's all right, Luke." I couldn't help smiling at him. The pants of his pajamas were a little baggy.

"I . . . I'll be back after I get dressed," he said, and quickly left the room.

Shortly after I awoke in the morning, old Doc Williams arrived. He had been our family doctor for as long as I could remember. He was a short, stocky man with curly peach-colored hair that was mostly gray now. When he walked into my room, he greeted me with a wide smile that made me feel relaxed. I didn't feel I was being prodded and poked like some laboratory specimen, and most importantly, there was no nurse hovering over his shoulder and scowling at my every question.

"Your pressure's good and your heart sounds fine, Annie. Of course, I gotta get hold of the X rays and reports from Boston. I'll do that right away, but I don't see any reason for you not to be walking."

"I started to stand on my own and even took a step

379

or two, Dr. Williams," I volunteered. "But they didn't want me to continue trying to walk."

"They didn't?" His eyes grew small and he pinched his chin between his thumb and forefinger as he stared at me. "I can see your reflexes are sharp. You have feelings in your limbs. Most of your problem is emotional now. They had no reason to confine you to a wheelchair and prolong your invalid state."

"So there's no reason not to continue trying to walk?"

"Not that I can tell. Just don't try to do too much and get yourself exhausted. Your body will be the best judge of that. I'll return soon as I get the information from Boston. Welcome home, Annie. I'm sure you'll be better soon."

"Thank you, Doctor." He saw the tears in my eyes and his face became fatherly, soft, his smile widening and his eyes brightening with love and concern.

"You know how I felt about your parents and how I feel about you. You've got to get strong now; you're going to have many new responsibilities." He pinched my cheek gently, the way he always did, and left.

Soon after, Luke swept into the room.

"Oh, I'm sorry," he said, turning about to leave again. "I thought they had gotten you up and about for breakfast."

"Now, Luke Casteel, you come right back here, pull up a chair and tell me everything you've done since I've been at Farthy. I want to hear all about your college experiences . . . especially about girlfriends." I remembered what he had told me on the plane, how he had been worrying about me so much he had kept to himself most of the time, but I also remembered Drake's stories and I had to hear it from Luke.

"Girlfriends?" He stepped back in and came closer to my bed. "When you mentioned girlfriends before, I didn't understand."

"Didn't you meet anyone special right away?" I questioned.

"Hardly. Between orientation, gathering books and materials, organizing my dorm room . . . and trying to get to see you, I didn't have time for much socializing."

"But I thought . . . Drake came to see you once, didn't he?" My heart was pounding now. Was Luke lying so I wouldn't feel bad? Should I force him to tell me the truth?"

"He came, for about ten minutes. I was in the dorm lounge reading," he said nonchalantly.

"By yourself?" I pursued. I was like a glutton for punishment, demanding to hear what I knew would break my heart.

"There were other students there, but we had hardly gotten to know one another. I told you, I was so concerned about you, I—"

"Drake thought you knew someone very well," I blurted out.

Luke looked confused. "Really? I didn't think he thought anything. He babbled about your condition, the need for you to be kept quiet and undisturbed, and then rushed off on some business errand, promising to keep in touch. I called him a number of times, and each time, his secretary told me he was out or involved in a meeting. I called Tony's office and usually met with the same response. Finally I called Farthy itself and spoke with Mrs. Broadfield. And as you now know, she wasn't encouraging.

"But I was so happy when my roommate gave me your phone message. Then . . . when Tony turned me away, I nearly knocked him over and rushed in anyway. All that kept me from doing it was fear of causing more trouble for you. Thank God my mother got that call and was on her way. Now tell me, what was all that about between you and Tony when we left Farthy . . . that confusion he spoke about?"

"Oh, Luke, it was painful, horrible and disgusting. I felt so helpless, so victimized, and what has added pain to it now is the knowledge that most of it didn't have to happen, that what I thought was being done as therapy or as good medical treatment was part of the madness I was surrounded by. I'll have nightmares forever!" I cried.

"No you won't, because when those bad memories return, I'll be here to drive them away," he promised, his eyes small and determined. "But tell me some of it. It might help to talk about it."

"Oh, Luke, it was so embarrassing, and now that I know some of the sick reasons for some of it, I feel dirtied and defiled." I shook myself to shake off the feelings and thoughts.

Luke took my hand into his. "Oh, Annie, what sort of things did he do?"

"He made me undress in front of him, and he insisted he help me with my bath."

Luke's face froze in astonishment.

"I couldn't resist him. There was no one to call to, no one to help me, and he seemed so . . . fatherly at the time. I let him wash my back, I let him . . . Oh, Luke, it's disgusting to think about it now." I covered my face with my hands. He slipped beside me on the bed and embraced me, holding me close to him and stroking my hair. Then he kissed my forehead and I lifted my face toward his.

"I'm so angry at myself for not coming to rescue you sooner."

"There was no way for you to know," I said. "But you were with me, helping me. During the darkest, most painful and lonely moments, I thought about you. Oh, Luke, I feel so secure with you, so safe again." Our faces were so close. We gazed deeply into each other's eyes. "I know it's not fair. I shouldn't make these demands on you and keep you from having a real girlfriend, but—"

He put his finger on my lips.

"Don't say anything else, Annie. I'm happy being . . . being with you."

He kissed my cheek. I closed my eyes, waiting, hoping, expecting his lips would press against mine, but he didn't do it. My body tingled in anticipation. I felt the blush come into my neck. My breast was pressed against his arm.

"Oh, Luke, I can't help feeling this way about you," I whispered.

"Nor can I help the way I feel, Annie." He pressed me to him again and we embraced for a long moment. "Anyway," he said, pulling back, "the horror is over. Who was it who called my mother? One of the handymen?"

I hesitated, wondering if I could share Troy's secret life with Luke. We had shared so many secrets before. I knew he was dependable and wouldn't do anything to hurt me.

"If I tell you, will you keep it a treasured secret and promise never to reveal it?"

"Of course. There are so many things between us kept under lock and key in my heart, one more won't matter."

"It was Troy Tatterton."

"Troy Tatterton? But I thought—"

"Troy Tatterton is not dead, Luke, but he wants people to think he is."

"Why?"

"He wants the anonymous life. He's had a very troubled, sad existence and he simply wants to be left alone."

"So he was the one who called my mother? Very lucky he did."

"I think it was more than luck. I think he decided he would look after me. He took me to see his cottage, and guess what, Luke? The replica," I said, pointing, "it's his cottage."

"Really?"

"While I was in his cottage he helped me stand and got me to take a few steps. I felt like a baby just learning how to walk, but that convinced me I should be trying harder right now, getting my legs to come back, to get used to holding my weight."

"Of course. We'll get your walker this morning and I'll help you as soon as you want."

"Help me into the wheelchair, please."

He looked about, helpless for a moment.

"Are you sure? I mean—"

"Of course I'm sure. I'm not a piece of fragile china, Luke Casteel."

He brought the wheelchair to my bed and gently pulled back my blanket. Then he slipped his left hand under my thighs and embraced me at the waist with his right arm.

"I'm not too heavy, am I?"

"Too heavy? You're as light as a warm, soft dream."

He held me in his arms for a moment. Our faces were so close that when I turned toward him, my lips nearly grazed his. We gazed into each other's eyes. I felt a warm glow move down my body, a magical, soft, silky tingle.

"I could hold you like this forever and ever," Luke whispered. His eyes were so intense, so fixed on mine, I felt as though he were looking into my soul.

"What if I told you to do that? To hold me forever and forever?" I asked him in a silvery, soft voice.

He smiled and kissed my forehead. I closed my eyes.

"I won't put you down until you tell me to."

"Let's pretend again," I said. "Pretend you found

me at Farthy asleep in that horrible room, under a spell cast by the wicked Devil. Put me back on the bed," I commanded. He smiled and did so. I put my arms at my sides and closed my eyes.

"I burst through the doors!"

"Yes," I said, excited that he had taken up the challenge. "And you see me and your heart is broken." I kept my eyes closed.

"Because I think you will never wake up and I have lost you forever and ever."

"But you remember the magic. A long time ago you were told this would happen and you must kiss the sleeping princess to wake her. Only, your kiss must be sincere," I added.

He didn't reply, and for a moment I thought the game was over, but I didn't dare open my eyes. First, I felt him leaning over me. Then I sensed his face coming closer . . . closer . . . until . . . his lips touched mine. And his kiss lingered on my hungry lips.

"Had to make it sincere," he whispered, and I opened my eyes. I wanted to reach up and pull him down to me, but I was so taken with my own feelings and the look in his eyes, I couldn't move. Then he smiled.

"It worked! You're awake."

He scooped me up into his arms again.

"My prince," I said, and embraced him more tightly.

"And now, to carry you off and away." He held me like that for a few long moments. If he were struggling, he didn't show it. Finally, I laughed.

"Okay, my prince, put me in the chair. I believe you," I said, thinking that someone could come into the room and find us like this.

He lowered me ever so gently and then stepped back.

"How do I look to you? Tell me the truth," I added quickly, afraid that I had changed dramatically and lost whatever beauty I had once possessed.

"Well . . . you're thinner. And I am having some trouble getting used to that hair color, I'm afraid."

"I'm changing back to my own natural color tomorrow."

"But other than that . . . you're no different. Just as pretty as ever."

"Luke Toby Casteel, you'd tell me I was pretty even if my face were covered with chicken pox," I said, trying to cover my obvious pleasure.

"I remember when it was and I did think you were still pretty, or at least, cute." He fidgeted about for a few moments. "You want me to wheel you anywhere?"

"No, I'll just stay here for a while."

He nodded, his dark blue eyes narrowing on me.

"When I just looked down at you, with your eyes closed like that, I . . . I didn't want to pretend. I wanted it to be a real kiss, Annie," he confessed.

"It was a real kiss," I said. "A wonderful kiss."

He nodded and then looked away quickly, knowing that if he didn't, we might say too much.

"Oh, Luke, I missed you so much."

He pressed his teeth down softly over his lower lip and nodded gently. I saw that he was holding back tears.

"Well now, I see ya up and ready to get started. That's good." Suddenly Fanny was in the doorway. "Want ta wash up and stuff and get ready for breakfast?

"Yes, Aunt Fanny."

"Okay then. You scoot off, Luke, and I'll get Annie up and dressed."

"I'll bring up her breakfast," Luke offered.

He started out.

"Luke," I called. He turned around quickly. "Thanks, but from now on, no more meals in bed. No more invalid."

He smiled. "Great. We'll work on your walking as many times during the day as you want." He looked at his mother.

"If ya two are gonna keep talkin' like this, I'll jist go back ta the livin' room and twiddle ma thumbs."

"I'm leavin'." He flashed a smile at me and walked out.

"Ya eva see anyone gab as much as that boy kin? Takes after his grandpappy Toby, all right. That man could sit out on the porch of that cabin whittlin' rabbits and jawin' till the sun dropped. Why, long after ma grandma Annie died, he still talked ta her as if she was still around, ya know."

"I understand why now, Aunt Fanny. It's hard to give up the people you love, and sometimes you just refuse to do it, no matter what reality tells you."

She stepped back and considered me. "I guess ya changed a lot, Annie. Grew in some ways 'cause of this tragedy and all that followed. Maybe ya learned things I neva learned 'bout people. Granny used ta say hard times kin wise ya up plenty. Know they did that fer Heaven. She was a lot smarter than me.

"Oh, I had hard times, too, but I was always feelin' sorry fer maself, so I didn't have time ta learn nothin'." She shook her head.

"Well, here I am jawin' away like Luke. Must run in the family. Let's tend ta ya bathroom needs and get ya dressed."

Mrs. Avery came in to help, too. The way she and Aunt Fanny fussed over me surely made me feel at home again. What a difference between their loving hands and soothing words and Mrs. Broadfield's coldly efficient and mechanical ways. All the money and elaborate medical attention in the world couldn't rival tender loving care. I should have known that from the start, and when Tony offered to get me the best doctors and the best medical care money could buy, I should have simply asked to go home.

In a short time I was bathed and dressed and Luke returned to help bring me downstairs.

"Ready?" he asked. Both Mrs. Avery and Aunt Fanny turned to me in anticipation. Would I back out and ask to have my meals brought up, or would I face the world without Mommy and Daddy? I turned to Luke. His eyes were full of determination for me. I knew he would be at my side.

"Yes," I said. "I'm ready."

And Luke moved forward quickly. He put his hand over mine and got behind the wheelchair.

"It's going to be all right," he whispered, and when Aunt Fanny and Mrs. Avery turned their backs to us, he kissed me on the cheek quickly.

TWENTY-TWO

By Love Blessed, or Cursed

As soon as we entered the dining room, my eyes shifted to my father's and mother's places. The empty seats stared back at me, and my heart folded in and shut itself away like a clam. For a moment no one spoke; everyone, including Luke, gazed down at me with faces soaked in pity.

And then everyone started talking at once . . . Aunt Fanny giving orders, Mrs. Avery complaining about this or that, Roland slapping his hands together and promising the best breakfast in Winnerrow. Even George, usually quieter than a storefront Indian, asked unnecessary questions like should he get another napkin holder? Was that the right pitcher for the juice?

"Everyone, please," I cried, "let's just enjoy the breakfast. It's not so important that everything be perfect. It's wonderful just to be back here with you all. I love you and missed you all very much."

They all looked down at me again, this time their faces full of love and affection.

"Well, then, let's eat," Aunt Fanny declared, "'fore it all gets colder than a spinster's bed."

"Oh my," Mrs. Avery said, pressing the palms of her hands against her bosom, and we all broke out into laughter and set ourselves around the table to begin.

"I made ya an appointment at the beauty parlor first thing this mornin'," Aunt Fanny announced.

"Well," Luke beamed. "It's a beautiful day. Why don't I wheel you down there."

"I'd like that."

Breakfast was cheerful. I couldn't remember ever eating as much, but Roland kept coming out of the kitchen with something else for me to try.

Right after breakfast Luke wheeled me slowly toward downtown Winnerrow, taking the same route we had taken all our lives: past the magnolia trees that lined the street, past the houses and other families I knew so well. It was a beautiful day, one of those rare late summer days when the sun was bright, the sky was crystal blue, and the air wasn't uncomfortably hot because a soft, cool breeze wafted down from the Willies. People waved from their porches; some came out to say hello and to express their sorrow over my parents' deaths.

"I feel a hundred years old and like I've been away seventy-five of them," I told Luke.

"Funny how different it looks once you go away and come back," Luke remarked. "I never realized just how small our Main Street really is. When I was little, it was as grand and as bright as Times Square, New York City, to me."

"Disappointed?"

"No. I rather like it. I think I'd like to come back here to settle down someday. What about you?"

"I suppose. First, I'd like to travel and see the world."

"Oh sure, me, too."

"Maybe your wife won't want to live in such a small town, Luke," I said, testing him with the painful reality I would wish to deny forever. But we were half brother and sister. Someday we would have to find someone else to love. Once Luke returned to college, I would have to face the fact once again that he wasn't always going to be here with me.

A pained look claimed his face. He squinted and wrinkled his forehead.

"She will if she wants to be my wife," he said angrily, despising the wife who wasn't me. He was so handsome and dangerous-looking when he lost his temper. Instead of turning crimson, his skin darkened and his eyes grew dazzling. "Besides, your mother returned to Winnerrow after living in a very rich and sophisticated world. If it was good enough for someone like her . . ."

I didn't want to tell him then what her real reasons were for returning.

"She was brought up here and she was coming back to a wonderful old house and a huge new business enterprise. But off in a college like Harvard, you're going to meet girls who come from cities and towns much larger and livelier than Winnerrow. They might think it's quaint, but they'll want to be where they can go shopping in fine, expensive stores, eat in fancy restaurants, and see theater and opera and other glamorous things." I hated to say these things, but I wanted him to confront the inevitable with me.

"I'm not interested in those kinds of girls," he snapped. "Besides, the same can happen to you. You'll meet a man who will want to take you away from here, a man who will be bored with this simple life."

"I know that, Luke," I said softly. It was so painful to think these thoughts, much less to say them aloud, but keeping them locked in our hearts was even more painful. It was one thing to fantasize and pretend, but it was another to lie to yourself. My short, horrible, painful and tormenting stay at Farthy taught me that.

"I know what," he chirped, suddenly looking bright and happy again. "Let the girl you think I'm going to marry and the man I think you're going to marry, marry each other. Then they'll be happy."

I laughed and shook my head. Luke wasn't ready to face the truth. Perhaps he felt he had to go on protecting me, that I was still too fragile.

"But Luke, what will happen to us then?"

"Us? You'll . . . you'll stay a spinster and I'll stay a bachelor and we'll grow old together in Hasbrouck House."

"But could we be happy that way, Luke?" I asked, wondering myself if we could.

"As long as I'm with you, Annie, I'm happy," he insisted.

"I feel as if I'm holding you back from a normal life, Luke."

"Don't ever say that," he pleaded. He stopped pushing my wheelchair. I looked back and saw the pain return to his eyes. He scowled like a little boy who was being teased and teased by older boys and was frustrated because there was nothing he could do to stop it.

"Okay. I'm sorry," I apologized, but he still looked as though he might cry. He shook his head.

"I mean it, Annie. I couldn't marry anyone unless she was just like you. And . . ." he added slowly, "there can't be anyone just like you."

He gazed at me so intently I felt my pulse begin to race. I quickly became aware that passersby and people in cars were looking our way.

"Well, when you find someone close, send her around and I'll give her lessons," I said, trying to lighten things up. But in my heart I couldn't help being selfish, wanting our lives to turn out just the way Luke predicted . . . neither of us finding anyone else and the two of us being together, forever and ever, being close and loving, even if we could never have what other lovers had—a marriage and children of their own.

We continued on toward the beauty parlor. They must have been waiting by the windows, watching for us, because just before we arrived, the owner, Dorothy Wilson, and her two assistants came rushing out to greet me.

"We'll take her out of your hands now, Luke," Dorothy commanded, getting behind the wheelchair.

All three of them fussed over me. While they worked on my hair, they gave me a pedicure and manicure and jabbered away, filling me in on all the local gossip. Luke went off to see some of his old friends and returned only moments after I was finished.

The girls didn't simply want to change my hair color; they talked me into a French braid as well. The sides of my hair were pulled back tightly and the back of my hair was woven into a thick rope of a braid. When Luke first stepped in and saw me, I could see that he liked it very much. His eyes widened and there was that smile that rippled slowly up his cheeks and settled around his eyes, that special smile I could remember on wonderful occasions like the time he gave me the charm bracelet and I gave him the ring.

"How do I look?"

"You're so very beautiful," he blurted. He looked at Dorothy and blushed because of how enthusiastically he had responded. "I mean . . . you look so much better in your own hair color. Everyone's going to agree, I'm sure. Well," he said, shifting his weight from one foot to the other, "we had better get back before my mother sends Gerald looking for us and he gets lost."

"You really like it?" I asked him as we started for Hasbrouck House.

"Very much. It makes you look like your old self again."

"I do feel so much better since I came home, Luke. I feel like I'm coming back to life after a long, long sleep. I want to try to walk again, Luke. When we get back, fetch the walker and I'll see if I've become any stronger or if it's all just in my imagination." My enthusiasm made him smile.

"Sure. Where do you want to try?" He slowed me down and I looked back at him. I didn't have to explain. Our eyes did all the talking. He nodded and we continued on.

When we reached the house, Luke went inside and came out carrying the walker. Then he pushed me down the path that ran around the side. He stopped at the steps of the gazebo and came up beside me to take my hand as we both stared up at it.

"First, I'll carry you up and set you on the bench."

"Okay." I could barely utter the sound; I was so happy to be here again with Luke.

He lifted me gently into his arms. I cupped my left arm around his neck and our cheeks touched. Then, carefully, slowly, he carried me up the steps of our gazebo and lowered me to the bench. He squatted before me, still holding my hand and looking up at me. I sat back and looked around.

"You're right about going away and coming back. Somehow it looks smaller, older."

"But we're both here again, together. Just close your eyes and remember it the way it was for us and wish and it will be that way again. I know it will. You know, I came here the day my mother and I returned from Boston after seeing you in the hospital."

"You did?" I looked down into his eyes, eyes that fixed so tightly on my own. It was as if we could see the deepest part of one another, go beyond our bodies and even our minds to press our souls together. He made me believe that we did share something special, something magical, something only we could know and touch.

"Yes. I sat here and closed my eyes and when I opened them, I saw you sitting across from me, laughing, your hair dancing in the breeze. You spoke to me."

"What did I say?" My voice was barely above a whisper.

"You said, 'Don't be sad, Luke. I'll get better and stronger and return to Winnerrow.' I had to close my eyes to see you, and when I opened them, something magical did happen, Annie."

"What?"

"I found this lying on the gazebo floor." He reached into his pants pocket and brought out a strand of pink satin ribbon I had used to tie my hair. "Oh, I know people would say it was always here, maybe hidden under the railing and finally blown out by the wind, but I didn't see it until I opened my eyes again."

"Oh, Luke." I took the ribbon into my hand. "It doesn't even look faded."

"I kept it with me, went to sleep with it at night. My roommate must have thought I was some kind of weirdo, but I didn't care. As long as I had it, I felt close to you. So you see, there is something magical here."

Magical, I thought. If love is magic, then this is magical. Oh, I knew it was wrong; I knew a young man and a young woman so closely related shouldn't be thinking of each other this way, shouldn't be looking at each other and wanting each other this way, but neither of us seemed able to stop it. Should we just confront it openly, declare our feelings freely and fully? Or should we go on pretending that we were only close friends as well as half brother and sister?

Would that end the longing I felt for him? Would it quell the racing of my heart everytime he touched me? Would I stop dreaming and fantasizing about him? If love was truly magical, then we were blessed, or cursed, by its spell.

Blessed because whenever I was with Luke, I felt alive; I felt like a woman should feel. Cursed because it was a torment to want and to need someone you were forbidden to fully love.

Perhaps it was better not to be touched by such magic.

"I want to be close to you, Luke," I whispered, "but—"

"I know," he said, putting his finger on my lips to lock in the words we both feared. He took his finger away and leaned toward me. My heart was thumping, my breath quickened.

"Luke . . ." I murmured, and he stopped, got hold of himself, and sat back quickly. He looked flustered for a moment and then he stood up.

"I'll get the walker. You're going to walk again without difficulty. You'll do it for us," he added, putting a higher value on my efforts. I grasped out quickly for his hand to make him pause.

"Luke, don't expect too much. I've just begun to feel my legs again."

He simply smiled down at me as if he knew things I didn't. I clutched the old pink ribbon to my breast and waited for him to unfold the walker and set it up in front of me. Then he stood back, crossing his arms just under his chest.

I reached up and took hold of the top of the walker. Then I pulled and pressed until my body began to lift from the bench. My legs wobbled but gradually straightened until I was in a standing position. My arms trembled. Luke looked concerned and took a step toward me.

"No. Just stay back. I've got to do it all myself."

A large cloud blocked out the sun and a shadow dropped over the gazebo like a great, dark curtain, shutting out the surrounding world. Even though it was warm, a chill traveled up the backs of my legs and into my spine. I struggled to get my back straighter and straighter and then I concentrated on moving my right foot forward. I felt the grimace of effort in my face as my lips tightened.

"Walk, Annie, walk," Luke urged.

I inched my foot forward with all my will until it completed a step. My heart pounded with joy and optimism and then I started my left leg. It was like reaching for something just an inch or two beyond you, like the gold ring on a merry-go-round, but stretching yourself and struggling until you went beyond the limits of space and strength and the tips of your fingers first grazed the gold ring and then seized it. My left foot found a step. The wheels of the walker turned. I opened my eyes. The cloud moved on and the sunlight lifted the curtain from the gazebo. I felt as if a great weight had been taken away from me, freeing me, ripping off the bindings around my knees and ankles. My legs seemed so much stronger, so much more themselves.

I smiled and moved my right foot again, this time farther. My left followed suit. The walker's wheels turned more. Each succeeding step was faster and longer. My back straightened even more, until I felt I was truly standing on my own power.

I was doing it!

"I'm standing, Luke! I'm standing! It's not just the walker!"

"Oh, Annie, I knew you would!"

I grew very serious and lifted my right hand from the walker.

"Wait, Annie. Not too much in one day."

"No, Luke. I can do it. I must do it!"

He started toward me, but I put my hand up.

"Don't help me."

"If you fall, my mother will shoot me."

"I won't fall."

Using only my left hand now, I moved the walker ahead so that I was nearly independent of it. When the walker was far enough from me, I straightened completely and then lifted my left hand from it.

I was standing on my own! Completely on my own! My legs were strong enough to hold me up again.

Luke held out his hands, only half a foot or so from me.

"Annie."

I closed my eyes and then opened them quickly. I was still clutching the pink ribbon in my left hand. Without further hesitation, I lifted my right foot and shuffled it forward a few inches and then followed with my left. Luke's face broke out into a wide, wonderful smile, and so did mine. I took a longer step and then another before my legs gave out with the effort, but before I had a chance to sink to the floor, Luke's arms were around my waist and he was holding me tightly to him and kissing my cheek.

"Annie, you did it! You did it!"

I was so happy I started kissing his face, too.

And then suddenly our lips met. The encounter was so quick and unexpected, neither of us pulled back before our lips pressed passionately together. Luke lifted his face from mine first.

"Annie . . . I . . ." He looked so guilty. We had passed through that veil between us, crossed that border, violated the prohibition.

"It's all right. I'm happy we kissed," I asserted.

He still held me tightly to him.

And then we both spun around at the sound of Drake's voice.

"Annie!" he screamed. His eyes were wide with shock and anger. I reached back to clutch the walker and pull myself from Luke's embrace. Drake ran up to the gazebo, his shoulders rising along with the fury in his face. He turned on Luke.

"I interrupted an important business trip when I heard what happened at Farthy, and now I'm glad that I did. Seems I got here just in time."

"And just what is that supposed to mean?" Luke demanded. They faced each other, their fists clenched.

"You and that hillbilly mother of yours had no right . . . no right to take Annie from Farthy, where she was getting the best medical treatment, where she had constant care, day and night, where she had the best equipment, where—"

"Drake, please," I interrupted. "You don't know what went on. I tried to tell you, but you didn't listen. Let me tell you now."

"Tell me what?" He sneered. I'd never seen him so angry. "How you wanted to come back here to play your . . . your fantasy games with him? I thought it was wrong then, and I especially think it's wrong now. But you're not to blame, Annie," he said, turning from me. "You've been taken advantage of in your weakened state."

"No, Drake. That's not true," I cried, but he stared hatefully at Luke, his dark eyes blazing like lit coals.

"I oughta break your neck once in for all," he said, his lips curling up and twisting his face into an ugly grimace, a grimace of hate.

"Maybe you should try once and for all," Luke responded, his face hard, his lips taut, his eyes small and determined, his whole face beet red.

"No, Luke! Drake, listen! I called Luke. I wanted him to take me from Farthy."

They stepped toward one another, both seemingly deaf to my cries.

"You don't surprise me now. I knew you'd turn out bad. How could you be anything else, living with a mother like that? It's rubbed off and it's finally showing itself. I saw the way you looked at Annie all these years."

"Drake, stop!" I was terrified over what he would say next.

"Well, it's going to end right here. It's going to—"

"Drake! Luke!" I pleaded.

The gazebo suddenly spun like a merry-go-round. The railing began to turn and turn. The walker began to roll on its own, moving too quickly for me to keep my balance. I felt myself spinning and dropped my head back. Before either of them got to me, I fell to the floor and all went dark.

I awoke in my own bed, a cold, damp washcloth on my forehead. Aunt Fanny and Mrs. Avery were standing beside me. Luke was seated in one corner and Drake was in the other, both sulking.

"I've sent fer Doc Williams. He'll be here any moment. Ya did too much, didn't ya? I knowed it would happen."

Both Luke and Drake turned to look at me, both looking sorry.

"I'm all right."

"We'll let the doctor decide that, Annie," Luke said softly.

Mrs. Avery replaced the washcloth with a colder,

damper one. Then Doc Williams arrived and everyone but he and Aunt Fanny stepped out of the room.

He checked my pulse, blood pressure, and listened to my heart. Then he sat back and shook his head, looking from Aunt Fanny to me, his bushy eyebrows lifted like two exclamation points.

"What happened here?"

"I guess she done too much, huh, Doc? We got her outta bed, let her eat at the table. Then Luke wheeled her down ta the beauty parlor and she was there a long time, and then she come back and he and her done some exercise on the gazebo with her walker."

"Did you push yourself too hard, Annie? I warned you about that." He shook his short, thick right forefinger at me in mock chastisement.

"I don't think so, Dr. Williams."

"Uh-huh. Well, your pulse and heartbeat are fine. Blood pressure is a little high, but not terrible. Just rest now and don't try to do too much. I finally got your Boston doctor on the phone and he promised to send your reports immediately. From what he told me, though, I think you're going to make a full recovery. It's just a matter of time."

"I know I will, Dr. Williams. Now I feel sure of it."

"Good, Annie." He stood up and turned to Aunt Fanny. "She'll be all right. Let her go easy for a few days."

"You hear the doctor?" Aunt Fanny warned.

"Yes, Aunt Fanny. Thank you, Dr. Williams."

"I'll stop by again soon." He smiled reassuringly and patted my hand.

Aunt Fanny started out with him.

"Aunt Fanny, please send Drake in. I must talk to him. It's all right for me to do that now, isn't it, Doctor?"

"Sure. Just as long as you rest, too."

Drake returned, his face glum, the anger still burning under the surface.

"Please, Drake, come sit here and let me talk to you. Dr. Williams said it was all right."

He remained in the doorway. Then he took a few steps forward, but I saw he wasn't going to sit down and listen calmly.

"You can't listen to what old Doc Williams says. The man is just a small-town doctor, Annie. Let me pack your things and take you back to Farthy."

"Drake, the last time you visited me at Farthy, you promised to help me leave if I insisted."

"I just said that because you were so overwrought from the medicine and all."

"Drake, it wasn't the medicine. The horror began with Mrs. Broadfield. She was a cruel, domineering woman. She thought I was some spoiled rich girl, and she resents rich people. She was terrible to me."

"So . . . Tony got rid of her, didn't he? He was about to get another nurse. That wasn't a problem."

"Tony is a problem, Drake. Tony was a big problem. He never wanted me to recuperate."

"What? Now listen—"

"No, you listen, please. Tony wanted me to be there forever. He wanted to imprison me in his dreams, in his twisted fantasies. He was deliberately not letting me do the things I should have been doing so I could get well. He was prolonging my invalid state deliberately so he could keep me in that bed, dependent upon him forever. Why, after I showed him I could get up and out of bed myself, he removed my wheelchair and walker from the room so I couldn't leave!"

"I'm sure he just didn't want you doing too much and hurting your chances for a full recuperation." He sat back smiling. "Sick people are often impatient with their recoveries and—"

"No, Drake, he wasn't thinking about my welfare. He was thinking only of himself."

"Now, Annie," he said, leaning forward, "I know—"

"He's not well!" I raised my voice and widened my eyes, and the abruptness and force with which I came back at him stopped him cold for a moment. "Drake, he . . . he came to me at night thinking I was my grandmother Leigh when Leigh was a young girl."

"What?" An incredulous smile took form in his face.

"Yes, he wanted to . . . to make love to me, thinking I was Leigh."

"Oh, Annie, surely your medicine must have created that ridiculous hallucination. Why Tony's . . . just a lonely old man. And that was why I came directly here," he said, taking on a reasonable tone. "You broke his heart when you let Fanny and Luke sweep you away from Farthy. He was practically crying to me over the phone. He doesn't understand why you left without saying good-bye to him. 'I did all I could for her,' he told me, 'and I would do more, do whatever she wants. I was rebuilding Farthy.' "

"Oh, Drake, why are you so blind to what's happening?"

"I'm not blind. I see a kindly old man eager to help us, giving me an important position . . . promising me the management of the Willies Toy factory here, as well as many other projects . . . someone who did all he could for you medically, willing to spend any amount to help you to get better. That's what I see.

"But I also see my slut half sister filling you with lies just to get you back here so she can live in this house and enjoy all of what Logan and Heaven had, and my perverted nephew eagerly pretending to be so self-sacrificing just so he can . . . can dominate your time.

He didn't waste any time getting you to the gazebo. Your magic place," he added with a sneer.

"He's not perverted, Drake. And I wanted to go there, to the gazebo. I believe in it."

"Annie, you're so vulnerable now . . . weak, your emotions naked . . . anyone can take advantage of you . . . Fanny filling you with ridiculous lies, Luke hovering over you, touching you . . . that's why I want you to return to Farthy where you'll be safe and—"

"Safe? Didn't you hear anything I said?"

Drake stared at me a moment, his dark eyes glowing.

"Luke's turned you against me . . . he's filling you with all this gobbledygook about fantasy games. That's why you won't listen to me and—"

"Stop blaming him. You're wrong about him. Luke has been wonderful, caring. He's even dropped out of summer school just to help me."

"You would defend him; you always did. No matter what I said or told you, you found a way to justify him," he accused, like someone who had felt slighted all his life.

"Drake." I reached out for him.

"No!" He backed away from my bed, shaking his head. "Heaven would be on my side. She would. She didn't like to see you with him so much."

"That's not true, Drake," I objected, though I knew it was.

"It is true," he insisted. "She was worried; she knew. Well, I won't remain here and watch this or put up with it. When you come to your senses, call me and I'll drop everything or anything I'm doing, no matter how important, and I'll come down here to fetch you and take you back where you belong. Farthy is yours; it's ours; it will all be ours!"

"But I don't want it! I want what I have here, Drake. Farthy is not what you think. My mother was right.

You were the one who didn't listen, not me. It's a . . . a graveyard full of sad memories. Don't go back there. Stay here. Work in the factory here and forget all that, Drake. Please," I begged.

"No. It's going to be mine . . . all mine. Tony promised. He promised. Remember what I told you. When you come to your senses, call me."

He turned and left my room.

"Drake!"

My scream died in an empty doorway. I buried my face in the pillow and sobbed. Drake looked so vicious, so angry. Gone was the kind of look a loving older brother would have. Gone was the softness in his eyes. Now his eyes were burning with jealousy and hate. All the Tatterton money and power and prestige had changed him. It was as if he had sold his soul to the Devil.

Luke didn't come up to see me after Drake ran off in anger, so I didn't know if there had been any more terrible words between them. Mrs. Avery asked me if I wanted to have lunch in the dining room, but I was too upset to be with people, so Fanny brought it to me. I asked her where Luke was.

"He said he had ta take a ride by himself ta think things ova. I didn't git in his way. When a Casteel man gits moody like that, it's best ta ignore him. If ya don't, they jist git mean and nasty."

"I never saw Luke mean and nasty, Aunt Fanny."

"Well . . . ya ain't seen him mad like I have. 'Course, I give him reason ta be mad sometimes. When he's with ya, he's different. Yer daddy's blood thinned out the hot Casteel blood, I guess, but ya neva know what kin happen. He'll go off and calm hisself down first."

"As soon as Luke returns, please tell him to come see me, Aunt Fanny."

She nodded and left me. To pass the time I went back to my last painting of Farthy, making the changes I thought would portray it more realistically. It was important for me to do that now, to put away some of my childhood fantasies. I added a man coming out of the maze. When I was finished and sat back, I saw that I had captured Troy's eyes, nose, and mouth so well, I was even impressed with my work myself. If ever I had been inspired, I was inspired now.

The work restored my strength and calmed me down, so I decided to have dinner in the dining room. Aunt Fanny came with Mrs. Avery to take me. I was disappointed to find that Luke had still not returned. Although Roland had prepared roasted Cornish hen with cherry sauce, one of my favorite meals, and had made a sumptuous-looking chocolate cream pie, I had little appetite. I kept looking at the doorway, hoping that Luke would arrive. But he didn't.

I watched a little television with Aunt Fanny, still keeping a part of my attention on the front door and listening keenly for the sound of a car driving up to the house, but the hours passed without Luke's return. Finally, tired and disappointed, I went to bed.

I fell asleep in short cycles, waking with a start each time and listening to the familiar sounds in the house, longing to hear Luke's footsteps. Sometime after midnight I awoke because I felt Luke's presence, and sure enough, when I opened my eyes and looked up, I found him standing in the pool of moonlight at the side of my bed, staring down at me.

"Luke, where have you been? Why did you stay away so long?" I cried. He stared down at me thoughtfully.

"I went to the cabin in the Willies, Annie, to do some thinking," he said softly.

"The cabin?" I sat up.

"I used to go there a lot when I was younger," he said quickly. Then he frowned, unable to hide the anger that boiled under the surface. "Is Drake still here?"

"No, he ran out. He's angry with me because I won't go back to Farthy and Tony," I explained.

"I was never so mad at him. I was hoping he would take a swing at me so I could swing back," Luke said, his eyes becoming cold and small with determination. Then he must have realized how hard and hateful he appeared, for his face softened and he relaxed his shoulders. "I suppose it's in my blood, and his blood, too. My mother has often told me about the Casteel temper." He sat down beside me. And then he smiled the smile I knew and loved so: his eyes bright, his lips soft. "I wish I was more like you, Annie. We have the exact same heritage, Stonewall and Casteel, yet you're so different, so tolerant, patient and understanding."

"Oh, Luke . . . we don't have the exact same blood. Tony wasn't just babbling nonsense when we left Farthy. Mommy wasn't a Casteel after all."

His smile froze for a moment and then evaporated. "How do you know for certain. Tony's so confused . . ."

I told him all Aunt Fanny had told me. He listened with rapt attention, but nodding slowly as if he had expected to be told something like this someday.

"So you're not my cousin and half brother, too. You're just my half brother," I concluded.

"Annie," Luke said, shaking his head like some tired old man and then sighing, "our lives are so twisted and confused. It seems that you and I have been left to bear all the suffering, a never-ending suffering."

"I'll get better Luke. I will," I promised. He looked so defeated, so overwhelmed. He wasn't my old, determined Luke, unafraid of facing the "tallest mountains." If he lost hope and faith, what would I do?

"I don't mean that kind of suffering, Annie." He looked down at his hands in his lap and then looked up. Even in the dim moonlight I could see that his eyes were wet with tears. "I was angry at Drake because he was so nasty to you, but I was even more angry at him because he . . . he said the truth. Annie . . ." Luke took my hand into his. "I can't help myself. I love you, and not like a half brother should love a half sister. I love you like a man should love a woman."

"Oh, Luke . . ." The walls between us crumbled in dust. My heart rose and fell. I couldn't help it. In my mind when Luke said the words aloud, he challenged the spell. He had done the forbidden and unleashed all the passion that had been waiting hopefully for just this moment, waiting for either of us to give in to what we truly felt.

He took on that familiar decisive look, his eyes fixed on me, his jaw tight. "I decided in the cabin that I would come here and say it all. Drake was right. I did look at you with longing, with passion all these years. No other girl made me happy. It's why I never really had any girlfriends. I dream about you all the time. It's wrong, I know, but I can't help it. That's why I ran away. It's painful, Annie. It's really very painful."

"Luke, I understand." I pulled myself up so that our faces were inches apart.

"Do you?" he asked, with the look of someone who had always known.

"I've had the same feelings, always had them, and they seem to have grown stronger since you came for me at Farthy," I confessed. For a long moment the air between us seemed more like a window through which we gazed into each other's eyes and against which we pressed our lips.

"I thought so," Luke whispered, his hands moving

up my arms to my shoulders. "I came so close to saying these things during the last day or so. I almost did it on the gazebo."

"So did I."

My nightgown slipped over my shoulders and hung precariously against my upper arms. Half my bosom was already exposed, but I didn't feel embarrassed. Luke's fingers, as if they had minds of their own, traced along my collarbone. He sighed.

"Oh, Annie, Nature has played such a dirty trick on us. I hate myself for loving you this way; but I don't know how to stop it, I don't even want to stop it!"

"Luke, don't hate yourself. I can't help it, either, but I don't hate myself."

"Annie . . ."

We could no longer keep our lips from touching. We both slipped through the imaginary window, and when his lips touched mine, my nightgown fell below my elbows and bared my breasts. His fingers traveled down to touch me. I moaned and searched for his lips again, but Luke pulled himself abruptly back.

"No, Annie . . . no, no. We can't do this. Drake was right about me. I don't belong here; I can't stay here. Whatever undercurrent of evil that has run through the Casteels is running through me now, too. If I stay here with you, I won't be able to stop myself and we'll become like some of my hillbilly ancestors . . . incestuous, like animals, ugly."

"Luke, we can't be ugly. This can't be wrong. I don't know why, but I feel it can't be."

"You're too good for someone like me, Annie. You don't deserve to have any evil curses dropped over your head just because I can't control the foul passion that runs freely through my Casteel veins. I'm probably no better than my mother used to be. Drake was right about that.

"I must stay away from you for a while, Annie, and

let you get better and stronger emotionally as well as physically." He backed away from my bed.

"No, Luke, I need you. Please, don't go." I reached out toward him, but he continued to back away.

"I must. God bless you, Annie. Get well."

He pivoted quickly and rushed out.

"Luke!" I struggled to get out of the bed. My legs trembled. Even so, I forced them to hold me enough so I could work my way around my bed and grab my walker. Using it, I made my way to the bedroom doorway. I got there just in time to hear the front door open and close.

"Luke!"

"Annie! What's wrong?"

Aunt Fanny rushed across the hallway.

"Oh, Aunt Fanny, hurry. Luke's run out. Stop him. He blames himself for everything, for what happened between me and Drake . . . for . . . for everything."

She nodded, but I saw she knew more than I thought.

"It was bound ta happen, child. Like Heaven, I could see it comin', but I didn't know how ta stop it." She guided me back to my bed.

"See it coming?" Did everyone know what we thought was kept so deeply secret in our own hearts?

"Saw the way he always looked at ya, saw the way ya were togetha. I saw the light in ya eyes and the light in his'n and I knew what was growin' between ya."

"Oh, Aunt Fanny, I didn't do it deliberately. I . . ." I sat on my bed, my hands in my lap, and shook my head.

"I know, honey." She sat beside me and took my hand. "I know ya wouldn't have let anythin' happen if ya could stop it. Love jist gushed outta ya and outta him. Can't blame nurther of ya fer it. Ya were both drawn ta one another at an early age, and like two flowers in the forest, hidden from everyone's shoes and sight, yer love grew free and wild until ya entwined. Yet, it's all wrong, so ya got ta untwine. It's goin' ta be somethin' painful, and fer it ta happen atop'a all the rest, it's goin' ta be doubly hard fer ya, but I'll be here ta help ya get through it, Annie."

"But Luke," I cried. He had no one to help and to comfort him.

"Ya got ta let him go his own way, Annie. I told ya. He ain't jist got Luke Casteel's name; he's got his blood. I loved ma pappy, but he was a man with a man's fire burnin' hot and heavy beneath those pretty eyes."

"Aunt Fanny, I feel so sick inside, so empty and alone. I just can't stand it," I moaned. She put her arms around me and held me to her for a few moments. Then she kissed my forehead and held me out at arm's length.

"Come on, Annie. I'll help ya back ta bed. Ya gotta think of yer own health now."

I let her help me. After I was under the blanket again, she leaned down and kissed me on the forehead and stroked my hair just like my mother used to.

"Git yerself some sleep, Annie. I'll be here with ya and help ya till ya get yerself on yer feet again."

"Thank you, Aunt Fanny."

"Us women gotta stick together now," she said, smiling and straightening her shoulders to indicate we would tough it out together.

She kissed me again and then she left me alone in the darkness with only the echo of Luke's voice beside me. I could still see his eyes close to mine.

"It isn't ugly; it can't be ugly," I chanted, and fell asleep with the memory of his kiss still on my lips.

TWENTY-THREE

The Secret of the Cottage

The next week and a half was difficult for me. In some ways it was even harder than the time I had spent at Farthy. Not that anyone was cruel to me; far from it. All of the servants and my aunt Fanny couldn't have been more concerned, loving, and considerate. But now, so soon after I had lost my parents, I had lost Luke, the one person in the world who I thought would always be there for me, the one person who made the struggle and the pain worthwhile. He was gone, and I felt as dead and as lost inside as I had when I had lost my parents.

Days were bleak and dark no matter how brightly the sun shone. I was forever cold and tired, wrapping my blankets around me and spending hours and hours simply staring up at the ceiling, not even wanting to put on the lights when twilight came. At times I felt numb, and at times I cried and cried until my chest ached. I cried myself to sleep, only to awaken to the realization that now all the people who had been close to me were gone. I had never felt so alone, not even when I was shut up in Farthy. At least when I was there, I still had my fantasies, my dreams.

Now even the dreams were gone. There were no more fantasies to pass the dreary time away. What was even worse, my memories of Luke and myself now seemed tainted. We were living a forbidden love, and all that had once been wonderful and beautiful to remember now seemed evil and wrong. That tore my heart and filled me with agony.

How horrible it was not only to lose the ones you love, but to lose the pleasure and joy of the memories of them as well. Fate had plundered my heart, come into my garden and plucked every blossoming flower, leaving only a plot of weeds and stems stripped naked of their beauty, their reason to be.

Many of my parents' old friends paid belated condolence calls, belated because I had been too far away for them to do so before. I appreciated their sympathy, but each time someone visited, I relived the tragedy, felt my loss afresh.

Some of my mother's friends broke into tears in my presence, and their sorrow cut into me sharply, opening wounds where scabs had formed. Nevertheless, I found myself being the stronger one and by necessity comforting them.

"It's jist what Heaven would do," Aunt Fanny remarked after one such episode. "In a pinch no one was stronger than yer ma. I was the one whinin' and bitchin', but it was her and Tom got us the food when we was nearly starvin', and it was her who nursed and cared for Our Jane when she was sickly."

These stories about my mother and stories like them gave me the determination and strength to work on my recuperation after Luke and Drake had run out on me. Aunt Fanny said Luke called frequently to ask about me, but each time she asked him if he wanted to speak to me, he told her he would speak to me another time. At least a half-dozen times I tried to compose a letter to him, but whenever I looked at what I had written, I tore it up because nothing seemed right, nothing expressed how I truly felt.

Doc Williams stopped by often to check on my progress. My legs grew stronger every day, and he assigned me a physical therapist to help me build them up, until I reached the point where I no longer needed the walker. Doc Williams gave me a cane to use just to keep my balance. A few days later I navigated stairs by myself and finally went outside by myself and sat on the gazebo, thinking about all the things that had happened to me and Luke. Aunt Fanny came out after me, insisting I put on a sweater.

"There's a chill in the air and ya still ain't fatted up ta where ya should be."

Autumn had crawled in quietly under the shadows, moving around us like a sleek, cool cat. Suddenly one morning I noticed that the leaves were nearly all rust and gold.

I remembered how much Mommy loved the fall. She told me it was especially pretty in the Willies. "I loved to wander through the forest then. Above me the trees were dazzling in the sunlight, the different trees different shades of yellow: amber, lemon, saffron; and different shades of brown: chestnut, ginger, and dark mahogany. Go to the forest in the fall, Annie," she told me, "and you'll get all your ideas for colors in your paintings."

She was right about that, but thinking about the forest and walking through the woods only reminded me of Luke because we had done that so many times together. How I wished he was with me now, now that I was back on my feet. But he was back at college trying to forget.

I began a painting of Luke. First, I drew the gazebo,

414

and then I drew him standing in it, looking over the grounds thoughtfully. While I worked on my painting of him, I eased the pain of his being away from me some, but as soon as I drew closer to finishing it, I felt a terrible loss. I delayed completing it, finding this and that to do, adding a detail here and changing something there. But soon I had no more to do and no way to avoid finishing it. When I finally put down my brush and stood back, I loved and hated the painting at the same time.

I had painted it from my heart and had captured him well, captured the way he always tilted his head a bit to the right whenever he grew deeply thoughtful, captured those strands of hair that always seemed to be over his forehead, captured the look in his eyes when he gazed at me and saw the love I had for him.

But the picture teased and tormented me. It made me long to hear his voice and feel his presence. This was the artist's passion and agony as well, I thought, to fall in love with what you create and yet never to truly possess it.

It made me feel so melancholy to think these thoughts. In the past when I had these depressions or became so deeply involved in something philosophical that it made my heart heavy and cheerless, I could go to Mommy and unload the burden my sad thoughts had placed on me. Mommy would greet me with the warmest smile, and almost immediately I was light-hearted and happy again. We would flip through the pages of fashion magazines and discuss the fads just like two teenage girls, giggling over something we thought silly, sighing over something we thought beautiful.

I still hadn't gone into my parents' bedroom yet. I didn't have the courage to go into the room where they had slept, where I had often gone whenever I had a nightmare or an unpleasant thought, and where I had been comforted and loved. I was afraid to look at their empty bed, see their closets and clothing, my father's shoes, my mother's jewels, the pictures, everything that had belonged to them.

But I knew that if I were to go on with my life and truly face the tragedy that had changed it so, I had to confront the things I loved that were gone; I had to face down the torment and the misery. Only then would I become strong enough to be the woman Mommy and Daddy wanted me to be, the woman I had to be for myself as well as for them.

I made my way slowly out of my room, guiding myself with the cane. I paused in the hallway, once more hesitating to turn to my right and go to their bedroom doorway, but this time my argument with myself was short. I was determined.

I opened the door. The curtains were open and the windows raised to air out the room. Everything was as neat and in place as it had been the night of the accident.

I stood in the doorway for a while and gazed at everything, visually digesting each and every morsel of memory. There on the vanity table were Mommy's powders and perfumes, a set of blue seashell earrings she had left the night of Aunt Fanny's fateful party, and the dark mahogany jewelry box Daddy had bought her one Christmas. Lined up neatly beside it were her pearl combs.

My heartrending gaze moved slowly across the room, pausing at the bed. Her soft red satin slippers peeked out from under it on her side, longing, I was sure, for the feel of her small feet slipping into them. A book she had been reading was still on the night table, a marker stuck between pages more than halfway through.

Of course, the painting of the cabin in the Willies was still above their bed. Looking up at it now made me think of Luke going there to think things over and conclude he should go back to college and stay away from me for a while. Perhaps the spirits of his grandpa Toby and grandma Annie had advised him. Maybe it was the right advice after all.

On Daddy's dresser was a large photograph taken of the two of them at their wedding reception at Farthy. Now I recognized the background. They both looked so young and so alive. Although when I studied the picture closely this time, it seemed to me there was also a longing in Mommy's face. From where they were standing, I knew they were facing the maze.

Thinking about the maze made me think about Troy and the cottage. And suddenly a wave of realization rushed over me. I returned to my room and gazed at the toy cottage Mommy had given me on my eighteenth birthday. The gift had meant so much to me because I knew how much it meant to her, but when I looked at it now, I found that it intermingled with images of the real cottage on the other side of the maze at Farthy, and I realized that it had to have been Troy Tatterton who had made the gift and had sent it to Mommy shortly after my birth. She had never talked about who had sent it. All she and Daddy had said was they assumed some Tatterton artisan had made it.

Was it that Mommy didn't know Troy was still alive and so couldn't imagine him making and sending it? Wasn't he afraid she might grow suspicious?

Thinking about him now brought another picture to mind: the way he sat in the chair talking to me . . . the way he had his hands behind his head. That was the pose the little man in the toy cottage had, too. Was that just a coincidence? And the little woman looked like Mommy, had her hair color, wore her kind of dress. She had to have known who sent this. Who else but Troy could have captured that scene? If she knew he was still alive and had sent the replica of the cottage, why did she keep that a secret?

I guided myself into the small chintz chair by my vanity table and set down my cane. Then, slowly, carefully, I lifted the roof of the toy cottage away, and instantly the tinkle of the Chopin nocturne began. It seemed to have been waiting all this time for someone to start it going again. I peered down at the small figures within and confirmed what I had thought: the man did look like Troy; the young lady was the tiny replica of Mommy.

Now that I had been in the real cottage, I saw things I had never noticed before: the wee toys the tiny man had been making, the teacups on the table in the kitchen, and the partially opened back door. Did the door actually open and close?

My fingers trembled as I reached in and touched the tiny door, which was only three inches tall. It swung open on its small hinges, and when I lowered my head to peer into it, I saw there was a flight of stairs going down. Something there caught my eye. A little ways down those mysterious stairs was a pale white piece of paper. My fingers were too large to fit through the doorway safely to reach in and retrieve whatever it was. There was only one way to do it, the way whatever it was had been put in there, I thought: with a pair of tweezers.

I found a pair in Mommy's vanity-table drawer, and with both a surgeon's eye and a surgeon's dexterity, I inserted the tip of the tweezers through the tiny doorway and took hold of the mysterious paper, inching it out carefully until I could see that it had been folded tightly until it had been small enough to hide.

I brought it up and out of the cottage and put it down on the tabletop. Then I placed the cottage roof back on to stop the tinkle of the music and began to unfold the paper. It was brittle, and yellowed with age, like those replicas of historic documents made to look authentic. The ends broke away and threatened to disintegrate in my fingers.

Finally I had it completely unfolded and placed before me on the table. It was a full letter-size sheet of paper. The creases were so deep, they made the words difficult to read, but I struggled through it.

My dear, dear forbidden love,

Now, more than ever, last night seems like a dream. So many times this past year I had the fantasy, that now, now that it actually came to pass, I find it hard to believe it really happened.

I sat here thinking about you, recalling our precious moments, the softness in your eyes and in your touch. I had to get up and go to my bed to search for strands of your hair, which, thank God, I found. I shall have a locket made for them and wear it close to my heart. It comforts me to know that I shall have something of you always with me.

I had hoped to remain here awhile longer, even though I recognized it would be a torture, and from time to time spy on you at Farthy. It would have brought me pleasure as well as some pain to see you walking over the grounds or sitting and reading. I would have been like a foolish schoolboy, I know.

This morning, not long after you left me, Tony came to the cottage and told me the news, news I expect you will be bringing to me, too. Only by the time you arrive I will be gone. I know it seems cruel of me to leave Tony at a time like this, but I gave him all the comfort I could while he was here and we had a chance to talk.

I did not tell him about us, about your visit last

night. He does not know you know of my existence. I couldn't add that to his troubles at this time. Perhaps there will be a time in the future when you feel he should know. I leave that to you.

You are probably wondering why I feel it necessary to leave so quickly after Jillian's death.

My dear Heaven, as hard as it may be for you to understand, I feel somewhat responsible. The truth is I enjoyed tormenting her with my presence. As I told you, she saw me a few times, and I knew it shocked her each time. I could have told her the truth, that I was not dead, that I was no ghost, but I chose to let her believe she was seeing a spirit. I wanted her to suffer some guilt, for even though it wasn't her fault you were born Tony's daughter, I always resented her for telling me, for exposing that horrible truth between you and me. She was always a very jealous person, resentful of the affection Tony had for me, even when I was just a little boy.

Now I feel terribly guilty about it all. I had no right to punish her. I should have realized it would only bring pain to Tony and even to you. It seems that I bring sadness and tragedy to everyone around me. Of course, Tony doesn't feel this way. He didn't want me to leave, but in the end I convinced him it was best.

Please stand by him during this time of great need, and comfort him as best you can. You will be acting for the both of us.

I expect you and I shall never set eyes upon each other again or touch each other the way we touched each other last night. But the memory of you is so engraved in my heart that I take you with me no matter where I go.

Forever and ever,
Troy

I sat back, dazed.

"Momma, did you know what you were bequeathing me when you gave me this cottage, the symbol of your love?" I whispered.

The unfairness, the sadness, the tragedy of it all struck me like a cold gust of wind. How horribly history had repeated itself. Something I had sensed in my heart, but hadn't quite put into words in my thoughts, had been true: Mommy and Troy Tatterton had been lovers, but their love was just as Troy had written at the top of the letter—forbidden. It was as forbidden a love as the love between Luke and myself, for Troy was Tony's brother, my mother's uncle. A blood relationship had made their love for one another foul, just as our blood relationship had made my love for Luke and his love for me foul.

So my mother always knew that Troy was still alive, but she could never speak to him, or write to him, or go to him again. Now I understood why Troy Tatterton had looked at me the way he had when he had first set eyes on me. I had surely roused his memories, especially with my hair colored the way Mommy's hair had been.

Much of what was written in the letter made sense to me, since I had been at Farthy. I understood the references to Jillian's madness, the idea of spirits wandering the big house, Tony's torment and the reason Troy had made himself invisible to the world around him. But what I didn't understand or know until this moment, of course, was Mommy's agony, for it seemed from the way Troy wrote, that she had loved him as much as he had loved her.

How well she would have understood what was happening between Luke and myself now, I thought; and now I understood why she was so concerned about the time he and I spent with one another. She anticipated all this because it had happened to her.

"Oh, Mommy," I whispered, "how I wish you and I could have just one more conversation. How much I need your counsel and wisdom. I would easily see that you had lived through this kind of pain and I would be guided by your words."

Until the first tear splattered on the letter, I did not realize I had been crying. Much of what Troy had written here to Mommy, Luke could have written to me. In fact, as I had read the words, I had heard Luke's voice.

I refolded the letter and lifted the roof from the cottage once again to return it to its special hiding place where it had been kept all these years. It belonged with the cottage; it was part of it. The music tore at my heart much the same way it must have torn at Mommy's whenever she sat alone and listened, for while it played, she surely saw Troy's face and heard his words of farewell, time after time after time.

Perhaps this had much to do with why she never wanted to return to Farthy. It wasn't only her anger at Tony. The memories of lost love were too painful. And all those times Luke and I talked about the maze and fantasized about Farthy . . . the pain we were inflicting on her without realizing it. Oh, Mother, I thought, forgive us. Our little fictions must have sent you back to this little toy cottage to mourn the love you had buried forever.

Just then Mrs. Avery knocked on my door. I called to her to come in. She looked unusually flustered and excited.

"There's a gentleman on the phone who says he's calling from Farthinggale Manor. He says it's very important."

Would I ever be free of Tony Tatterton and his mad hallucinations and confusions? Bubbles of anger began to boil in me. "Well, you'll have to tell Tony Tatterton—"

"No, Annie, it's not Mr. Tony Tatterton. He says it's about Mr. Tony Tatterton. He says he thought you ought to know."

"Know? Know what?" My heart stopped and then began to pitter-patter.

"He didn't say, Annie. He asked to speak directly to you and I came looking for you."

"Oh. Tell him I'm coming." I took a deep breath and drove back the cold shiver that had started to climb my spine.

I followed Mrs. Avery as quickly as I could. Now that I was up and about, I was frustrated by my slow and awkward gait.

Mrs. Avery handed me the telephone receiver and I sat down to speak.

"Hello," I said in a tiny frightened voice. I thought the pounding of my heart could be heard over the phone; it was that loud to me.

"Annie," he said. I had no trouble recognizing the voice, just as I imagined Mommy would have had no trouble had she heard it after years and years. "I thought you would want to know and might want to come to the funeral."

"Funeral?" My heart paused and I held my breath.

"Tony passed away a few hours ago. I was at his bedside."

"Passed away?" Suddenly I felt sorry for him, pining away at Farthy, thinking the woman he loved had left him again. Through me he had relived his own tragedy. I had unwillingly been an actress in a play cast years and years ago. Like some understudy, I had stepped into a role Mommy had been forced to play, too. Now, finally, mercifully perhaps, the curtain had been brought down, the lights had been turned off, the players had all left the stage. For Tony Tatterton, the agony had come to an end.

But Troy's voice was filled with sincere sorrow, not

relief. He had lost a brother who had once been more of a father to him.

"Oh, Troy. I'm sorry. I didn't think he was physically unwell. You were with him?"

"I had just made up my mind to make myself more visible and give him some comfort at a time in his life when he desperately needed someone to care for him, for what I had told you was true—he did care for me whenever I was sick. And," he added, his voice cracking, "he did love me very much. Ultimately, we had no one but each other."

My throat closed up and I couldn't swallow for a moment. I felt my eyes fill with tears. It was not difficult for me to imagine Troy at Tony's bedside, Tony's hand in his, Troy's head bowed, his shoulders shaking with sobs when the life left his older brother.

"How did he die?" I finally asked, my voice so thin it was nearly in a whisper.

"It was a stroke. Apparently, he had had a minor one some time back, but I never knew."

"Drake called me recently and told me he had spoken with him, but he didn't mention he was seriously ill."

"He shut himself up in his room, so that even Rye didn't know what was happening. By the time he realized it, it was already too late. At least I was with him at the end. He babbled a great deal, confusing people. After a while I wasn't sure he knew who I was, but he did mention your name and he made me promise I would look after you and be sure you were all right.

"I . . . I know that he had been going through strange mental torments, and I imagine you witnessed some of it, but he was harmless. He was just someone searching for love and a way to make up for his sins . . . something we all end up doing one way or another."

"I know." I wondered if he could hear in the way I had said that just how much I already did know. "I know who Tony really was to me, Troy. He shouted it out as I was leaving, and my aunt Fanny confirmed it."

"Oh. I see." His voice drifted off. "I'm not making any excuses for him, but he did have a complicated and difficult marriage."

"Yes." I wasn't eager to talk about all that now. "But Troy, I want to come to the funeral. When is it?"

"Day after tomorrow, two o'clock. Everything will be at the family cemetery. From what your maid just told me, I understand you've been improving steadily. I'm happy for you, Annie, and I don't want anything to set you back, so if making such a journey is too much of a strain—"

"It won't be, and I won't have a setback. I'm . . . anxious to see you again. I never had a chance to thank you for calling my aunt Fanny and having Luke and her come and get me. It was you who did that, wasn't it?"

"I didn't want to see you go; I was hoping we would have more opportunities to be together, but I saw what was happening to you here and I knew you really belonged with the people you loved, even though I can imagine how painful it must have been for you to go home. I remember Tony telling me how it was for him when he came to my cottage a long time ago, thinking I was dead and gone."

"It was painful. I wish I had a cottage to hide away from sadness and pain like you do with a maze to keep unwanted people away."

"Tragedy has a way of discovering the right turns and finding you anyway if it is meant to, Annie. I've learned that too well," he said sadly.

"I know." My voice was barely audible, just a shade above a whisper. I was about to say more, perhaps even mention the secret letter in the toy cottage. He

425

must have sensed something, for he spoke quickly to end our conversation.

"I'll see you day after tomorrow, Annie. I'm happy you'll be there with me. Good-bye until then."

"Good-bye, Troy."

I cradled the receiver slowly, my thoughts turning to Tony. Despite the madness and the lies, I couldn't help cry for him. Troy had been right: even though Tony was rich beyond imagination, he was lonely and lost, and very much like everyone else, searching for someone to love who would love him back.

Perhaps Rye Whiskey was right about the spirits at Farthy. Maybe they had finally ended Tony's torment by claiming him as one of their own.

Aunt Fanny was upset when I told her I planned to attend Tony's funeral.

"No one know'd he was yer grandpappy, Annie. No one expects ya ta travel all the way ta see 'im buried."

"I know who he was, Aunt Fanny. I can't forget him and hate him. He did try to help me in his own way."

"That place is poison. All them rich people destroy themselves one way or t'other. Not that I don't want ta be rich; it's jist the way those beantown phonies lived, thinkin' they was better'n everyone else. Makes them mad as hatters. I wish ya'd change yer mind 'bout it."

She complained all day, but she saw I was adamant. Shortly after I spoke with Troy and learned of Tony's death, I phoned Luke. I almost didn't speak when he answered the phone. He sounded so sad and alone. My hand trembled at the sound of his voice, but I closed my eyes and spoke up. As soon as he heard my voice, his voice regained its strength and lightness.

"I've been trying to write you a letter for days, Luke, but nothing seems right."

"I know. It's why I haven't spoken to you or written to you myself. But I'm glad you called. I'm trying to keep busy and to keep you out of my thoughts, but it's not easy. I'm so happy to hear your voice, Annie."

"As I am to hear yours, but I'm not calling with happy news," I said, and told him about Tony's death and Troy's phone call. "Your mother is angry about my going and says she won't go back there. She's hoping I won't want to go myself, but I will. I can get around now with my cane, so traveling is easier."

"I'll be there that morning to take you to Farthy," Luke replied quickly.

"Oh, Luke, I knew you would."

"I love you, Annie. I can't help it. I'll live with it and suffer with it until the day I die."

"And so will I, Luke." Neither of us spoke for a moment. My throat closed up so tightly anyway, I wasn't sure I would be able to get any more words out. Finally, after a deep sigh, I looked at the painting of him I had done and regained my strength. "Oh, Luke, I painted a picture of you standing in the gazebo."

"Really? Can I have it to hang in my dormitory room?"

I wanted it for myself, but I thought that was too selfish a thing to say.

"Of course."

"I'll see it when I come to pick you up. Don't worry about anything. I'll handle all the travel arrangements."

"Thank you, Luke."

"Annie, it's so hard to deny what I feel for you."

"I know. It's been the same for me."

"I'll see you soon." Both of us had to end the conversation for the same reason. Each word was like a sharp, heavy sword, stinging as it struck us, right through to our hearts.

Later in the afternoon Drake called. He was surprised I already knew about Tony's death, and even more surprised when I told him I would be at the funeral. He didn't even ask me how I had found out, so I didn't mention Troy at all. He put me off with his cold businessman's tone of voice.

"Well, if you thought you wanted to come, you should have called me. But it's not too late. I'll make arrangements for you."

"It's all being done. Luke's coming along, too."

"I should have known."

"Please, Drake. For Tony's sake, for his memory, let's keep peace," I pleaded.

"You're right. Of course, I'll act dignified. Everyone who's anyone in the business world will be there, I assure you."

"I didn't mean—"

"Anyway, you can't imagine what's left to do now. I haven't got the time to waste on Luke. It's fortunate I began here before all this happened. I might as well have been Tony's son, the way people are turning to me. I was going to surprise you with the news, but I might as well tell you now. Before he died, Tony gave me a large percentage of the stock in his corporation." He paused, and then dryly added when I didn't congratulate him quickly enough, "I thought you would be happy to know."

"I know it's what you want, Drake. I know you're happy."

He was disappointed with my thoughtful and controlled reaction.

"Yes. Well, I'll see you at the funeral."

"Yes, Drake." He seemed more and more a stranger to me.

Luke was at the house very early the morning of Tony's funeral to take me to the airport. I was dressed and ready when he came to my room. I stood without the cane. For a long moment we stared at each other. Finally, he shifted his eyes to the painting I had done of him.

428

"Wow, that is really good."

"I was hoping you would like it."

"Like it? I love it. You're a wonderful artist, Annie. People will pay thousands for your paintings, I'm sure. I know I will."

We stared at each other again. It seemed that whenever one of us finished a sentence, there was sure to be a long pause during which our eyes did the talking. Right now mine were telling him how much I loved and needed him and how much I felt cheated by destiny. His said the same.

I thought Aunt Fanny would relent and join us, but she had as much of that Casteel stubbornness in her as she said Drake and Luke had. She broke our tormenting silences by coming to the doorway of my bedroom, her hands on her hips, her head thrown back in her characteristic manner.

"Can't believe ya traveled down here ta take her ta that place, Luke. Ya shouldn't have encouraged it."

"I would have gone with or without him, Aunt Fanny."

"Yer motha ran away from that place and that man, Annie."

"I know." I gazed at one of the pictures of her on my vanity table. It was one of my favorites because in it she was gazing off toward the Willies, one of her few good memories of that life brightening her cornflower-blue eyes. "But she had a way of seeing the rainbows after the rain. I think she would have gone to Tony's funeral, too, Aunt Fanny." I turned back to her, my gaze as sharp and as determined as Mommy's could be. Aunt Fanny saw that.

"I've got to go for both of us."

TWENTY-FOUR

My Prince, at Last

$\mathbf{A}$s we started for the airport, I couldn't help imagining what it would have been like for us to be going to a plane that would take us on our honeymoon. What if we defied Fate and defied everyone and ran off to get married? This would have been our most romantic and loving journey. Airline attendants and other passengers would have looked at us snuggled beside each other and smiled to themselves, thinking how wonderful young love could be, how it opened the world and made life dazzling, exciting, hopeful, and warm.

When I looked into Luke's face now as he helped me into the car taking us to the airport, I couldn't help but think we did belong together. How tragic and quick life could be, I thought. Look at what had happened to my parents; look at the agony Tony had lived through. Why shouldn't we choose happiness?

During the ride to the airport in Virginia and the flight itself, I debated whether or not I should tell Luke about the letter I had found in the toy cottage.

Luke had been very polite, almost formal during the journey so far. I knew he was acting this way in order to build a wall between his feelings and me, but it was a torment for both of us. We quickly ran out of small talk, and every time his eyes met mine, our hearts thumped so hard both our faces became crimson. The passion within us wouldn't be denied. It would be easier to harness the ocean tide or smother the lightning that streaked across the summer sky.

Because what happened between Troy and Mommy seemed so similar to what was happening between Luke and me, I thought he had a right to know and to understand what they had suffered. Surely it would help him appreciate why Mommy was so fearful about our relationship.

I began by reminding him of the toy cottage, and then I described my discovery. When I recited some of Troy's words, tears appeared in the corners of his dark sapphire eyes.

"I can understand his loneliness and why he wanted to drop out of the world and live by himself on the other side of the maze," Luke said. "I feel the same way."

"No, Luke. You can't deny your life the way he has denied his. You must go on to become a doctor like you dreamed you would and find someone you can love cleanly, wholely, without guilt of any kind. You deserve it."

"And you?"

"I'll do the same. . . ."

"You're not a good liar, Annie. Your blue eyes betray you."

"Well, I'm going to try," I insisted.

He smiled that smile of Casteel arrogance, Drake's smile, too.

"Luke Toby Casteel, you don't know everything."

After my reprimand, his face became soft, sad, like a little boy's face.

"I know what I feel in my heart and what you feel in yours, and I know what that means."

"I'm going to try anyway, and so should you," I repeated in a smaller voice. I turned away from him so he wouldn't see my tears. Luke dozed on and off for the remainder of the trip and I stared out the window at the tiny houses and highways below, once again wishing we lived in a Tatterton toy world where fantasies could come true.

At the airport in Boston we rented a car and began the drive to Farthy. I couldn't help but remember Tony's excitement during my first journey to Farthy after I had been released from the hospital. He was so happy and eager to help me. How could I have ever anticipated what was soon to pass? Perhaps if Mommy had had a chance to tell me more about her past, I would have avoided the hardship and turmoil.

By the time we arrived at Farthy, the throng of mourners were gathered at the front of the house. Besides Miles and Curtis and Rye Whiskey, there were dozens of Tony's business associates, as well as many people who worked for Tatterton Toys. Most were formally dressed in black and gathered in small cliques, greeting one another, shaking hands, kissing cheeks and talking softly.

It was a warm, but overcast fall day, a perfect funeral day, I thought. Everything looked grayer than ever, and the bleakness emphasized how rundown Farthinggale Manor was. I couldn't help but remember the proud way Tony had described it when we had first driven out here . . . his ancestral home, improved and expanded by every succeeding Tatterton heir. How ironic it was that he had an heir who would truly follow in his footsteps but who had no relationship to him at all, for Drake was Luke Casteel's son, the man from whom Tony had bought his own daughter. And now, in every sense of the word, he had bought Drake, bought himself an heir.

And Drake had indeed taken charge. He stood up front by the hearse, dressed in an ebony-black tuxedo. His face was as somber and dark as an undertaker's. The people he hired to conduct the funeral were quietly checking with him for instructions. There were people directing cars and handing out small prayer and hymn cards.

Luke pulled his car into line and I gazed up at the main house again, the mystery and excitement of the big, old gray-stone building gone, replaced with unpleasant memories. The window of what had been my room was dark. All the curtains had been drawn, the panes becoming mirrors reflecting the dismal, cloudy sky.

The servants came to greet me first. Curtis looked shattered, his blue lips trembling; Miles looked stunned, his cheeks cold, his eyes distant. Even Rye looked very old to me. Bereavement had aged him quickly; he and Tony Tatterton had been together for so many years.

Drake approached us soon after, ignoring Luke and coming directly to my side of the car.

"How are you, Annie?"

"I'm fine, Drake." I was determined to be my mother's daughter and keep my dignity and strength.

"It will all begin soon." He leaned closer to me. "Do you know who is here? Who is alive after all?"

"Yes."

He recoiled with surprise.

"You do?"

"If you would have let me talk to you calmly instead of accusing me of being ungrateful and accusing Luke of terrible things, I would have been able to tell you I had met him here and he was the one who called Aunt Fanny and told her to come to get me."

"But . . . why?"

"Because he saw what was happening, Drake. He knew some of the things you refused to see," I said, not attempting to hide my anger.

Drake glanced at Luke and then turned to me again.

"Well . . . I . . . did what I thought was best for you, Annie. I'm sorry," he said remorsefully.

"Let's put it behind us, Drake, and do what we've come here to do," I said firmly.

"Yes. Of course." One of the undertakers signaled him. "I'll talk to you later."

He went back to the hearse. I looked everywhere for Troy but I didn't see him. Where was he?

My question was answered after the line of cars pulled away from the house and wound its way to the family cemetery. He was already there, saying his private good-bye. He came directly to our car as soon as we arrived. His dark, melancholy eyes brightened when he saw me.

Now that he was dressed in a black suit and tie, I was able to see the resemblances between him and Tony more clearly. However, where Tony's eyes had been bright and excited by his confusion and sadness, Troy's were calm.

"Hello, Annie. Was the trip all right?"

"Yes, Troy. Troy, this is Luke."

"Oh yes." They shook hands. I saw from the way they looked into each other's eyes that they liked each other instantly, and that warmed my heart. When I opened my door, they both rushed to help me, but Luke got there first. Troy stepped back and watched him help me out of the car.

"Just a cane now. That's good," Troy said when

Luke handed it to me. "How much of a difference tender loving care can make."

Luke, Troy, and I moved to the front of the crowd. I saw how Troy's eyes followed Luke's hand as it grasped mine. Troy watched us in a most peculiar way, his eyes growing smaller, his face darkening. He nodded gently to himself and then turned to hear the clergyman's words.

Drake delivered a short eulogy afterward, describing Tony as a pioneer businessman whose imagination tapped new markets and created an entirely new industry. I was impressed with how experienced and knowledgeable he appeared. He looked years and years older, and I thought Tony had been right about him—he was executive material.

The clergyman then asked everyone to sing the hymn written on the cards we were all given. During the hymn my eyes shifted from Tony's monument to my parents' monument. Graveyards have a way of making all life's struggles seem simple and meaningless, I thought. All family squabbles die and are buried here, too: Jillian's madness, Tony's lusts and confused passions, my grandmother Leigh's flight from who she was, my mother's frustrated and lost love . . . all of it was put to rest. Only those of us who remained had to struggle still.

For a long moment Troy and I looked at each other, and I think he knew I understood why he would want to ride into the ocean that fateful day. He looked from me to Luke and back to me. As soon as the hymn ended and the clergyman said his final words, Troy turned to us.

"Won't the two of you come to my cottage for a little something to eat and drink before you start back?"

"I'd like that," Luke replied. I simply nodded. I

looked for Drake, but he was busy greeting business associates, shaking hands and discussing actions to be taken in the near future. I didn't think he even noticed we had left.

I had the strangest feeling when we drove up to the cottage, approaching it on a road off the rear of the cemetery. It was as if we had all become miniaturized and we were about to enter the toy cottage, become citizens of a toy world, a world of magic and make-believe, the world Luke and I had lived in for so much of our lives. Troy, the master creator of the Tatterton Toy world was our magician. He would touch us with his magic wand and make the ugly and the sad world go away.

Luke loved the cottage and was fascinated with all of Troy's new creations, especially the medieval village. Troy prepared sandwiches and drinks for us, and he and Luke talked about college, Boston, and some of the things he was creating. I sat back and listened, happy the two of them were getting along so well.

Finally, Troy sat back, a gentle smile on his face as he looked from me to Luke.

"Tell me what your plans are now."

"Plans? Luke's back in college. He'll go on to be a doctor. I suppose I'll travel through Europe as my parents originally planned for me to do, so I can study the Great Masters, and then I'll attend college myself to develop my art talent. We'll go our separate ways and do what we can to make our lives meaningful."

"I see." He looked away, the smile lifting off his face and disappearing like smoke. When he looked back at us, his face was full of sorrow and pain again. "I must confess that I have brought you here with ulterior motives in mind. Believe me when I tell you I

436

have agonized for days over these things. The greater temptation is to bury the past alongside Tony and Jillian, Heaven and Logan, and live out my days as I am now . . . ghostlike, apart from the real world, involved only in my make-believe, my toys.

"How safe and secure the make-believe world is. But I have the feeling that is something you two already know, for you have found it to be a safe haven for your true feelings." He looked at us knowingly, and I wondered how someone who had seen and spoken with me only a short time could understand me so well and perceive my secret anguish so quickly.

He turned to his tiny creations.

"I can imagine a whole life for myself, populate it with the kinds of people I like and design events to fit what I want to happen. It's my particular madness, I suppose; not as debilitating as Tony's madness was, but nevertheless, a form of escape.

"But after seeing you two, I realize I can't do it; I can't forget and bury myself here. Even though it uncovers terrible emotional wounds and forces me to face sad reality, I must; for I must not let what happened to Heaven and me happen to you and Luke."

"Troy, you don't have to do this to yourself." I looked at Luke. "We already know."

"Know?"

"I was looking closely at the toy cottage you sent my mother shortly after my birth. It was you who sent it, wasn't it?" He nodded. "And I happened to peer closely into the door at the rear of the kitchen . . . the same door that you have in there," I added, pointing.

"And I found the letter you wrote to my mother the day Jillian died and you decided to leave."

Instead of the surprise and perhaps the embarrassment I expected, Troy merely nodded, a strange, small smile forming at the corners of his mouth, his eyes suddenly taking on a faraway look.

"She kept that, did she? How like her to do that, and how like her to hide it away in the cottage by the stairway. Oh, Heaven . . . my darling Heaven." He turned back to me, his gaze sharply focused on me now. "So you found out that your mother and I were lovers, secret lovers."

He stood up, went to one of the front windows, and gazed out so long, I thought he was not going to say another word. Luke reached for my hand and we waited patiently. Suddenly all the clocks struck the hour and a light blue music-box clock that was shaped like the cottage opened its front door and the tiny family within emerged and then retreated to the sweet, haunting melody I had come to know so well.

"Troy . . ."

"I'm all right," he said, and returned to his seat. "Some of what I am about to tell you, your mother might have told you herself.

"Years ago, when she lived the hard life in the Willies, she met your father and they became young lovers, pledging their hearts to one another. If your mother had remained in the Willies, she might very well have married your father and lived a quiet, happy life in Winnerrow, but Fate would not have it so.

"After Luke Casteel broke up his family by selling off his children, your mother lived with a very selfish, jealous woman, Kitty Dennison, and her husband Cal. It was a hard life for her because Kitty became jealous of your mother, and Cal . . . eventually took advantage of her. It's not hard to understand how such a thing could happen. Your mother was young and desperately searching for someone to love and cherish her. Cal, an older man, a father figure, sensed that.

438

"For a while that soured Logan, and even after Kitty's death, when your mother came to Farthy to live while he was going to college in Boston, he rejected her. She led a lonely life here. I was in the midst of a very bad time myself, convinced I would not live long. I was bitter and withdrawn. Your mother and I met, and for a time she filled my life with hope and happiness. We talked about marriage and made wonderful plans.

"Then Heaven left to pursue her lost family, and while she was away, as you know from the letter you read, Jillian told me the truth: Tony was Heaven's father; she was my niece. Knowing we could never marry, I wrote her a letter and left Farthy to travel and try to forget.

"I returned while she was away and, as you know, rode Jillian's horse Abdulla Bar into the ocean, convincing everyone, even Tony, I was dead.

"And I was dead, dead to anything warm and hopeful, just wandering about, waiting for the inevitable end of my wretched existence.

"But it didn't come. I lived on past the time I had dreamt I would die. Once again, hopeful, even renewed, I returned, dreaming of some kind of existence with Heaven, but by then she had reunited with Logan and they had married. I was living in the cottage secretly and secretly watched their wedding reception at Farthy, my heart shriveling.

"For a while I wandered about the grounds and even entered the building surreptitiously, behaving as one of Rye Whiskey's spirits, just so I could see her unobserved. Your mother sensed my presence and came to the cottage. I tried to hide from her in the tunnels, but she pursued and . . . discovered me, discovered I was really still alive.

"We both mourned the love we had lost, but"—his

439

eyes lifted to gaze upon my face—"we didn't leave it at that, even though we parted and determined we could never see each other again. She returned that night. God forgive me, I hoped and prayed she would. I even left my door open.

"She came and we had one last loving night together, a special, precious night, Annie, for there is no doubt in my mind as I look upon you now that your birth was a direct result of that stolen night of love."

My tears were streaming down my face throughout his tale, but when he said those final lines, my heart paused and Luke squeezed my hand as though he had been abruptly woken from a deep sleep.

"What . . . what are you saying?"

"I'm saying you are my daughter, Annie; my daughter, not Logan's. I'm saying you and Luke are not blood related. Fanny and Heaven were not sisters and Logan was not your father, although I'm sure he loved you as much as any father could love a daughter, even though deep in his heart he might have known.

"Believe me, I agonized over telling you all this, for I feared you would think less of your mother because of it, but I finally concluded Heaven would have wanted me to tell you so that you and Luke would not lose one another as she and I did.

"If there is truly a curse on the Tattertons, it is born out of our refusal to be honest with our hearts, and I will not let that happen to you.

"Lift the dark shadows from Farthy; shine a light of life over it, Annie. Understand and forgive people who were turned and twisted by cruel Fate, whose only fault was they longed too hard and too much for love."

He lowered his head, exhausted from his revelations. For a long moment neither Luke nor I spoke. Then I reached forward and slowly took my father's hand. He looked up to meet my eyes, and in his eyes I saw Mommy's face. I saw her smiling, beautiful face. I felt her comfort and her love, and I knew that everything Troy had told us was born of love, words from the heart.

I hated no one; I faulted no one. Actions taken long ago had determined that two families as different as night and day would cross paths and destinies. The turmoil that resulted swept up both houses, kept them forever in the midst of winds of passion and hate, driving some mad, shaking the very foundations of both families.

Now Luke and I stood alone in this confusion. Now my true father had decided it was time to end it. He showed us the way out of the maze.

"We don't hate and there is no one to forgive."

He smiled through his tears.

"There is so much of Heaven in you. I believe what you have of her will be strong enough to overcome any melancholy you have inherited from me.

"For a long time, I lived in shame, regretting that night of love Heaven and I shared, but when I saw how beautiful you were and realized what your life could be if you were free of all the lies and deceptions, I decided to give you the best, the only gift I could . . . the truth."

"It's the most beautiful gift of all. Thank you . . . Father." I stood up to embrace him. We held each other tightly, and when we parted, he kissed me on the cheek.

"Go now and live, free of all the shadows."

He shook Luke's hand.

"Love and cherish her as your father came to love and cherish Heaven."

441

"I will."

"Good-bye."

"But we'll come to see you, again and again," I cried.

"I'd like that. It won't be hard to find me. I'll always be here. My flight from life is over now."

He escorted us out and we kissed and embraced once more. Then Luke and I got into his car. I looked back once to wave good-bye. The melancholy part of me made me worry that I would never see him again, projected me forward to a time when I would return to a cottage empty but for the unfinished toys. But my happier, and hopefully stronger, side, shoved the dark pictures away and replaced them with images of an older Troy, still working on his toys, greeting me and Luke and our children.

Luke reached across the seat to squeeze my hand.

"Stop at the cemetery one more time, please, Luke."

"Of course."

After he did, I got out and he and I went to the monuments. We stood before them silently, holding hands.

In the distance the great stone house loomed as majestic and tall as ever. Sunlight found an opening in the clouds and widened and widened it until bright rays washed over the grounds and the building.

Luke and I looked at each other. In my memory our fantasy words replayed themselves: ". . . maybe it becomes whatever you want it to become . . . if I want it to be made of sugar and maple, it will be."

"And if I want it to be a magnificent castle with lords and ladies-in-waiting and a sad prince moping about, longing for his princess to come, it will be."

"Be my princess, Annie," Luke said suddenly, as if he heard my thoughts.

"Forever and ever?"

"Forever and ever."

"Oh yes, Luke. Yes."

He put his arm around my waist and then we turned away and went back to the car.

I smiled to myself, positive that back in the cottage, Troy was listening to the tinkle of a Chopin melody.

The Phenomenal
V.C. ANDREWS®

- ☐ FLOWERS IN THE ATTIC..................72941-1/$6.99
- ☐ PETALS ON THE WIND...................72947-0/$6.99
- ☐ IF THERE BE THORNS..................72945-4/$6.99
- ☐ MY SWEET AUDRINA....................72946-2/$6.99
- ☐ SEEDS OF YESTERDAY..................72948-9/$6.99
- ☐ HEAVEN..............................72944-6/$6.99
- ☐ DARK ANGEL.........................72939-X/$6.99
- ☐ GARDEN OF SHADOWS..................72942-X/$6.99
- ☐ FALLEN HEARTS......................72940-3/$6.99
- ☐ GATES OF PARADISE..................72943-8/$6.99
- ☐ WEB OF DREAMS......................72949-7/$6.99
- ☐ DAWN...............................67068-9/$6.99
- ☐ SECRETS OF THE MORNING............69512-6/$6.99
- ☐ TWILIGHT'S CHILD...................69514-2/$6.99
- ☐ MIDNIGHT WHISPERS.................69516-9/$6.99
- ☐ DARKEST HOUR.......................75932-9/$6.99
- ☐ RUBY...............................75934-5/$6.99
- ☐ PEARL IN THE MIST.................75936-1/$6.99
- ☐ ALL THAT GLITTERS.................87319-9/$6.99
- ☐ HIDDEN JEWEL.......................87320-2/$6.99
- ☐ TARNISHED GOLD.....................87321-0/$6.99
- ☐ MELODY.............................53471-8/$7.50
- ☐ HEART SONG.........................53472-6/$7.50
- ☐ HEAVEN (Limited time offer at special price)
                                        01005-0/$3.99

Simon & Schuster Mail Order
200 Old Tappan Rd., Old Tappan, N.J. 07675
Please send me the books I have checked above. I am enclosing $_____ (please add
$0.75 to cover the postage and handling for each order. Please add appropriate sales
tax). Send check or money order—no cash or C.O.D.'s please. Allow up to six weeks
for delivery. For purchase over $10.00 you may use VISA: card number, expiration
date and customer signature must be included.

POCKET
BOOKS

Name _____

Address _____

City _____ State/Zip _____

VISA Card # _____ Exp.Date _____

Signature _____ 752-21

Algae

A Problem Solver Guide

by Julian Sprung

Book Design by Daniel N. Ramirez

Published by Ricordea Publishing
Miami, Florida 33133 USA

W9-CAI-969

Oceanographic Series™
Algae: A Problem Solver Guide

Copyright © 2002 Ricordea Publishing.
All rights reserved under International and
Pan-American Copyright conventions.

Except for brief quotations for review purposes, no part of this publication may be
reproduced, stored in a retrieval system, optically scanned or transmitted in any form
or by any means, electronic, mechanical, photocopying, recording or otherwise,
without prior permission of the publisher and author.

First Printing July 2002
10 9 8 7 6 5 4 3

Published by Ricordea Publishing
Miami, Florida, USA

Distributed by Two Little Fishies, Inc.
4016 El Prado Blvd., Coconut Grove
Florida, 33133 USA

Printed and bound by Artegrafica, Verona, Italy.
Design and production by Daniel N. Ramirez
Photographs by Julian Sprung except where noted otherwise
Back cover photo: Leon Corry

ISBN 1-883693-02-0

Solutions

Simple, Elegant, Practical, Useful...

Two Little Fishies

SeaElements®
Julian Sprung's Reef Formula
Some trace elements accumulate in marine aquariums, but SeaElements avoids contributing to this problem by including only elements that are typically depleted, such as iron and manganese, iodine, strontium, boron, bromine, and others. Developed by Julian Sprung for Marine and Reef Aquariums. 250 ml (8.4 fl oz) bottle.

Kalkwasser
Julian Sprung's Reef Formula
Calcium Supplement Mix. For replenishing calcium and maintaining alkalinity, for corals, clams, and calcareous algae that build skeletons of calcium carbonate. It also helps maintain pH, precipitates phosphates and enhances protein skimming. Available in 1 lb bottle and 4 lb bucket.

Strontium Concentrate™
Julian Sprung's Reef Formula
For aquariums with dense growth of reef building corals, this supplement provides a concentrated boost of strontium to enhance the formation of their calcareous skeletons. Economical concentrated formula. 250 ml (8.4 fl oz) bottle.

HydroCarbon®
Julian Sprung's Reef Formula
Granular Activated Carbon designed specifically for water purification. Removes dissolved organic compounds that turn the water yellow. The extremely porous granules are the optimum size for use in high capacity filters, allowing high flow at minimal backpressure. Positively does not leach phosphates. Available in 1 Liter bottle and 4 Liter bucket.

Iodine Concentrate™
Julian Sprung's Reef Formula
Use this supplement to provide an extra boost of this important element and observe the positive effects. Great for growing *Xenia*, other soft corals and delicate red and brown seaweeds. Made from potassium iodide and seaweed extracts (source of organic iodine). 250 ml (8.4 fl oz) bottle.

C-Balance®
Two-part solution that makes replenishment of calcium and alkalinity easy. Adjusts calcium, magnesium and strontium ions to Natural Seawater ratios, and achieves a balanced ionic residual, for the optimal conditions for stony corals and coralline algae. Packaged in two 16oz. bottles, or the economical concentrate in two 1 gallon bottles.

FloraPlan™
Julian Sprung's Freshwater Formula replenishes essential trace elements and other micronutrients, providing them in special compounds that are easily utilized by plants and fish. FloraPlan fosters the development of colorful foliage, healthy roots and stems. It also enhances biological filtration and benefits fishes. Nitrate & phosphate free! 250 ml (8.4 fl oz) bottle.

PhosBan™
Synthetic ferric oxide hydroxide granules with an extremely high capacity for adsorbing phosphate from saltwater and freshwater. Also adsorbs silicate, and does not leach adsorbed substances. Recommended by Julian Sprung for long-lasting and easy control of phosphate levels on a permanent basis.

CombiSan
CombiSan® is a bio-activator that contains essential trace elements in special compounds easily absorbed by invertebrates, micro-organisms, and marine fish. CombiSan has been used throughout the world by scientists and marine aquarium hobbyists who keep and propagate stony and soft corals, other invertebrates, and fishes. Nitrate & phosphate free! Made in France. 250 ml (8.4 fl oz) bottle

MarineSnow® Plankton Diet
A first of its kind product that reproduces the special biogenic suspended matter found in natural seawater, including "marine snow" aggregates. A food for filter-feeding marine invertebrates that feed on particulate and dissolved organic matter, phytoplankton and zooplankton. Formula based on components of ocean plankton. Available in 250 ml (8.4 oz) and 500 ml (16.8 oz) bottles.

Water Conditioners

Julian Sprung's SeaVeggies®
Red Seaweed (*Palmaria palmata*)
Super nutritious natural Red Seaweed. Ideal for marine herbivores such as Tangs and Surgeonfish, Moorish Idols, Parrotfish, Angelfish, large Butterflyfish, and herbivorous freshwater fishes, such as Cichlids and Goldfish. Now available in new foil packaging and in two sizes: 30g (1 oz) and the New 12g (0.4 oz)

Julian Sprung's SeaVeggies®
Mixed Seaweed Flakes
(*Porphyra, Palmaria,* and *Ulva* spp.)
For herbivorous Marine or Freshwater Fish. Chopped natural seaweeds, harvested and dried to preserve their high nutritional value. Ideal for Tangs, Angelfish, some large Butterflyfish, Cichlids, Goldfish, Plecos, and Livebearers. NET WT. 30g (1 oz) Now available in Pro Bulk Pack 750g (1.65 lb)

Julian Sprung's SeaVeggies®
Purple Seaweed (*Porphyra umbilicalis*)
Super nutritious natural Purple Seaweed. Ideal for marine herbivores such as Tangs and Surgeonfish, Moorish Idols, Parrotfish, Angelfish, large Butterflyfish, and herbivorous freshwater fishes, such as Cichlids and Goldfish. Now available in new foil packaging and in two sizes: 30g (1 oz) and the New 12g (0.4 oz)

Julian Sprung's SeaVeggies®
Green Flakes (*Porphyra yezoensis*)
Super nutritious Natural Green Seaweed chopped into Flakes. Ideal for marine herbivores such as Tangs and Surgeonfish, Moorish Idols, Parrotfish, Angelfish, large Butterflyfish, and herbivorous freshwater fishes, such as Cichlids and Goldfish. NET WT. 30g (1 oz)

Julian Sprung's SeaVeggies®
Green Seaweed (*Porphyra yezoensis*)
Super nutritious Natural Green Seaweed sheets. Ideal for marine herbivores such as Tangs and Surgeonfish, Moorish Idols, Parrotfish, Angelfish, large Butterflyfish, and herbivorous freshwater fishes, such as Cichlids and Goldfish. Now available in new foil packaging and in two sizes: 30g (1 oz) and the New 12g (0.4 oz)

Julian Sprung's SeaVeggies®
Red Flakes (*Palmaria palmata*)
Super nutritious natural Red Seaweed chopped into flakes. Ideal for marine herbivores such as Tangs and Surgeonfish, Moorish Idols, Parrotfish, Angelfish, large Butterflyfish, and herbivorous freshwater fishes, such as Cichlids and Goldfish. NET WT. 30g (1 oz)

SeaVeggies Clips™
This unique plastic clip with a large suction cup securely holds Julian Sprung's SeaVeggies™. Attaches easily and holds firmly to the aquarium glass. Unlike other clips, ours floats, so it is easy to retrieve and won't get lost in the aquarium decorations. No metal parts. For freshwater and marine aquariums.

Julian Sprung's SeaVeggies®
Purple Flakes (*Porphyra umbilicalis*)
Super nutritious natural Purple Seaweed chopped into flakes. Ideal for marine herbivores such as Tangs and Surgeonfish, Moorish Idols, Parrotfish, Angelfish, large Butterflyfish, and herbivorous freshwater fishes, such as Cichlids and Goldfish. NET WT. 30g (1 oz)

PhytoPlan® Advanced Plankton Diet. PhytoPlan is a spray dried blend of several strains of phytoplankton. PhytoPlan is a food for filter feeding invertebrates and a great supplement to enrich the nutritional value of dried and frozen fish foods, or live *Artemia*. Rich in vitamins, trace elements, amino acids, and highly unsaturated fatty acids. NET WT. 30g (1 oz)

ZoPlan™ Advanced Zooplankton Diet. ZoPlan is a blend of dried crustaceans and other sea creatures in a size range that makes an ideal food for marine invertebrates such as soft and stony corals, seafans, anemones, zoanthids, clams, scallops, featherduster worms, and other filter feeders. Also for plankton eating fishes or larval fishes. Rich in vitamins, trace elements, amino acids, and lipids. NET WT. 30g (1 oz)

Two Little Fishies

Two Little Fishies Inc.
4016 El Prado Blvd.,
Coconut Grove, Florida 33133 U.S.A.
Tel (+01) 305 661.7742
Fax (+01) 305 661.0611
eMail: info@twolittlefishies.com
www.twolittlefishies.com

© 2003 Two Little Fishies Inc.
Two Little Fishies is a registered trademark of
Two Little Fishies Inc.

All illustrations, photos and specifications
contained in this brochure are based on the latest
product information available at the time of
publication. Two Little Fishies Inc. reserves the
right to make changes at any time, without notice.

Printed in Italy

PhosBan™
Granular Filter Media

Problem Solved.

PhosBan is synthetic ferric oxide hydroxide granules with such a high capacity for adsorbing phosphate that it can keep phosphate levels in aquariums low for MONTHS, not just days. PhosBan also adsorbs silicate, and does not leach adsorbed substances. Recommended by Julian Sprung for long-lasting and easy control of phosphate levels on a permanent basis. Got phosphate? **Ban it!**

I wrote this book to solve a problem. Not specifically any particular algae problem, what I wanted to solve was how much time I was spending teaching aquarists how to solve their own individual custom-tailored, genetically-modified, unstoppable, maddening, keep-me-up-at-night, "Help me, do something, DO something, please, please, please put me out of my misery now!" algae problem that was ruining their aquarium and disturbing the peace in their neighborhood. I figured that if I simply put what I knew into a short book I might save myself a fair amount of time: Algae problem? Read my book!

Definition of "problem" algae

To show their disdain for someone or something, ancient Romans sometimes used the description, "vilia alga," which roughly means more vile than sea slime. Many aquarists share this opinion of algae. I do not want to be accused of brainwashing readers into believing that algae are universally bad things. On the contrary, algae are essential features of the natural environment and our aquariums. Algae are primary producers that serve as food for fishes and invertebrates. In addition they filter the water in recirculating aquariums, removing ammonia, nitrate, phosphate, and heavy metals. Some algae fix nitrogen and are important sources of nutrients in nutrient-poor habitats. Furthermore they may release organic compounds into the water that are beneficial to fishes and invertebrates, and some are ornamental, enhancing the appearance of an aquarium.

Notwithstanding the aforementioned positive sides of algae, there can be some negative ones. Some algae grow explosively under the right (for them) conditions. Thus their growth can ruin an aquarium by covering every exposed surface and smothering sessile invertebrates. Some algae release toxic compounds that may damage or kill the tissues of sessile invertebrates, usually upon contact with the algae. Others, such as dinoflagellates, can be toxic to fishes and mobile invertebrates, including herbivores. At some point every aquarist encounters a problem with algae. Solving the problems and controlling the algae can be a real test of ones patience and skill.

Under specific conditions just about any seaweed, turf alga, phytoplankton or cyanobacteria can bloom and become "problematic." In this book I focus on the varieties that commonly do so in aquariums. I identify them by Latin and common name, with photographs showing their typical appearance and important features that can be seen when viewed under the microscope. For each entry I offer hope of salvation to weary algae bloom sufferers through a combination of aquarium husbandry practices and/or the use of herbivores specifically suited to graze the different problem algae.

Aquarists wishing to solve a particular algae "problem" seek the "cause" of it. Those who give them advice often focus on things such as lighting, nutrients, filtration, and herbivores. I explain all of this and more in this book, but wish to promote the idea that the "cure" of a given problem often does not involve a single big "fix," but many small ones instead, and a bloom may take time to subside after corrective action is taken. Steering a living biological system in the direction you want it to go is a different matter from controlling algae in one's swimming pool with a measure of chlorine.

The Chapter on algal biology and the chapter introductions for the different algae are intended to provide a brief overview of algal taxonomy, life history, and morphology. More detailed information on these topics can be found in the literature cited in the Bibliography, and through various internet sites dedicated to phycological research.

This book is the third in the Oceanographic Series™, and follows the quick reference style used in the first two, *Corals: A Quick Reference Guide and Invertebrates: A Quick Reference Guide.* We chose a more compact format for this book because the topic is shorter and more focused, but nonetheless of great importance to aquarists.

Acknowledgements

For their help in obtaining or having algae or other things I needed to photograph, thanks to Joy and her staff at Harbor Aquatics, Valparaiso, IN, Karen, Bob and the staff at Exotic Aquariums in Miami, Millie, Jean, Mabel, Nene, Eilene, and all the rest at All Seas Fisheries, Miami, George and his staff at Gables Aquarium, South Miami, Rick and the gang at Rick's Fish and Pet, Frederick MD., Joe and Jan Genero at Fish World, Richmond VA., Mike and Jan at Living Seas, Chicago, Scott Lebowitz at Fishnet, Lancaster PA.

For a variety of small and large favors for this book, thanks to Nadine Alexis, Robert Brons, Anne Fielding, Sanjay Joshi, Daniel Knop, Cory Pittman, Pauline Fiene-Severns, Peter Wilkens, Jim and Kaye, and the crew of Spirit of Solomons, Jim Norris and Walter Adey from The Smithsonian Institution in Washington D.C. Thanks to Mike Schmale and Pat Gibbs at the University of Miami's Rosenstiel School of Marine and Atmospheric Sciences who helped me with some of the microscope images, and a special thanks to Helen, Robbie, Eric, and the rest of the library staff at RSMAS.

Thanks also to my beautiful girlfriend Lluvitza, who helped me gather and photograph some of the algae in this book, and to my brother Elliot Sprung for his work on some of the images.

Thanks to Daniel Ramirez for making it all look so good.

The Biology of Algae

his book focuses on tropical photoautotrophs in several groups: The "Green Algae" Chlorophyta; "Red Algae" Rhodophyta; "Brown Algae" Phaeophyta; "Blue-Green Algae" Cyanophyta; Diatoms Chrysophyta; and Dinoflagellates Pyrrhophyta. This chapter provides an overview of what algae are, how they reproduce, their physical and chemical requirements, and special features of their structure and biology. I offer more detailed information about the distinguishing features of these different algae groups in Chapter three.

What are algae?

The algae (plural of the singular alga) are a diverse assemblage of organisms sharing the following attributes: all have the pigment chlorophyll, all produce spores as one of their modes of reproduction (some unicellular algae may themselves function as gametes), and most are aquatic, though many are terrestrial or subterranean.

We commonly think of algae as "plants," but the term algae is used to describe organisms belonging to the first three of the five kingdoms of life listed here: Plantae (eukaryotic, multicellular, autotrophs); Monera (prokaryotic, unicellular, autotrophs or heterotrophs); Protista (eukaryotic, unicellular or simple multicellular autotrophs or heterotrophs); Animalia (eukaryotic, multicellular, ingestive heterotrophs); and Fungi (eukaryotic, multicellular, absorptive heterotrophs).

Algae range in form from microscopic unicellular phytoplankton to multicellular seaweeds that may grow more than 50 meters long. Most are photosynthetic (photoautotrophs), some are facultative or obligate heterotrophs, and a few are phagotrophic! Some algae are symbiotic, living on or within animals, fungi, or other plants, and some are parasitic. Seagrasses, often confused with seaweeds because both are aquatic, are flowering vascular plants, not algae.

Evolution of algae from Prokaryotes to Eukaryotes

The name eukaryote in Greek means "true nut," but "eukaryote" is not just a name you might cleverly use to describe some difficult people you know. All people are members of this "true nut" society. The "nut" refers to the well-defined nucleus found in eukaryotic cells. The nucleus is a sac with a membrane, and it contains the cell's DNA. Unlike prokaryotes such as bacteria, cyanobacteria, and archaea, eukaryotes have their DNA in linear pieces bound up with special proteins called histones, forming the structures known as chromosomes. Eukaryotes also have a cytoskeleton composed of a network of protein filaments anchored to the cell membrane, and criss-crossing the cell periphery. The cytoskeleton provides a structural framework, giving the cell a shape, and stabilizes or selectively exerts tension on the membrane systems, which makes it possible for the cell to move. These protein filaments are involved in the separation of chromosomes during mitosis, and contraction of these protein filaments also makes muscles able to function.

Nearly all eukaryotes contain other complex structures called organelles that perform functions within the cells. Mitochondria are organelles that give the cells power. They employ aerobic respiration to generate energy, breaking down food in the presence of oxygen, and producing water and carbon dioxide as byproducts. In plants and many protists, organelles known as plastids use photosynthesis to manufacture food from carbon dioxide and water in the presence of light energy. Chloroplasts are plastids that contain the green pigment chlorophyll.

The chloroplast in plant cells is actually a cyanobacterium living within the plant's cells. Sometime in the late Proterozoic, or early Cambrian period, cyanobacteria began to take up residence within certain eukaryote cells, a lifestyle known as endosymbiosis. They made food for the eukaryote host in exchange for a home and other benefits. The bacteria became so dependent on their host that they no longer lived apart. Dinoflagellates known as "zooxanthellae," *Symbiodinium* spp. now live in symbiotic association with such animals as corals, anemones, and tridacnid clams in a way reminiscent of the early relationships that made possible the evolution of plants and other eukaryotes.

Plastids and mitochondria use their own prokaryotic DNA to replicate independently, a fact that supports the idea that these organelles are descendants of symbiotic bacteria that once lived inside the cells of a eukaryote host. Eukaryotes may thus be thought of as colonies rather than just evolved single organisms, something to keep in mind the next time you don't want to accept sole responsibility for your actions.

Cyanobacteria or Blue-Green Algae?

Because they superficially resemble algae, are photosynthetic and live in water, cyanobacteria are called "blue-green algae." However cyanobacteria are relatives of the bacteria. They are not eukaryotes. It is only the *chloroplast* in eukaryotic algae to which cyanobacteria are related. In a similar vein, some dinoflagellates contain a second nucleus that is believed to be part of a membrane-bound endosymbiont within the cytoplasm of the dinoflagellate. The presumed endosymbiont's cytoplasm contains not just this nucleus, but also chloroplasts, mitochondria and ribosomes. Thus some groups of algae may have obtained chloroplasts from other symbiotic eukaryotic algae instead of from symbiotic prokaryotes (Darley, 1982).

Primary production
The process of photosynthesis converts light energy into chemical energy that is stored as organic matter in compounds such as carbohydrates, proteins, and lipids. The amount of this stored organic matter produced by algae and other autotrophs is known as primary production, and it supplies food for many creatures, and for the creatures that feed on these creatures, and so on. Algae are thus referred to as the grass of the sea, as they form the base of the food chain.

Leaching of Organic Exudates
Algae are not just consumed directly, they also excrete into the water nutritious organic substances including polysaccharides, complex organic nitrogenous matter, vitamins, proteins, enzymes, DNA, RNA, and phenolic compounds (Bold and Wynne, 1985). Some of the dissolved organic matter contributes to the water staining in near-shore habitats and in recirculating aquariums. In the natural environment some of the exudates aggregate to form large particles in the water column, part of the material known as "Marine Snow." This is besides the contribution by algae of particulate organic matter in the water column, generated from erosion and grazing. Rates of exudation increase with photosynthesis during the light period and decrease in the dark (Ragan and Jensen, 1979) and, as for corals with symbiotic zooxanthellae, a significant amount of the carbon budget for seaweeds may be lost (exuded) as dissolved organic carbon (Hatcher et al., 1977).

Red algae have halogen-containing metabolites (bromine and/or iodine, sometimes even chlorine) in their tissues, and it is believed that they serve anti-bacterial functions in addition to a function in deterring herbivory. These compounds indicate allelopathic interaction between red algae and their environment (Fenical, 1975). Other algae may have similar positive or negative affects on other organisms. In aquaria with additions of iodide or iodine, the growth of such red seaweeds may curb the growth of fungi, pathogenic bacteria, other algae or cyanobacteria.

Reproduction
Algae employ several modes of reproduction. The simplest mode is vegetative: growth and division, or fragmentation. Another reproductive mode involves the formation of spores. Unicellular algae employ simple cell division to produce motile "zoospore" cells or non-motile "autospore" cells. Filamentous and other multicellular algae may liberate zoospores by division of regular vegetative cells, or from special structures such as sporangia. Algae also form gametes and thus have sexual reproduction. Some algae have life cycles characterized by quite different looking "adult" plants that may reproduce by different means (spore forming or gamete forming). Such a life history is called alternation of generations, also a feature of the life history of ferns.

Reproduction and life cycle in *Bryopsis* and *Derbesia*
In *Bryopsis* the gametophyte (which forms flagellated gametes) is a branched, tubular system of siphons with a familiar feather-like thallus. The filamentous thallus in *Derbesia* is the sporophyte phase (which forms diploid zoospores) and it has distinctive sac-like

sporangia. The gametophyte in *Derbesia* is usually a sac-like vesicle. However, there is such a close relationship between *Derbesia* and *Bryopsis* that at least one form of *Derbesia* has a "species" of *Bryopsis* as its gametophyte phase!

The sac-like gametophyte in most *Derbesia* spp. was at one time described as a separate Genus of alga, *Halicystis*. It resembles "bubble algae" *Valonia* and *Ventricaria*, but is solitary, small, and inconspicuous. In aquaria *Derbesia* my proliferate by asexual fragmentation of filaments, and the *Halicystis* phase may be absent. In this case there is direct development of sporophytes from the zoids of sporophytes, as reported in Sears and Wilce, (1970).

Bryopsis has a diplohaplontic life cycle, showing alternation of generations, almost exactly like that of *Derbesia*. Unlike *Derbesia*, *Bryopsis* is able to form homothallic microthalli (Bruck and Schnetter, 1997). During sexual reproduction a single *Bryopsis* plant with genetically identical gametes is able to mate with itself. Therefore it was separated from Derbesiaceae and placed in the family Briopsidaceae,

Siphonous Green Algae
Bryopsis is a member of the order Caulerpales that, along with the orders Cladophorales and Dasycladales, are called siphonous algae. This refers to their unique structure. Siphonous algae do not have cell walls dividing up their cytoplasm and organelles. *Bryopsis* has many nuclei within its branched, tubular thallus but no cell divisions. This condition is called coenocytic, or multinucleate. Although most unicellular organisms are microscopic, *Bryopsis* contains no cell walls within its internal structure and is therefore unicellular. The algal body is full of lens shaped chloroplasts that move around the cell. Menzel, (1986) showed that *Bryopsis* has an elaborate cytoskeleton made up of long protein filaments called actin and microtubules, which conducts organelle movement.

Bryopsis is given its shape by a single fluid-filled vacuole that extends throughout the center of the thallus. The cytoplasm, cytoskeleton, and all cellular organelles therefore occur only in a narrow region between the vacuole and the outer cell wall.

Clotting in Siphonous Green Algae
In multicellular algae, damage to the outer plant wall is not a serious problem because the damage only extends to those cells that have been ruptured. In siphonous alga, the smallest tear in the cell wall risks spilling the contents of the entire plant. In defense against this, siphonous algae developed a clotting factor similar to that of human blood. Within the cytoplasm multiple small protein masses collect at the opening when the cell wall is torn, and they form a new cell membrane (Fritsch, 1965).

Clotting factors also assist vegetative reproduction. If the plant is severed by turbulence or grazing, clotting factors in the fragment seal the opening and the fragment can drift and settle in a new location. A rhizoid develops at the base of the fragment, and a thallus forms at the top. Fragments maintain this "apico-basal" orientation. Thus the cell is said to have polarity, which means that two very different structures may arise from two ends of one cell. The rhizoid growing out of one end displays negative phototropism, which means that it bends away from a light source. The thallus displays positive phototropism, bending toward light (Iseki and Makoto, 1995).

Growth in algae

While siphonous algae grow by forming extensions of a single-celled thallus, in multicellular algae new tissues are added by a variety of processes involving division of cells within a localized part of the thallus. In parenchymatous growth cell division occurs in many directions, producing broad sheets or thick tissues. In intercalary growth the cell divisions occur in the middle of a set of tissues, usually near the base of the stalk, as in most Kelp species. This is in contrast to the apical growth (growth at the tips) that occurs in land plants and some brown seaweeds in the Fucales and Dictyotales.

Structures of the thallus

Flat photosynthetic structures in algae are called lamina or blades, and these may be attached by a narrow region called a stipe or stalk. The point of attachment to the substrate at the base of the stalk is called the holdfast. Root-like rhizoids aid attachment in sand and mud for some siphonous algae, particularly members of the genus *Caulerpa*. Some brown seaweeds such as kelps or Sargassum weed develop gas-filled bladders to keep their blades near the surface or at least facing the light.

Water Chemistry and Algae

Although they have some capacity to alter the quality of the water that surrounds them, algae are also strongly affected by the water chemistry. The following section gives an overview of water parameters that affect algae.

Salinity

Algae may adapt to a wide range of salinity, but many species do not tolerate a large sudden change in salinity. Unfortunately, with few exceptions the nuisance algae are not among the intolerant algae. If they were, controlling them would be as simple as performing a water change to drop or raise the salinity. For some varieties of cyanobacteria this may in fact resolve a problem bloom, but for most it does not, and filamentous green and red algae tolerate salinity changes quite well. *Caulerpa* species, however, do not tolerate wide fluctuations in salinity, and it might be possible to eliminate a problem species affecting some rocks in the aquarium by removing the affected rocks and exposing them to a specific gravity change of .010 points difference in a holding tank. Maintain the rocks at this specific gravity for a few hours before replacing them in the aquarium. For example, if the aquarium has a specific gravity of 1.024, make a batch of seawater at a specific gravity of 1.014 or 1.034 in the holding tank. Beware that this change will also kill many coralline algae, as well as sponges on the live rocks.

Alkalinity

The alkalinity of the water in an aquarium plays a role in managing algae growth for several reasons. High alkalinity promotes calcification, and thus encourages the rapid growth of calcifying algae such as red coralline algae or green *Halimeda* spp. High alkalinity combined with calcium dosing promotes the precipitation of phosphate, and thus limits algae growth.

Carbon

Carbon may be derived from Carbon dioxide, carbonates, bicarbonates, or organic compounds.

Carbon dioxide is present in various forms in water, as shown in the equation:

$$CO_2 + H_2O = H_2CO_3 = HCO_3^- + H^+ = CO_3^{-2} + 2H^+$$

Below pH 5, CO_2 is the main species, between 7 and 9 bicarbonate is most present and above pH 9.5 carbonate begins to dominate. Above pH 9 calcium carbonate precipitates.

Carbon dioxide

Carbon dioxide is a fertilizer for plants, being an essential component of the process of photosynthesis. Dissolved carbon dioxide occurs as carbonic acid, and its presence in the water lowers the pH. This is the reason for the measurable fluctuation in pH in aquariums. During the day, when the plants are illuminated and photosynthesis is occurring, the dissolved CO_2 is taken up from the water and thus the pH rises. At night, the dark aquarium has no photosynthesis to mop up the CO_2 produced by respiration, so the CO_2 accumulates and the pH is falls.

Enriched air

Standard indoor home aquarium designs have the aquarium exchanging gasses with the atmosphere of the room where they are located. If the room is small and does not have rapid ventilation with the outdoors, it may have an atmosphere quite different from natural air. In crowded offices, for example, the CO_2 accumulation from the respiration of many people causes a measurable drop in the pH of the aquarium water. This can also be demonstrated at a party when a pH meter is on the aquarium. The more people in the room the lower the pH will be in the aquarium. If the room where the aquarium is located has poor air exchange and a chronically high population of people (as in an office) the effect can promote the growth of algae, given the presence of other fertilizers such as phosphate, ammonium, and iron.

Phosphorus

Algae utilize inorganic phosphorus in the form of orthophosphate (PO_4^{-3}), either taking it up directly, or by obtaining it from various forms of organic phosphate. Algae use enzymes called alkaline and acid phosphatases to hydrolyse the organic phosphates and liberate the usable inorganic orthophosphate. Algae also accumulate phosphate beyond their immediate nutritional needs, a process known as "luxury consumption." They store the excess phosphate as polyphosphate in the form of granules in the cytoplasm. They keep the phosphate as a reservoir to help them survive when this essential nutrient is limited in their environment. Under phosphate limited conditions they not only use up their stores, they also increase the activity of phosphatase enzymes to obtain phosphate from as many sources as possible. Furthermore, some algae live in association with bacteria that liberate phosphate from the substrates on which the algae and bacteria are growing.

Phosphate and Kalkwasser Dosing

Reef aquarium hobbyists commonly add daily to the aquarium a saturated aqueous solution of calcium hydroxide (a.k.a. "Kalkwasser") as top off water. This top off water not only supplies calcium ions for coral growth, it also has a side benefit of precipitating phosphate from the water when it is added.

Dissolution of phosphate

When phosphate precipitates as calcium phosphate it is insoluble at typical aquarium pH. It may therefore accumulate heavily in the bottom substrate and in live rocks in an aquarium. While many aquarists have speculated that this reservoir of precipitated phosphate may, in time, cause algal blooms, the dissolution of calcium phosphate requires a sufficiently low pH such that it effectively does not occur in aquariums. If dissolution of precipitated phosphate were to occur deep within a substrate where the pH might reach a low level, the phosphate would still not be accessible to the plants living up in the bulk water.

One way that precipitated phosphate can be made available is if the substrate is used in a calcium reactor that utilizes carbon dioxide to lower the pH and dissolve the substrate. The effluent of such reactors may contain measurable amounts of phosphate. Much of this phosphate spontaneously precipitates as calcium phosphate again when it enters the aquarium that has a high pH and an abundance of calcium ions. Some of it, however, may be available to algae and promote their growth.

Another way that precipitated phosphate can be made available to algae is through the use of phosphatase enzymes. Algae may secrete these enzymes to break down organically bound phosphate, liberating usable orthophosphate. Symbiotic bacteria associated with algae may also secrete phosphatase enzymes.

Phosphate and activated carbon
Activated carbon is used in aquariums to remove water-staining organic compounds. The source of activated carbon is important for reef keeping aquarists who want to limit phosphate inputs to the aquarium because some sources of activated carbon leach phosphate. This can be tested by simply placing several grains of a particular activated carbon into a test vial with pure water (distilled, de-ionized or reverse osmosis) and phosphate reagent from a commercially available phosphate test kit. The carbon must first absorb water and sink before the test can confirm the

release of phosphate, which may take as much as 45 minutes. If the carbon leaches phosphate, a blue color appears in the test water, confirming a positive test result for phosphate.

Nitrogen
Most algae use nitrate (NO_3^-), nitrite (NO_2^-) or ammonium (NH_4^+) as sources of nitrogen. Some cannot use nitrite, while others (pers obs.) seem stimulated by it. Ammonium (NH_4^+) is preferred over nitrate (NO_3^-), and concentrations of ammonium above 1 micromol/liter may inhibit uptake of nitrate by some algae. Algae also are able to utilize a wide variety of organic sources of nitrogen, such as urea, and seaweeds may store nitrogen (as nitrate) in their thalli. Nitrates accumulate in the vacuoles of marine algae. *Derbesia* may have nitrate levels 500 times natural seawater and *Valonia* 2000 times natural seawater level (Round, 1965). Although marine algae generally prefer to use nitrogen in the form of ammonium, nitrate is a food for algae, and its presence in the aquarium water can stimulate algae growth.

Nitrate uptake in photosynthesis
Nitrate appears to act as an alternate hydrogen acceptor in photosynthesis (Round, 1965). When Chlorella is grown in the light with glucose and nitrate but with no available CO_2, it gives off oxygen, which indicates reduction of nitrate. Closed system marine aquariums with zooxanthellate corals and/or large standing stocks of algae may have little available CO_2 when brightly illluminated. Under such circumstances the algae may effectively reduce nitrate concentrations in the aquarium.

Sources of Nitrate
The principal sources of nitrogen in aquariums are food additions for the fishes. Dry foods

especially have a high protein content and thus provide a high concentration of nitrogen. The fish, invertebrates, and microorganisms that eat these proteins and amino acids produce nitrogen-rich waste ammonium. Aerobic nitrification accomplished by bacteria within the aquarium substrates and filters converts ammonium to nitrite and nitrate. Bacteria living in low oxygen zones within the substrate can break down nitrate into nitrogen gas and free oxygen, a process known as denitrification. Reef aquariums employing Jaubert's thick substrate and plenum method or deep sand beds often have no nitrate accumulation because of the strong biological denitrification that occurs in thick substrates.

Since algae will consume ammonium before bacteria convert it to nitrate, algae growing in an aquarium tend to limit the formation of nitrate by bacteria. Algae also use nitrate, so they may reduce the accumulation of nitrate in the water directly. Conversely, a strong biological filterbed (as in Jaubert's system) can process ammonium and denitrify the water so effectively that algae are left limited by the lack of available nitrogen (pers. obs.).

Cyanobacteria fix nitrogen

Aquarists have the opportunity to observe an ecological phenomenon that is important in the global cycling of nitrogen. Cyanobacteria are able to collect dissolved atmospheric nitrogen and store it in their tissues. When they die and decompose or when they are eaten by herbivores this stored nitrogen returns to the water as ammonium, thus supplying food to other algae. In this way an aquarium with no fish and no food additions can, with a population of cyanobacteria and an aerobic biological filter, develop high levels of nitrate accumulation.

Silicate

Diatoms use silicate in the form of orthosilicic acid, $Si(OH)_4$, to form their siliceous skeletons, known as frustules. They also utilize silicate in DNA synthesis. Other algae in the chrysophyta and chlorophyta are also known to accumulate silicon or form siliceous scales. The concentration of silicate-silica in natural seawater ranges from a trace to as much as 4 mg/l. In natural freshwaters the silicate concentration may also have this range, but in some localities it may exceed 50 ppm.

Aquarists try to limit the input of silicate into the aquarium by purifying (usually by reverse osmosis or deionization) the freshwater used for top off of evaporation. Since one might expect an R.O. filter to remove about 90% of a particular ion, if the source tap water has 50 ppm of silicate, there will still be 5 ppm left in the purified water. Therefore it is important to know the level of silicate in your tap water to be sure that the water filter can be effective at limiting silicate. In the above example, a secondary deionization filter placed after the R.O. filter would bring the silicate down to .5 ppm, an acceptable level for top-off water.

In marine aquariums with infrequent water changes, using purified top-off water, diatom grazing by herbivorous snails and fishes, and export (through siphoning or protein skimming) of the waste fecal pellets of the herbivores, the silicate level in the water can fall to levels that limit diatom growth. There will always be some silicate available in glass aquariums because a small amount is supplied by dissolution of the glass itself, in addition to the small amount supplied with top-off water and food. Silica is only slightly soluble in seawater, and its cycle in nature is limited by the fact that diatoms that use it are basically insoluble except under very alkaline situations. For this reason diatom growth slows with time as an aquarium ages. A large water change, which may significantly elevate the silicate level, normally produces a short-term bloom of diatom growth, usually appearing as a brown coat on the glass a day or so after the water change and lasting for only about a week.

Diatoms are important in food webs in marine ecosystems, and some authors of aquarium literature have pointed out that allowing them to grow (with sufficient herbivory) may be beneficial (Bingman, 2000). Supplementation with silicate or with unfiltered tapwater has been suggested for supplying trace quantities of silicate to promote not only diatom but also sponge growth. Although it is true that many sponges use silicate to form spicules, the main limiting factor for growing some sponges in captivity is their food source (large quantities of dissolved organic matter), not silicate.

Magnesium

Since magnesium is a component of the pigment chlorphyll, it is required for all pigmented algae. Magnesium is also required for the formation of the enzyme catalase (Round, 1965), which serves the protective function of breaking down hydrogen peroxide into oxygen and water. Magnesium is unlikely to be a factor limiting the growth of algae in seawater aquariums due to its high concentration in seawater.

A possible exception to this regards the use of magnesium by coralline algae, which deposit it along with calcium carbonate in their skeletons in the form of calcite. Coralline algae skeletons contain from 7 to 30% magnesium carbonate. There are anecdotal reports of die-off of coralline algae due to magnesium levels in the aquarium being well below natural seawater values (about 1300 ppm at a specific gravity of

1.025). It is important to remember that natural seawater values are measured at a specific gravity of 1.025. Aquarists with low specific gravity in the aquarium often erroneously believe the magnesium level is low when it really isn't. At a specific gravity lower than natural seawater, the magnesium concentration will be proportionately lower than 1300 ppm, and this is not a sign of deficiency.

Calcium

Calcium is required by many algae, though generally in small amounts, much less than is readily available in seawater (Round, 1965). Of course calcifying algae such as *Halimeda* or red coralline algae take up larger quantities of calcium from the water.

Potassium

Potassium is required for all algae thus far tested (Round, 1965).

Trace elements

Trace elements such as iron, manganese, molybdenum, cobalt, and zinc (Axler et al., 1980, Round, 1965) are known to enhance algae growth. It is not necessarily a specific concentration of these elements that is needed; rather it can simply be the availability of them, something that is affected by environmental factors. Naturally ocurring chelating substances, organic ligands, form dissociable complexes with metal ions, keeping them in solution and maintaining concentrations of free ions. One may think of them as "buffers" that maintain metal ions at optimal levels. Humic substances in natural waters are believed to have this benefit. A similar capacity is achieved with the synthetic chelator EDTA. Adding EDTA alone to culture water has been shown to enhance the growth of algae (Darley, 1982). Its effect is probably both to increase the availability of trace metal ions already present in the water and to decrease the toxic levels of excess free metal ions. Excess EDTA (over-chelating) can be used to reduce the availability of free metal ions to levels that limit algal growth (Darley, 1982). In aquariums the use of activated carbon to remove dissolved organic substances from the water may thus have an affect on algae growth, since it may strongly reduce the availability of these chelating substances, and therefore trace element availability. Conversely, allowing a system to become very rich in dissolved organic matter may limit the growth of algae by the over-chelating effect.

Some trace metals accumulate over time in aquariums and may be responsible for sudden blooms or die-offs of algae. For example, copper is required by some algae in minute concentrations, while slightly higher concentrations are known to kill many algae.

Molybdenum

Nitrogen fixation by Blue-Green algae requires Molybdenum. (Round, 1965). Molybdenum is also believed to be involved in phosphatase activity. (Round, 1965). There are anecdotal claims in aquarium literature that molybdenum supplementation stimulates the growth of cyanobacteria, but this has not been tested.

Iron

Iron is a component of the cytochrome molecule, and is thus a critical requirement for algae. Iron deficiency lowers the rate of photosynthesis. In alkaline waters (e.g. seawater) the amount of free iron in solution remains very low, but it can be available in colloidal form (Round, 1965). Iron is strongly limited in most marine aquariums. It can be

supplied with unfiltered top-off water, trace element or iron supplements, and with some foods. It is essential to add iron to aquariums for the health of corals, anemones, and other marinelife, but when the growth of undesirable algae is strong, iron supplementation can further promote this growth, even though it is not itself the cause. Hydroxides of iron can be used to precipitate or absorb phosphate, and thus can be used to limit algae growth.

Manganese

Manganese is involved in nitrogen metabolism, and its addition to algal cultures stimulates photosynthesis and growth. Manganese is required for growth in the light in some algae, and may also be required by zooxanthellae. Manganese is often limited in marine aquariums and should be added via supplements.

Boron

Small quantities of Boron are included in algal culture mediums as it has been observed that Boron deficiency may cause pigment loss in certain algae. Borate is included in many commercially available buffers (often in excess) and in some trace element supplements.

Sulphur

Sulphur is present in all plant cells, but algae are the only plants that form sulphated polysaccharides. However, most algae are probably not limited by the availability of sulphur under normal seawater conditions. Cyanobacteria such as *Oscillatoria* utilize hydrogen sulfide as a hydrogen donor (Round, 1965). Silica assimilation by some diatoms may depend upon the presence of water-soluble sulphur in the cell membrane (Round, 1965).

Vitamins

Vitamin B12, thiamine, and biotin are known to be limiting to some algae that require an exogenous source of these vitamins. Some algae synthesize vitamins endogenously and secrete them into the environment (a fact that may be responsible for the positive effects of some algae on the health of fish and invertebrates). Secretion of vitamins synthesized by one type of algae can make it possible to maintain in the same aquarium another type of algae that requires but cannot synthesize these vitamins. Some algae produce and secrete a glycoprotein that binds to vitamin B12, making it unavailable to algae that require this vitamin (Pinter and Altmeyer, 1979). This is but one of many ways an alga may gain a competitive advantage and dominate over other algae.

The addition of vitamin supplements to the aquarium water should be done sparingly, as it may promote excessive growth of some algae. Generally it is best to reserve the use of such supplements to soaking foods in them for the purpose of enhancing the foods' nutritional value just before feeding them to fishes or invertebrates.

Dissolved organic substances

Besides vitamins, other dissolved organic substances such as acetate, sugars, and various amino acids may stimulate excessive growth of algae.

Chemo-organotrophy

Many algae use organic compounds as a source of energy. Some of the compounds they may use include hexose sugars, acetic acid, alcohols, amino acids, peptones, and proteins. The use of foam fractionation (protein skimming) and biological filtration, described in chapter two effectively reduces the availability of such organic food sources and thus effectively limits the growth of algae. Bacteria that use the same organic compounds, given sufficient substrate to grow on, are also able to compete with algae for the organic food and limit their growth. Facultative chemo-organotrophic algae have chlorphyll but may absorb and use high energy organic compounds, allowing them to grow with or without light. Chemo-organotrophy may allow algae to live at very low light intensities. This heterotrophic growth is a means by which phytoplankton may supplement low rates of photosynthesis at greater depths. Chemo-organotrophic algae may also produce extracellular enzymes to digest large organic molecules that they would not be able to use otherwise.

Chemolithotrophy

The use of inorganic compounds as a source of energy is rare in algae, but common in bacteria and some cyanobacteria.

Other Parameters That Affect Algae

Light

Phototrophic algae utilize light wavelengths mostly between 400 and 700 nannometers as an external source of energy in addition to the organic and inorganic compounds they require. The light is absorbed by a variety of pigments, mainly (but not exclusively) found in the chromatophores. The pigments are sensitive to light of not only particular wavelengths (spectrum) but also intensity. The composition of pigments in a particular alga is a result of the ambient light it receives and can change according to changes in lighting, within certain limits. The subject of photosynthesis, while essential to the understanding of the biology of algae, is a topic of great complexity and not essential to the purpose of this short book. Explanations of the processes involved can be found in Round (1965), Adey, and Loveland (1991), Lee (1980), Trainor (1978), as well as numerous textbooks on the subject of biochemistry.

Old bulbs

As fluorescent and metal halide bulbs are used, they don't maintain their spectrums over time. Following the idea that some light spectra promote certain algae to grow more rapidly, the spectrum-altering effects of long-term use on light bulbs has been implicated as a cause for algae blooms.

Changes in intensity and spectrum emitted from the bulbs may promote the growth of some algae, in addition to the reduced efficacy for the photosynthetic corals, anemones, and other light-loving invertebrates. It is important to replace fluorescent tubes and metal halide bulbs according to manufacturer's recommendations for "bulb life," even though the bulbs continue to emit light. The replacement times vary. For many bulbs, daily use of approximately 12 hours per day cause a loss of spectrum and intensity that necessitates replacing the bulbs every six to twelve months. Some metal halides hold their spectrum and intensity for longer periods, and the new T5 format fluorescents claim to have very long life.

Temperature

Temperature affects on algal growth follow the usual relationship between temperature and biological activity. The alga exhibit increased growth rate with increases in temperature up to some optimum temperature, after which the growth declines, often sharply. Temperature optima vary for different algae, and algae have some capacity to adapt to grow at suboptimal temperatures. There is a relationship between temperature and light. Under high light intensities an increase in temperature raises the point at which light saturation occurs.

Water Motion

The movement of water is a physical factor that has numerous effects on the growth of algae. Strong water motion has the ability to move sand and gravel substrates, thus preventing the development of microalgae mats there. The shearing effect of strong water motion likewise may lift algal mats from soft or hard substrates, and can prevent the growth of some loosely attached types of green filamentous algae. Slow water motion promotes settlement and accumulation of nutrient-rich detritus. Combined with strong illumination, slow flow can thus promote the development of algal mats.

Water flow and Nutrient uptake

The quantity of nitrogen and phosphorus compounds in the water on a reef is low, but the supply is limitless given the continuous replenishment of water (Adey and Loveland, 1991). The nutrient levels in the water may vary little, but the supply may vary quite a bit. This state is termed dynamic equilibrium (Delbeek and Sprung, 1994). The dissolved nutrients in the water are only a portion of its nutrient package that is continuously replenished with new water. Live phytoplankton and zooplankton are nutrient sources that, upon being eaten and digested, supply additional nutrient input to the reef. The faster the water moves past a point on the reef, the more nutrients are available to it (Atkinson, et al., 2002). Furthermore, the motion of water can prevent the development of nutrient-depleted water in the micro-layers surrounding algal filaments, the so-called boundary layers that can isolate an object (or plant or animal) from the surrounding water. Strong water flow disturbs and thus replenishes this layer from which the plant absorbs nutrients.

An aquarium works in a different manner. It is a more static equilibrium. The nutrients are more tightly recycled and may either become limited or accumulate. Biological filtration tends to "buffer" the nutrient level to a static position. An aquarium that has nitrogen and phosphorus levels matching reef water may thus be nutrient limited if sufficient food inputs are not made. Aquarists trying to "duplicate reef parameters" often miss this important point. Water flow also affects the accumulation of detritus.

Filtration and algae

Filtration by definition refers to purification of the water by some means that separates or alters the impurities so that they are easily removed from the water. Various modes of filtration have an affect on algae, either directly or indirectly. Indirect effects include the limitation of nutrients that promote algal growth, while direct effects include mechanical removal of algal spores or filaments, or destruction of waterborne algae by ultraviolet wavelengths in a UV sterilizer. In chapter Two I briefly describe the filters, filter media, and their affect on algae.

Algal Succession

Algae grow in aquariums following a predictable pattern from the time the aquarium is started and as it matures. It is important for a beginning aquarist to understand that the occurrence of certain algae (diatoms, cyanobacteria, and *Bryopsis,* for instance) is normal during the first several weeks the aquarium is set up. The lack of their occurrence during the "break-in period" would be exceptional. Delbeek (1990 a and b) and Fossa and Nilsen (1996) offer accounts of the succession of algae that bloom during the break-in period and afterwards.

When live rock is added to a newly established aquarium with illumination, the growth of diatoms on the rock and walls of the aquarium begins by the second day. It obstructs the view through the windows and, if the water flow is not sufficiently strong to prevent it, covers the sand or gravel. This phase lasts about two to three weeks and is followed by the appearance of red cyanobacteria on the rocks and glass, and light green filamentous *Bryopsis* on the glass. The *Bryopsis* may be accompanied by *Enteromorpha* and *Chaetomorpha*. If the alkalinity and calcium levels are maintained at or slightly above natural seawater values, and phosphate accumulation is managed with protein skimming, adsorption media, or algal filters, coralline algae will begin to grow rapidly on the glass and plastic pipes after about one to two months. Under ideal circumstances the diatoms, cyanobacteria, and *Bryopsis* will spontaneously disappear and coralline algae will continue to grow, followed by the appearance of seaweeds such as *Caulerpa, Halimeda, Sargassum, Dictyota, Lobophora, Halymenia, Hypnea,* and many others. The presence of large herbivores such as surgeonfishes and *Diadema* urchins limits the occurrence of the larger seaweeds and tends to leave the live rocks with a more bare-looking coat of coralline algae. In larger aquariums the affect of these grazers is less pronounced.

Ways to Control the Growth of Algae

If the control of algae could be achieved by one magic substance this book would hardly be necessary, and this chapter would be titled "The way" instead of "Ways" to control the growth of algae. In fact there are useful creatures, substances, and methods that can make algae vanish like magic, but not in every case, and usually not instantaneously. When the various methods and herbivores described here are used, in time the control of algae is achieved.

Herbivores are an "in-house" means of algae control. The simplest invertebrate grazers are microscopic protozoans. Many ciliates can be seen zipping about if one places a sample of algae under a dissecting microscope. Some of these are herbivores, and they may play a very important role in the presence or absence of some forms of algae in aquariums. One unidentified ciliate is so large that it can be seen by the unaided eye (at least by those people with good eyes!). It is a dark reddish elongated creature that could easily be mistaken for a small worm. It occurs in large numbers on the aquarium walls, where it appears to feed on diatoms and other microalgae. Its presence is delineated on an algae-coated viewing window by a zone of cleared algae, often in a circular shape. The ciliates are located at the edge of the zone, and they proceed to graze from this front. They must also occur on live rocks and sand and surely play a role in the grazing of microalgae in these areas.

Copepods

Copepods are very small crustaceans, most being smaller than a grain of sand, though larger species exist. They are abundant in aquatic ecosystems and are an important source of food for fish larvae and planktivorous fishes. While many copepods live in the water column where they feed on phytoplankton and particulate organic material, there are also many varieties of copepods that live in sediments and especially in algal turfs and mats. These copepods may feed directly on the algae or on organic material trapped by the algal filaments. Fishes that feed heavily on copepods (mandarinfish, pipefish) may reduce their populations in a small aquarium, and this can promote the growth of algae.

Unidentified red ciliate with the diatom *Nitzschia*.

Copepod on red slime algae.

Copepod on *Derbesia*.

The unidentified red ciliates can just barely be seen by the unaided eye en-masse on the glass.

A typical amphipod.

When a newly imported piece of live rock has sponges and algae on it that have died in transport, the rotting mass often stimulates a prolific bloom of copepods. They swarm over the decaying areas and consume them. When they have consumed all the decaying matter, the population of copepods collapses due to the lack of available food. Many of these copepods are herbivores in addition to their affinity for decaying food. It is possible that the addition of an organic food source that stimulates them to bloom could encourage the development of sufficient copepod populations to have an effect on undesirable algal species. Hoff and Snell (1993) provide details for how to culture copepods. Select herbivorous copepods could be cultured to be applied in aquaria as a means of controlling various algae.

Amphipods

Small dorsoventrally flattened flea-like or shrimp-like creatures that scurry along the substrate are crustaceans known as amphipods (or "pods" on internet bulletin boards, where the English language is often mutilated). They are among the most important grazers and scavengers in a reef aquarium. Looking at the aquarium with a flashlight after the lights have gone off reveals amphipods scurrying on the rocks and gravel. They feed on detritus and algae.

Mollusks

Various sea slugs may be used for the control of algae (Delbeek and Sprung, 1994, Sprung, 2001). The main drawback to using sea slugs for grazing algae in aquariums is the fact that they are readily drawn over surface-skimmers and into the suction intake strainers of pumps.

Most *Aplysia* spp. grow very large.

Dolabrifera usually starves in captivity.

Aplysia parvula, a small useful herbivore.

Bursatella or *Stylocheilus*. Pauline Severns.

Dolabella, a large seaslug that eats algae.

Elysia diomedea from the Eastern Pacific.

Elysia crispata from the Caribbean.

Elysia sp.

Aplysia spp. are mainly large and unsuitable for aquariums because of their ability to release a violet colored substance when disturbed. There are some small species of *Aplysia*, however, that may be worthwhile herbivores for the control of a variety of algae, including cyanobacteria and filamentous green and red algae. The related genus *Bursatella* grows to a moderate size and is a good control for red slime algae (cyanobacteria). It may also release a violet colored substance when disturbed. Another related genus is *Dolabella*, which grows to enormous size. It feeds on a variety of algae, but it may starve in aquaria when the supply of algae runs out.
Dolabrifera is another *Aplysia*-like slug that feeds on diatoms and filamentous algae. It is not very hardy in aquariums, probably due to starvation and preference for particular algae.

The lettuce slugs, *Elysia* spp. are the most popular sea slugs for controlling green filamentous algae (*Derbesia* and *Bryopsis*). These slugs incorporate in their tissues chloroplasts from their food source. They need both algae and light to grow. Other sealugs may also be used for the control of filamentous green algae. *Ercolania endophytophaga* from the Indo-West Pacific is a recently named seaslug found inside the large cells of the green alga *Struvea plumosa* in Western Australia, and inside the giant cells of *Valonia* on the Great Barrier Reef. It has a single row of dark green cerata down each side of the body. *Ercolania boodleae* and *Ercolania coerulea* are reported to eat *Valonia*. *Ercolania fuscata* is a small (8mm) seaslug with a transverse pattern of dark green to black pigmentation arranged in irregular bands. It occurs from Florida, the Gulf of Mexico

Unidentified *Stilliger?* sp. Cory Pittman.

Placida cremoniana. Cory Pittman.

Stilliger sp. Pauline Fiene-Severns.

Unidentified *Stilliger?* sp. Cory Pittman.

Snails, Limpets, Chitons

Numerous snails are utilized in reef aquariums for controlling the growth of algae. The most popular snails are "Turban" snails of the genera *Turbo, Astraea*, and *Trochus. Trochus* spp. are being farm raised for the aquarium hobby. These snails are collected or raised in huge numbers for reef aquariums. As a rule of thumb, aquarists use 1 *Astraea, Turbo,* or *Trochus* snail per (3-5 gallons) 10-15 liters. Other snails, such as Ceriths, Nerites, and Stomatellids, are harvested incidentally or come as hitch-hikers on live rock. Limpets are good herbivores, and some varieties reproduce in aquaria. Larger species have the risk of occasionally feeding on coral tissues (Sprung and Delbeek, 1996, Sprung, 2001). Chitons are primitive herbivorous molluscs with 8 articulated shells. They feed on diatoms and bacteria, and some multiply in aquariums (Sprung, 2001). *Strombus alatus* the fighting conch, is now commercially raised for aquariums. This small conch is a superb sand sifter that feeds on detritus and algal films (cyanobacteria and diatoms) on sand and gravel. *Strombus gigas,* also available tank raised, grows large but is a good herbivore.

and the East coast of North America up to Canada. *Ercolania fuscata* feeds on *Cladophora* and *Chaetomorpha*, piercing the cell wall with its radula and sucking out the cell contents. *Caliphylla mediterranea* eats *Bryopsis*, as do *Placida dendritica, P. kingstoni, P. viridis*, and *Limapontia capitata. Stilliger* spp. feed on filamentous greens and possibly *Valonia* spp. *Cyerce* spp. are also known to feed on filamentous greens. *Hermaea* spp. look like *Stilliger* and *Limapontia* spp., but are reddish instead of green, and they eat red filamentous algae.

Jensen (1980, 1997) reviews the diets of sacoglossan sea slugs. She believes the evolution of the slugs' mouth and radula anatomy increased their adaptive radiation to feeding on more varieties of siphonaceous green algae that have different cell wall composition.

Astraea tectum.

Trochus fenestratus.

Turbo sp. from the Eastern Pacific.

Turbo sp. from the Pacific.

Trochus cf. radiata

Nerite sp. from the Red Sea.

Young tank-raised Strombus alatus from ORA at Harbor Branch Oceanographic Inst. T. Smoyer.

Turbo castanea, the Chestnut Turban snail from Florida.

Stomatella varia from Indonesia.

A Keyhole Limpet, Diodora sp.

Tank-raised Strombus gigas feeding on algae on the aquarium window.

Crabs

Several crabs are useful herbivores. *Mithraculus sculptus*, the Emerald Crab, is popular for the control of green bubble algae (*Valonia*). *Percnon gibbesi*, the Sally Lightfoot, is a good grazer of filamentous algae. Both are omnivorous and will eat meat, including fishes, given the opportunity. In the case of *Percnon*, which grows to a large size, there is a significant risk for small fishes housed in the same aquarium.

Pitho sp. The female has smaller claws.

Pitho cf. aculeata eats turf algae and *Valonia*.

Mithraculus spp. feed on various algae.

Mithraculus sculptus claws snip algae.

Percnon gibbesi feeds on filamentous algae, but may also attack small fishes.

Pitho spp. crabs are residents of nearshore rocky reefs and seagrass beds in Florida, and feed on filamentous algae and bubble algae (*Dictyosphaeria* and *Valonia*).

Hermit crabs

Small hermit crabs of the genera *Clibanarius*, *Calcinus*, *Phimochirus*, and *Paguristes* are very good herbivores that feed on cyanobacteria, green and red filamentous algae. They are particularly useful for controlling filamentous algae in between coral branches, where they can reach with their pincer-like claws. *Clibanarius tricolor*, the "Blue-legged Hermit" from seagrass beds, rocky shores and tidepools in Florida and the Caribbean is also good for controlling cyanobacterial mats on sand and gravel. For an aquarium with an algal problem, adding a large number of hermit crabs as a "cleanup crew" can be effective. Once they have grazed down the algae, however, it becomes necessary to reduce the number of hermit crabs so that they don't starve.

These hermit crabs are not exclusively herbivorous. They may attack, kill and eat snails on occasion to obtain not only a bite to eat but also a new and larger shell. Sick or dying tridacnid clams will also be mobbed and consumed by hermit crabs. Nevertheless, under most circumstances these small hermit crabs serve a very useful function in a reef aquarium.

Paguristes cadenata, the Red-legged hermit crab.

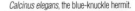
Clibanarius tricolor, the Blue-legged hermit.

Calcinus elegans, the blue-knuckle hermit.

Mespilla globulus, the tuxedo urchin is a useful grazer for smaller aquariums.

Diadema setosum is a useful herbivore for many tough algae, and it is not very destructive.

Urchins

Many, but not all sea urchins feed on algae. *Diadema* spp., the long-spined urchins are the most useful. The downside to them is that their spines easily (and painfully) puncture the skin, so one has to be careful around them, and they sometimes graze away coral tissue. The small globe or tuxedo urchin, *Mespilla*, is both adorable and useful for algae control. It has the added benefit of remaining small enough to be used in reef aquariums under 20 gallons.

Sea urchins can knock rocks or corals over while trying to graze algae, hence their reputation as "bulldozers." *Diadema* and *Mespilla* are not particularly bad in this respect. Sea urchins also consume coralline algae, rasping it from the rock and leaving bare white areas. Under normal conditions (high calcium and alkalinity) the growth rate of coralline algae exceeds the grazing by the urchins.

Herbivorous Fishes

Parrotfish

Some Parrotfish feed on corals, but most feed on filamentous algae. Many grow to a large size and require a lot of algae to thrive. They are suitable as herbivores for large reef aquariums only.

Blennies

Several genera of Blennies are specially adapted to scrape algae from hard substrates. Their charming smile and overbite consist of a fleshy upper lip and a broad brush-like upper

Parrotfish have a reputation for biting corals, but many are good herbivores in a large aquarium.

Cirripectes filamentosus.

Ophioblennius sp.

occasionally bite the mantles of tridacnid clams, presumably feeding in part on the zooxanthellae. *Ecsenius* spp. (except *E. midas*) have likewise been observed eating the tissue of stony corals for the same reason. The Leopard Blenny, *Exallias brevis* feeds on stony corals, mainly of the genus *Porites* and *Pocillopora*, and thus is unsuitable and should not be harvested for aquariums.

Most Blennies remain small, with a maximum size under 15 cm, so they are ideal choices for controlling algae in small reef aquaria. In larger reef tanks, several specimens may be housed together, but they may fight due to shortage of their food resource. Occasionally blennies are aggressive, chasing and even nipping at other fishes. For example, the Red-Lipped Blenny from Florida and the Caribbean, *Ophioblennius atlanticus*, is a hardy and a very good herbivore, but it can be a fin nipper, especially at feeding time. The Rock Blenny, *Salarias fasciata* also referred to as Jewelled Rockskipper, Lawnmower Blenny, Jewelled Blenny, or Sailfin/Algae Blenny is a good herbivore but less hardy, and very shy. *Salarias* sometimes refuses to take prepared foods and starves in small aquaria where the algae may quickly be stripped away by its feeding. In larger aquaria, a single specimen may be able to get enough to eat whether or not it takes prepared foods.

dentition. They leave kiss-like marks on the algal film growing on viewing windows as they eat diatoms, cyanobacteria, detritus, and soft filamentous algae. Blenniid algae eaters include *Atrosalarias, Cirripectes, Ecsenius, Entomacrodus, Istiblennius, Ophioblennius, Salarias* and *Scartella*. The Midas Blenny, *Ecsenius midas,* feeds on zooplankton only and, though one of the most wonderful additions to any aquarium, it does not feed on algae.

Many blennies are omnivores. Some, however, are strictly herbivorous, and will starve in an aquarium if not offered sufficient algae to graze. They may also occasionally mistake corals for algae, nipping at the polyps of *Xenia* or *Briareum* spp. Sometimes they harm other sessile invertebrates. *Cirripectes, Ecsenius, Ophioblennius, and Scartella* are reported to

Salarias fasciata. The "Lawnmower Blenny."

Atrosalarias sp.

Tangs

Members of the genus *Ctenochaetus* have fleshy upper lips with brush-like dentition that they use like the blennies to scrape algae from the substrate. Their feeding behavior is a bit more delicate than the "head-pounding" blennies. *Ctenochaetus* spp. seem to kiss the substrate. What they feed on is detritus and algal films, including diatoms, dinoflagellates, and Cyanobacteria. Some short filamentous turf algae may also be taken, but *Ctenochaetus* spp. are not as effective at eating filamentous algae as their long-snouted cousins, the *Zebrasoma* sp. tangs. *Ctenochaetus* spp. are rather prone to breaking down with *Amyloodinium*, aka velvet disease, which is actually caused by a parasitic dinoflagellate.

Surgeonfishes

The most popular algae eating fishes belong to the family Acanthuridae, commonly known as "Tangs" or surgeonfishes. Their popularity is due not only to their ability to eat algae, but also to their coloration and charming personality. However, many tangs are especially prone to parasitic infections, and they require large quantities of food to maintain optimal health. In a small aquarium they may easily graze all available algae and slowly starve if not fed sufficient supplemental algae. Furthermore, most species grow large and require ample swimming room, making tangs unsuitable for very small aquariums.

The genus *Zebrasoma* contains the most hardy species in aquariums, such as the

Ctenochaetus hawaiiensis, the Chevron tang, feeds on detritus, diatoms, and cyanobacteria.

Acanthurus spp. can be delicate.

Zebrasoma desjardinii is a robust herbivore.

Ctenochaetus striatus, the Kole tang, feeds on detritus, diatoms, and cyanobacteria.

The eternal favorite herbivore, *Zebrasoma flavescens*, the yellow tang.

popular Yellow tang from Hawaii, *Zebrasoma flavescens*, which grows to about 20 cm, and *Z. xanthurum* the Red Sea Purple tang. Other members of the genus grow considerably larger. The Sailfin tangs, *Z. veliferum* and *Z. desjardinii*, for example, grow twice as large.

It is possible to keep several specimens of *Zebrasoma* together in larger aquaria if they are introduced at the same time and they have plenty to graze on. Otherwise they will fight. The Yellow tang and its relatives are excellent grazers of filamentous algae, *Caulerpa*, *Halimeda*, and other fleshy species. They also accept prepared commercial foods. Spirulina flake food and dried seaweeds are useful to keep them fat and healthy when there is not much algae to graze in the aquarium.

Naso
Members of this genus grow very large. The most popular *Naso* sp. is *Naso lituratus*, with coloring that make it appear to be wearing lipstick and eyeshadow. Due to its large size and need for plenty of swimming room, *Naso lituratus* is suitable only for larger reef aquariums. They take all kinds of prepared foods, including meaty foods, but are good grazers of red filamentous algae and brown seaweeds such as *Dictyota* and *Sargassum*. Some specimens may eat bubble algae, *Valonia*, *Ventricaria*, and *Borgesenia* spp. as well as *Bryopsis*, though they don't prefer the taste of these latter four algae and will choose other algae and foods first. To keep *Naso lituratus* healthy be sure to also offer it dried seaweeds, now commonly available from your pet dealer.

Acanthurus
Tangs in this genus are delicate to acclimate to captivity, and they are prone to infestations with the parasites *Amyloodinium* and *Cryptocaryon*, but once acclimated they are pretty sturdy fish. They graze all kinds of filamentous turf algae.

Paracanthurus hepatus, the Blue, Regal, Hepatus or Hippo Tang is also an algae grazer, though in nature it feeds heavily on zooplankton. Nevertheless it can be an effective grazer for a reef aquarium, and it should be offered dried seaweed to supplement its diet if it has little algae to graze.

The Convict Tang, *Acanthurus triostegus*, feeds on all kinds of filamentous algae.

Lo vulpinus, the Foxface Rabbitfish is a superb herbivore for large aquariums.

Foxface and other Rabbitfishes
The rabbitfishes, family Siganidae, are closely related to the surgeonfishes. Members of the genera *Lo* and *Siganus* are very good herbivores useful for controlling filamentous algae and other tough algae that other herbivores won't eat, including bubble algae. They grow to large

Rabbitfishes are excellent herbivores for a large aquarium.

The flame angelfish is a small omnivore that feeds primarily on algal films and turfs.

size (about 20 to 50 cm) and are therefore unsuitable for small aquariums. Both genera are toxic, having a poison in their sharp dorsal spines that may inflict a painful wound. One downside to these fishes, particularly *Lo vulpinus*, is that they may feed on soft corals.

Angelfish

All angelfish feed on algae to some extent, even though they may feed on a variety of invertebrates, including sponges and corals. The pigmy angels, genus *Centropyge*, feed on algae to a much larger extent than other angelfish genera, and some of them are fairly good herbivores for reef aquariums. The downside of including angelfish in a reef aquarium is the possibility that they will feed on corals or tridacnid clams. Corals of the genera *Cynarina*, *Trachyphyllia*, and *Lobophyllia* are most likely to be targeted by these fish. Other corals are likely to be ignored.

Centropyge spp. angels feed on detritus, diatoms, and cyanobacteria, in addition to small invertebrates found living among the algal filaments. They may take some soft varieties of turf algae, but are not very effective for the control of hair algae.

Yellow Rabbitfish.

Amblyogobius decussatus Solomon Is.

Amblyogobius

Several members of the genus *Amblyogobius* are good herbivores for a reef aquarium. *Amblyogobius phalaena*, *A. rainfordi*, and *A. hectori* are the most popular and readily available species. These fish have a downwardly turned mouth that they use to suck up sand, detritus and algal filaments. *Amblyogobius phalaena* is useful for cleaning sand substrates. The other two are effective for controlling filamentous algae, including *Derbesia*. In the absence of filamentous algae these fish may starve, unless they adapt to taking prepared fish foods.

Biological Controls

Biological filtration

The use of biological filtration for water purification is universal in closed recirculating aquariums. Bacteria proliferate in the sand, gravel, rock and other substrates. Heterotrophs convert amino acids to ammonia and Aerobic nitrifyers convert ammonia to nitrite and nitrate. Facultative anaerobic bacteria also known as denitrifying bacteria break down the nitrate and liberate free nitrogen gas. These processes have direct impact on the availability of nutrients to algae. The formation of ammonia from amino acids and proteins is the first step, and it produces a strong response in algal growth since algae prefer ammonia as a source of nitrogen. The buildup of nitrate that occurs later on supports algae that can utilize this nitrogen source, but it also may limit the growth of some algae that prefer ammonia. Furthermore the formation of nitrate is a process that tends to acidify the water, an effect that can promote the growth of algae that prefer lower pH and alkalinity. Denitrification removes nitrogen from the system, lowers the nitrate level, and thus limits algal growth.

Algal filtration

The use of algae grown in a filter chamber attached to the aquarium has paradoxically among its benefits the ability to limit the growth of some types of algae within the aquarium. The use of algal turfs in this manner to filter the water in recirculating aquariums has been promoted by Dr. Walter Adey of the Smithsonian Institution (Adey and Loveland, 1991). The algae are grown on screens in shallow illuminated refugia attached to the display aquarium. The screens are scraped regularly (weekly) to harvest the

Algal turf filter with wave dump-bucket and screen, based on the design of Walter Adey.

algae from the system, thus removing with the algal mass all the assimilated nutrients, as well as excess trace elements.

The illumination is on an opposite timing cycle with the display aquarium, a technique called reverse daylight photosynthesis, or RDP. This technique serves to balance the concentration of dissolved carbon dioxide and thus stabilizes pH, and it also ensures that the night-time oxygen level does not fall precipitously, which it often does in systems not employing RDP.

Algal turf filters supply an abundant source of algal reproductive spores, which is food for many filter feeding invertebrates. This food source and the refugium habitat also promote the development of zooplankton, further benefitting filter feeding invertebrates.

An additional benefit of algal filters is that the algae cultivated on the screens filter out dissolved inorganic nitrogen and phosphorous so efficiently that they limit certain types of algal growth in the display aquarium. However, algal turf filters may leach some dissolved organic exudates, so that some algae that utilize organic nutrients will continue to thrive despite the turf filter's competition for inorganic nutrients. One more benefit of using algae as a filter is their ability to accumulate trace elements. Certain trace elements may accumulate to levels well above natural seawater values in recirculating aquarium systems, and the algae can slow this process or prevent it altogether.

Caulerpa and other higher algae

The use of algal filters employing green algae of the genus *Caulerpa* as well as other algae has come into fashion lately, though it has been practiced in the aquarium hobby for at least 40 years. The popularity of refugium filters and the "mud system" of Leng Sy has stimulated renewed enthusiasm for this method, and generated interest in the effect not only of the plants but also of the substrates they grow in.

The "mud filter" borrows from Dr. Adey's turf filter design, but has several differences. The algae are illuminated continuously, which means they are on a reverse light cycle with respect to the display aquarium at night, affording similar advantages. Among other differences, the algae used are grown in a live substrate rather than on screens, and their growth is much slower. In Adey's turf filter, algae are used more effectively for nutrient export since they grow faster and are harvested regularly. The *Caulerpa* filters, including the mud system, acheive nutrient export as well when the *Caulerpa* is harvested and via denitrification that certainly occurs in the substrate.

Aquarists who grow algae in refugia note positive effects on the aquarium that can be attributed to several factors, including the effects on nutrient availability and water chemistry already mentioned. One possible additional

An illuminated refugium aquarium with *Caulerpa* and mud substrate.

effect relates to a feature described in the chapter on algal biology, that red seaweeds accumulate halogen-containing metabolites in their tissues. These metabolites released into the water may impede the growth of pathogenic bacteria as well as other algae. When red seaweeds are cultured in aquariums their metabolites give the water that distinctive fresh aroma of the sea. Another positive effect of growing algae in refugia is an increased live food supply to the aquarium and the formation of so-called "food webs" (Adey and Loveland, 1991). The algae themselves release spores in the water that are eaten by filter feeders, and these spores also stimulate the development of zooplankton that feed on them, which are in turn fed upon by other invertebrates.

Mangroves

Like the rise in popularity of algae filters, the incorporation of red mangroves (*Rhizophora* spp.) in marine aquariums has become popular, just as the interest in refugium aquariums and natural ecosystem models has grown (Adey and Loveland, 1991). Published photographs of beautiful systems featuring the trees growing out of the water helped to further this direction (Sprung and Delbeek, 1996).

Mangroves are a part of coastal ecosystems that can also benefit natural system aquariums.

Seagrasses can be maintained in aquariums, but herbivores are needed to crop epiphytic algae.

Discussions on the internet about mangroves have promoted the idea that they might be used to filter the water in much the same way algae are used in refugia to filter the water. In fact, algae are by far more efficient at removing nutrients from the water than mangroves are. The effect on water quality from one or several

mangroves is negligible. The substrate they might be planted in, however, can have a significant effect, as it is a site where biological denitrification can take place. Older, larger mangrove trees develop extensive root systems in the substrate and may ultimately have the ability to remove significant amounts of plant nutrients from the substrate and interstitial water.

Seagrasses
Like mangroves, seagrasses are not as fast growing as algae, and are therefore not as effective in controlling nutrients in recirculating aquariums. They have ornamental value and, as with mangroves and *Caulerpa* filters, the substrate they grow in provides strong nitrification and denitrification capacity, which has the ability to limit algal growth. A densely planted seagrass display or refugium is still likely to need herbivores (fishes, snails) to keep the seagrass blades free of epiphytic algae, and may need predatory fishes to control populations of amphipods that might graze the seagrass blades.

Giant Clams
That tridacnid clams can be used to remove ammonia and nitrate from the water is well known (Fitt, et al, 1993, Knop 1996) and this

Giant clams such as this *Tridacna maxima* are not only beautiful, they also filter the water.

When coral cover approaches 100% there is less surface where competing algae can grow.

fact has promoted the notion that they could be used as a means of limiting the accumulation of nitrate in recirculating aquarium systems. Since the clams are included in aquariums as ornamental features, and since they are expensive and sometimes delicate, they are unlikely to be used in sufficient numbers to be relied on as filtration for an aquarium. However, some species attain large size (*T. gigas*, *T. derasa*, and *T. squamosa*) and a large specimen of any of these may have a significant impact on water chemistry in a small to moderately sized aquarium. The loss or removal of a large clam in a moderately sized aquarium commonly is followed by a marked increase in the growth of algae (pers. obs.) indicating that tridacnid clams can indeed compete for the same nutrients and limit algal growth. Although interest in use of clams as filters has focused primarily on their capacity to remove ammonia and nitrate from water, they may also be lowering the levels of phosphate and dissolved organic material, both of which are plant nutrients.

Corals

Corals compete with algae, algae compete with corals. Given low nutrient high illumination and otherwise proper conditions (temp, alkalinity and salinity) for coral growth the balance between algae and corals is usually tipped in favor of whichever is most abundant on the substrate. Having an aquarium with live rock and just a few corals is a delicate balance to maintain. The more corals you have the less likely that algae will dominate. The less corals there are the more likely that algae will some day dominate.

Corals produce anti-fouling substances that inhibit the growth of algae on them. Some corals (for example *Porites*, *Sarcophyton*, *Lobophytum*, *Sinularia*, and many gorgonians) produce a waxy film that is shed periodically to remove algal spores that settle on their surface. Most other corals simply shed copious amounts of mucus. Corals also inhibit algal growth by shading. The expansion of their tissues during the daylight hours shades nearby surfaces and thus limits algal growth adjacent to the corals. Since the tissues are translucent they do not totally block out light, so some algae do survive in these shaded zones, particularly red coralline and filamentous red species. Stony corals also use digestive filaments to kill algae adjacent to them. This can be seen clearly when corals (for example, *Acropora* spp.) grow on the glass of the aquarium. The front of new growth emits tiny white string-like mesenterial filaments that kill algae adjacent to the coral tissue. The mechanism that kills the algae is presumably through digestive enzymes.

Standing stocks of leather corals (*Sarcophyton, Lobophytum*) may have the ability to compete with algae for sources of dissolved organic nutrients. Pore-like polyps called siphonozooids located in between the larger autozooids in these corals serve to irrigate the colonies with fresh seawater and also draw in dissolved and particulate organic material which is consumed (Fabricius and Dommisse, 2000, Fabricius and Alderslade, 2001). Nevertheless such corals also exude dissolved organic material, so their ability to compete with algae for organic food may be negligible. They do consume inorganic nitrogen, however, as do other corals with symbiotic zooxanthellae.

Soft coral farming

Some zooxanthellate soft corals (members of the family xeneidae, for example) grow about as quickly as higher algae do and can therefore compete with them for the same inorganic nutrients. These soft corals also utilize organic food sources, and thus compete for these nutrients as well, perhaps more efficiently than algae. Harvesting soft corals from the display aquarium or from an attached refugium can be utilized as a means of nutrient export, as is done with algal filters.

Zoanthids

Zoanthids or "button polyps" (*Zoanthus, Palythoa*, and *Protopalythoa* spp.) are colonial anemone-like creatures that proliferate vegetatively and spread quickly over rocky surfaces. By covering the rock substrate they limit the surfaces upon which algae may take

hold. Furthermore, they secrete substances that inhibit algal growth, thus preventing some algae from growing over them. Their ability to do this is limited, however. Some algae, *Derbesia* and *Bryopsis*, for example can grow among the polyps and may even smother zoanthids. Generally that only occurs when there is sufficient nutrients available in the water, or under low-flow and low light situations. Strong illumination keeps the polyps open (which shades the spaces between polyps) and strong water flow washes away clinging algal filaments.

Feather Duster Worms

Small feather-duster worms of the genus *Bispira* are common inhabitants of reef aquariums, being introduced with live rock or on macro-algae. These worms multiply profusely by fission, and may coat the undersides of live rocks. It has been the author's experience that the cessation of a *Derbesia* (green hair algae) bloom often occurs simultaneously with a bloom in the population of *Bispira*. The worms use detritus to build their tubes, and it may be that by trapping the detritus this way they can limit the growth of *Derbesia*, which also traps detritus and apparently obtains nutrients from it.

Bacteria, Viruses and Fungi

Viruses, cyanophages, and myxobacteria are known to cause lysis of blue green algae (Fogg et al., 1973). Fungi are known to form symbiotic partnerships with or parasitize marine algae (Dawson, 1966). The growth of algae may be altered (Provasoli and Pintner 1980) or stopped by viruses, bacteria and fungi (Bold 1985, Round 1965, Lovejoy, et al. 1998, Mitsutani, et al. 1992). This area has not been thoroughly investigated and holds the potential to simplify the control of algae in

Ball fungus? associated with dying *Derbesia*.

Cyanobacteria on dying *Derbesia*.

Feather dusters use detritus to build tubes.

Diatom associated with dying *Derbesia*.

recirculating aquariums. The sudden disappearance of algae in aquariums may at times not be associated with a change in water quality or with the sudden bloom of a particular herbivore or competing organism. Lacking a better explanation the author hypothesizes that in these cases a bacterium, virus or fungus may be responsible for the sudden cessation of algal growth.

Chemical Controls

Chemical controls of algae may include substances added to the aquarium that directly affect algae or indirectly affect algae by limiting nutrient availability, filtration media that limit the availability of important plant nutrients. Water change, food and trace element inputs, and the use of filtered top-off water. can also be viewed as controls that affect water chemistry and algae growth.

Use of purified freshwater

One of the first steps in controlling the growth of algae in aquariums is limiting sources of nutrients added with the water. Tap water can contain significant amounts of nitrate, phosphate, silicate, and plant micronutrients. In some localities the water is suitable for use without filtration, but in many places the water needs to be filtered to remove substances that would harm an aquarium or simply promote the growth of algae. It is standard practice to use Reverse Osmosis (R.O.) filtration and deionization for purifying the tap water used for mixing artificial seawater and topping off evaporation. Reverse osmosis filters leave approximately 10 percent of the original concentration of many water contaminants. Under most circumstances this amount is negligible, but a high initial concentration of an undesirable contaminant may necessitate post-filtration with a deionization filter to remove most of the remaining 10%.

Activated Carbon

Bituminous coal and lignite processed with steam becomes a highly porous "activated" carbon. Activated carbon is used for removing dissolved organic substances that lend a yellow cast to the water. The organic substances are adsorbed onto the carbon, which has an extremely high surface area because of its highly porous structure. It removes many varieties of substances, including some that promote algae to grow. Therefore the use of activated carbon is one small factor in keeping algal growth limited.

The use of activated carbon also has the ability to curb the growth of some types of algae, probably due to adsorption of chelating substances from the water (see chapter one) or the absorption of other organic substances that promote algae growth. Because it soaks up so many organic compounds, activated carbon also quickly becomes a site for biological filtration (both aerobic nitrification and anaerobic denitrification), and a sufficient quantity of it in continuous use could thus limit the availability of nitrogen to algae.

Organic substances that tint the water filter the light and reduce the amount of light reaching the creatures living in the aquarium. The removal of water-tinting compounds by activated carbon allows for strong light penetration in the full range of wavelengths of the light source, especially ultraviolet wavelengths that are filtered by yellow water. This increase in light may promote the growth of some seaweeds and stop the growth of others.

Aluminum hydroxide

Aluminum hydroxide is used in wastewater treament to remove phosphate from the water. It has been applied for this purpose in aquariums and is effective, but there are anecdotal reports of it affecting some soft coral species.

Ferric Hydroxide

Granules of Ferric hydroxide (GFH) are used in wastewater treatment to remove arsenic and phosphate, and can be used in aquariums to control phosphate levels. GFH is very effective for this purpose, and it does not leach any harmful substances. Its use makes keeping large fish populations in aquariums together with live corals possible, without harmful phosphate accumulation.

Calcium Hydroxide (AKA Kalkwasser)

pH boosting and phosphate precipitation with Calcium Hydroxide has been observed to limit the growth of cyanobacteria and filamentous algae. High pH also seems to limit the growth of dinoflagellates. Based on the advice of Peter Wilkens, Delbeek and Sprung (1994) recommend adding kalkwasser (calcium hydroxide solution) as a means of curbing the growth of dinoflagellates. The effect may also be due to the precipitation of phosphate by the calcium hydroxide, and the enhanced protein skimming caused by the pH elevation from kalkwasser dosing.

Potassium permanganate

Although I haven't personally used potassium permanganate as a means of algae control, there is some reference to it in aquarium literature. According to Thiel (1998), a way to reduce dissolved organic carbon (DOC) is to add controlled dosages of a 5 % solution of potassium permanganate diluted in water to the aquarium. The exact dosage is not given. Be very careful with the amounts added because even small amounts of $KMnO_4$ increases the redox potential rapidly, and that can shock the corals and fish.

Mechanical filtration

When most people hear the word filtration they think of mechanical filtration. The filter on your air conditioner is a mechanical filter. It traps dust particles. In an aquarium the removal of detritus and algal filaments can be achieved with a mechanical filter such as a canister and cartridge filter, sand filter, diatomaceous earth filter, fine mesh bags or simple sponge or floss pad filters. In reef aquariums it is best to use such devices only intermittently for periodic routine maintenance lasting no more than a day or two. If used continuously, mechanical filters not only remove the food of filter feeding invertebrates, they also develop colonies of aerobic bacteria that digest the trapped material, which consumes oxygen, and return dissolved inorganic nutrients back into the tank, which promotes algae growth.

UV sterilizers

The use of germicidal wavelengths of ultraviolet light in contact chambers known as UV sterilizers is common practice in aquarium keeping, mainly for the purpose of lowering populations of pathogenic organisms in the water in recirculating systems for fish. UV sterilizers are also employed effectively on outdoor sunlit pond systems to control blooms of phytoplankton that might otherwise turn the water into what looks like green pea-soup. Reef keeping aquarists who use ultraviolet sterilizers report reduction in the growth of cyanobacteria and filamentous algae. Since the UV light from a UV sterilizer does not directly affect the algae within the tank, its effect is principally on the floating spores and filaments in the water that passes through the sterilizer. A second possible effect is that UV sterilizers produce a small amount of ozone and may produce residual hypobromate or chlorine in small quantities, possibly sufficient enough to curb the growth of some algae.

Protein Skimming

Protein Skimmers, a.k.a. foam fractionators employ a column of tiny bubbles that scrub the water of organic substances that stick to the interface between air and water. These compounds form a frothy foam that gathers in the skimmer's collection cup and collapses into a thick brownish fluid. The dissolved material collected from the water includes carbohydrate substances, amino acids, lipids, and a fair amount of phosphate bound organically. This removal of amino acids, (which contain nitrogen that would ultimately become ammonium and nitrate) and phosphate is a way to limit the supply of nutrients that algae need to grow.

Protein skimming not only traps organic compounds, but also phytoplankton, algae spores and filaments, and fine detritus. The export of detritus is a means of limiting phosphate accumulation in the aquarium, and the trapping of phytoplankton, algal spores and filaments is a nutrient export mechanism as well, not to mention a direct way of limiting the spread of algae.

Ozone and Redox potential

Ozone is sometimes used in protein skimmers or other contact chambers as a water purifying measure. It is produced by a spark that converts the oxygen, O_2 in air into O_3. The O_3 molecule is unstable, and the extra oxygen atom readily combines with organic compounds, with an effect like chlorine bleach. Ozone is a powerful oxidizer, and its use in aquariums is best managed with a redox potential meter and an experienced aquarist. Elevating the redox potential has been associated with changes in algal composition in aquariums and with elimination of some nuisance species, particularly cyanobacteria (Paletta, 1990, 1991). Redox potential affects algae because oxidation of organic plant nutrients limits food to algae, and loss of dissolved trace micronutrients such as iron is another factor.

Antibiotics

The use of antibiotics to control cyanobacteria is a practice that has gained popularity with some aquarists. Various forms of Erythromycin have been used primarily to stop the growth of red slime algae. The downside of this regimen is that it is not a permanent solution and has the potential to develop strains that resist treatment. These two features should dissuade anyone from using a "quick fix" such as antibiotic treatment, but unfortunately they don't. The indiscriminate use of antibiotics in aquariums should be avoided. Control of cyanobacteria is easily accomplished by directly attacking its causes: by removing or oxidizing dissolved organic compounds, increasing water flow, and limiting dissolved phosphate.

Clean-up Aids

Several aquarium accessories as well as common household items can be used to manage algal growth in a reef aquarium. This short section explains what these are and how to use them to keep your aquarium looking good.

Toothbrush
An old toothbrush is one of the handiest tools for a reef aquarist. It can be used to clean algae from the corners of the tank, or filamentous algae (such as *Derbesia*) from a stubborn place where it always seems to persist on the rocks.

Sometimes a good brushing is all that is needed to turn the tables on a green filamentous algae problem, allowing the herbivores a chance to get ahead of the growth instead of letting the algae keep the upper hand. Be sure to keep the old toothbrush in a place far apart from your bathroom!

Credit Card
An old credit card (or any similar plastic card, for example those used as hotel keys) makes a great algae scraper to clean diatoms or other sheeting algae from the aquarium viewing windows.

Toothpick or wooden skewer
When filamentous algae grow in between the polyps of zoanthids or encrusting soft corals such as *Briareum* spp., the easiest way to remove the mass of filaments is with a narrow wooden stick such as a toothpick or skewer. The rough edges of the stick catch the filaments. Simply twirl the stick in the algae and lift it out to remove the algae.

Razor blade window scraper
Calcareous algae and precipitated calcium carbonate on the viewing windows can only be removed from glass by means of a sharp razor blade. Plastic window scrapers with disposable metal blades can be used for this purpose.

Chaetomorpha turf and spontaneously precipitated calcium carbonate. Use a razor to remove.

Useful cleaning tools, L to R, Razor, toothbrush, credit card, magnet scraper, non-grit scrub pad.

Chapter Two

Blades are not suitable for use on the viewing windows of acrylic aquariums, which would be scratched by them.

Magnets
Probably the easiest mechanical means of keeping the viewing windows free from algal growth is to use commercially available magnetic algae scrapers, one located outside the aquarium, the other inside with some sort of scraper or pad affixed to it. This allows the aquarist to remove algae from the glass without getting wet. A side benefit is that the micro-algae and diatoms scraped off the glass are a natural food source for filter feeders.

Siphon
Quite a lot of algae can be removed from an aquarium with a siphon hose when performing routine water changes. *Derbesia* is often loosely attached, as are various cyanobacteria. For a dinoflagellate bloom it is best to let the bloom run its course and not siphon them out, since they grow back quickly and disturbances to the aquarium tends to promote their growth.

Mechanical filter and pump
A tank-cleaning mechanical canister filter and pump allows a powered up version of the siphon for sucking up and removing algae. In this case the water is recirculated and the algae is trapped on a cartridge. Under normal circumstances such a set-up is not necessary for routine maintenance, but it is very useful for cleaning up an aquarium that is overrun by algae.

A submersible powerhead
Small but powerful submersible centrifugal pumps can be used in periodic maintenance to "blast out" pockets of detritus that may

Detritus settles where the water velocity is low.

accumulate in low water velocity pockets within live rock. The powerheads can be hand-held and moved around in an aquarium to direct water jets into holes sending clouds of detritus into the water. During this "storm activity" a mechanical filter may be used to trap the detritus so that it can be removed from the aquarium. This procedure helps to reduce the accumulation of detritus in the aquarium, a factor in limiting the occurrence of algae blooms. Be sure to use a GFI outlet and wear shoes to prevent yourself from being electrocuted when performing routine maintenance such as siphoning or hand-held powerheads for blast cleaning in the aquarium.

Green Algae

The "greens" are the most diverse grouping of algae, with more than 7000 species. The designation of the group as a single entity is a matter of tradition rather than an indication of a relation among all "green algae." Of the two major lineages of green plants, one consists of most of what are considered green algae, including microscopic and larger green seaweeds. The other lineage includes several groups of green algae more closely related to land plants. Because the two lineages are monophyletic, they are contained in a single group called green plants, Chlorophyta, in the subkingdom Chlorobionta (Bremer, 1985).

Chlorophyta, like land plants, have chlorophyll a and b, store energy as starch, and have cell walls composed of an outer pectin layer and an inner cellulose layer. They are usually green or yellowish, but other pigments may be present that may give them a bluish or reddish hue.

Tropical marine green algae include unicellular microscopic forms, coenocytic forms, membranous sheets, filamentous turfs, parenchymatous forms, calcified forms, and forms that resemble seagrasses.

The green algae reproduce with alternation of generations. Unlike higher plants, however, the alternation may be isomorphic. In isomorphic alternation of generations the gametophyte and sporophyte phases are indistinguishable. Asexual reproduction is by vegetative fragmentation and by spore formation (both zoospores and aplanospores). Sexual reproduction is by motile gametes (isogametes, anisogametes, eggs, and sperm). Life histories are haplontic, diplontic, or diplohaplontic.

Turf-forming green algae include the most frustrating of all "problem algae" in aquariums. They are ubiquitous, fast-growing, very tolerant of a wide variety of water parameters, produce foul-tasting substances to ward off grazing by herbivores, and smother corals and other sessile invertebrates. They also tend to promote their own proliferation by trapping particulate organic material within the filaments, and using the decomposed products of this matter for food.

Green Phytoplankton (various Genera)

Common Name: Green Water

Description: Cloudy green water that persists for hours or days, caused by the bloom of planktonic green algae. Another cause can be the release of spores by *Caulerpa* or *Halimeda* spp., but that event is temporary, usually lasting for only several hours, beginning the moment the lights come on in the morning. A true planktonic algae bloom can persist for weeks if not controlled.

Similar: Pea Soup

Desirable/undesirable features: Good for use in the culture of invertebrate and fish larvae, and a food for filter-feeding invertebrates. Bad for display aquarium because it obstructs the view and may cause low night-time oxygen levels.

Controls: An ultraviolet sterilizer will rapidly eliminate planktonic algae blooms. To eliminate the nutrient source that promoted the bloom, use phosphate export via protein skimming, algae filters, or phosphate absorbing media. Also use reverse osmosis water for top-off to reduce input of plant nutrients.

Herbivores: Herbivores are not used to control planktonic algae blooms, though many copepods, rotifers, and protozoans may be cultured in green water.

A bloom of microscopic algae turns the water a light opaque green.

Ostreobium

Common Name: Green Algae

Description: Dark green extremely fine filaments forming a network living within limestone rock (endolithic), including the skeletons of live corals.

Similar: There is a red endolithic alga also common in coral skeletons.

Desirable/undesirable features: Slow growing. May harm corals under conditions that promote its proliferation (Wilkens, 1990). The damaging effect on corals works this way: Nitrate and phosphate stimulate the alga to grow, while phosphate slows the deposition of the coral skeleton. As the algae proliferates in the coral skeleton it may cause the coral tissue to recede from its point of attachment to the skeleton. Schlichter, et al. (1997), and Schlichter, et al. (1995) discuss potential benefits of *Ostreobium*, including transfer of photoassimilates to coral tissue.

The green stain on this coral skeleton is produced by the boring alga *Ostreobium*.

Controls: Reduce nitrate and phosphate levels that promote growth in this alga.

Herbivores: *Diadema* grazes it from exposed rock surfaces.

The structure of *Ostreobium* revealed by dissolving a piece of coral skeleton with acid.

Enteromorpha

Common Name: Green Hair Algae

Description: Light green fat or fine hollow soft tubular filaments, attached at a central holdfast. Some forms quite like *Ulva* (Sea lettuce) but rolled into a tube.

Similar: *Bryopsis, Chaetomorpha, Boodlea, Derbesia, Ulva, Ulvaria*

Desirable/undesirable features: Good substrate for amphipods, copepods, worms, and other foods for mandarinfishes (*Synchiropus*). Very palatable to most herbivorous fishes. Can bloom explosively, especially in new reef aquariums with high phosphate level due decomposition from uncured rock.

Controls: Maintain Alkalinity above 8 dKH, Use phosphate export via protein skimming, algae filters, or phosphate absorbing media. Herbivores.

Herbivores: Hermit crabs, Amphipods, Surgeonfish, Rabbitfish, Angelfish, *Diadema* Urchin, Tuxedo Urchin, Limpets, *Elysia* spp. Seaslugs.

Enteromorpha spp. have tubular filaments.

The structure of *Enteromorpha* sp. filaments at 100x magnification.

Ulva

Common Name: Sea Lettuce

Description: Light or dark green thin translucent sheets attached at a central holdfast. Growths look like lettuce.

Similar: *Anadyomene, Ulvaria*

Desirable/undesirable features: Very palatable to most herbivorous fishes. Can bloom explosively, especially in new reef aquariums with high phosphate level due decomposition from uncured rock.

Controls: Use phosphate export via protein skimming, algae filters, or phosphate absorbing media. Herbivores.

Herbivores: Surgeonfish, Rabbitfish, Angelfish, *Diadema* Urchin, Tuxedo Urchin.

Ulva sp. growing from live rock in a newly established reef aquarium.

Ulvaria and *Ulva* are similar. The former has a softer, thinner thallus.

Derbesia

Common Name: Green Hair Algae

Description: Dark green extremely fine filaments, loosely attached under low velocity water movement, tightly adhering under strong water flow. Filaments usually have distinctive grape-like sporangia, visible under magnification of a microscope. The alternate (gametophtye) generation of some *Derbesia* spp. is a small grape-like plant called *Halicystis*, which resembles *Valonia* and *Boergesenia*.

Similar: *Bryopsis, Enteromorpha, Chaetomorpha, Boodlea*

Desirable/undesirable features: Good substrate for amphipods, copepods, worms, and other foods for mandarinfishes (*Synchiropus*). Otherwise this is a nuisance algae that is not very palatable to most herbivorous fishes. It can be difficult to control for extended periods.

Controls: Maintain Alkalinity above 8 dKH, Use phosphate export via protein skimming, algae filters, or phosphate absorbing media. Use toothbrush to remove small patches. Herbivores.

Herbivores: Hermit crabs, Amphipods, Surgeonfish, Rabbitfish, Angelfish, *Diadema* Urchin, Tuxedo Urchin, *Trochus* Snail, *Turbo* Snail, *Astraea* Snail, Limpets, *Elysia* spp. sea slugs.

Derbesia quickly overgrows corals.

Halicystis phase of *Derbesia*, ca. 3 mm long.   A mature sporangium of *Derbesia*.

Derbesia filaments without sporangia.   The thick-branched *Derbesia* shown below.

Derbesia on the trunk of a *Sarcophyton* sp. leather coral.

Distinctly different forms of *Derbesia* from one aquarium.

Derbesia can smother all kinds of sessile invertebrates, including zoanthids.

Bryopsis

Common Name: Bryopsis, Green Hair, Feather, Plumose Algae

Description: Green or bluish filaments, usually with pinnate (feather shaped) tips. Each branch is constricted at the point of origin, and the lower portion of each filament does not have lateral branching. Attached at a holdfast-like point with branched hair-like rhizoids or proliferating with numerous attachment points. Produces secondary metabolites that inhibit herbivores from eating it.

Similar: *Enteromorpha, Chaetomorpha, Derbesia*

Desirable/undesirable features: Good substrate for amphipods, copepods, worms, and other foods for mandarinfishes. This nuisance algae is not very palatable to most herbivorous fishes. It can be difficult to control for extended periods.

Controls: Seems to proliferate when there is some ammonia and or nitrite available. Strong biological filtration (nitrification and denitrification) limits its growth. Herbivores. Manual removal.

Herbivores: Rabbitfish, *Diadema* Urchin, Tuxedo Urchin, *Mithraculus* crab, Sea slugs: *Elysia* spp., *Caliphylla mediterranea, Placida dendritica, P. kingstoni, P. viridis,* and *Limapontia capitata.*

Typical appearance of *Bryopsis*. Note the bluish hue.

Closeup photo of a pinnate branch tip of *Bryopsis*.

This dark *Bryopsis* sp. growing on an *Astraea* snail shell does not have the typical pinnate tips.

This pale *Bryopsis* sp. commonly grows on new aquarium windows the first month or two.

Boodlea

Common Name: Green Hair Algae

Description: Light green extremely fine filaments, loosely attached under low velocity water movement, tightly adhering under strong water flow. Spongy crisp texture.

Similar: *Bryopsis, Enteromorpha, Chaetomorpha, Derbesia*

Desirable/undesirable features: Good substrate for amphipods, copepods, worms, and other foods for mandarinfishes (*Synchiropus*). Otherwise this is a nuisance algae that is not very palatable to most herbivorous fishes.

Controls: Maintain Alkalinity above 8 dKH, Use phosphate export via protein skimming, algae filters, or phosphate absorbing media. Herbivores. Remove by hand.

Herbivores: Hermit crabs, Amphipods, Surgeonfish, Rabbitfish, Angelfish, *Diadema* Urchin, Tuxedo Urchin.

Boodlea sp. Solomon Islands.

The structure of *Boodlea* sp. filaments.

Chaetomorpha

Common Name: Green Hair Algae

Description: Dark or light green stiff fine or coarse banded hair-like filaments that grow in loose clumps like locks of curly hair. Also grow on glass, forming a low bright green turf when heavily grazed.

Similar: *Cladophora, Rhizoclonium*

Desirable/undesirable features: Not palatable to many herbivorous fishes. Fast growing and easily maintained in a refugium or algal filter. An ideal genus for use in algae filters to control nutrient levels.

Controls: Herbivores.

Herbivores: Surgeonfish, Rabbitfish, *Diadema* Urchin, Tuxedo Urchin.

Chaetomorpha cf. *antennina*. Indonesia.

Chaetomorpha spiralis.

Chaetomorpha sp. from aquarium window.

A grazed fine *Chaetomorpha* sp. on glass.

Cladophora

Common Name: Green Hair Algae

Description: Light or dark green fine tough filaments, often forming turfs or cushion-like growths.

Similar: *Bryopsis, Chaetomorpha, Rhizoclonium, Cladophoropsis, Valoniopsis*

Desirable/undesirable features: Good substrate for amphipods, copepods, worms, and other foods for mandarinfishes (*Synchiropus*). Not very palatable to most herbivorous fishes. Can bloom explosively, especially in old reef aquariums with low alkalinity and high phosphate level due poor phosphate export.

Controls: Maintain Alkalinity above 8 dKH, Use phosphate export via protein skimming, algae filters, or phosphate absorbing media. Herbivores.

Herbivores: Surgeonfish, Rabbitfish, *Diadema* Urchin, Tuxedo Urchin, *Mithraculus* crab.

Large *Cladophora* with *Valonia* attached.

Large *Cladophora* at 100x magnification.

Cladophora sp. with fine filaments.

Cladophora sp. with fine filaments at 100x.

Cladophoropsis sp.

Cladophora sp. on an aquarium wall.

Cladophora sp.

Structure of the filaments of *Rhizoclonium*.

Valoniopsis is similar to *Cladophoropsis*.

Valoniopsis at 100x magnification.

Cladophoropsis spp. form spongy cushions.

Cladophoropsis.

Valonia, Ventricaria, and *Dictyosphaeria*

Common Name: Green Bubble Algae

Description: Green spherical or club-shaped rigid bubbles. *Ventricaria* bubbles are usually solitary and large. *Dictyosphaeria cavernosa* forms sheets or hollow pillows of attached spherical bubbles, giving the impression of the compound eye of an arthropod. It seldom blooms in aquariums. *Boergesenia* forms light green club shaped bubbles or clusters of bubbles that are occasionally forked. It is common on Indo-Pacific live rock and seldom blooms. *Ventricaria* and *Valonia* spp. bloom in aquariums, reproducing mainly by two methods: vegetative budding growth, and formation of daughter cells within each "bubble." The reproductive cells become clear and the tiny newly formed daughter cells can be seen inside. The original cell wall becomes soft and breaks, releasing thousands of new bubble algae.

Similar: *Boergesenia, Dictyosphaeria, Halicystis.*

Desirable/undesirable features: Not palatable to most herbivorous fishes. Slow growing. May smother stony corals.

Controls: Low nitrate levels. Removal by hand or siphoning. Herbivores. Some authors warn that popping the bubbles should be avoided because it risks releasing thousands of new bubble algae. While this is technically true, controlling a *Valonia* bloom by manual removal and the use of herbivores (that pop the bubbles as they eat them) can nevertheless be very effective.

Herbivores: Surgeonfish, Rabbitfish, *Diadema, Mithraculus* and *Pitho* spp. crabs, *Ercolania* and possibly other seaslugs.

Valonia macrophysa.

Boergesenia top and *Valonia,* bottom right.

Ventricaria ventricosa.

Ventricaria reproduction.

Valonia utricularis.

Dictyosphaeria ocellata.

Dictyosphaeria cavernosa growing over a branch of *Acropora.* Solomon Islands.

Caulerpa

Common Name: Caulerpa, Grapeweed

Description: Green algae distinguished by root-like rhizome used for attachment to rock, gravel, mud, or sandy substrates.

Similar: Seagrasses.

Desirable/undesirable features: Palatable to many herbivorous fishes. Some species unpalatable. Has a positive effect on water quality, and most species are safely maintained as an ornamental plant or in refugium filters. However, some species may directly injure corals by contact, and most can shade, or smother them. *Caulerpa lentillifera* and a dwarf variety of *C. nummularia* are particularly difficult to control, and they injure corals.

Controls: Removal by hand, Herbivores.

Herbivores: Surgeonfish, Angelfish, *Diadema* Urchin.

Caulerpa racemosa overgrowing corals. Solomon Islands.

Caulerpa cf. *nummularia* can smother corals.

Caulerpa lentillifera is difficult to control.

Halimeda

Common Name: Cactus Algae

Description: Crisp (due to calcium deposition) flattened circular, angular, or bead-like segments arising from a common holdfast or from numerous points of attachment.

Similar: *Udotea.*

Desirable/undesirable features: Palatable to some herbivores. This alga blooms in aquariums under good water quality conditions, and it seems to have a positive effect on water quality, though it may shade and smother corals.

Controls: Reduce nitrate level. Removal by hand, Herbivores.

Herbivores: Surgeonfish, Angelfish, *Diadema* urchin.

Halimeda opuntia can overgrow corals and shade or smother them. Aquarium photo.

Halimeda discoidea sometimes proliferates in aquariums. It is attractive, but may shade corals.

Brown Algae

The brown algae, Phaeophyta, are members of the kingdom-level taxon Chromista, which also includes diatoms, "water molds," and coccolithophorids. Phaeophyta are the largest Chromista, and include species such as Kelp, which grow over 50 meters in length.

Phaeophytes are photosynthetic protists, not closely related to land plants. They are yellowish to brown in color because of the carotenoid pigment fucoxanthin. They also contain chlorophyll a and c. Unlike the green algae, brown algae don't produce starch. The products of their photosynthesis are stored as laminarin and mannitol.

Phaeophyta do have a complex life cycle like plants and many protists. Reproduction is usually by alternation of gametophyte and sporophyte generations, except in the Fucales. Vegetative reproduction occurs by fragmentation and by abcission of special reproductive branches called propagula. In some phaeophytes chemical signals called pheromones aid the sperm in their search for an ovum.

Almost all Phaeophyta are marine. While there are many microscopic brown algae that grow as epiphytes on other underwater plants and substrates, as branched filaments, or low crusts, none are unicellular or colonial. All Phaeophyta are multicellular. The cell walls are composed of cellulose and alginic acid, and other polysaccharides. Larger more developed forms are parenchymatous (fleshy), like land plants, with cells that divide in various planes to form true tissues. Species such as *Sargassum* have specialized gas-filled structures for flotation.

Some species are intertidal, being exposed to the air at low tide. Brown algae produce compounds such as algin, a viscous gel that absorbs and retains water, to deal with aerial exposure and prevent dessication.

Dictyota

Common Name: Dictyota

Description: Brown, yellow, green, or blue cushions composed of flattened Y-shaped branches.

Similar: *Dictyopteris*, which has a midrib.

Desirable/undesirable features: Not palatable to most herbivorous fishes. Fast growing. This alga blooms in aquariums under good water quality conditions, and it seems to have a positive effect on water quality, though it may shade or smother corals.

Controls: Removal by hand, Herbivores.

Herbivores: *Diadema* Urchin, *Mithraculus* crab.

Dictyota sp.

Dictyota sp.

Dictyota sp.

Dictyopteris sp.

Lobophora and Pseudolithoderma

Common Name: Lobophora, Brown Wafer Algae

Description: *Lobophora* forms brown, circular encrusting tiers and fan-shaped fronds or ruffled lettuce or potato-chip like clusters. The underside of the fronds has a felt-like surface, while topside is smooth. *Pseudolithoderma* (*=Ralfsia*) forms brown, circular crusts on rock and glass. Though similar in appearance, the two plants are not closely related.

Similar: *Distromium, Mesopora, Peyssonnelia* (a red alga), *Padina, Zonaria*.

Desirable/undesirable features: Not palatable to most herbivorous fishes. Fast growing. These algae bloom in aquariums under good water quality conditions, and seem to have a positive effect on water quality, though they may shade or smother corals.

Controls: Remove *Lobophora* by hand. Remove *Pseudolithoderma* (*=Ralfsia*) from glass with a blade. Herbivores.

Herbivores: *Diadema* Urchin, *Naso lituratus*.

Lobophora variegata. The reddish spots are flatworms. Aquarium photo.

Pseudolithoderma (=Ralfsia) with red coralline algae on the glass window of an aquarium.

Sargassum

Common Name: Sargassum Weed, Gulf Weed

Description: Though some species can occur as floating rafts, most occur attached by a strong disc-shaped holdfast with a primary axis and numerous branches bearing leaf-like appendages and gas-filled spherical bladders.

Similar: *Hormophysa, Turbinaria, Cystoseira*

Desirable/undesirable features: Not palatable to most herbivorous fishes. Fast growing. This alga blooms in aquariums under good water quality conditions, and it seems to have a positive effect on water quality, though it may shade or smother corals.

Controls: Removal by hand, Herbivores.

Herbivores: *Diadema* Urchin, *Naso lituratus*

Sargassum spp. are common on rocks from Fiji. They are attractive but can shade corals.

Hincksia

Common Name: Brown Hair Algae

Description: Very fine soft brown filamentous cotton-candy-like tufts.

Similar: *Ectocarpus, Feldmannia.* (see Littler and Littler, 2000). The green filamentous alga *Derbesia* when coated by epiphytic diatoms looks like brown filamentous algae. Several genera of cyanobacteria can be brown and filamentous.

Desirable/undesirable features: Not palatable to most herbivorous fishes. Fast growing. Filamentous brown algae bloom in temperate or cold-water aquariums, seldom affecting tropical aquariums. In the natural environment tropical genera are more common in winter when the water is cooler.

Controls: Siphon them off the substrate. Use phosphate absorbing media and protein skimming to limit phosphate.

Herbivores: Unkown. Possibly herbivorous slugs such as *Aplysia* or *Dolabrifera* will eat some species. Sea urchins may also eat these brown filamentous algae.

Hincksia sp. Biscayne Bay, Florida. This brown filamentous alga is not common in aquariums.

The structure of *Hincksia* sp. filaments.

Red Algae

he Rhodophyta include unicellular as well as multicellular forms that may be filamentous, parenchymatous (fleshy), membranous sheets, or rope-like. Some are calcified. Red algae lack flagella at all stages in their life history, and some have multinucleate cells. There are more than 5000 species, some inhabiting fresh water, but most are marine. Rhodophytes are generally reddish due to water-soluble pigments called phycobilins. The dominant red pigment, r-phycoerythrin, reflects red light and absorbs blue light. Because blue light penetrates water to a greater depth than light of longer wavelengths, the red pigments allow rhodophytes to photosynthesize and live at greater depths than most other algae. Rhodophyta also contain chlorophyll a and d, carotenes, lutein, zeaxanthin, and r-phycocyanin. Some rhodophytes have very little phycoerythrin, and may appear yellow, green, or bluish from the chlorophyll and other pigments present. They store products of photosynthesis as floridean starch.

Simple forms reproduce asexually through cell division and production of non-flagellated spores, but most Rhodophyta have complicated life histories, with three phases, one phase (sexual) producing gametes and two producing spores (carpospores and tetraspores).

Haploid tetraspores germinate into gametophytes. The gametophytes develop attached eggs that are known as carpogonia, and release sperm (spermatia) into the water. The fertilized egg develops into a carposporophyte that produces diploid carpospores. The carpospores germinate into tetrasporophytes that release tetraspores. The spores and gametes are non-flagellated.

Calcifying reef-building rhodophytes called coralline algae have contributed far more to reef structure than other organisms, even more than corals on some reefs.

Halymenia

Common Name: Red Leaf Algae

Description: Red, pink, Orange or yellowish slippery leaf-like plants attached at a central holdfast.

Similar: *Cryptonemia*, which grows slowly and is not slippery.

Desirable/undesirable features: Ornamental. Palatable to many herbivorous fishes. This alga seems to have a positive effect on water quality, but it may shade corals.

Controls: Reduce nitrate level. Removal by hand, Herbivores.

Herbivores: Surgeonfishes, *Diadema* Urchin.

Halymenia floresia is an attractive plant that can bloom in nitrate-rich aquariums.

Halymenia durvillei. Solomon Islands.

Nitophyllum

Common Name: Red "Dictyota"

Description: Red, pink, or yellowish (if sun bleached) thin flat dichotomously branched soft membranous plants with overlapping branches all in one plane, the branches being about 3-6 mm broad and having a ruffled edge.

Similar: *Dictyota*, which is a brown seaweed that can be yellow, green, or bluish. *Haraldiophyllum* does not have ruffled edges. *Branchioglossum* and *Hypoglossum*, which have a midrib and proliferating branches, not dichotomous.

Desirable/undesirable features: Ornamental. Palatable to many herbivorous fishes. This alga blooms in aquariums under good water quality conditions, and it seems to have a positive effect on water quality, though it may shade corals.

Controls: Removal by hand, Herbivores.

Herbivores: Surgeonfishes, *Diadema* Urchin.

Nitophyllum sp? growing on the leather coral *Sarcophyton* in an aquarium.

Closeup showing dichotomous branching

Branchioglossum on *Cladophoropsis.*

Polysiphonia

Common Name: Red Hair algae

Description: Grows as a low fine red turf on coral branches or as centrally attached branchy tufts similar to *Bryopsis*, but red or brown.

Similar: The sporophyte stage of *Asparagopsis*. *Ceramium* and *Centroceras* are filamentous and bushy, but the filaments are banded.

Desirable/undesirable features: Palatable to some herbivorous fishes. *Polysiphonia* spp. bloom in aquariums under certain conditions, which appear to include nitrite availability (pers. obs.). This genus is a common, beneficial turf grown on screens in algal turf filters, but it can damage corals if it grows on their skeletons.

Controls: Biological filtration that removes nitrite. Removal by hand. Herbivores.

Herbivores: Surgeonfishes, *Diadema* Urchin, Hermit crabs, Seaslugs: *Aplysia*, and *Hermaea*.

Large *Polysiphonia* sp. on *Dictyota*.

Close up of the same large *Polysiphonia* sp.

Turf of *Polysiphonia* sp. on *Acropora*.

Mixed turf of *Polysiphonia* and *Ceramium*.

Asparagopsis (sporophyte stage)

Common Name: Red Hair algae

Description: Dull or bright reddish low turfs or centrally attached cotton-candy-like tufts. The blooming form is one phase in the alternation of genrations life cycle of this alga. It may reproduce in this phase in perpetuity in aquariums.

Similar: *Polysiphonia*. *Ceramium* and *Centroceras* are filamentous and bushy, but the filaments are banded.

Desirable/undesirable features: Not palatable to most herbivorous fishes. This alga blooms in aquariums under certain conditions, which appear to include nitrite availability (pers. obs.).

Controls: Biological filtration that removes nitrite. Removal by hand. Herbivores.

Herbivores: *Diadema* Urchin. Seaslugs: *Aplysia*, and *Hermaea*.

Asparagopsis sporophyte stage.

Asparagopsis sporophyte stage.

This is the appearance of the gametophyte stage of *Asparagopsis*.

Hypnea

Common Name: None

Description: *Hypnea pannosa* forms dark purple, pink, gray, or bluish crisp cushions of tangled branches with pointed tips. Color is iridescent and changes depending on angle of view. Other *Hypnea* species are brown, green, or dull red.

Similar: *Coelothrix*, which is tougher and brighter blue, *Acanthophora*.

Desirable/undesirable features: Ornamental. Palatable to many herbivorous fishes. This alga blooms in aquariums under good water quality conditions, and it seems to have a positive effect on water quality, though it may shade or smother corals.

Controls: Removal by hand. Herbivores.

Herbivores: Surgeonfishes, *Diadema* Urchin.

Hypnea pannosa. Aquarium photo.

Hypnea pannosa. at the water surface.

Hypnea pannosa. growing between the branches of *Millepora* sp. Solomon Islands.

Gelidiopsis

Common Name: Wire Algae

Description: Red or brown tough wiry filaments.

Similar: *Coelothrix*, which has a bluish cast. *Gelidium* has more flattened branches. *Pterocladia* is like *Gelidium* but larger and more fern-like.

Desirable/undesirable features: Palatable to many herbivorous fishes. Slow growing, but can smother corals and tends to grow over damaged edges.

Controls: Removal by hand. Herbivores.

Herbivores: Surgeonfishes, *Diadema* Urchin.

Gelidiopsis on the base of a stony coral, *Turbinaria* sp.

Gelidiopsis on live rock.

Closeup of a filament of *Gelidiopsis*.

Ceramium

Common Name: Red Hair Algae

Description: Red or brown turfs composed of fine annulate filaments with claw shaped ends.

Similar: *Centroceras.*

Desirable/undesirable features: Palatable to many herbivorous fishes. Good for nutrient export in algal turf filters. Fast growing. Can smother corals.

Controls: Removal by hand. Herbivores.

Herbivores: Surgeonfishes, *Diadema* Urchin.

Ceramium turf on a damaged surface of the stony coral *Favia*, Solomon Islands.

Ceramium at 100x magnification. Note banding of filaments and claw-shaped tips.

Coralline Algae

Common Name: Coralline Algae

Description: Red, pink or brown flattened circular encrusting or foliaceous calcified plants.

Similar: *Pseudolithoderma*

Desirable/undesirable features: Atractive. Slow growing, but can smother corals and tends to grow over damaged edges. Inhibits growth of some filamentous green algae. Difficult to remove from acrylic aquarium windows.

Controls: Removal by hand. Herbivores. Remove from glass with a blade.

Herbivores: *Diadema* Urchin.

Thick plating growth of coralline algae at the National Aquarium in Baltimore.

Coralline algae can quickly block the view.

Coral larvae settle on coralline algae.

Diatoms

The diatoms, Bacillariophyta, are one of several photosynthetic groups of Chromista with siliceous skeletons. Others include the Prymnesiophyta and Silicoflagellata. The skeleton or "frustule" of a diatom is made of silica with an organic coating. The frustule is divided into two parts, an epitheca that overlaps the hypotheca like a lid over a box. The epitheca and hypotheca are each made up of two or more parts: a hoop-like rim called a cingulum, which surrounds a valve. Diatoms in the class Pennatibacillariophyceae are elongate (pennate), with a bilateral plane of symmetry. The Centrobacillariophyceae are round and radially symmetrical (centrate). Some diatoms are slightly asymmetrical, but generally they fall into one of these two classes.

Diatoms are a major component of plankton, but not all diatoms are planktonic; many cling to surfaces such as aquatic plants, sediments, and other substrates. Some occur as individual cells, while others grow in long chains. They are abundant in freshwater and marine habitats, but also occur in soils or on moist mosses.

About a quarter of the earth's organic carbon fixation (photosynthetic transformation of carbon dioxide and water into sugars) is accomplished by living diatoms. Diatoms are therefore also a major source of atmospheric oxygen, in addition to being a major food resource for marine and freshwater microorganisms and animal larvae.

Naturally occurring toxic marine phytoplankton includes diatom species such as *Pseudonitzschia* that produce domoic acid, a naturally occurring amino acid that strongly binds to the glutamate receptors in the brain where it causes nerve cells to transmit impulses continuously until the cells die. Most diatoms occurring in aquaria are not toxic. However, blooms of toxic diatoms may occur in aquaria.

Diatoms form delicately beautiful but durable microfossils, with an extensive fossil record going back to the Cretaceous. Deposits formed almost entirely of fossil diatoms are known as diatomite or diatomaceous earth.

Nitzschia, Licmophora, and *Triceratium*

Common Name: Diatoms, Brown slime algae.

Description: Brown, yellow, or rust colored films on glass, sand, gravel, rocks, or among filamentous algae, often with trapped bubbles of oxygen produced by photosynthesis. Diatoms often bloom in newly established aquariums, and subside after a few months. Disturbances may stimulate temporary blooms. Silicate supplied with top-off water or newly mixed seawater can stimulate blooms.

Similar: Superficially resemble dinoflagellates and cyanobacteria, which also form films that can be brownish and have trapped oxygen bubbles.

Desirable/undesirable features: Palatable to many herbivores. Fast growing.

Controls: Strong water flow to prevent its growth on sand, Herbivores, limitation of silicate.

Herbivores: *Astraea, Turbo, Trochus. Strombus alatus* for eating diatoms on sand. Blennies, *Ctenochaetus* spp. tangs.

Nitzschia sp. collected from the window of an aquarium.

Nitzschia on *Derbesia.*

Licmophora on *Derbesia.* Such blooms make the green filamentous algae look brown.

Unidentified centrate diatom on *Cladophora.*

Licmophora on *Derbesia.*

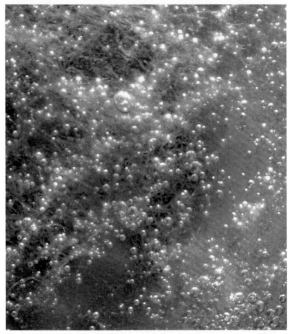

Nitzschia among green filamentous algae on an aquarium window produces oxygen bubbles.

The star-shaped diatom *Triceratium*, found among filaments of *Lyngbya* in an aquarium.

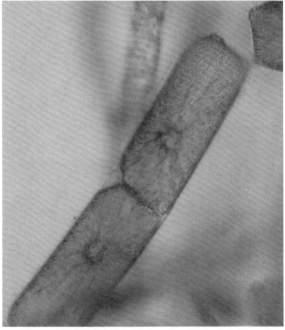

This diatom is associated with dying *Derbesia*. It can be found within dead hollow filaments!

Diatoms lend a golden hue to filamentous green algae in a damselfish territory. Solomon Is.

Diatoms are pioneers that often coat the substrate in new aquariums during the first weeks.

Dinoflagellates

Dinoflagellates are unicellular protists that exhibit a great diversity of form. There are nearly 2000 known living species classified in about 125 genera. The largest, *Noctiluca*, may be 2 mm in diameter! Dinoflagellates include photosynthetic and non-photosynthetic species; about half are in each category. Non-photosynthetic species of dinoflagellates feed on diatoms, other dinoflagellates, other protists, and the eggs of vertebrates and invertebrates. Though there are many freshwater species, most dinoflagellates are marine plankton, and photosynthetic dinoflagellates are second only to diatoms as primary producers in coastal waters. Some are benthic, some are parasites of fish, algae, or other protists. Some coastal marine species "bloom" during the warm summer months in such great numbers that the water can be colored golden or red by them. Such "red tide" dinoflagellates may produce a neurotoxin that affects muscle function in susceptible organisms, including humans.

Dinoflagellates are sometimes called Pyrrhophyta, meaning "fire plants" because some species produce light through bioluminescence, glowing like fireflies when agitated. The name "Dinoflagellate" refers to the two dissimilar "whirling flagella" they have that cause the dinoflagellate to slowly turn on its axis as it moves through the water. Dinoflagellates have a complex shell called the amphiesma, which consists of outer and inner continuous membranes. Between them lie a series of flattened vesicles that contain thickened cellulose thecal plates in armored forms. In "naked" species this armor is lacking, and some species shed their theca depending on environmental conditions. Some species have ridges or crests, and the crests may be hollow to house symbiotic cyanobacteria that provide fixed nitrogen to the host, especially beneficial in oceanic habitats that are nitrogen-poor.

The Dinoflagellate nucleus has unique features. For example, the DNA has repeated sequences as in other eukaryotes, but lacks histones, and dinoflagellates have more DNA in their nucleus than other eukaryotes. Some dinoflagellates contain a second nucleus that is believed to be part of a membrane-bound endosymbiont within the cytoplasm of the dinoflagellate. The presumed endosymbiont's cytoplasm contains not just this nucleus, but also chloroplasts, mitochondria and ribosomes. The discovery of this feature suggests that some groups of algae may have obtained chloroplasts from other symbiotic eukaryotic algae instead of from symbiotic prokaryotes (Darley, 1982). The triple membrane around the plastids and small nucleus-like structure inside them suggests a case of secondary endosymbiosis, the "plastid" being a swallowed diatom or chrysophyte, since it contains chlorophyll "c," otherwise found only in the Chromista.

The endosymbiosis doesn't stop there. Some photosynthetic dinoflagellates form symbiotic partnerships with other organisms. In these remarkable forms of symbiosis the host organism swallows the dinoflagellate and incorporates it into its own tissues without harming it. Zooxanthellae associated with corals, anemones, jellyfish, and giant clams are dinoflagellates. Other photosynthetic dinoflagellates take up residence within flatworms, ciliates, foraminiferans, and colonial radiolarians.

Photosynthetic dinoflagellates have light-sensitive organelles called eyespots, composed of lipid droplets packaged within stacked layers of membranes. They contain light-excitable carotenoid pigments, that allow the dinoflagellate to detect the direction of the light. Some species have a more eye-like light-sensing structure called an ocellus, which has a refracting lens that focuses a projected image onto a retinoid lining membrane. Dinoflagellates are obviously highly evolved little creatures.

The most common mode of reproduction in dinoflagellates is asexual cell division, and a few genera grow as filaments made up of chains of cells that don't separate after dividing. Sexual reproduction begins with the formation of free-swimming gametes by mitosis. The fertilized egg (zygote) also actively swims, and, under unfavorable conditions it may form a durable cyst.

High pH seems to limit the growth of dinoflagellates in aquariums. Based on the advice of Peter Wilkens, Delbeek and Sprung (1994) recommend adding kalkwasser (calcium hydroxide solution) as a means of curbing the growth of dinoflagellates in aquariums. The effect may also be due to the precipitation of phosphate or trace metals by the calcium hydroxide, and the enhanced protein skimming caused by the pH elevation from kalkwasser dosing. Humic substances may promote growth in some dinoflagellates, so the use of activated carbon in aquariums may also help to limit their growth.

Gambierdiscus

Common Name: Brown Slime algae, Dinoflagellates

Description: Golden brown gelatinous sheets or strings on substrate or glass, with trapped bubbles of oxygen produced by photosynthesis. *Gambierdiscus toxicus* is toxic to Turban snails. Common in new or biologically unstable aquariums.

Similar: Diatoms, brown cyanobacteria, other dinoflagellates.

Desirable/undesirable features: This toxic dinoflagellate blooms in aquariums under certain conditions, and blooms may last for weeks or months.

Controls: Let it run its course. Discontinue water changes for the duration of the bloom. Boost alkalinity with buffers or calcium reactor. Use kalkwasser for top off water. Use activated carbon to reduce humic substances that promote dinoflagellate growth. The use of algal turf filters may limit dinoflagellate growth via competition for nutrients. Specific bacteria may also be used to control dinoflagellates (Nagasaki et al. 2000).

Herbivores: Most herbivores will not eat dinoflagellates. Snails (*Turbo, Astraea*) may be harmed by them, rolling over and dying. Remove affected snails from the aquarium at once! Dead snails release nutrients back to the water that promote the algal bloom.

Gambierdiscus toxicus coating gravel in an aquarium.

Cells of *Gambierdiscus toxicus* from an aquarium. They multiply, and swim rapidly.

An unidentified dinoflagellate that produces oxygen bubbles and forms gelatinous mats.

Prorocentrum sp. is a harmless dinoflagellate found in an aquarium after a die-off of *Derbesia*.

The unidentified dinoflagellate at 100x magnification. It is an extremely small species.

Cyanobacteria

Cyanobacteria a.k.a. blue-green algae are aquatic photosynthetic bacteria that left the oldest known fossils, more than 3.5 billion years old. Oxygen generated by cyanobacteria shaped the course of evolution and ecological change on earth, and endosymbiosis by cyanobacteria within eukaryotic cells is responsible for the development of higher plants. Furthermore, cyanobacteria are one of very few organisms that convert atmospheric nitrogen into nitrate or ammonia, which are utilized by plants. Cyanobacteria form symbiotic relationships with other organisms, and with fungi they form complex symbiotic organisms known as lichens.

Blue greens are the only algal group that has prokaryotic cellular organization. That they have chloropyll a and produce oxygen via photosynthesis distinguishes them from other prokaryotic autotrophs, and this is the reason they are often referred to as algae. Nevertheless cyanobacteria are related to only the *chloroplast* within eukaryotic algae. Blue-green algae may occur as single cells, colonies of single cells, or filamentous cell chains, often surrounded by a gelatinous or mucilaginous sheath. They do not have sexual reproduction, but under unfavorable conditions, they produce specialized thickened cells called akinetes that are full of food reserves.

Blue-green algae get their color from the phycobiliprotein known as phycocyanin, though some species are purple or reddish due to the pigment phycoerythrin. Their color is variable depending on the abundance of one pigment or another, which is affected by light spectrum and intensity.

Some cyanobacteria are capable of movement. *Oscillatoria*, for example, gets its name from the "swaying" motion of its filaments.

The cyanobacterium *Spirulina*, now a popular "health food," has long been valued for its high protein content, and ease of cultivation in ponds. Many other cyanobacteria are toxic to humans and animals. Aquarists call cyanobacteria slime algae and consider them a nuisance.

Lyngbya

Common Name: Slime algae, Hair algae

Description: Brown, yellow, dark green, or red filaments forming turfs on rock, sand, gravel, or among filamentous algae.

Similar: Superficially resemble green filamentous algae such as *Derbesia*.

Desirable/undesirable features: Not palatable to many herbivores. Not very fast growing. *Lyngbya* spp. sometimes bloom in older aquariums, usually under nutrient-poor conditions.

Controls: Herbivores. Manual removal.

Herbivores: *Diadema*.

Lyngbya sp. that resembles *Derbesia*.

Lyngbya sp. with the diatom *Triceratium*.

Derbesia-like *Lyngbya* sp. Solomon Islands.

Lyngbya sp. Solomon Islands.

Phormidium

Common Name: Slime Algae

Description: Dark red or brown encrusting gelatinous growths with trapped air bubbles.

Similar: Several other genera of cyanobacteria may have this gelatinous form.

Desirable/undesirable features: Not palatable to many herbivores. Very fast growing. This alga sometimes blooms in aquariums, usually under nutrient-poor conditions. May smother corals and damage coral tissue upon contact. "Black Band Disease" in corals involves attack of coral tissue by a *Phormidium* species. The occurrence of *Phormidium* in aquariums seems to limit the occurrence of *Derbesia,* or the change in nutrient concentration in the aquarium may be marked by a transition from *Derbesia* to *Phormidium*.

Controls: Strong water flow to phyically prevent growth on coral. Remove by hand or siphon. Higher food inputs to encourage stronger coral growth.

Herbivores: Hermit crabs such as *Clibanarius tricolor.*

Mats of this *Phormidium* sp. proliferate in brightly illuminated tanks with low nutrient levels.

The filaments in this *Phormidium* sp. are stuck together by an amorphous mucilage.

Oscillatoria

Common Name: Slime algae

Description: Red, green, or brown films composed of fine filaments, forming encrusting tissue-paper-like growths on rock, sand, gravel, soft corals, or among other algae, often with trapped bubbles of oxygen produced by photosynthesis. When viewed under a microscope the filaments slowly sway in the light.

Similar: *Calothrix, Hydrocoleum, Schizothrix, Blennothrix.*

Desirable/undesirable features: Not palatable to many herbivores. Very fast growing. A red form of this genus sometimes blooms in aquariums, usually under organic nutrient-rich conditions. A bright green form is common on aquarium lids and in nutrient-rich aquariums.

Controls: Herbivores. Strong water flow to prevent growth on sand. Use of protein skimming, activated carbon, ozone, strong water circulation or other means of increasing redox potential of the water and reducing the accumulation of dissolved organic compounds. Elevate alkalinity.

Herbivores: Hermit crabs such as *Clibanarius tricolor;* Some *Aplysia* sp., *Bursatella, Strombus alatus* and Turban snails. Blennies, *Ctenochaetus* spp. tangs.

Red Slime algae growing on detritus. This plague species likes nutrient rich aquariums.

Red slime algae viewed at 100x has very fine filaments held together in a matrix.

Brown *Oscillatoria* floats to the surface

Brown *Oscillatoria* filaments.

Green slime algae looks like red slime algae.

A bright green *Oscillatoria* sp., Solomon Is.

Oscillatoria can damage gorgonians.

Red *Oscillatoria* on *Halimeda*. Solomon Is.

A red *Oscillatoria* sp. that has "bleached" green. It appears to be killing a coral. Solomon Islands

autotroph - an organism capable of self nourishment, using inorganic nutrients (carbon from CO_2) and photosynthesis or chemosynthesis as a source of energy.

algin - the sodium salt of alginic acid, a polysaccharide produced by brown seaweeds.

alternation of generations - life cycle involving an alternation between a haploid,gamete-producing vegetative phase (gametophyte) and a diploid, spore-producing vegetative phase (sporophyte).

anastomose - cell walls are united by cross connections, net-like.

anisogamous - gametes differ in size, the large being female, the smaller male.

annular, annulate - having rings or bands.

antheridium - male sex organ containing male motile gametes.

aplanosporangia - sporangia that produce non-motile spores.

aplanospore - non-motile spore, distinguished from autospores, which are non-motile miniatures of the cells from which they are derived.

axis - a longitudinal support on which other parts are arranged.

blade - erect leaf-like extension of the thallus.

bifurcate - dividing into two branches.

caespitose - forming dense turfs.

calcified - having hardened cell walls impregnated with calcium carbonate, as in *Halimeda* spp.

carpogonium - female sex organ in Rhodophyta.

carpogonium - a basal, egg-bearing portion of the female reproductive organ in red algae, usually with a projecting trichogyne to which male gametes attach.

carpospore - a diploid spore produced terminally by a gonimoblast, and germinating into a diploid tetrasporic plant, in red algae.

carposporophyte - a genration that results from sexual fusion in the red alga family Florideophycidae. It consists of gonimoblast filaments with attached carposporangia.

chemotroph - an organism that oxidizes inorganic or organic compunds as its principle source of food.

chloroplast - green plastid.

clavate - club shaped.

coenocytic – multinucleated single cell resulting from nuclear division without a corresponding cytoplasmic division, the cell having few or no crosswalls.

conceptacle - an organ formed by a pocket that encloses reproductive bodies.

crustose - forming a thin crust or hard coating.

cystocarp - the "fruit" produced by fertilization in red algae.

dichotomous - forked regularly with equal-length divisions, like a Y.

diplohaplontic - life cycle with an alternation of haploid and diploid generations and sporic meiosis.

diploid - having double the basic (haploid) number of chromosomes in each nucleus; 2N.

endospore - spore of cyanobacteria.

epiphyte - a plant growing on another plant but not parasitic.

eukaryote - an organism whose cell or cells is characterized by specialized organelles in the cytoplasm and a membrane-bound nucleus enclosing DNA bound into chromosomes.

facultative - having the ability to live under more than one specific set of environmental conditions or lifestyle modes.

floridean starch - the storage product of red algae.

filamentous - thread-like.

foliaceous - having the form of a leaf.

frustule - the siliceous wall of a diatom.

gametangia - an organ or body that produces gametes.

gamete - an active sexually produced cell that combines with a compatible cell to produce a zygote. Egg or sperm.

gametophyte - gamete-producing phase in an alternation of generations; usually haploid.

gonimoblast - In red algae, a filament that arises from the fertilized carpogonium.

haploid - having a single set of chromosomes per nucleus; 1N.

haptera - basal multicellular structures that form part of the holdfast.

heterocysts - clear, thickened cells that occur at intervals on the filaments of cyanobacteria, believed to be the site of nitrogen fixation.

heterotroph - an organism that requires organic compounds as its principle source of food.

holdfast - the point of attachment that anchors a plant to a hard substrate.

intertidal - (n) the part of the shore that is exposed and covered again by tidal changes. (adj.) living in the intertidal zone.

isogamous - having gametes that are morphologically indistinguishable.

karyogamy - fusion of two nuclei.

midrib - a thickened longitudinal axis on a blade.

monostromatic - having cells in a single layer only.

obligate - opposite of facultative. Restricted to a specific set of environmental conditions or lifestyle.

parenchyma - tissue made of cells functioning in food storage or photosynthesis.

parenchymatous - plants with thickened tissue made of cells functioning in food storage or photosynthesis.

pericarp - a sterile envelope that surrounds a cystocarp.

phagotrophic - Organisms such as certain dinoflagellates that ingest particulate bits of food drifting in seawater.

photoautotroph - an organism that uses light energy for food synthesis and carbon dioxide as its principle source of carbon.

phycobilin - biliprotein pigments found in red algae and cyanobacteria.

plankton - free-floating microorganisms of marine or freshwater environments.

prokaryote - any cellular organism that lacks a nuclear membrane, has DNA in the form of single continuous strands that form coils or loops, and has no organelles in the cytoplasm except for ribosomes.

rhizoid - branch composed of non-pigmented cells; usually functions in attachment.

rhizome - horizontal stem located underground.

secondary metabolites – Chemical deterrents that plants give off in order to avoid predation.

sheath - in Cyanophyta, a coating in addition to the cell wall.

sporangia - cells within which spores are produced.

spores - specialized, thick-walled, single asexually produced reproductive cells that can develop into a new plant when it is released from the parent plant.

sporophyte - spore-producing phase in an alternation of generations; arises from a zygote and is usually diploid.

stipe - stem-like portion of the thallus located above the holdfast.

tetrasporangia - reproductive cells that produce tetraspores.

thallus - the plant body in an alga, including holdfast, stipe, stolons, blades, etc. Although it may have structures that look like roots and leaves, the tissues are undifferentiated.

vesicle - a bladder-like structure.

zygote - a cell arising from the union of two gametes.

Atkinson, MJ, Falter, JL, and CJ Hearn. 2001. Nutrient dynamics in the Biosphere 2 coral reef mesocosm: water velocity controls NH4 and PO4 uptake. *Coral Reefs* 20(4):341

Adey, W.H. and K. Loveland. 1991. *Dynamic Aquaria*. Academic Press. San Diego, CA. USA.

Bass, A.L. 2001 (Apr 23) Re: *Ercolania fuscata* from Florida *[Message in] Sea Slug Forum*. http://www.seaslugforum.net/find.cfm?id=4226

Bingman, Craig. 2000. Silicon, Foe or Friend? *Aquarium Frontiers* www.animalnetwork.com/fish2/aqfm/2000/feb/features/1/default.asp

Bold, Harold C. & Michael J. Wynne. 1985. *Introduction to the Algae*. Prentice-Hall, NJ.

Bremer, K.. 1985. Summary of green plant phylogeny and classification. Cladistics 1:369-385.

Brown, V., Ducker, S.C. and K.S. Rowan, 1977. The effect of orthophosphate concentrations on the growth of the coralline algae (Rhodophyta). *Phycologia* 16:125-131.

Bruck, B. and Schnetter, R. 1997. Life History and Karyology of *Bryopsis plumosa* from the Canary Islands. *Phycologia*, volume 36, pp. 128-137.

Calumpong, H.P., and Menez, E.G. 1997. *Field Guide to the Common Mangroves, Seagrasses and Algae of the Phillipines*. Bookmark Inc.

Carmelo R. Tomas et al. 1996: Identifying Marine Diatoms and Dinoflagellates. Academic Press Inc., New York, 598pp.

Carr, N.G. and Whitton, B.A. (eds) 1973 *The Biology of Blue-Green Algae*. Blackwell Scientific Publications, Oxford.

Cribb, A.B. 1996. *Seaweeds of Queensland. A Naturalist's Guide*. The Queensland Naturalists' Club Inc., Brisbane. Australia.

Cox, E.R. (ed) 1980. *Phytoflagellates*. Elsevier/North-Holland, New York.

Darley, W.M. 1982. *Algal Biology: a physiological approach*. Blackwell Scientific Publications, Oxford.

Dawson, E. Yale 1966. Marine Botany; An Introduction. Holt, Rinehart, Winston. NY.

Delbeek, J. C. 1990. Live Rock Algal Succession in a Reef System. *Atoll*. Vol 3. Num 4.

Delbeek, J. C. 1990. Live Rock Algal Succession in a Reef System. *Freshwater and Marine Aquarium*. 13(10):120-135,179.

Delbeek, J.C. and J. Sprung 1994. *The Reef Aquarium*. Ricordea Publ., Coconut Grove, FLA. pp 544.

Doucette GJ, McGovern E, Babinchak J (1999) Bacterial influences on HAB population dynamics: I Algicidal bacteria active against the Florida red tide dinoflagellate, Gymnodinium breve. *J Phycol* 35:1447-1454

Emmens, C.W. 1991. Algae. *Freshwater and Marine Aquarium* 8/91.

Fabricius, K.E. and Dommisse, M. 2000. Depletion of suspended particulate matter over coastal reef communities dominated by zooxanthellate soft corals. *Marine Ecology Progress Series*. 196: 157-167

Fabricius, K.E. and Alderslade, P. 2001. *Soft Corals and Sea Fans. A comprehensive guide to the tropical shallow-water genera of the Central-West Pacific, the Indian Ocean and the Red Sea*. AIMS and MAGNT.

Fenical, W. 1975. Halogenation in the Rhodophyta- a review. *J. Phycol.* 11: 245-259.

Fenner, Bob 1989. Some notes on algae and their control. *Freshwater and Marine Aquarium* 6/89.

Fitt, W.K., Heslinga, G.A. and T.C. Watson. 1993. Utilization of dissolved inorganic nutrients in growth and mariculture of the tridacnid clam *Tridacna derasa*. *Aquaculture* 109:27-38.

Fossa, Svein. *Algae Eating Animals* May 31, 1998 on #reefs

Fogg, G.E., Stewart, W.D.P., Fay, P. and A.E. Walsby 1973. *The Blue-Green Algae*. Academic Press, New York.

Freshwater, D. W., et al. 1994. A gene phylogeny of the red algae (Rhodophyta) based on plastid rbcL. Proc. Natl. Acad. Sci. USA Vol. 91: 7281-7285.

Fritsch, F.E. 1965. *The Structure and Reproduction of the Algae: Volume I*. Cambridge University Press: Cambridge.

Gamble, Sam. 1995. Algae curse: a new view. *Freshwater and Marine Aquarium* 8/95.

Garibaldi, Lou. 1973. Seaweeds are not weeds. *Marine Aquarist* 4(4):73.

Gibbs, S.P. 1978. The chloroplasts of *Euglena* may have evolved form symbiotic green algae. *Can. J. Bot.*, 56, 2883-9.

Giovanetti, Thomas A. 1989. *Caulerpa* enemy of the miniature reef aquarium? *Freshwater and Marine Aquarium* 10/89.

Glodek, Garrett 1993. A lesson in plant taxonomy and systematics. *Freshwater and Marine Aquarium* 11/93.

Glodek, Garrett. 1996. All you ever wanted to know about marine plants (selected bibliography). *Freshwater and Marine Aquarium* 1/96.

Goemans, B. 2000. *Marine Algae Control Secrets*. Marc Weiss Companies, Inc.

Graff, R. (1991) The Problems Associated With Controlling Micro Algae in Reef Tanks. *Atoll*. Vol 4. Num 4.

Graff, R. (1992) The Problems Associated With Controlling Micro Algae in Reef Tanks. *Atoll*. Vol 5. Num 2.

Graff, Rick. 1993. Getting control of microalgae; how to deal with this problem in reef tanks. *Freshwater and Marine Aquarium* 1/93.

Hamann, Mark T. and Scheuer, Paul J. 1993. Kahalalide F: A Bioactive Disipeptide from the Sacoglossan Mollusk, *Elysia rufescens* and the Green Alga *Bryopsis* sp. *J. Am. Chem. Soc.* 115:5825-5826.

Hatcher, B.G., Chapman, A.R.O., and K.H. Mann 1977. An annual carbon budget for the kelp *Laminaria longicruris*. *Mar. Biol.*, 44, 85-96.

Hoff, Frank. 1988. Coral reefs of Florida, part II; the algae. *Freshwater and Marine Aquarium* 1/88.

Hoff, F. and T. W. Snell, 1993. *Plankton Culture Manual*. Florida Aqua Farms. Dade City, FL.

Imai I, Sunahara T, Nishikawa T, Hori Y, Kondo R, Hiroishi S (2001) Fluctuations of the red tide flagellates Chattonella spp. (Raphidophyceae) and the algicidal bacterium *Cytophaga* sp. in the Seto Inland Sea, Japan. *Mar Biol* 138:1043-1049

IOC Taxonomic Reference List of Toxic Algae, Intergovernmental Oceanographic Commission of UNESCO. www.ioc.unesco.org/hab/data4taxlist, 2002.

Irving, D.E.G. 1984. *Systematics of the Green Algae*. Academic Press Inc. London.

Iseki, M. and Makoto M. 1995. Positive Phototropism in the Thallus of the *Bryopsis plumosa*. *Plant Cell Physiol*. 36 (6):971-976.

Iseki, M. and Makoto M. 1995. Negative Phototropism in the Rhizoid of *Bryopsis Plumosa*. *Plant cell Physiol*. 36(6): 977-982.

Bibliography

Ishio S, Mangindaan RE, Kuwahara M, Nakagawa H (1989) A bacterium hostile to flagellates: identification of species and characters. In: Okaichi, Anderson, Nemoto (eds) *Red tides: biology, environmental science, and toxicology*. Elsevier Science Publishing, p 205-208

Jensen, K.R. 1980. A Review of Sacoglossan diets, with comparative notes on radular and buccal anatomy. *Malacological Review* 13: 55-77.

Jensen, K.R. 1997. Evolution of the Sacoglossa (Mollusca, Opisthobranchia) and the ecological associations with their food plants. *Evolutionary Ecology*, 11: 301-335.

Jensen, K.R. 1999. A new species of Sacoglossa (Mollusca, Opisthobranchia) from Rottnest Island, Western Australia. *[In]*: D.J.Walker & F.E.Wells (Eds). *The Seagrass Flora and Fauna of Rottnest Island, Western Australia*. Western Australian Museum, Perth: 377-383.

Knop, D. 1996. *Giant Clams: A Comprehensive Guide to the Identification and Care of Tridacnid Clams*. Dahne Verlag, Ettlingen, Germany. 255 pp.

Lee, R.E. 1980. *Phycology*. Cambridge University Press, Cambridge.

Littler, D.S., Littler, M.M., Bucher, K.E., and J.N. Norris, 1989. *Marine Plants of the Caribbean*. Smithsonian Institution Press.

Littler, D.S., Littler, M.M. 2000. *Caribbean Reef Plants*. Offshore Graphics. 542 pp.

Lovejoy C, Bowman JP, Hallegraeff GM (1998) Algicidal effects of a novel marine *Pseudoalteromonas* isolate (class Proteobacteria, gamma subdivision) on harmful algal bloom species of the genera *Chattonella, Gymnodinium,* and *Heterosigma*. *Appl Envir Microb* 64:2806-2813

Lüning, K. 1990. *Seaweeds: Their environment, biogeography, and ecophysiology*. Wiley, New York.

Mattox, K. R. & Stewart, K. D. 1984. Classification of the green algae: A concept based on comparative cytology. In: *Systematics of the Green Algae*. Irvine, D.E.G. & John, D.M. [Eds.] Academic Press, London, pp. 29-72.

McCourt, R. M. 1995. Green algal phylogeny. *Trends in Ecology and Evolution* 10:159-163.

Meyer, K.D.; Paul, V.J.; Sanger, H.R.; Nelson, S.G. 1994. Effects of seaweed extracts and secondary metabolites on feeding by the herbivorous surgeon fish *Naso lituratus. Coral Reefs*. 13:105-112.

Michael, Scott 1995. All that algae; If it makes you feel any better, this is a common problem. *AFM* 8/95.

Minor, K. I. 1995. What is that? part II: Valoniaceae. *FAMA* 6/95.

Mitsutani A, Takesue K, Kirita M, Ishida Y (1992) Lysis of *Skeletonema costatum* by *Cytophaga* sp. isolated from the coastal water of the Ariake Sea. *Nippon Suisan Gakkaishi* 58: 2159-2169

Nagasaki K, Yamaguchi M, Imai I (2000) Algicidal activity of a killer bacterium against the red tide dinoflagellate *Heterocapsa circularisquama* isolated from Ago Bay, Japan. *Nippon Suisan Gakkaishi* 66:666-673

Paletta, Michael. 1990. Eliminating problem algae. *SeaScope* v. 7 Fall 90.

Paletta, M. 1991. The Relationship of Redox Potential to Micro Algae. *SeaScope* Vol. 5, Winter 1998.

Pickett-Heaps, J.D. 1975. *Green Algae: Structure, Reproduction and Evolution in selected Genera*. Sinauer Associates, Sunderland, Massachussets.

Prasek, Ed. 1995. Mirror & slime algae; are they driving you crazy too? *TFH* 7/95.

Provasoli and Pintner 1980. Bacteria induced polymorphism in an axenic laboratory strain of *Ulva lactuca* [Chlorophyceae], *J Phycol* 16: 196-201

Ragan, M.A. & A. Jensen 1979. Quantitative studies on brown algal phenols. III. Light-mediated exudation of polyphenols from *Ascophyllum nodosum* (L.) Le Jol. *J. Exp Mar. Biol. Ecol.*, 36, 91-101.

Ragan, M. A., et al. 1994. A molecular phylogeny of the marine red algae (Rhodophyta) based on the nuclear small-subunit rRNA gene. Proc. Natl. Acad. Sci. USA Vol. 91: 7276-7280.

Raven, P.H. 1970. A multiple origin for plastids and mitochondria. *Science*, 169, 641-6.

Raven, P. H., Evert, R. H., Eichhorn, S. E. (1992) *Biology of Plants*. 5th Edition. Worth Publishers, New York.

Rippka, Rosmarie, Josette Deruelles, John B. Waterbury, Michael Herdman & Roger Y. Stanier 1979. Generic Assignments, Strain Histories and Properties of Pure Cultures of Cyanobacteria. *Journal of General Microbiology* Vol. 111 p. 1-61

Round, F. E., 1965. *The Biology of the Algae*. St Martin's Press. New York.

Rudman, W.B., 2000 (March 3) *Ercolania endophytophaga* Jensen, 1999. *[In] Sea Slug Forum*. http://www.seaslugforum.net/ercoendo.htm

Rudman, W.B., 2001 (Apr 18) *Ercolania fuscata* (Gould, 1870). *[In] Sea Slug Forum*. http://www.seaslugforum.net/ercofusc.htm

Schlichter, D. & H. Kampmann, S. Conrady 1997. Trophic Potential and Photoecology of Endolithic Algae Living within Coral Skeletons. *Marine Ecology*, 18 (4): 299-317

Schlichter, D. & B. Zscharnack, H. Krisch 1995. Transfer of Photoassimilates from Endolithic Algae to Coral Tissue. *Naturwissenschaften* 82, 561-564

Searles, R.B. 1980. The strategy of the red algal life history. *Am. Nat.*, 115, 113-20.

Sears, J.R. and R.T. Wilce. 1970. Reproduction and Systematics of the marine alga *Derbesia* (Chlorophyceae) in New England. *J. Phycol.* 6: 381-392.

Sprung, J. 2001. *Invertebrates: A Quick Reference Guide*. Ricordea Publishing. Miami, Fl USA.

Stewart, K.D. and Mattox, K.R. 1975. Comparative cytology, evolution, and classification of the green algae with some consideration of the origin of other organisms with chlorophylls a and b. *Bot. Rev.*, 41, 104-35.

Stewart JR, Brown, RM (1969) Cytophaga that kills or lyses algae. *Science* 164:1523-1524

Thiel, Albert. *Nutrient Control and Algae Control in the Marine Aquarium* August 9th, 1998 on #reefs

Trainor, F.R. 1978. *Introductory Phycology*. John Wiley & Sons, New York.

Trowbridge, C.D. 1992. Phenology and Demography of a Marine Specialist Herbivore: *Placida dendritica*.

Werner, D. (ed) 1977. *The Biology of Diatoms*. Blackwell Scientific Publications, Oxford.

Whittaker, David. 1993. Characteristics of blue-green algae. *TAG* 6(3):5,6

Whittaker, R.H. 1969. New concepts of kingdoms of organisms. Science, 163, 150-60.

Wilkens, Peter. 1990. *Marine Invertebrates. Stone and False Corals, Colonial Anemones*. Engelbert Pfriem Verlag, Wuppertal, Germany.

Wilkens, Peter. 1992. Green water in the aquarium; the sexual reproduction of *Caulerpa* algae. *TFH* 2/92.

Womersley 1984. *The Marine Benthic Flora of Southern Australia*, Part I. (Fig. 100A, p. 291. *Derbesia tenuissima*).

Index

You should be able to find this book in your local library, book store, aquarium shop, pet store, or public aquarium. If you cannot find it locally, please contact:

Publisher
Ricordea Publishing
Miami, Florida, USA
Tel 305 477.1150 Fax 305 477.5650

Distributed by
Two Little Fishies, Inc.
4016 El Prado Blvd.,
Coconut Grove, Florida, 33133 USA
Tel 305 661.7742 Fax 305 661.0611
eMail: info@twolittlefishies.com
Website: www.twolittlefishies.com